About the Authors

USA TODAY bestselling author **Lynne Graham** was born in Northern Ireland and has been a keen romance reader since her teens. She is very happily married to an understanding husband who has learned to cook since she started to write! Her five children keep her on her toes. She has a very large dog who knocks everything over, a very small terrier who barks a lot, and two cats. Visit her on the web at www.lynnegraham.com.

Michelle Smart's love affair with books started when she was a baby, when she would cuddle them in her cot. A voracious reader of all genres, she found her love of romance established when she stumbled across her first Mills & Boon book at the age of twelve. She's been reading – and writing – them ever since. Michelle lives in Northamptonshire, England, with her husband and two young Smarties.

USA TODAY bestselling and RITA® Award–nominated author **Caitlin Crews** loves writing romance. She teaches her favourite romance novels in creative writing classes at places like UCLA Extension's prestigious Writers Programme, where she finally gets to utilise the MA and PhD in English Literature she received from the University of York in England. She currently lives in California, with her very own hero and too many pets. Visit her at www.caitlincrews.com.

Ruthless Revenge

COLLECTION

July 2018

August 2018

September 2018

October 2018

November 2018

December 2018

Ruthless Revenge: Ultimate Satisfaction

LYNNE GRAHAM

MICHELLE SMART

CAITLIN CREWS

MILLS & BOON

Published in Great Britain 2018
by Mills & Boon, an imprint of HarperCollins*Publishers*
1 London Bridge Street, London, SE1 9GF

Ruthless Revenge: Ultimate Satisfaction © 2018 Harlequin
Books S.A.

Bought for the Greek's Revenge © 2016 Lynne Graham
Wedded, Bedded, Betrayed © 2016 Michelle Smart
At the Count's Bidding © 2015 Caitlin Crews

ISBN: 9780263268119

09-0718

BOUGHT FOR THE GREEK'S REVENGE

LYNNE GRAHAM

For my readers, who have given me endless
support throughout my career.
Thank you.

CHAPTER ONE

NIKOLAI DRAKOS SCANNED the photo with a frown and enhanced it. It couldn't be the same woman; it simply couldn't be! There was no way that his quarry, Cyrus Makris, could possibly be planning to marry a woman from a humble background.

Bemused, Nikolai lifted his arrogant dark head high and once again studied the picture of the ethereal redhead. No way could it be the same little temptress he had once met working as a parking attendant. The world wasn't that small. Even so, he was aware that Cyrus owned a country house in Norfolk. A deeper frown lodged between his level dark brows, his quick and clever brain taking a rare hike into the recent past.

For all her diminutive size the woman he had met had had attitude, lots and *lots* of attitude, certainly not an attribute Nikolai sought from the transient beauties who shared his bed. But she had also had aquamarine eyes and a mouth as soft, silky and pink as a lotus blossom. A sizzling physical combination, which had taken a hell of a lot of forgetting on his part. His wide sensual mouth compressed with dissatisfaction. After she had blown him off, another man might have tried to find her again to make another attempt but Nikolai had refused to do so. He didn't chase women, he didn't do sweet talk or dates or flowers or any of that stuff *ever*. He walked away. The mantra by which he lived insisted that no woman was irreplaceable, no woman unique, and he didn't believe in love. She had simply caught his imagination for a few intoxicating moments but he had refused to allow lust to seduce him into pursuit. Since when had he had to pursue a woman?

And although it was generally known that Cyrus's elderly father was putting pressure on his forty-five-year-old son and heir to take a bride, it was a challenge to credit that Cyrus *could* be planning to marry the feisty little redhead who had scratched the paintwork on Nikolai's cherished McLaren Spider. Besides, only pure and untouched female flesh excited Cyrus, as Nikolai's late sister had learned to her cost. And no way could that sparkling little redhead still be that pure and untouched.

Flexing his lean muscles as he sprang upright, Nikolai swept up the file he had been studying. The investigator he used was a consummate professional and the report would be thorough. He studied the photos afresh. He was willing to admit that the likeness between the two women was startling. Curiosity at a height, he began to read about Prunella, known as Ella. Yes, that night he had definitely heard her boss using that name, he conceded grimly. Ella Palmer, aged twenty-three, a former veterinary student who had once been engaged to Cyrus's dead nephew, Paul. Now there was a connection he could not have foreseen for Cyrus, who rarely bothered with relatives.

Nikolai read on, unexpectedly hungry for the details. It had been a year since the nephew had died of leukaemia and two years since Ella's father, George Palmer, had had a stroke. The older man was currently drowning in debt. Nikolai marvelled that Cyrus, who was rich but tight, had not stepped in to help Ella's family, but perhaps he was holding that possibility in reserve as a power play.

Nikolai, on the other hand, immediately grasped that it was *his* optimum moment for action and intervention. He called his team of personal assistants and issued his instructions even while he was still struggling to work out why Ella Palmer could be in line to become Cyrus's bride.

What was so special about her? For a couple of years at least she had evidently hovered on the outskirts of Cyrus's life. As his nephew's fiancée she would have been untouchable, the unattainable always a powerful temptation to a male who thrived on the challenge of breaking the rules. Now she was alone and unprotected and Cyrus appeared to be playing a waiting game. However, it was equally possible that Ella was eager to marry Cyrus, because although he was old enough to be her father he was also a prominent, and wealthy, businessman.

But what, other than innocence, could be attracting Cyrus? Ella Palmer had neither money nor connections to offer. She was a beauty, but could a formerly engaged young woman *still* be a virgin in this day and age? Nikolai shook his arrogant dark head in wonderment. Was that even possible? And had she the smallest concept of the kind of male she was dealing with? A man who was excited by sexual violence? And who, given the opportunity, would cause her irreparable harm? Would she consider a wedding ring adequate compensation for brutal mistreatment?

Whatever, Nikolai's objective was to take her off Cyrus. Cyrus was a dangerous man and Nikolai knew exactly how addicted he was to the seamier side of life. By utilising bribery, intimidation and hush money, Cyrus had so far contrived to escape justice. Nikolai had long been forced to pursue a more subtle form of revenge. Being both extremely rich and extremely clever, Nikolai had tracked his quarry's every move in the business world and had regularly snatched lucrative deals from right under Cyrus's nose. That had been easy because Cyrus was better at making enemies than keeping friends and making connections. But it wasn't nearly as satisfying as striking out at Cyrus on a more personal level would be. Losing Ella Palmer, seeing her choose his greatest rival over him, would really hit Cyrus hard where it hurt. And anything that caused Cyrus pain made Nikolai happy.

As for how his actions would affect Ella Palmer and her family, Nikolai ruminated darkly, did he really care? They would simply be collateral damage in Nikolai's battle. But, at the same time, her family would be freed from crippling debt while Ella would be protected from Cyrus. Nikolai's burning desire for revenge was fuelled by ruthless resolution and by the knowledge that all Cyrus's victims had been cruelly denied justice. Yet there was also a weird personal feel to the challenge that made his teeth grit because, try as he did to stay cool and in control and essentially uninvolved, unholy rage gripped Nikolai at the thought of Cyrus getting his slimy hands on Ella and *hurting* her...

* * *

'It's bad, Ella,' Gramma said heavily.

'How bad?' Ella prompted, dry-mouthed.

George Palmer, Ella's father and Gramma's son, sighed heavily. 'I'm a terrible failure of a man when it comes to my family… I've lost everything.'

'The business, yes…perhaps it's too late for anything to be saved there, but that doesn't make you a failure,' Ella conceded in a wobbly voice, because they had known for ages that the shop was doing badly. 'But, at least, the house—'

'*No*, Ella,' Gramma cut in, her lined face pale and stiff with self-discipline. 'This time the house has to go as well—'

'But how can that be?' Ella exclaimed incredulously. '*You* own the house, not Dad!'

'My divorce from Joy took half the business,' the older man reminded her.

'And the house was the only asset we had left. Your father couldn't get the business loan he needed to pay off Joy without backing it up with the house,' Ella's grandmother, Gramma, a petite white-haired lady in her seventies, told her tightly. 'So, we put the house on the line and hoped for the best.'

'Oh, my…goodness,' Ella gasped after carefully searching for a word that would not make her grandmother flinch.

Thinking of her stepmother, the volatile Joy, Ella tried to reflect on the reality that since the divorce her father was a much happier man. His wife had been a very demanding woman, and although the older man had made a decent recovery from the stroke that had laid him low two years earlier, he now used a stick and the left side of his body remained weak. His wife, Joy, had walked out on him during his rehabilitation. She had deserted him as soon as his once comfortable income had declined. Her father had not been able to afford the services of a good lawyer in the divorce that followed and it had been a shock when his estranged wife had been awarded half the value of his furniture shop in the settlement. That pay out had led them straight into their current dire financial straits.

'Taking that risk with the house hasn't worked out for us but I'm trying to console myself with the idea that at least we *tried*,' George Palmer said wryly. 'If we hadn't tried we would always have wondered if we should have done. Now it's done and dusted and, unhappily for us, my creditors need to be paid.'

Ella's mood was not improved by the older man's accepting attitude. George Palmer was one of nature's gentlemen and he never had a bad word to say about anyone or anything. Her attention fell instead on the letter lying on the kitchen table and she snatched it up. 'That's what this is about? Your creditors?'

'Yes, my debts have been sold on to another organisation. That's a letter from the new owner's solicitors telling me that they want to put the house on the market.'

'Well, we'll just see about that!' Ella snapped, scrambling upright and pulling out her phone, eager to be able to do something at last, for sitting around bemoaning bad situations was not her style.

'This is business, Ella.' Gramma gave her feisty grandchild a regretful appraisal. 'Appealing to business people is a waste of your time. All they want is their money and hopefully a profit out of their investment.'

'It's not that simple…it's our *lives* you're talking about!' Ella proclaimed emotively, stalking out of the kitchen to ring the legal firm and ask for an appointment.

Life could be so very cruel, she was thinking. Time and time again misfortune and disappointment had made Ella suffer and she had become so accustomed to that state of affairs that she had learned to swallow hard and bear it. But when it came to her family suffering adversity, well, that was something else entirely and it brought out her fighting spirit. Her father couldn't regain his full health but he did deserve some peace after the turmoil of his divorce. She couldn't bear him to lose his home when he had already been forced to adjust to so many frightening changes.

And what about Gramma? Tears flooded Ella's bright green eyes when she thought of Gramma losing her beloved home. Gramma's late husband had moved her into this house as a bride in the nineteen sixties. Her son had been born below this roof and she had never lived anywhere else. Neither had Ella or her father, Ella reflected wretchedly. The worn but comfortable detached house sat at the very heart of their sense of security.

George Palmer had fallen in love with Ella's mother, Lesley, at university and had hoped to marry her when she became pregnant with Ella. Lesley, however, had been less keen and shortly after Ella's birth she had left George and her daughter behind to pursue a career in California. A brilliant young physicist, Ella's mother had since gone on to become a world-renowned scientist.

'I obviously lack both the mum and the wife gene

because I have no regrets over being single and child-free even now,' Lesley had told Ella frankly when they first met when Ella was eighteen. 'George adored you and, when he married Joy, I assumed it would be better for me to leave you to be part of a perfect little family *without* my interference...'

Ella dragged her mind back from that ironic little speech that she had received from her uncaring mother. Lesley hadn't recognised that her complete lack of interest in Ella and absence of regret would hurt her daughter even more. In addition, George, Joy and Ella had not been a perfect family because as soon as Joy had become George's wife she had made her resentment of Ella's presence in their home very obvious. Had it not been for George's and Gramma's love and attention, Ella would have been a deeply unhappy child.

And Joy, Ella thought bitterly, had done very nicely out of the divorce, thank you. However, she cleared her mind of such futile reflections and concentrated on thinking instead about her family's predicament while she outlined her request to the very well-spoken young man who accepted her call after she had been passed through several people at the legal firm. She was dismayed to then walk into a solid brick wall of silence. With a polite reference to client confidentiality, the solicitor refused to tell her who her father's creditor was and pointed out that nobody would be prepared to discuss her father's debts with anyone other than her father, although he did at least promise to pass on her request.

As she replaced the phone and checked her watch in dismay Ella's eyes were stinging with tears of frustration, but she had to pull herself together and get to work, her small income being the only money currently entering the household aside of Gramma's pension. As she pulled on her jacket an idea struck her and she paused in the kitchen doorway to look at the two older people. 'You know…er…have you thought of approaching Cyrus for help?' she asked abruptly.

Her father's face stiffened defensively. 'Ella… I—'

'Cyrus is a family friend,' Gramma stepped in to acknowledge. 'It would be very wrong to approach a friend in such circumstances simply because he has money.'

A flush of colour drenched Ella's heart-shaped face and she nodded respectful agreement, even though she was tempted to remark that matters were serious enough to risk causing offence. Perhaps her relatives had already asked and been refused help or perhaps they knew something she didn't, she conceded uncomfortably. In any case approaching Cyrus was not currently possible because Cyrus was abroad on a lengthy trade-delegation tour of China.

She climbed into the ancient battered van that was her only means of transport. Butch went into a cacophony of barking on the doorstep and she blinked, very belatedly recalling her pet, who normally went to work with her. She braked and opened the car door in a hurry to scoop the little animal up.

Butch was a Chihuahua/Jack Russell mix and absolutely tiny, but he had the heart and personality of a much bigger dog. He had been born with only three legs and would have been euthanised at birth had Ella not fallen in love with him while she had been working on a placement at a veterinary surgery. He settled down quietly into his pet carrier, knowing that his owner frowned on any kind of disturbance while she was driving.

Ella worked at an animal sanctuary only a few miles from her home. She had volunteered at Animal Companions as a teenager, found solace there while the man she loved had slowly succumbed to the disease that would eventually kill him and had ended up working at the rescue centre when she had been forced to leave her veterinarian course before its completion. One day she still hoped to be able to finish her training and become a fully qualified veterinary surgeon with her own practice, but Paul's illness and her father's stroke had been inescapable events that had thrown her life plan off course.

Not such a bad thing, she often told herself bracingly at times when it seemed that her desire to work as an animal doctor was continually destined to collapse in the face of other people's needs. She had gained a lot of experience working at the rescue centre and was using the skills she had acquired during her training by functioning as an unofficial veterinary nurse. To think any other way when her presence at home had achieved so much good would be unforgivably selfish, she told herself firmly. Gramma and her dad had badly needed her assistance during that testing time. And she was painfully aware of all the advantages that their loving support had given *her*.

Her boss, Rosie, a generous-hearted woman in her forties with frizzy blonde curls, surged out to the car park to greet Ella. 'You'll never believe it… Samson's got a home!' she gasped excitedly.

Ella started to smile. 'You're kidding—'

'Well, I haven't done the home visit yet to check

them out but they did seem very genuine people. Just lost their own dog to old age, so I didn't think they'd want another oldie but they're afraid that a young dog could be too much for them to handle,' Rosie told her.

'Samson really deserves a good home,' Ella said fondly, for the thirteen-year-old terrier had been repeatedly passed over because of his age by other prospective owners.

'He's a very loving little chap...' Rosie paused, her warm smile dwindling. 'I heard your father's shop closed down last week. I'm so sorry for your dad—'

'Well, can't be helped,' Ella responded, hoping to forestall further comment because she couldn't discuss her family's financial affairs with Rosie, who was a hopeless gossip.

While Rosie talked about the rise of the big furniture chain stores working to the detriment of smaller businesses, Ella made polite sounds of agreement while she checked that the kennel staff had completed their early morning cleaning routine. That done, Ella put on overalls and concentrated on sorting out an emaciated stray with matted hair brought to them by the council dog warden. When she had finished she peeled off the overalls, washed and fed the poodle mix and settled her down in a run.

She heard a car and assumed that Rosie had set off to do her home visit to check out Samson's new potential owners. She went into the office where she worked between times, being better at paperwork than Rosie, who was more driven by her need to rescue animals and rehome them than by the equally important requirement of meeting all of a recognised charity's medical, legal and financial obligations. As a team, however, she and

Rosie were efficient because their abilities fitted neatly together. Rosie was fantastic at dealing with the public and fundraising while Ella preferred to work with the animals in the background.

Indeed Ella had been very uncomfortable at the fancy charity auction that Cyrus had persuaded her to attend with him only a month earlier. Champagne, high heels and evening dresses were really not her thing. But how could she have said no when Cyrus had been so very good to Paul while he was ill? Acting as Cyrus's partner at a couple of social occasions was little enough to be asked to do in return, she ruminated wryly, wondering as she often had why Cyrus had never married. He was forty-five years old, presentable, successful and single. Once or twice she had wondered if he was gay but Paul had got very annoyed at her for trying to make something out of what he insisted was nothing.

Rosie entered the office, rudely springing Ella from her momentary loss of concentration. The older woman looked flustered. 'You have a visitor,' she announced.

Her smooth brow furrowing, Ella stood up and moved round the desk. 'A visitor?' she prompted in surprise.

'He's a *foreigner*,' Rosie stage-whispered as if that fact were terribly mysterious and unusual.

'But he went to school in the UK and speaks excellent English,' a very masculine voice commented from the door that still stood open on the small outer hall, where he had evidently been left to hover.

Ella's lower limbs succumbed to nervous paralysis as she froze where she stood, a tiny disbelieving quiver running down her spine because, incredibly, she *recognised* that voice even though she had only heard it on one previous occasion almost a year earlier. It couldn't be but it was…it was *him*, the gorgeous guy with the fancy car and the very short temper and the eyes that reminded her of melted caramel. What on earth was he doing visiting her at Animal Companions? Had he tracked her down?

'I'll just leave you in…er…privacy,' Rosie pronounced awkwardly, backing out of the office again as the very tall, dark man behind her strode forward without taking any apparent note of her still-lingering presence.

Rosie arched a pale brow. 'Do we need privacy?' she asked doubtfully.

Nikolai studied her fixedly. She was incredibly tiny and delicate in build. He remembered that. He remembered the long curling tangle of her bronze-coloured hair as well because the shade was unusual, neither brown nor red but a metallic shade somewhere between the two. She bore a ridiculously close resemblance to a pixie he had once seen in a fairy-story book, he thought, feeling oddly numb, oddly dry-mouthed as his keen dark gaze roved over her, reluctant to miss out on a single detail of that petite, pixeish perfection. No, of course she wasn't perfect, no woman was, he reasoned, striving to be more lucid, but that flawless porcelain skin, those glorious green eyes and that lush mouth in that beautiful face were quite unforgettable. Memory hadn't exaggerated her beauty, but his brain had persuaded him he had to prevent himself from chasing after her, he decided in exasperation.

'We do,' Nikolai confirmed, firmly shutting the door in Rosie's wake. 'We weren't introduced at our last meeting.'

'No, you were far too busy shouting at me,' Ella reminded him doggedly.

'My name is Nikolai Drakos and you are?'

As he extended a hand Gramma's strict upbringing brought Ella's own hand out to grip his. 'Prunella Palmer. Most people call me Ella. What are you doing here, Mr Drakos? Or are you here about that stupid car?' she asked witheringly.

'You pranged that stupid car,' Nikolai pointed out, unamused.

'I inflicted a minuscule rubbing mark on one wing. I didn't dent or scratch it,' she traded drily. 'I can't believe you're still complaining about it. Nobody got hurt and no real damage was done.'

Nikolai was very tempted to tell her how much that 'rubbing' mark had cost to remove. She had scraped the car past a bush when she'd accelerated too fast. His teeth ground together. It was healthy to be reminded just how very annoying she could be, he told himself warningly. Complaining? He had never complained in his life, not when his father beat him up, not when he was bullied at school, not even when his sister and only living relative had died. He had learnt at a very young age that basically nobody cared what happened to him and nobody was interested enough to listen to what he had endured. Nothing in life had ever come easy to Nikolai.

Ella couldn't take her eyes off him. He was so physically large in both height and breadth that he ate up every inch of space in Rosie's little office and made it feel crowded and suffocating. Tension held her rigid while she watched him like a rabbit mesmerised by a hawk ready to swoop down on her. Nikolai Drakos—

the ultimate female fantasy with olive skin, black hair and spectacular dark eyes. His tailored charcoal-grey business suit couldn't hide the reality that he was built with an athlete's lean, muscular power and he moved with long-legged easy grace, she registered, struggling to pinpoint exactly what continually drew her attention to him. He was very, very good-looking but it wasn't just the looks. He had amazing bone structure though and would probably still be turning heads in his sixties. Maybe it was the electrifying quality of the raw, masculine sex appeal he exuded. Twelve months earlier his sheer charisma had struck her like a thunderbolt and utterly humiliated her.

'I'm not here about the car,' Nikolai said very drily. 'I'm here because you *asked* to see me…'

Ella was thoroughly disconcerted by that statement. 'I don't know what you're talking about. How could I ask to see you when I have no way of contacting you? And why would I contact you when I haven't had the slightest desire to see you again?' she enquired tartly, her whole bearing suggesting that such a belief could only have come from an intolerable egotist.

A sardonic smile curved Nikolai's wide sensual mouth as he gazed down at her with scantily leashed satisfaction. *She* had approached *him*. She had come looking for him first and that felt very much like the helpful hand of fate working on his behalf.

'You did request my attention,' he told her again.

Bewilderment gripped Ella but it was swiftly followed by a surge of frustrated fury. So far she had been having a very bad day and she was not in the mood for big arrogant male surprises and particularly not one who had offended her by offering her a one-night stand before he had even enquired what her name was! Yes, act first, *think* afterwards, that was how Nikolai Drakos functioned around women, she reflected scornfully. He had made her feel bad about herself and she allowed no man to do that to her. Yet when she gazed back at him and rated the uncompromising light in his eyes and the hard resolution etched in his strong-boned features, she could suddenly see that he was not the weak, frivolous and impulsive male she had first assumed him to be and that threw her off balance...badly.

'I've had enough of this nonsense!' she told him bluntly. 'I want you to leave.'

Nikolai compounded his sins by slowly raising a beautifully drawn ebony brow. 'I don't think so.'

The rage that Ella always struggled to control broke through her cracking composure because she hated bullies and it seemed to her that he was trying to intimidate her. 'I *know* so!' she slammed back at him, half an octave higher. 'And if you're not out of here by the time I count to ten, I'm calling the police!'

'Go right ahead,' Nikolai advised, lodging his wide-shouldered frame back against the door and folding his arms with the infuriatingly cool poise of a male who had no intention of going anywhere. As she almost bounced in fury, she reminded him of a hummingbird dive-bombing a flower. Tiny but also colourful, intense and vibrant.

An unholy flash of hostility lit up Ella's emerald-green eyes. 'I mean it!'

Nikolai sighed. 'You only *think* you mean it. Be aware that that temper of yours is a major weakness.'

Incensed by that crack, Ella said, *'One—'*

'When you allow yourself to lose your head, you surrender control.'

'Two—'

'And you're not thinking rationally either,' Nikolai told her smoothly.

'Three!'

'How could you be?' Nikolai continued. 'Right now I can read your face like a map. You want to jump on me and thump me but you're not physically up to that challenge, so you're stuck acting illogical and childish—'

'Four! And shut up while I'm counting! *Five!'* Ella added jerkily, her throat muscles so tight, she could barely get the words out.

'The performance you're putting on for me now is why I never allow myself to lose my temper,' Nikolai told her, thoroughly enjoying himself for the first time in a long time because she was that easy to rile. He would be able to wind her up like a clockwork toy and control her…*so* easily.

'Of course, you could try asking yourself why you're being this unreasonable. As far as I'm aware I did nothing worthy of this reception,' Nikolai murmured smooth as glass, his wide, expressive mouth quirking round the edges.

'Six!' But that fast she remembered his mouth on hers, hard and demanding and passionate, rather than playful and shy and sweet. He was the only man apart from Paul to ever kiss her. The core of steel deep inside her reached a furnace heat of hatred and temper and shame but her body still betrayed her. Her nipples pinched into tight little buttons that stung, and lower down in a place she didn't even want to think about she

felt that almost forgotten liquid, hot, sliding sensation. It made her teeth grind together in vexation.

'*Seven!*' she launched and reached for the phone on the desk, almost desperate to see him go, her brain a morass of angry, tumbling impressions and images.

'We're going to get on like a house on fire…*literally*,' Nikolai told her with sardonic bite. 'Because while I may control my temper, I am demanding, stubborn and impatient and if you cross me you'll know about it.'

'Out!' she spat at him furiously, outraged by the fact that she couldn't get him to react to her threat in even the smallest way. 'Get out of here!'

'Eight…maybe even nine,' Nikolai pronounced for her. 'When you know why I'm here, you'll *beg* me to stay.'

'In your dreams…*ten*!' Ella countered in a ringing tone of finality as she lifted the phone with a flourish.

'I'm the man who bought your father's debts,' Nikolai admitted and watched her freeze and lose all her animated angry colour while her arm slowly lowered the phone back on its rest and her hand fell back from it in dismay.

CHAPTER TWO

'THAT'S NOT POSSIBLE,' Ella whispered unevenly. 'It would be too much of a coincidence.'

'Coincidences happen,' Nikolai countered, for he had no intention of taking her into his confidence and sharing his ultimate plan.

'Not one this unlikely,' Ella argued, backing away from the desk while her brain endeavoured to regroup to this most surprising change of circumstance.

'You rang the firm who handle my legal work and asked to see me,' he reminded her levelly. 'Here I am.'

'I wasn't prepared for a personal visit, maybe a phone call or an appointment,' she muttered uncertainly, barely knowing what she was saying because the temper that was often her strength had subsided in fear like a pricked balloon. No, she couldn't possibly shout at or drive off her father's main creditor. Even angry, she wasn't that stupid.

The silence lay between them as thick and heavy as treacle. She stared at him, incredulous at such a piece of unwelcome happenstance as the combination of events that had brought Nikolai Drakos back into her life again. A man she had naturally assumed she would never see again, a man she had *prayed* she would never see again! And she had preferred that reality, had needed to know she could bury that silly little episode and wipe it from her mind as an insane moment while she was still grieving for the man she had loved. Being confronted by him again was a real slap in the face and she could feel her face warming and prickling as though she had sunburn.

'As you say...here you are,' Ella acknowledged woodenly. 'You can't be surprised that I'm shocked that my father's creditor is someone I've met before.'

'Would you call it a meeting? A brief encounter in a car park would be more accurate,' Nikolai murmured with a dry mockery that made her yearn to knock his teeth down his throat, for he made it sound as though they had shared rather more than a kiss.

And had she been willing, they would have done. She had no doubt of that. He was a player, the kind of male who did what he wanted when he wanted and he had certainly been in the mood for sex. Her face flamed at the awareness that, had she agreed and had it been physically possible, they could well have enjoyed a sordid, sweaty encounter there and then in his car and she would never have made it back to the misleading respectability of the hotel he had suggested. Inwardly she cursed her fair skin as mortification burned her cheeks, while he studied her with a measured attention that warned her he was picking up on her every reaction.

'So, you own Dad's debts,' Ella recapped, striving to push onward past the personal aspect and withstand the odd tingling heat that infiltrated her every time she clashed with Nikolai's stunning dark, black-lashed eyes. It was attraction. What else could it be? And it made her hate herself.

'You wanted the chance to speak to me,' Nikolai reminded her levelly. 'I have no idea what you want to say to me...apart from the obvious. If you're planning to pluck the violin strings, it won't work on me. Let's cut to the bottom line: this is business, nothing personal—'

'But it *is* personal to my family!'

'Your family is no concern of mine,' Nikolai declared with unapologetic assurance. 'But I do, as it happens, have another option to offer you.'

Tension made Ella rise slightly on her toes. 'Another option?' she queried breathlessly.

Nikolai gazed into those luminous green eyes and read the hope writ large there and for some reason it made him feel like a bastard. He crushed that foreign sensation and irritably squashed down his conscience. What was it about her? That air of vulnerability? Her physical delicacy? The shocking naivety that could persuade her to look at a stranger hoping that he was about to play the good Samaritan? How could she still be that trusting at her age? Sadly, he was not a soft touch, never had been, never would be and there was no point in even trying to pretend that he was. He didn't get close to anyone; he didn't connect with other people. He had been that way for a very long time and he had no plans to change his basic nature. When you let yourself care about anyone, you got kicked in the teeth and it had happened to him so often when he was a boy that he had learned his lesson fast.

'There is one situation in which I would be prepared to write off your father's debts,' he admitted.

In the unearthly silence that dragged, her tension heightened and her tummy gave a nervous flip. 'Well, what is that situation?' she pressed impatiently.

'You move in with me in London for a period of three months,' Nikolai outlined smoothly.

Her eyes opened wide and rounded in bewilderment. '*Move in* with you? And exactly what would that entail?'

'What it usually entails when a man and a woman live together,' Nikolai countered, wondering why he wasn't just spelling the terms out with his usual directness.

Possibly he was a little squeamish about the terms. Her reactions, the unmistakeable shyness she couldn't hide, were persuading him that, unlikely as it seemed, she might indeed be a virgin. He would very much like to take her to bed but he really didn't want her there on sufferance. He didn't particularly want to be the man who deflowered her either, although, when he thought about that aspect, he realised that he didn't want any other man to do it for him.

All of a sudden his brain was leaping about in directions he hadn't counted on, throwing up objections to what had seemed perfectly simple and straightforward only an hour before. And all that had changed was that Ella Palmer was now in front of him, and, instead of being merely a step in an ongoing project, was becoming very much a *lust* object in her own light.

Nikolai was confounded by that too because she was not his usual type. He went for tall, curvy blondes and Ella was tiny, skinny and almost as bare of curves as a teenaged boy. So, he had no understanding of precisely why he had developed a throbbing hard-on the instant a slight movement made her tiny, unfettered breasts shift below her T-shirt. Now he could see pointed nipples poking through the thin fabric and his body was eager to see a lot more of that slender but highly feminine body of hers. However, that was sex, nothing more, and he had many more convenient options in that line, didn't he? *Diavole*, why was he thinking such thoughts? What was the matter with him? He had never allowed himself to be driven by what lay south of his belt.

'You want me to be your girlfriend...?' Ella mumbled in wonderment, barely crediting that they were truly having such a conversation.

Nikolai winced. 'I don't have girlfriends... I have sex.'

'So, you're a man whore,' Ella pronounced before she could think better of it, for in her experience there were only two types of men available. One type was open to the possibility of meeting the *one* and commitment while the other type only wanted to sleep around with the maximum possible number of women.

His dark-as-jet eyes flashed like golden flames. 'Don't apply that label to me!'

'Oddly enough I wasn't trying to be insulting. I just meant that you only want sex and I know there are women like that too, so, although I shouldn't have said it, I was simply stating a fact.' Ella finally fumbled to a perspiring halt, her skin dampening below her clothing while she inwardly acknowledged the foolishness of saying anything he could find offensive. 'I'm only trying to interpret what you suggested as an option— if *not* girlfriend...?'

'Mistress,' Nikolai slotted in cool as ice.

Ella blinked, thinking he did not just say that...*did he*? Such a delightfully old-fashioned role for such a modern man. But then what did she know about Nikolai Drakos? She turned away from him, wandered over to the window and was surprised to see a big glossy dark limousine complete with driver parked outside. The limo could only belong to him, which meant that Nikolai was rich and privileged and that the concept of having a mistress to cater to his sexual needs might not seem as much of an anomaly to him as it was to her.

Unhappily, shock had welded Ella's tongue to the roof of her mouth because he was sexually propositioning her and nothing could have prepared her for that possibility. She wasn't drop-dead gorgeous…ironically, *he* was! Male heads didn't tend to swivel when Ella walked down the street because she had neither the length of leg nor the curves usually deemed necessary to attract such attention. Why on earth could he be making *her* such an offer?

'But we don't even know each other,' she framed dazedly. 'You're a stranger…'

'If you live with me I won't be a stranger for long,' Nikolai pointed out with monumental calm.

And the very sound of that inhuman calm and cool forced her to flip round and settle distraught eyes on his lean, darkly handsome face. 'You can't be serious about this!'

'I assure you that I am deadly serious. Move in and I'll forget your family's debts.'

'But it's a *crazy* idea!' She gasped, having failed to get him to acknowledge that reality and floundering against his restrained silence. It was obvious that he was determined to behave as though such a proposition were an everyday occurrence.

'It's not crazy to me,' Nikolai asserted. 'When I want anything, I go after it hard and fast.'

Her lashes dipped. Did he want her like that?

Enough to track her down, buy up her father's debts, and try and buy rights to her and her body along with those debts? The very idea of that made her dizzy and plunged her brain into even greater turmoil. 'It's immoral…it's blackmail.'

'It's definitely *not* blackmail. I'm giving you the benefit of a choice you didn't have before I came through that door,' Nikolai Drakos fielded with glittering cool. 'That choice is yours to make.'

'Like hell it is!' Ella fired back. 'The choice you're offering is totally unscrupulous.'

'When did I say I had scruples?' Nikolai asked almost conversationally. 'I want what I want and I want you in London to take out and show off.'

'But…*why*?' she interrupted, helpless in the grip of her desire to know that answer. 'Why pick me? I said no that night…was that all it took to fire you up? For you to suggest this?'

'I'm not going to answer those questions. I don't need to,' Nikolai told her without apology. 'My motivation is my own. Either you want to consider the option I've offered or you don't. It's entirely up to you.'

'But a mistress…!' A driven laugh fell from Ella's convulsing throat because she was struggling to accept that he could have confronted her with such an insane choice. 'Don't you understand that even if I wanted to say yes I couldn't?'

He frowned. 'What are you talking about?'

'My father wouldn't live with himself if he knew I was sleeping with a man just to get him out of trouble! No, the mistress option is a total impossibility as far as I am concerned.'

'That's for you to decide.' Nikolai settled a business card down on the desk. 'My phone number. I'll be staying at the Wrother Links Hotel until tomorrow.'

'I've already made my decision and it's a no,' Ella hastened to tell him.

Nikolai flashed her a slow wicked smile that radiated charisma. 'Think about it properly before you say no but if you discuss it with anyone else, I'll withdraw the offer,' he warned her smoothly. 'It's a strictly confidential option.'

'You know, you can't simply ask a woman you don't know to live with you,' she bit out, fit to be tied at his sheer nerve and nonchalance.

Black curling lashes screening his shrewd gaze, Nikolai shrugged a broad shoulder. 'I believe I just did.'

'But it's barbaric!' she exclaimed. 'A complete cheat of a supposed offer!'

Nikolai sent her a gleaming sideways glance. 'No, the real cheat was you kissing me the way you did last year and then saying no and acting as if I had grossly insulted you,' he murmured with lethal quietness.

'You *did* insult me!' Ella flung back, her cheeks hot as fire while she wondered if her refusal that night had started off his whole chain reaction. What else could possibly be driving him?

Nikolai straightened lazily as he opened the door. 'If you take offence that easily, maybe it's just as well that the answer is no.'

Strangely that wasn't what she wanted to hear and she didn't understand that truth, nor the feeling that his departure was somehow a low point rather than something to be celebrated. She watched the limo drive off, her thoughts miles away, trailing back down the timeline to the moment she had first met Nikolai Drakos…

* * *

Her stepmother's best friend, Ailsa, had been a wedding planner and when one of Ailsa's part-time workers had taken ill, Joy had insisted that Ella step in. Ella could have declined but she had been too well aware that if she crossed the older woman Joy would throw a tantrum and rain down misery on the whole family. And she had always hated listening to her stepmother torment her father with nasty, sneering comments. When Ella had arrived at the country house that evening she had been startled to be asked to park cars rather than wait tables as she had dimly expected. And, truth to tell, with an advanced driving test under her belt and a love of fast cars, parking the luxury models driven by the wedding guests would have been fun, had her foot not slid off the pedal of that McLaren Spider, causing the wing of it to be grazed against an overhanging bush.

Nikolai had started shouting and Ailsa had come running out to smooth over the incident. Unfortunately, Ella's immediate apology had had no effect and Ailsa had made a big deal out of supposedly sacking Ella simply to comfort Nikolai. That was when Nikolai had suddenly cooled off, dismissed the matter and insisted that he didn't want Ella sacked before striding into the house to join the rest of the guests.

It had been much later that night before she'd seen Nikolai again. She had been outside the ballroom listening to the DJ playing for the evening party while half dancing to the beat of the music to keep warm in the cold. And when she had heard something behind her, she had spun and he had simply been standing there watching her, dark eyes glowing golden as melted caramel in the reflected lights.

'If you want your car, you can fetch it for yourself,' Ella told him.

'You're right. I wouldn't allow you behind the wheel of it again,' he admitted, strolling almost soundlessly closer to gaze down at her. He had moved very quietly for such a big male. 'When do you finish tonight?'

'I'm finished now. I'm waiting for a lift home from one of the bartenders.'

'Could be a long wait,' he murmured softly.

'Could be.' Lifting her head, Ella shook her hair back from her face because the breeze was blowing it into her eyes.

'You have gorgeous hair,' he breathed.

'Thank you…' In the light flooding through the windows behind her, she could see his lean dark features with clarity and all she could think at that moment was that he was definitely the most gorgeous man she had ever come across.

'And stunning eyes…but, you're a rubbish driver.'

'My shoe slid on the pedal. I have an advanced driving test.'

'Don't believe you.'

Ella lifted her chin. 'Your problem, not mine.'

'My problem is that I want you,' Nikolai said boldly. 'I saw you dancing by the window and it gave me a high.'

Sharply disconcerted, Ella reddened. 'Oh—'

'Oh?' he mimicked with derision. 'That's it, that's all you've got to say?'

'What do you want me to say?' Ella rolled her eyes expressively. 'I'm not looking for a man right now.'

'And I'm not looking for a woman... I'm looking for *one* night,' Nikolai admitted silkily, lean brown fingers reaching up to curl into the fall of her hair and urge her closer than she would have chosen to be, had she been in her right mind.

As for that, what happened next proved to her that she was not in her right mind when Nikolai was around her because he closed his other hand to her spine and tilted her forward into sudden searing contact with his long, hard body. Within seconds he was kissing her as she had never been kissed before, forcing apart her lips with the hard pressure of his, sliding in his tongue, and sending such a jolt of wild excitement through her that her head swam and her knees buckled. He was passionate and demanding and all-male hungry, every sinuously sexual movement of his lean hips and powerful thighs against her warning her that a kiss could be almost as sizzlingly intimate as a naked embrace.

He lifted his handsome dark head and the chill of the night air on her back contrasted with the heat of his powerfully aroused body against hers. Immediately, Ella remembered who she was and where she was and the chill on her skin slivered inside right down to her stomach, and sickened her.

'Thanks, but no, thanks,' she said tartly, pulling free and starting to walk away.

'You can't be serious,' he breathed, his surprise audible because he knew she had been fired up just as much as he.

But what he didn't know was that Ella had never been that aroused...*ever*. And mere weeks after she had watched the love of her life being laid in the ground at twenty-four years of age, that truth hurt so bad that she almost sobbed over it. She had believed she truly wanted Paul but Paul had never made her feel like that and the pain of that acknowledgement tore into her grief and ate her alive with guilt.

'Watch me go,' she told Nikolai thinly, walking towards the back entrance of the country house where she would wait for her lift...regardless of how long because it would be infinitely safer than going any place with the male who had just kissed her. Kissed her until there was no yesterday and no Paul in her mind. Kissed her for now, for the moment, for a cheap pickup and one-night stand. She knew she was in a big enough emotional mess without making that mistake and doing something she would undoubtedly regret...

As she filed paperwork to tidy Rosie's desk, Ella drifted back from that powerful memory and shivered. She had blown him off. Even though it hadn't been intentional, she had given him the impression that she was with him every step of the way during that kiss and then she had changed her mind. But a woman was entitled to change her mind and she had exercised that right. Yet had she become that much more desirable after she walked away? How many women had said no to Nikolai? Ella reckoned that score would be low because he was very handsome and evidently wealthy into the bargain. Nikolai was a hard hitter, an achiever. Had she challenged his male ego?

Was it really pure coincidence that he now owned her father's debts? He hadn't answered her questions. He had said he was giving her a choice she hadn't had before he arrived, and, although she didn't like to see it that way, she saw that it was the unwelcome truth.

The father and grandmother she adored were on the brink of losing everything they had left. How could she stand back and let them suffer when she had been given an alternative?

Throughout the day her mind seethed with wild ideas. She was willing to do just about anything to save the roof over her family's head. Freed from the burden of those awful debts and Joy's extravagance, her father would finally be in a position to make a reasonable living again. Although he had lost the furniture shop, he remained a qualified accountant and the ability to work again would give him his self-respect back.

Yet while Ella might want to help her family, Nikolai Drakos had put her in an impossible situation. Her father would never accept such a sacrifice on her part. So, how could she get around that obvious stumbling block?

Well, one possibility would be offering Nikolai the intimate night she suspected he felt cheated out of. She shuddered at the prospect of having sex with anyone in such circumstances but just as quickly told herself off for being a drama queen. Why make a three-act tragedy out of a perfectly normal feature of life? If possessing her body meant that much to the man, he was welcome to it.

It was not as though she were still a virgin because she had actively chosen to embrace that state. She had waited for Paul, for the miraculous day when he would be 'well enough', only that opportunity had failed to arrive. Now and not for the first time she wished Paul had not been so exacting in his wishes, so determined that everything be right and perfect before they became intimate, because going to bed with Nikolai would have been much less intimidating had Ella already acquired some sexual experience. One night, she told herself bleakly, yes, she could do one night if it saved her family. Were there any other options?

Well, instead of making her a mistress, Nikolai could *marry* her, lending their entire arrangement the sort of respectable patina that would allow her father to accept his debts being paid off, because a son-in-law was a family member while a lover who was a stranger was something else entirely. Somehow she didn't think Nikolai would want to go for the wedding-ring option. In fact a reluctant giggle was forced from between Ella's tense lips at even the idea of making such a suggestion. The man who didn't date and only had sex was unlikely to warm to the prospect of holy matrimony...

At the end of her working day, Ella called the number on the business card Nikolai had left her and before he could even speak said, 'I want to come and see you this evening.'

Taken aback by that bold declaration, Nikolai frowned. 'You've changed your mind?'

'I want to talk...'

Nikolai was dubious. He had already wondered how sure she was of Cyrus's support if she was willing to turn *his* offer down without hesitation. Had his old enemy already proposed to her? Yet wouldn't she have thrown that information at him?

'There's nothing to *talk* about,' he countered.

'Where there's a will, there's a way,' Ella quoted Gramma in her desperation to get him to listen.

Ten minutes later, Ella walked into the exclusive Wrother Links Hotel. Rather belatedly she became conscious of her shabby work clothing, which consisted of a tee and worn skinny jeans thrust into sensible ankle boots. Perhaps she should have gone home first and changed and used some make-up, she reflected uneasily. But then Nikolai had outlined his outrageous proposal at the start of her working day when she was looking far from glamorous. Her smooth brow indented.

What did the wretched man want from her?

The obvious, she told herself irritably as the receptionist directed her into the lift with a curious appraisal. Just because she had never viewed her body as a means of negotiation didn't mean Nikolai felt the same. He had to want her for something and her body was the most likely explanation, Ella reasoned uncomfortably. Over the years she had listened to friends insist that men saw sex as being of crucial importance, which had left her confused, dealing with Paul's rigid self-discipline.

Even so, it was an enormous challenge for Ella to credit that suave, sophisticated Nikolai Drakos could possibly see a woman like her in some irresistible had-to-possess-her light. When she had first gone to uni to study, she had been bombarded by sexual approaches. In many ways that was why meeting Paul, initially only a friend, had been such a relief. Paul had valued her for the person she was, not for her body or the physical pleasure he assumed she could give him. Paul, however, had been a very special case, she reminded herself with regret.

A young man who introduced himself as Nikolai's employee opened the door of the suite and ushered her in. The desk in the room was scattered with papers, a laptop sitting open on it. She got a glance at the columns of figures on the screen before the employee closed it down and gathered the papers into a file to take his leave.

'Mr Drakos will be with you shortly,' he assured her as he departed.

Ella stared out of the window at the renowned golf course and, in an effort to steady her leaping nerves when she heard a sound somewhere behind her, she said, 'Do you play golf?'

'No. Not my game,' Nikolai proclaimed as he shook out his shirt. 'Why are you here, Ella?'

Ella spun round and focused in consternation on Nikolai's incredibly well-defined muscular abs and stomach as he pulled on a shirt. Clearly he was fresh from the shower with his black hair still curling damply and his hard-boned jaw clean-shaven, but the bronzed expanse of naked male flesh on show above the belt encircling his lean hips sharply disconcerted her. Cheeks warming, she glanced away. 'Is it inconvenient?'

'Let's call it unexpected,' he replied, his brilliant dark eyes resting on her.

Well, there was nothing of the seductress in her appearance, Nikolai acknowledged wryly. He had assumed she would dress up but she hadn't made the effort, which for some strange reason irritated him. Wasn't he worth that much effort? In the shower he had reminded himself that approaching Ella Palmer had always been a long shot. After all, if she had already had one rich man in the palm of her hand why would she accept another dictating terms to her? And yet the fact remained that, astonishingly, Cyrus was evidently not coming to his supposed future wife's rescue and had taken himself off on a long trip to China. Maybe the tip-off Nikolai had received about Cyrus's marital plans was rubbish, maybe Cyrus was simply playing with Ella…as he did in the initial stages of his games with such women, when he played the honourable respectful male to perfection to lull any suspicion of his true intentions.

'The unexpected doesn't always have to be bad,' Ella fenced while he buttoned his shirt. Her cheeks were hot because the little peepshow he had unthinkingly subjected her to had made perspiration break out on her skin below clothes that suddenly felt too tight and constricting.

'I believe you're acquainted with Cyrus Makris,' he remarked.

Startled, Ella glanced at him. 'Yes. He's a family friend. I was engaged to his nephew, Paul, until he died,' she told him, wondering how he had known about her acquaintance with Cyrus before a vague association occurred to her. 'Your name… I should've guessed. You're Greek as well, aren't you?'

'I am. Would you like a drink?'

'No, thanks.' Ella simply wanted to get what she had to say said and then run. 'Can't stay long anyway. I left my dog outside in the van.'

'So…?' Nikolai prompted, watching a strand of bronze hair fan out across her white throat as she lifted her head high, her pale skin accentuating the luminous green of her eyes and the succulent pink of her lips. He tensed, fighting the incipient throb at his groin with annoyance.

'Would…?' Ella breathed in deep and straightened her spine. 'I'm here to ask if one night would do.'

'One night of what?' Nikolai queried blankly.

'You know, sex, for goodness' sake!' Ella launched back at him in furious embarrassment. 'I mean, if that's all you want, I hardly need to go to London and live with you for it!'

Nikolai surveyed her in shock and it took a great deal to shock him. 'Let me get this straight…you're offering me a night of sex instead?'

'Don't make it sound so sordid!' Ella lashed back at him.

'It wasn't me who made the offer. No, the night of sex wouldn't meet my…requirements.' Nikolai selected the word and voiced it smooth as silk. 'I also assume by that offer that you're not a virgin?'

'And why would you think I was at my age?' But Ella thought better of lying because there was always the hope that the truth would be a total turn-off for him. 'Actually, I am inexperienced but…'

Distaste at the entire conversation was filling Nikolai. Of course she had assumed he wanted her for sex. What else was she supposed to think? But he wasn't a ball of sleaze like Cyrus, who treated women like toys he enjoyed breaking. And as it occurred to Nikolai what a challenge making that offer must have been for an innocent like her, he almost swore and had to fight back an angry sense of discomfiture. For the very first time he appreciated that he had recklessly plunged himself into a scenario that was not at all his style.

'One night won't work for me,' Nikolai admitted in a driven undertone.

Ella's heart was thumping at what felt like a mile a minute behind her breastbone. Relief and dismay assailed her in equal parts. Naturally she was very relieved not to be asked to immediately deliver on the

shameless proposition she had just made, but she was
taken aback by the speed and power of his repudiation
as well. What did he really want? What on earth more
could he possibly want or expect from her?

'Then I only have one other…suggestion to make,'
she murmured tightly. 'You marry me.'

'*Marry* you?' Nikolai exclaimed after an unnerv-
ingly protracted pause while he studied her with incredulous force. 'Are you out of your mind?'

She had finally got an honest and true reaction out
of Nikolai Drakos, Ella realised, and a curious feeling
of triumph mingled with her mortification. The idea
of getting married had shattered him, scoring colour
along those amazing high cheekbones, widening his
stunning dark-fringed golden eyes. Evidently he had
not been prepared for that idea.

CHAPTER THREE

'It was a purely practical suggestion from my point of view,' Ella told him curtly.

'You need to change your point of view,' Nikolai retorted with sardonic bite.

Her face was burning with embarrassment and her hands had closed into tight little fists of restraint. If he couldn't be more frank about exactly what he needed from her, then he could take the rough with the smooth and it would be his own fault. 'I can't. You would have to marry me to persuade my father that it was acceptable for you to write off his debts. He's no freeloader.'

'There is no way that I will marry you to get what I want!' Nikolai cut in with a raw edge of impatience to his dark deep drawl.

'Then that concludes our discussion,' Ella stated without heat, simply desperate to escape the opulent hotel suite and forget that she had ever met him. As her father had said when he had put the family home on the line and lost it, well, at least he knew he had tried. Well, she now knew what it was like to try hard and still fail too.

'*Diavole*, Ella!' Nikolai bit out as she reached the door. 'There *has* to be another way!'

Ella spun round. 'No, there honestly isn't. My father couldn't live with the idea that his daughter would move in with some man to clear his debts.'

His melted caramel eyes suddenly flashed as brilliant a gold as sunlight. 'You have the rare ability to make everything sound sleazy!'

'No, you just don't like plain speaking...unless it's you doing it. And you talk in riddles. You asked me to be your mistress yet you say no to the chance to sleep with me.'

'Obviously I want more from you than sex. I can get sex anywhere, any time,' he assured her dismissively.

Frustration roared through Ella. 'I'm not a secret heiress, am I?'

'What the hell are you talking about?'

'I thought I might be the sixth cousin of some distant relation who's worth a fortune and that you had found out and that maybe—'

'Your imagination is more inventive than mine. But in that situation a man would want marriage to secure his share of the inheritance. However, in *this* instance...' Nikolai compressed his wide sensual mouth.

Marriage, even a fake marriage, was out of the question. Nikolai had never wanted to get married. From the little he remembered of his irresponsible parents, they had fought continually and spent their money on alcohol and drugs while neglecting their two children. He probably wouldn't have survived early childhood without the loving care of his older sister, who had had a real live baby to look after instead of a doll. No, Nikolai would be perfectly happy to leave the world without descendants of his own. Nor could he imagine wanting one woman for the rest of his life and shunning all others. He barely repressed a shudder because he set a high value on his freedom of choice.

'In this instance?' Ella prompted.

'I need you with me in London.'

'But as I've already explained, you can't have me without a wedding ring. You know, I don't want to marry you either,' Ella admitted shortly. 'But if it makes my family happy and secure again, I would do it for their sake.'

'I wouldn't even consider it. *I* will deal with your family,' Nikolai said flatly.

'What on earth do you mean?'

What it really came down to was how far he was prepared to go in his efforts to punish Cyrus, Nikolai reflected. A fleeting image of his sister's gentle smile, brought to the surface by memories of his background, froze him in place. There should be and there would be *no* limits to his desire for revenge. If others got caught up in the backlash, what was that to him? He could not afford to have a conscience. Ella was a pawn, nothing more.

'I will tell your family that we've been seeing each other and that now we want to be together in London,' Nikolai explained smoothly. 'Your father cannot struggle to settle debts that no longer exist. He will not have the luxury of choice.'

'You think it's a luxury for me to be able to *choose* to be your mistress?' Ella launched at him furiously, rage bubbling up through her slight body like a hot spring at the prospect of that indignity. 'But I've already said no to that option!'

'Which is wasting my time and your own! You can't renegotiate the terms just because you don't like them.

I won't let you. There will be no single night, no marriage either,' he asserted in a harsh undertone, his lean, darkly handsome features forbidding in cast, his stunning eyes hard as black diamonds. 'Either you come to London to be with me or I walk away. That's the *only* choice you have!'

The raw tension straining the atmosphere sent a wave of dizziness through Ella. Consternation brought her defensive barriers crashing down. He had ruthlessly rejected her options. Her head swimming a little, she closed her hands over the back of a tall chair to force her body to stand steady. She stared back at him with a sinking heart. It was the moment she had been fighting to avoid since he'd first confronted her earlier that day. The 'grit your teeth and deal' moment when there was no room left to wriggle. Perspiration dampened her skin.

'Your sole source of interest here should be the payoff,' Nikolai reminded her drily. 'And learning to do as you are told.'

In the rushing silence, Ella wrinkled her nose. 'If I don't agree with something, I'm hopeless at doing what I'm told.'

'But you can learn,' Nikolai sliced in, his tone as glacial as ice water. 'Don't sign up for this if you can't respect the rules.'

'Perhaps you could tell me how I'm supposed to respect a man who wants me even though I don't want him?' Ella shot back at him in scornful challenge.

'Do you always lie in preference to telling the truth about yourself?' Nikolai enquired dangerously softly as he strode closer.

Ella found herself backed up against the door before

she could grab the opportunity to make the swift exit she had originally planned. 'I'm not lying—'

Nikolai rested the palm of one hand against the door and gazed down at her with hard dark eyes. 'The worst of it is that you know you're lying...but I don't play that game.'

'I want to leave.'

'Not until I say you can,' Nikolai fenced, so big he was like a wall blocking the rest of the room from her view and cutting out most of the light, so that for the first time she wished she were wearing heels to cut the ridiculous height differential between them to a more reasonable level.

Ella turned up her face, chin tilted at an obstinate angle, green eyes sparkling. 'I could use my knee to persuade you.'

'Why would you damage a part of me you hope to enjoy?' Nikolai countered.

'It would take an avalanche to crush your ego, wouldn't it?'

'If I was modest you would walk all over me with pleasure.' Nikolai was entranced by the glorious green of her eyes against the smooth, fine grain of her porcelain skin. 'But that's not what you want from me, is it? You'd much prefer me to take your choices away and give you the excuse to *be* with me.'

'That's rubbish!' Ella gasped, barely able to credit that he had made such an allegation. 'I don't want or need an excuse to be with you!'

'*Ne*...yes, you do,' Nikolai insisted, pinning her up against the door in blatant entrapment. 'You want excuses and persuasion and, sadly, you're not going to get them from me. That's not how I am with a woman.'

'Fascinating as this dialogue no doubt is to a man who likes to listen to the sound of his own voice, I'm not interested.'

'Every time you lie to me I'll punish you.'

'Punish me?' Ella parroted, blinking in bewilderment.

Nikolai bent down and scooped her up, disconcerted by how very light she was. Yes, she was small and slight in build but he was convinced she weighed too little to be healthy. Nikolai walked through the room into the bedroom with her in his arms. 'You'll like the way I punish you.'

'What are you doing?' Ella exclaimed as he swept her off her feet.

'Sealing our agreement.'

'What agreement?' she demanded rawly as he dropped her down on a bed so well sprung that she bounced.

'Your agreement to be my mistress.' He savoured the word.

As Ella made a sudden sidewise motion intended to remove her from the bed Nikolai came down and imprisoned her with the vastly superior weight and strength of his big, powerful body. 'Get off me. Let go of me...*right now*!' she raked at him.

'I really hate being shouted at,' Nikolai confided a split second before his hard, sensual mouth claimed hers.

And for that same split second it was as though Ella's world stopped turning and she was jolted off course, sent breathless and spinning into the unknown. Heat surged up through her like an invasive weapon. He eased her out from under him but kept her trapped in his arms. Irritation flamed through her because inexplicably she had liked his crushing weight on hers. Her fists struck at shirt-clad shoulders as unyielding as rock. The tip of his tongue flicked inside her mouth and she shivered violently, the clenching at her secret core almost painful in its intensity. He nipped at her lower lip, sucked and soothed it with his tongue. She wanted more, she wanted more so badly it hurt to be denied and the rushing tide of that hunger shocked her back into her mind again.

His kisses were like nothing she'd ever experienced before. A lean hand tunnelled below her tee and closed round a small, high breast, long fingers stroking the throbbing tip and lingering to rub and tug until her spine arched in response and her hips jerked up and a helpless sound of craving was released from low in her throat.

He pushed up the T-shirt and replaced his fingers with his mouth. She was so sensitive there that she quivered beneath every lash of his tongue, every teasing brush of his teeth, and the molten heat pulsing between her thighs was swelling and swelling in an unstoppable rise. Her hips shifted, the driving need for relief powering her every instinctive movement, and then the surge at the heart of her became so urgent, so utterly overpowering that a jagged climax took her by storm. The wave of excitement that jerked her in his hold left her sobbing for breath and mental clarity as shock seized hold of her instead.

In a driven movement that took him by surprise, Ella rolled off the bed and yanked down her T-shirt with shaking hands. Her face was hot as a fire and her entire body was throbbing and trembling in the backwash of an orgasm more powerful than anything she had ever experienced. Her nerves were shot to hell. She couldn't even breathe normally. Momentarily she closed her eyes tight, praying for self-control. He could make her want him. He touched her, he kissed her and everything, including her proud protest of indifference, went haywire. Her body raged wildly out of control around him, which was just one more reason for her to hate him.

Dry-mouthed, Nikolai studied her, fighting his raging libido. He literally *ached*. He wanted to haul her back to the bed and pin her under him to drive into the hot, sweet release of her tiny body, and the intensity of his desire sent a chill of recoil snaking through him. He didn't do intense in any form. He didn't get excited about sex. He didn't do exclusive. He steered clear of entanglements and complications. Revenge and work motivated him. He had never *needed* anything else. He had never needed a woman and, if he had anything to do with it, he never would.

'I'm leaving,' she told him flatly while she fought harder than she ever had in her life to rescue some kind of composure. After quivers of reaction were still travelling through her treacherous body, while she tried not to question her total loss of control, keen not to think along such demeaning lines in his presence.

Nikolai sprang off the bed, shoving his shirt back below his belt. 'I'll follow you back.'

'Follow me *where*? What are you planning to do?'

'Ease your move to London.'

'Don't you dare go near my family!' Ella warned him furiously. 'You're a stranger to them.'

'But I won't be a stranger for long,' Nikolai asserted, picking up a jacket.

'You don't know what you're doing. They're not stupid. They're never going to believe that I've been seeing some man in secret!' she told him with scorn.

Nikolai elevated a fine black brow. 'People believe what they want to believe and they'll be relieved that you've started living again.'

Ella's face shuttered. 'I don't know what you're talking about.'

'I'm not stupid either. You're a woman and most women are dramatic. I bet you swore you'd never love again after your fiancé died. I bet you've hugged your grief to you like a security blanket ever since,' Nikolai opined.

Ella had turned white as bone. She flung him a look of loathing. 'How dare you drag Paul into this? How do you even know about him?'

'I know enough about you to make an educated guess or two,' Nikolai drawled coolly.

'Well, you got it wrong, badly wrong,' she assured him, but she was lying because although she would never have admitted it he had got it all frighteningly right. In fact his accuracy was both uncanny and mortifying. She *had* sworn that she would never love again, that she would never date another man after Paul. Her grief had been so great that she had voiced bitter self-destructive sentiments that had contained little common sense. The last thing she needed to hear now was Nikolai Drakos implying that she had acted like a drama queen craving sympathy and attention.

'So, quite naturally, your family will be delighted to believe that you have moved on after your loss and their pleasure in that reality will help them gloss over any inconsistencies in our story. They will *want* us to be real,' Nikolai declared with a sardonic smile. 'Your only role is to act happy about moving to London to see more of me.'

Something akin to panic assailed Ella's breathing process, tightening her chest, closing her throat. Act happy? She wasn't sure she knew how to do that. Life had been too challenging in recent years to offer many such opportunities but she had learned to smile and fake it for her family's benefit. No, it was the idea of moving to London and an unfamiliar environment to *be* with Nikolai that shocked and dismayed her most. And the concept of living with a man, being *intimate* with a man like Nikolai Drakos utterly unnerved her. Yet if she didn't agree to Nikolai's demands her family's life would be ruined. And after the setbacks and upheavals her father and Gramma had already lived through, how could they possibly cope with more at their age?

Almost three hours later, Ella let Gramma herd her into the kitchen for a private chat. She went reluctantly because she was straining to eavesdrop on the conversation that Nikolai was having with her father in the dining room the older man had long used as an office. The men's voices rose and fell, Nikolai's deep-pitched drawl soothing the rising note in her father's audible objections.

'I want Ella happy and she won't be happy if she's worrying herself sick about her family back home,' Nikolai asserted forcefully.

Ella paled. Nikolai would be saying all the right things and wearing all the right expressions, she reflected bitterly. He was clearly a consummate liar and smooth as molasses in a situation that would have sent nine out of ten men running for the hills. In action he was a breathtakingly quick study. He had arrived just after the family finished dinner and joined them for tea and carrot cake. He had grasped Ella's hand to declare that they had been seeing each other for months, ever since they had met the night she was parking cars. He had been very convincing, very persuasive and she had little doubt that he would soon crush her father's protests and persuade him to accept that his debts were being written off.

'Do you know what surprised me most about all this? Nikolai is *so* different from Paul,' Gramma remarked as Ella began to load the dishwasher to keep her restive hands busy. 'He's a real man's man.'

Ella's soft mouth compressed. The older woman had a traditional outlook. She liked men who could hunt a wild boar before breakfast and reduce a pile of logs to wood chips by dinner time. Paul's lack of interest in traditional male pursuits had bemused Gramma. She had liked him and treated him like a son but she had never understood him, Ella conceded with regret.

'I never thought that you would go for someone like Nikolai. Of course, he's very good-looking and obviously successful. Are you sure you know what you're getting into with him?' the older woman pressed. 'I know living together is very popular these days but I noticed that there was no talk of an engagement in the future or anything like that.'

'Let's see how it goes first. We may be too different. It may not work out between us,' Ella commented, dropping the first hint towards her eventual breakup with Nikolai. 'Who can tell when we haven't been able to spend much time together here?'

'Why didn't you tell us about him?' Gramma demanded for at least the third time. 'Are we so unapproachable?'

'I said a lot of stupid stuff after Paul died,' Ella muttered numbly.

'You were hurt, grieving. It was normal for you to feel that way,' Gramma assured her. 'I only want to be sure you're not leaping into this too fast with Nikolai. You're turning your whole life upside down for him. I did like the fact though that he said you might choose to pick up and continue your veterinary training again.'

Yes, if there were any right impressive things to say, Nikolai had contrived to corner the market on those sentiments, Ella ruminated bitterly. He came, he saw, he conquered. Her father and her grandmother had sat in awe while Nikolai shared his supposed thoughts. Acting as though he loved her had come so very naturally to him that it had spooked Ella. He had never said the words, but his behaviour had convinced his receptive audience that he cared deeply for Ella and only wanted her happiness.

'He's what you need,' the older woman murmured. 'A fresh start somewhere new. However, I suspect that this development is going to come as a huge shock to Cyrus.'

'I expect so,' Ella remarked uncertainly, thinking that it had come as a huge shock to her as well, although she could hardly admit the fact.

'You haven't a suspicion, have you?' Gramma grimaced. 'I don't think Cyrus sees you only as Paul's former fiancée. In fact I believe his interest is a lot more personal.'

Ella studied her grandmother's troubled face in consternation and winced. 'No, you're totally wrong about that. What on earth gave you such a *horrible* idea?'

'It *would* be horrible to you, then…' The older woman gathered with a hint of relief. 'For a while I was a bit worried that his attentions might be welcome?'

'There hasn't been any attentions,' Ella contradicted defensively.

'The flowers…the lunch dates…that big charity do…him asking you to check his house while he's away.'

'For a start, Cyrus has only sent me flowers a couple of times and the charity thing was a special favour. There's only been a couple of lunch dates and those were only casual catch-ups,' Ella protested. 'And me calling in to check his house when he has a resident housekeeper was just Cyrus being plain silly! I think he got all riled up about that spate of country-house robberies last year. Honestly, Gramma, Cyrus has never done or said anything that would give me the idea that he sees me as anything other than his late nephew's fiancée and a family friend.'

'Well, I think you've missed the signs. I don't like the way he looks at you and I wouldn't let your father approach him for a loan because I was worried it might come with strings attached,' Gramma confided uncomfortably.

Had Ella been in the mood to laugh, she would have laughed then at the irony of her grandmother's misgivings. Evidently the older woman had misread Cyrus's motives and distrusted him but she had offered Nikolai and his honeyed hollow lies a red-carpet welcome.

'Ella…?' Nikolai called her from the hall.

Grudgingly she went to the doorway. Butch pushed

out past her to caper round Nikolai's feet. From the instant of first laying eyes on Nikolai the tiny dog had been inexplicably smitten and craving his attention.

'Show me out. I need to get back to the hotel and start organising everything. That animal is insane,' he breathed, stepping carefully to avoid his canine companion.

'What do you have to organise?' Ella queried, shooing her pet away while wondering why Butch wasn't picking up on her hostility towards his new idol.

'Arrangements for your move,' Nikolai advanced, pulling open the front door with a lean, powerful hand and stepping out into the cool evening air.

As Ella closed the door in the little dog's face he began to fuss and bark in annoyance. 'You think you've won, don't you?' she whispered bitterly as soon as she was free from the risk of being overheard by her family.

Nikolai swung round, dark golden eyes as bright as torches, a satisfied half-smile lifting his sardonic mouth. 'I *know* I've won and you should be pleased. Everyone's happy.'

'Everyone but me,' Ella cut in curtly.

'I'll make you happy. You'll have fabulous clothes and fabulous jewellery,' Nikolai assured her, one hand splayed across her spine to hold her still in front of him as he lounged back against the wing of his spectacular sports car.

Ella bristled like a cat stroked the wrong way, scorn lightening her bright green eyes to palest jade. 'Those things aren't going to make me happy.'

'What about the even more fabulous sex?' Nikolai husked, both arms locking her into place in front of him, his keen gaze watching the rise of colour in her cheeks.

He couldn't stop touching her. He couldn't stop noticing things about her either. It was as though he went into supercharged observation mode in her presence. She was blushing and for some reason he revelled in having that effect on her even while he was continually surprised at the level of her innocence. How could she have been engaged and yet remain so naïve? True, the fiancé had been ill but the couple had been together for years. It must've been quite a particular relationship, he reflected in sincere puzzlement.

After all, Ella seethed with so much outright passion. At the hotel she had flared from a spark into a wild hot flame in his arms and her fiery generous response had been incredibly exciting. Indeed it was years since Nikolai had found *any* aspect of sex exciting. On a scale of one to ten his hunger for Ella had now veered into the seriously uncomfortable zone. The image of her lying against him quivering and gasping with release, her languorous green eyes pinned to him, would stay with him for ever. He didn't think he had ever wanted a woman so much and that seriously bothered him. Did it bother him enough to stop the whole scheme in its tracks?

He was promising her fabulous sex. Of course he was, Ella reflected in exasperation. Nikolai was incredibly confident of his own abilities. And maybe there was some excuse for that, she conceded as her body leant forward seemingly of its own volition, drawn by the heat and dominance of his sizzling sexual charisma.

Nikolai bent his head and kissed her. It was a slow claiming as the tip of his tongue traced the lush fullness of her lower lip and then delved gently between. A breathy little gasp erupted from her parted lips and she stepped closer. His arms snapped round her and it was the work of a moment for him to swing round and press her back against the car, his sensual mouth driving down hard on hers, his lean, powerful body crushing her against the unyielding metal.

Her every skin cell seemed to erupt into life as heat raced through her bloodstream and a bolt of naked yearning surged from low in her pelvis. His mouth was all she cared about. She couldn't get enough of him, was convinced she would never get enough of him. She gloried in the thrust of his arousal against her, the knowledge that Nikolai Drakos wanted her and couldn't hide the fact.

I want this man, she acknowledged, shocking herself rigid. Not someone she loved or respected or even liked. He exerted a primitive pull on her senses, which she could only compare to an utterly mindless desire to put her hand in a fire. But was it so destructive? So *wrong*? Wasn't it normal, even natural, that the physical side of her nature, which she had long been forced to suppress, should finally demand expression? And Nikolai was magnificent...

Nikolai wrenched himself free of her, breathing hard. She made him feel like a teenager with his first girl. It unnerved him and made the equivalent of defensive barriers of iron bars spring up inside him to police his very thought and reaction. She knocked him off balance, tore his control to shreds and he hated it. 'I'll be in touch,' he said without any expression at all.

Ella backed on hollow legs to the doorstep and watched him drive off. He had behaved as if nothing had happened. The hard, high planes of his lean dark features had betrayed no emotion. His eyes had been veiled by those ridiculously long lashes of his and his voice had been cool in tone. So where did that leave her?

Set on the road to making the biggest mistake of her life? Or to making the biggest discovery? She would make that choice, Ella promised herself squarely, *not* him. Wanting him wasn't going to make a fool out of her. She was bright enough to see that what he made her feel had nothing to do with love and caring. She wouldn't let him hurt her. She wouldn't let him use her. If there was any using to be done, *she* would be the user. And if he thought otherwise, he was in for a very big surprise...

CHAPTER FOUR

ELLA HAD TO smother a yawn while her nails were being done because she was bored stiff. A car had collected her and Butch early that morning and ferried them down to London. Parting from her father and grandmother had been tough but the knowledge that the family home was now safe and that her father was already making cheerful plans to open up a home office to work as an accountant had soothed her nerves. She had done the right thing, she was *doing* the right thing, she told herself urgently.

As soon as she had arrived in London it had been clear that her entire day had already been mapped out for her. Ella had been dropped off first while Butch and her luggage had travelled on to the town house where she would apparently be staying.

It was hours since she had arrived at the exclusive beauty salon where she had been waited on hand and foot, wrapped in fleecy towels and generally treated like an animated doll to be beautified. So far there was not one part of her that had not come in for some form of improving attention. She had been waxed and moisturised and polished to perfection. Her hair had been washed and conditioned and trimmed and now fell in silky waves round her shoulders.

In his office across the city, Nikolai couldn't concentrate. She was within reach, in *his* home. He had never lived in his late grandfather's house, however, and Ella would pretty much live there alone because Nikolai had no intention of giving up the privacy of his apartment. But his plan was coming to fruition. This very evening, Cyrus Makris would be back in London to attend the annual dinner being held to raise funds for Nikolai's favourite charity. Cyrus was, of course, a generous benefactor. He always made a point of giving money to organisations that took care of the victims of abuse. His good reputation was of unparalleled importance to him and invariably his first line of defence. But whatever else he got, he wasn't getting Ella, Nikolai reflected exultantly.

An older man wearing a bow tie and a smart black jacket opened the front door of the imposing town house. 'Miss Palmer...please come in. I'm Max, Mr Drakos's steward. I look after everything here.'

Ella walked into a surprisingly dark and ornate hall and looked around in surprise. She had somehow assumed that Nikolai would live in a very contemporary setting. But as she glanced into a massive, equally dark reception room and rolled her eyes at the clutter on every surface, she could see that indoors the clock of time had reset to the late Victorian Gothic era of interior decoration.

'My late employer, Mr Drakos's grandfather, didn't like change. This was originally his wife's family home and he kept everything the way it was after his wife passed. He got very annoyed if I moved anything.'

'My goodness; with all this stuff, how did he even notice something had been moved?' Ella exclaimed, spinning round to gape at her surroundings.

'Like the present Mr Drakos, he was a very clever and very observant man,' Max told her. 'Let me show you to your room.'

'Where's Butch…er…my dog?' Ella asked.

Max led her silently into a room with a tiled floor and a log burner. A scruffy terrier with flyaway ears lay sprawled across a rug there with Butch nestled against her. She was about twice Butch's size but Ella's pet showed no fear of the other animal. 'Good grief,' Ella framed as Butch leapt up and charged at her, his little eyes bright with welcome. His companion slowly sat up, voiced a half-hearted gruff bark before dropping her head down again, her attention welded to Butch.

'That's Mr Drakos's dog, Rory. Officially she's called Aurora. Rory took an immediate liking to Butch and has been cuddled up to him ever since. I expect she's enjoying the company.'

'I didn't know Mr Drakos had a pet.'

'She travels a lot with my employer. I'll show you upstairs now.' Max led the way up the elegant staircase.

The bed in the spacious bedroom was new, she was relieved to note, but the elaborate ebonised furniture followed the same theme as the ground-floor décor. Max opened a door to show off a high-tech en suite and she smiled. 'That must be a recent improvement.'

'When the electric and plumbing were being re-newed Mr Drakos took the opportunity to install bath-rooms and replace the kitchen. The redecoration project is awaiting the attention of the new mistress of the house,' Max remarked, flicking her a conspiratorial sidewise glance that made her stiffen as comprehension set in.

Seemingly the older man had misinterpreted her role in Nikolai's life and had assumed she was destined to be a wife, who would eventually take charge of the household. That was so far from the truth that it pained Ella like a nagging toothache. Max brought up her luggage and then reappeared with a beautiful long dress sheathed in a protective covering, other packaged items and several jewel boxes.

'Deliveries from Mr Drakos,' he announced. 'He phoned to say that he would collect you at seven.'

Ella raised a brow and said nothing.

Unfurling her phone, she called Nikolai when Max had left the room. 'It's Ella. Are we going out tonight?'

'Yes, I'm taking you to a gala dinner. I sent a dress, accessories and jewellery for you to wear. Haven't you received them yet? Didn't Max mention my call?'

'Yes…and yes. But you should've informed me in person.'

Nikolai compressed his hard, sensual mouth. This was why he didn't do relationships with women. He didn't want the petty squabbles, the clingy expectations or the too easy taking of offence to disrupt his day. 'I'm very busy,' he told her honestly.

'Since when have you been buying me clothes?'

'This is your new life, Ella. There'll be big changes. Get used to it.'

Seething at his stubborn, uncompromising stance, Ella ended the call. She unzipped the garment bag to reveal a designer gown. Although sleeveless and conservative in style, it was composed of the most beautiful white fabric overlaid with a shimmer of gold that glistened in the light. It was what Ella would have described as a dress fit for a princess and she was a little surprised it wasn't pink in colour and very puffy in shape. Was this what mistresses were wearing this season? Surely something sleek and black with a plunging neckline would have been more appropriate? Then it occurred to her that she had very little to show off in a plunging neckline and she squirmed.

Her cheeks fired up at the acknowledgement that she *had* agreed to be Nikolai's mistress. She studied the low, wide bed with its pristine white bedding and groaned out loud. Indecision was tearing her in two. Suddenly she felt as if she didn't know herself any more because one half of her was beyond excited at the prospect of sharing that bed with Nikolai while the other half of her was shocked and panicky. Which of those halves was her true self? In that instant she felt plunged into emotional turmoil.

Could she do it? Have meaningless sex without making a fuss about it? She wanted him, didn't she? The tightness in her chest eased at the acceptance of that fact, which made her feel more in control. Nikolai had forced a hard choice on her but what she made of the next step was solely her department. And if she was about to officially become a mistress there wasn't much point in slinking about as though she were ashamed of herself. Her family was secure again and she was grateful for the fact. She would use Nikolai for experience. The giving wasn't going to be all one-sided, she told herself firmly. She would be benefitting from his expertise. She wouldn't let herself feel anything for him either, anything *at all*. When it was over she would walk back into her own life and take it up again. That was why it was so important that she return to her veterinary training and complete it, she thought ruefully. Her career would give her a firm foundation on which to build a fresh future and it would provide her with a focus as nothing else could.

In the midst of that thought she flipped open one of the jewellery boxes and blinked in amazement at the flash of an extravagant emerald and diamond pendant. Evidently Nikolai wanted to display her like an expensive trophy, a rich man's toy. But why? She had assumed that for him it was all about sex, but now, instead of trying to take immediate advantage, he was marching her out to some formal public event. That didn't make sense. *He* didn't make sense. Nothing he did made sense. Why on earth had he settled on her in the first place?

Simply because she was free and available at the right time for a price he was willing to pay? Or because he had really, *really* wanted her last year and would do just about anything to have her? A surprising sparkle lightened her troubled gaze. She knew which option she preferred. Nikolai's proposition, his sheer, unscrupulous determination to get her into bed at any cost, was strangely flattering to a woman whose fiancé had resisted her supposed attractions at every turn.

As she went for a shower her eyes stung and misted with tears on that wounding thought.

'It doesn't have to be perfect,' she had told Paul once. 'I mean, I know it's not going to be perfect the first time. I'm not stupid. But perfect doesn't matter to me.'

Unfortunately it had evidently mattered a great deal to Paul. Yet sex wouldn't be any more perfect with Nikolai, she reasoned ruefully before sensibly shutting down her memories. Nikolai wouldn't expect perfect and something told her that he would take imperfect in his stride. He was complex but adaptable and she would have said he was less hung up on image had he not selected a dress and jewellery for her and ensured that she spent the day having her appearance tuned up at a beauty salon. Nikolai wanted her to look the very best she could and why shouldn't he?

Nikolai stilled in the hall as Ella descended the stairs with the caution of a woman wearing very high heels. The chandelier high above her head glittered over her metallic-bronze hair, picking out the deep auburn and gold strands and enhancing the radiance of her skin. The gown lengthened and shaped her tiny frame and the emerald pendant and earrings threw her luminous green eyes into striking prominence. A slow smile of satisfaction slashed Nikolai's forbidding mouth. He was very much looking forward to the evening ahead. It would *kill* Cyrus to see the woman he wanted with his mortal enemy.

And that was what the entire exercise was all about, he reminded himself darkly. Striking a blow at Cyrus was the goal, *not* taking Ella to bed. He tensed. Taking Ella to bed to taste that soft white skin, play with those luscious little breasts and sink so deep into her that she wouldn't know where he began and she ended. The erotic images sizzled through his brain, cutting through rational thought. Hunger thrummed through him instead, kicking off the pulse at his groin until he throbbed with hungry need. His even white teeth gritted while he fought the reaction because this wasn't how it was supposed to be.

On the bottom step, Ella collided with Nikolai's scorching dark golden eyes and her heart started banging like crazy inside her chest, every sense switching to super-sensitive levels. He was so beautiful it hurt. The luxuriant black of his hair, the sculpted slant of his hard cheekbones, the clean-shaven shadow outlining his strong jaw and wonderfully sensual and kissable lips. Taken aback by her own susceptibility, she sucked in a hasty breath and walked out to the waiting limousine with him.

'I understand that this was your grandfather's house. How long is it since he died?' Ella asked quietly.

Nikolai tensed, long tanned fingers curling against a powerful thigh. 'Five years.'

'Were you close?'

'No, I never met him...'

'Never?' Ella studied him wide-eyed. 'And yet he left you his house?'

'And his vast business empire. He wasn't a sentimental man but having an heir of his own blood was tremendously important to him,' Nikolai divulged grudgingly, loathing the topic of conversation but too proud and private to admit his sensitivity to it.

He had long since come to terms with his grandfather's essential indifference to him as a human being. The old man had paid for his education, and thanks to that Nikolai had been able to build on his strengths and advance in life, he thought. Sadly his grandfather had not been equally generous to Nikolai's sister, Sofia, because his sole interest had been in his *male* grandchild.

Nikolai's conscience was still weighted by the knowledge that his only sibling had had to leave school young, work in menial jobs in Athens and scrimp and save for survival. Even more regrettably he had come into his inheritance too late to protect or help the young woman who had been more of a mother to him than a sister. Sofia had died before he could express his gratitude or show his affection, because as a boy and young man he had been thoughtless and selfish, taking his only sibling for granted while making his home in London where he studied and worked for a pittance in those early years.

'How strange,' Ella remarked and, having picked up on his distaste for the subject, she said no more. She settled into the plush interior of the car.

'This evening if you're asked any nosy questions about our relationship just ignore them. We met last year and now we're together. That's all anyone needs to know,' he told her flatly.

What Nikolai had mentioned was as much as she knew herself, which made it impossible for her to betray any secrets. And were there secrets? Oh, yes, she felt in her bones that there were. But prying was forbidden because she was only with Nikolai for her family's benefit, she reminded herself firmly. She wasn't planning to get involved with him or his life or his secrets. Neither was she about to take an interest in his preferences or his moods. As far as possible she would keep herself as detached as he was. In the circumstances that was her first and only line of defence.

'Have you got that?' Nikolai prompted in the silence.

'Right. Got it,' Ella made a teasing zipping motion along her mouth. 'No chatterbox here to worry about.'

Nikolai studied her in surprise. With that dancing

sparkle in her eyes and the cheeky tilt to her chin below
the almost smiling, upward curve of her lush lips, she
looked radiant. Involuntarily his gaze lingered. 'You're
beautiful,' he said without meaning to.

Disconcertion widened her eyes and she flushed,
turning her head away to look out at the city streets
flashing past the window. In the flare of the street lights
his eyes had changed from onyx dark and guarded to
that melted caramel shade she was so partial to and
butterflies had fluttered in her tummy. Butterflies, as
if she were a blasted schoolgirl! she scolded herself
in disgust. Was there some foolish part of her trying
to romanticise his plans for her? Yes, Nikolai Drakos
wanted her...but only for a little while. He didn't want
her to keep. He didn't want to get to know her concerns
or share them. Sex would be superficial, fleeting. She
had to stay sensible or she would get hurt because he
was a terrifyingly attractive man, whose mystery simply gave him added depth.

As they left the limousine Nikolai banded a hand to
her back. Her spine was rigid. She was as tense as he
was. 'By the way, you might see your old friend Cyrus
Makris tonight.'

Ella frowned. 'Cyrus isn't back from China yet.'

'He is,' Nikolai contradicted. 'But if he's here tonight you don't speak to him.'

Aghast at the command, Ella twisted round to look
at his lean dark features, recognising the hardness
etched there. 'But—'

'No argument. You're with me now. You cut him
dead,' Nikolai instructed harshly.

'Nikolai, that's not fair.'

'I never promised to play fair,' he murmured impatiently as a stout older woman clad in a sequinned dress hailed him with enthusiasm.

Nikolai seemed to know everyone and a great wave of introductions engulfed Ella. Pre-dinner drinks were being served when a woman moved to a podium to make a speech about the victims of domestic abuse. By the time she had finished speaking, Nikolai had embarked on a conversation with two men and with a whisper Ella headed off to find the cloakroom.

And that was the moment when she finally saw Cyrus. He crossed the foyer to intercept her. He was smaller, slighter than Nikolai, blond and blue-eyed with wings of grey at the temples. 'Ella... I couldn't believe it was you. What on earth are you doing here?'

Ella reddened, uneasy with the intensity of his stare and the angry flush on his cheeks. 'I was planning to ring you but we haven't spoken since you left.'

'Your grandmother told me you were in London but said she didn't have your address.'

'I haven't had the chance to give it to her yet. I only arrived here today,' she told him uncomfortably, forced to come to a halt when he closed a hand round her wrist, his grip painfully tight. 'I've met someone, Cyrus.'

'How is that possible? You hardly go out.'

'You were always telling me to go out,' she reminded him.

'*Not* to find another man!' he disclaimed angrily. 'Who is he?'

'Nikolai Drakos...he's a—'

Cyrus's grip on her went limp and then fell away altogether. He frowned in disbelief. 'You're here in London with Drakos?'

Ella nodded slowly, watching a further flush of colour redden Cyrus's face while his mouth flattened into a livid line. 'We have to talk about this. Drakos is a complete bastard with women! He's notorious. How the hell did this happen?'

'Ella...'

The voice was cold as ice but she already knew it as well as she knew her own. A shiver of cold ran down her spine as she turned her head slowly and saw Nikolai glowering at her from several feet away.

'Cloakroom,' she mumbled and fled.

Cyrus simply walked away as fast as he could. He had never stood up to Nikolai, never allowed the younger man the opportunity to confront him. He was a little weasel, brutal with those physically weaker but a complete coward with other men.

'Well, that was a very special viewing. Cyrus is devastated,' an older woman paused by Nikolai's elbow to remark. 'It's only been a couple of weeks since I sent you that email. You certainly don't let the grass grow under your feet.'

'No, I got the girl,' Nikolai conceded. 'Does that make you happy, Marika?'

'Seeing my brother suffer always makes me happy,' she admitted, her dark eyes even colder than Nikolai's. 'And you're a hero. Pat yourself on the back. You've saved the girl from whatever disgusting plans he had for her. I don't think there's enough money in the world to compensate a woman for what life with Cyrus would entail.'

As Nikolai hovered awaiting Ella's reappearance, he acknowledged that the very last thing he felt just then was heroic. Naked rage had stormed through him when he saw Cyrus touching Ella, fondling her wrist like the dirty old man he was. He had almost forgotten where he was and his innate aggression had almost spilled over into violence. And that reality deeply disturbed him.

Why had he got so worked up? On the rare occasions that he saw Cyrus, he was accustomed to blanking him and Cyrus made it easier still by avoiding him. But somehow seeing Ella that close to Cyrus had outraged and revolted him. Hadn't he warned her not to speak to him? Didn't she ever listen? Had she no sense of self-preservation? Nostrils flaring, Nikolai gritted his teeth on a fierce surge of temper.

He knew he was no hero. A real hero would have *saved* his sister. His abject failure in that department had devastated him. He knew that, accepted that, was aware he had never really felt anything emotional since Sofia's death. Nor did he want to feel anything because feeling love was a weakness and it made you a target.

CHAPTER FIVE

ELLA FRESHENED UP in the cloakroom.

Her hands were shaking and her wrist ached where Cyrus had held it too tight. The instant she had seen his anger Gramma's warning had come back to haunt her. An old friend might have been annoyed by being left out of the loop about her move to London but Cyrus had been enraged, incredulous. In the past he had repeatedly urged her to socialise more but apparently not to find *another* man, he had angrily declared.

Suddenly everything Ella had believed she knew about Cyrus had been thrown into turmoil. Surely she was wrong, surely she had to be wrong?

Troubled, she looked back on the history of their relationship. Before Paul's illness was diagnosed he had applied to Cyrus for a working placement in one of the older man's businesses.

'Yes, I'm trying to pull strings because he's my uncle but why shouldn't I?' Paul had said defensively. 'My mother was the daughter of a very rich Greek but she was thrown out of the family for marrying my father because he was British and poor by their standards. Cyrus is her brother. I'll have to hope that he's not as prejudiced as his father.'

Ella had been with Paul the first time he'd met his uncle and Cyrus had given him the placement. Later he had invited them both to his country house and had pledged his support while Paul was ill. He had not let them down either, Ella recalled unhappily. Yes, Cyrus had been different with her tonight but wasn't there some excuse for his anger? He was a friend but she certainly hadn't treated him like a friend. She could've told him she was coming to London with Nikolai, but she hadn't because Nikolai had insisted that no one other than her family and Rosie was allowed to know that she was leaving home.

Ella glided back to Nikolai's side and within minutes they were being seated at their table. There was no opportunity for any private conversation but Nikolai's grim profile and clipped speech spoke for him. Nikolai was angry with her and what remained of the evening passed in an uncomfortable blur. He had told her to cut Cyrus dead and she had disobeyed. But how could she cut dead the man who had found Paul an apartment close to the hospital where he had been receiving treatment? The man who had housed him and hired a nurse to care for him while he was dying? The man who had been by her side when Paul had breathed his last? Tears burned at the backs of Ella's eyes.

Cyrus had said that Nikolai was a complete bastard with women, *and* notorious. And wasn't his treatment of Ella the living proof of that? Was that immoral choice he had given her to be his get-out clause? Her body in return for her family's security and happiness? But she had agreed and, what was more, had sworn she would not make a big drama over it. So where did that

leave her? Up the creek without a paddle, she reckoned wretchedly.

'You're furious with me,' she breathed to break the
intolerable silence in the limousine returning them to
the apartment.

'We'll discuss it when we get back to the house,'
Nikolai breathed darkly, lounging back in his corner
of the limo and splaying his lean, powerful thighs as
he surveyed her.

She had defied him in spite of his instructions. Mu-
tiny was etched in the set of her delicate jawline, obsti-
nacy in the jut of her determined little chin. And damn
her but it made him want her more than ever! How was
that possible when she was crossing him at every turn?
It was irrational and he was not an irrational man. He
could, of course, have told her the truth about Cyrus,
but she probably wouldn't believe him because he suspected she had seen a side of Cyrus granted to few. He
could not risk telling Ella anything because how could
he possibly know that he could trust her?

But his inability to trust wasn't uppermost in his
mind at that moment. Acting on impulse, he slid along
the passenger seat and gathered her stiff little body
into his arms.

'What the—?' Ella gasped, jerking in stark disconcertion.

'He shouldn't have touched you,' Nikolai growled
against her parted lips. 'You're not *his* to touch.'

And he crushed her soft, full mouth under his with
all the hunger powering him. She went limp and kissed
him back, a little whimper escaping her as his tongue
flicked against hers. He felt her arms come up round
his neck and he almost smiled. Talking was a vastly

overrated exercise. Sometimes action talked louder and she was his, indisputably *his* when he touched her, her lithe little body curling into him, one hand stroking his shoulder, the other delving into his hair.

Nikolai thought of lifting the skirt of her gown, swivelling her round, ripping off her panties and sating the overwhelming need that was making him ache. Black lashes lifting, he wrenched his mouth free of the clinging passion of hers and released a long shuddering sigh.

'I'm burning up for you. I spent the day planning what I want to do with you in bed.'

'I spent the day bored out of my mind at that beauty salon,' Ella confided helplessly. 'What did you plan to do?'

Nikolai whispered and her bones melted like honey, desire clenching her feminine core and tightening her nipples into straining buds.

'Not to be recommended even in a limo,' Nikolai concluded as he settled her circumspectly back in her corner of the seat. 'But a guy can dream...'

Ella smoothed down her skirt and fought to catch her breath. His words had undone her. She was with a male who could be bold and unconventional when he felt the urge. The price? Now she was all overheated and quivery and wanton and shocked at herself. Only minutes earlier she had been resentful and confused and unbearably tense but he had contrived to release that tension in the most unexpected way.

Nikolai followed her into the truly hideous drawing room with its swagged and canopied drapes and looming dark furniture. It put him in mind of a funeral parlour and he wished he had had the time to throw in an interior decorator to modernise the place. 'So, tell me,' he urged ruefully. 'What were you playing at tonight with Cyrus?'

'I spoke to Cyrus because he's a friend.'

Nikolai reacted as fast as a whip. He grabbed her hand and turned up her slender wrist where the skin was now showing purpling black fingerprints. 'A *friend* did this?' he growled in disbelief.

'It was an accident. He was angry because I hadn't told him that I was leaving home. I'm sure he didn't mean to hurt me!' Ella protested, snatching her hand back protectively. 'What's it to you anyway?'

'I'm the one responsible for your safety and, let me tell you now, you are *not* safe with Cyrus. Don't ever be alone with him anywhere,' Nikolai bit out forcefully.

'That's a ridiculous thing to say,' Ella framed in bewilderment. 'He warned me off you too.'

Nikolai threw back his head. 'Did he indeed?'

'He said you were a complete bastard with women, *notorious*,' she recited curtly.

'If being honest about my lack of honourable or long-term intentions is being a bastard, then I'm guilty as charged. Do you want a drink?'

'White wine,' she muttered. 'Th—thanks.' Her voice tripped on the word as he pressed a wine glass into her hand.

Nikolai tipped back his brandy in an unappreciative gulp. 'I need you to do as I ask, Ella, not as you want.'

'I need you to be human…seems we're both destined to disappointment,' she whispered round the rim of her glass.

'I don't handle disappointment well. For your own

sake, stay away from Cyrus,' he breathed in a driven
undertone.

Ella studied him and wondered how he could expect her to trust him over Cyrus when Cyrus had already earned her trust. Incomprehension assailed her
because Nikolai was by no means slow on the uptake.
The two men disliked each other; she had got that message loud and clear from both of them. The difference
between them was in her reaction. Cyrus's behaviour
had confused and troubled her but, inexplicably, Nikolai's reaction tore her up inside. And she didn't know
why. She had no more idea why when she looked at
his lean, darkly handsome features and sensed vulnerability, because from the outside Nikolai didn't have a
vulnerable bone in his big, powerful body.

Max knocked at the door and offered supper. Both
of them declined and the pitter-patter of running paws
on the tiled hall floor announced the entry of the dogs.
Rory hurled herself joyfully against Nikolai's legs
while Butch bounced around Ella, stayed just long
enough to get a pat and then went to join Rory.

'I was surprised you had a pet,' Ella admitted abstractedly.

Nikolai glanced at her and straightened from greeting the shaggy little mongrel at his feet. 'I can't take
the applause for that. Rory belonged to my sister. She
called her Princess Aurora…my sister had a love of all
things fairy tale,' he murmured stiffly, his lean, strong
face shadowing. 'After she died, I couldn't bring myself to part with her dog, so I kept her.'

'I didn't know you'd lost someone,' she muttered as
the dogs raced out again in pursuit of Max.

'Most of us have by the time we reach our third decade.'

'Doesn't make coping with it any easier,' Ella remarked.

A phone rang and Nikolai dug a cell out of his pocket and answered it. As soon as he did she saw his face change, paling and clenching hard. 'I'll be there as soon as I can.'

'What is it? What's happened?'

'There's been a fire…at my hotel. I need to get over there.'

'My goodness…is there anything I can do to help?' Ella exclaimed.

'No, just go to bed. I'll see you later…most probably tomorrow.'

After his sudden departure, Ella walked out to the cosy room off the kitchen where Max was watching television with the dogs at his feet. He stood up. 'Did you change your mind about supper?'

'No. I didn't.' Ella told him about the fire. 'I didn't know Nikolai owned a hotel.'

'The Grand Illusion. He worked in the bar there when he was a student,' Max told her. 'It was also his first big business project. He bought it and turned it into one of the most sought-after boutique hotels in Europe. I hope it's not too badly damaged. He's very attached to the place.'

Ella slid into the big white bed upstairs. The sheets were cool and silky against her skin. She was alone, reflecting wryly that she had not expected to be alone in bed tonight. She was too tired to agonise over the long eventful day but her body quickened and heated when she remembered Nikolai's mouth on hers in the limo and what he had whispered. There was nothing wrong with wanting him, she told herself drowsily. He was extraordinarily sexy and her response was simply natural and normal. Why did she feel guilty about what couldn't be helped? After all, no power on earth could bring back Paul or the future life she had once dreamt of sharing with him. Less troubled than she had been earlier, she finally slept.

When she wakened it was almost nine and she was very hungry. She discovered that Max had unpacked her clothes into one of the built-in closets off the passageway that led into the en suite and she picked out jeans and a long-sleeved tee before she went for a shower. Nikolai had not returned during the night. Either he had slept elsewhere or he was still dealing with the aftermath of the fire. While she applied a little make-up, her nose wrinkling at that newly acquired vanity, she was still thinking about that passionate kiss in the limousine and questioning how one kiss could possibly be that special.

As she emerged from the bathroom the bedroom door opened and Nikolai appeared. He looked exhausted and he brought with him the acrid smell of smoke. He stared at her with red-rimmed eyes and for a split second it was as though he didn't know who she was or what she was doing there.

'How was it?' she asked uncertainly.

Momentarily he closed his eyes and a faint shudder racked his lean, strong frame. 'Horrible...' he finally rasped, kicking back his shoulders to shrug off his jacket. 'I stink of smoke. I need a shower.'

'Was anyone hurt?' she pressed.

Halfway through unbuttoning his shirt, he looked at her, dark deep-set eyes semi-closed with no lightening flare of gold. 'Yes. I was at the hospital before I came back. Three of my staff are injured. One has...' his voice roughened '...life-changing injuries.'

'I'm sorry, Nikolai. You knew him personally?' she prompted sickly.

As the shirt fell to the floor he nodded in silence. 'I worked with the kitchen and bar staff as a student. The fire started behind the hotel. There was an explosion. Two assistant chefs were hurt. The bar manager has severe burns and he's facing years of surgery,' he completed gruffly.

'I'm so very sorry,' she said again, because she could see by the fierce tightness of his facial muscles that it had all been almost more than he could bear. He was literally fighting to stay in control and, shamefully, the tears glimmering in his dark eyes fascinated her.

'It could've been worse,' he said as if he was reminding himself of that reality in an effort to stave off too much negativity. 'The guests all got out in time. The hotel's wrecked but bricks and mortar can be rebuilt. It's lives that can't.'

He toed off his shoes, yanked off his socks and peeled off his trousers in his determined path to the shower. She could see that he wasn't even conscious that he was stripping naked in front of her. The lithe bronzed perfection of his lean, powerful body was revealed and she strove to respect his lack of awareness by not staring. He was drained and devastated and in a state she had never expected to see him in.

'Can I get you anything?'

'Max met me on the way in. He's bringing up breakfast…not sure I'll be able to eat,' he mumbled thickly.

Ella became braver. She moved into the bathroom doorway. 'It's not your fault this happened, Nikolai.'

'It's someone's fault!' he ground out rawly. 'The police suspect arson. An accelerant was used. Plastic bins shoved up against the oil tanks caused the explosion. It was no accident.'

'Oh, my word,' she whispered, moving back to the bedroom.

Max brought a covered tray and told her that he had included her in the food order. Butch pranced round her feet with Rory, both of them wanting to stay, but she asked Max to take the dogs back downstairs.

'He's shattered. He needs to rest,' Max agreed. 'Sleep makes everything look less dire.'

Nikolai reappeared, a towel wrapped round his narrow waist, damp black hair flopping untidily over his brow. Ella poured coffee and thrust a knife and fork at him as he sank down in one of the chairs by the table at the window.

'Eat,' she urged. 'You need fuel for energy.'

His wide, sensual mouth quirked as he met anxious green eyes. She was all warmth and softness but her sympathy unnerved him. He had learned to get by without leaning on anyone and it had protected him over and over again from making dangerous mistakes. If he didn't give his trust, it couldn't be broken. If he didn't open up to other people, he couldn't get hurt. Well, OK, he was hurting now, but that couldn't be helped because that was the kind of damage that life threw at everybody. Only this time, someone had personally choreographed that damage, he reminded himself grimly. Who hated him enough to target a packed hotel with an arson attack? Nikolai knew how fortunate it was that so many people had escaped the fire unscathed.

He drank the coffee and ate some bacon but admitted that he had no appetite. Ella wanted to ask him more about the fire but reckoned that a tactful silence was more welcome.

'I'll go to bed. I have to go back to the police station later,' Nikolai told her wearily, walking back to the bathroom.

She heard drawers open and close and when he reappeared he had disposed of the towel and donned a pair of tight-fitting white cotton boxers. For an instant she stared because he was so beautifully built, from his well-defined pectorals to the inverted V of muscle above his hips. She was surprised to see an elaborate tattoo adorning one masculine shoulder. It depicted a winged goddess…and a tiny *unicorn*? What was that all about? Her mouth drying, she swallowed hard and snatched up the book she had abandoned beside the bed the night before.

'I'll see you later,' she said breathlessly as she scooped up the big tray to take it downstairs in the lift.

Fatigue overwhelmed Nikolai. There were things he had wanted to say to Ella but he couldn't remember what they were. Instead he found himself recalling the tenderness, the caring in her shimmering green eyes while she tried to nag him into eating. It had reminded him of the way his sister had looked at him when he was sick as a little boy. With a savage curse he blocked out the disturbing image of both.

* * *

Ella settled at the kitchen table while Max baked a cake and talked about his army days. The dogs trotted in and out of the back garden. When the doorbell buzzed, she followed him out to the hall and then hovered, unsure why she had done so. When she saw Cyrus smiling on the doorstep she stiffened in dismay, but then he saw her and smiled warmly at her and she discovered that she couldn't hold spite against the man over bruises that were already fading from her wrist.

'Cyrus…' she said, moving forward.

'I hoped that I'd find you home today,' Cyrus remarked, extending a huge bouquet of flowers, which Ella passed uneasily to Max.

The whole situation felt wrong to her and she was very uncomfortable. Cyrus and Nikolai thoroughly disliked each other and she knew without even being told that Nikolai would be furious that Cyrus had entered his home. Yet Cyrus's calm manner and friendly smile were far more familiar to her than the angry man he had been the night before.

'Come in,' she said, struggling to feel more welcoming.

'I'll make you some tea before I leave to do the shopping,' Max promised.

'I knew you wouldn't be expecting me.' Cyrus followed her into the dark drawing room where he glanced around and rolled his eyes without comment. 'But I couldn't leave things the way they were when we parted last night.'

'It was awkward,' she conceded.

Cyrus took a seat and asked her about her family. She was very careful about what she said, fearful that he would ask difficult questions about her father's failed business because she had promised Nikolai that she would not discuss the matter. In actuality Cyrus made no reference to the debts or of the fact that the shop had closed and she realised that it was perfectly possible that he had no idea of the financial mess her family had been in.

'I have a question to ask you and it may surprise you,' Cyrus warned her as Max brought in a tray.

Taken aback, Ella studied him uncertainly. 'Is it likely to upset me?'

'I hope not.' Cyrus smiled again while she poured the tea. 'I've known you over four years, Ella. Recently, however, it's become a challenge for me to be the friend you want and if I've seen less of you that is why.'

Ella was becoming increasingly tense but she said nothing.

'You're worth much more than some tawdry affair with Drakos. I want to take you away from here *today*,' he told her emphatically. 'I want you to marry me. I'm asking you to be my wife.'

Her tummy gave a queasy lurch at the mere concept of that but she was careful to keep her face composed because, no matter how outlandish and inappropriate she found his proposal, she was still reluctant to hurt him. 'I'm afraid I've never seen you in that light, Cyrus. I think of you as Paul's uncle and a good friend.'

'Clearly I've played the waiting game too long and too well,' Cyrus said drily. 'I didn't want to make our relationship uncomfortable.'

Ella had never felt more uncomfortable with Cyrus than she did at that moment. She didn't like the way he was looking at her. If he had feelings for her, she could not return them and there was no way to wrap that wounding fact up as a compliment. 'I do like and respect you.'

'I should've spoken up sooner. You being here with Drakos suggests that I waited too long to tell you how I feel.' Cyrus could not hide his loathing for Nikolai or his contempt as he voiced his name. 'But I couldn't help being aware that you had an abnormal relationship with my nephew and I didn't want to put pressure on you.'

Ella had fallen very still. 'Abnormal? In what way?'

'Well, it certainly wasn't normal for the two of you to be in a celibate engagement,' Cyrus declared with a caustic derision that sent mortified colour flying into her cheeks. 'You should know that by the time of his death Paul had no secrets from me.'

Severely discomfited, Ella turned from red to bone white and curved her hands tightly round her cup as if savouring that warmth.

'But that wasn't your fault…it was *his*. I was tempted to tell you what I knew after the funeral but I didn't see that telling you that late in the day would be doing you any favours.'

Frowning, Ella leant forward in a sudden movement and put her cup back on the tray with a sharp little snap. 'Telling me what, for goodness' sake?'

'Paul was involved in a homosexual relationship before he met you.'

Ella stared at him in complete disbelief. 'That's a total lie!' she gasped.

'I don't know if he was gay, bisexual or simply confused, but Paul was definitely not attracted to women in the usual way,' Cyrus continued in the same hectoring tone of superiority. 'And once Paul realised he was ill, he clung to you for comfort and support and you gave it unstintingly. That's why he asked you to marry him. He was terrified of losing you and being alone.'

'It's not true,' Ella insisted in shock. 'It *can't* be true.'

'I'm afraid it is true,' Cyrus told her, curtly impatient. 'And that background made it very difficult for me to know how best to proceed.'

Ella stood up in the hope of hastening his departure. 'There was nothing to proceed with,' she muttered in fierce rebuttal. 'Even if it is, I'm not attracted to you as a man.'

Cyrus rose as well and moved closer. 'How would you even *know*, Ella? You've never been with a *real* man.'

Rage finally filtered through Ella's shock and freed her to speak her mind. 'Paul was more of a real man than you'll ever be! A good relationship isn't necessarily dependent on sex.'

'Let me show you what you're rejecting out of misplaced loyalty!' Cyrus grated, reaching for her. 'Did you even listen to me? I did you the honour of asking you to marry me!'

'Don't touch me!' Ella stepped sideways, only to be entrapped by the hand that closed roughly into her hair and yanked. Tears sprang to her eyes because it hurt. 'Let go of me!'

Cyrus had gone all red and his face was a mask of offended fury. 'I have every right to touch you!' he hurled down at her, his other hand biting into her slight shoulder. 'I spent a fortune helping Paul but it was all for *your* benefit. Are you aware that Drakos is the son of a drug dealer and a whore? Doesn't that matter to you?'

With every angry word he was pushing her back-wards and her calves hit the base of the sofa and his bullying momentum toppled her down on top of it.

'I'm going to show you what you've been missing,' he intoned viciously.

CHAPTER SIX

UPSTAIRS, NIKOLAI HAD stirred when the doorbell had rung and had then flinched when the front door had slammed loudly on Max's exit. When his cell phone began ringing beside the bed, he groaned in frustration and gave up the attempt to continue sleeping.

He checked his watch as he lifted his phone. He had had a couple of hours and that would have to do, he reasoned, springing out of bed and raking his fingers through his tousled black hair. Talking on the phone, he strode into the bathroom to splash his face and froze halfway there as his brain kicked in and he recognised the controlled distress in the voice he was listening to. His shoulders slumped as he voiced his sympathy at yet another piece of bad news and then he tossed his phone down in disgust. The bar manager had passed away shortly after Nikolai had left the hospital.

He had pulled on jeans and was wandering barefoot back into the bedroom when a flash of bright colour outside attracted his attention. The drapes hadn't been pulled properly. A very distinctive car was parked on the other side of the road. It was a bright yellow Ferrari and Nikolai knew exactly who that car belonged to. For a split second he couldn't credit the coincidence and then it dawned on him that Ella was in the house and he couldn't relax until he had checked on her. He raced downstairs, saw the drawing-room door ajar, heard Ella's muffled shriek of pain and kicked the door wide.

Suddenly the weight pinning Ella to the sofa was gone. She blinked in bewilderment and shock as Cyrus went flying back against the wall opposite where Nikolai had flung him after dragging him off her. She sat up just as Nikolai punched the older man hard in the stomach and shouted at him in Greek. Cyrus had attacked her, had torn at her jeans and she was bruised and sore and shaken and frightened. Only the fear that Nikolai might kill Cyrus made her intervene. She stumbled across the room and wrenched at Nikolai's arm.

'No...no, don't hit him again. You've hurt him enough!' she gasped as Cyrus, blood running down his face, which was already swelling from several hits, dragged himself up clumsily from the floor and stumbled frantically towards the door.

'He *hurt* you!' Nikolai vented between gritted white teeth as he strode after the fleeing older man.

Again, Ella grabbed his arm to hold him back and give Cyrus enough time to make it out through the front door. 'If you kill him you'll go to prison for it... is that what you want?'

A string of Greek curses erupted from Nikolai as Ella slammed the door protectively in his enemy's wake. 'I should've warned you about him.'

'You told me not to be alone with him. I didn't pay any heed,' she mumbled guiltily.

'He's been accused of getting rough with women before,' Nikolai divulged.

Blood dripped down onto the polished wooden floor

and she grabbed his hand to examine his bruised and bleeding knuckles. 'You need cleaning up,' she said, angling him towards the stairs.

'What happened before he attacked you?'

'He asked me to marry him and when I told him I wasn't interested he went off in a rage,' she told him in a daze. 'If Gramma hadn't already hinted to me that she thought he had a more than personal interest in me, I would've been gobsmacked. As it was, I tried to be polite. It never once occurred to me that he could be thinking of me like that.'

So, Cyrus had proposed. He *had* intended marriage. It should've been a moment of triumph for Nikolai but it fell resoundingly flat. He had wounded his opponent but Ella had been wounded too. He was appalled that Cyrus had contrived to violently assault Ella and he felt incredibly guilty about that reality. After all, he knew exactly what Cyrus was like and he had virtually set Ella up as a target for the older man's frustrated rage. She could've been raped just as his sister had been and the mere concept of Ella enduring such a violation made Nikolai feel sick with guilt and self-loathing. He was supposed to be in control of events, but somewhere along the line of his plotting he had become selfish and reckless and Ella had very nearly paid the ultimate price. How irresponsible was that?

Even worse, Ella was now valiantly trying to urge him up the stairs as if he were the injured party and in need of the support of her tiny frame. In another mood he would have laughed at the incongruity of her sympathy for him at that moment. But he was not in a laughing mood any more than he was in a triumphant one.

'What did he do to you?' Nikolai demanded, thrusting open the bedroom door.

'He was trying to kiss me and I twisted my face away and he yanked at my hair. I swear he pulled a handful of it out by the roots,' she whispered, massaging her sore scalp. 'He flattened me on the sofa and started pulling at my clothes. I never thought of him as a big, strong man but he was much stronger than me. I don't think I could've got him off me without your help... Thank you.'

'No, don't thank me,' Nikolai said with distaste. 'This is all my fault.'

'I don't see how,' Ella pronounced, dabbing the blood from his hand and applying an antiseptic she had found in the cabinet. She was still trembling in shock from Cyrus's assault and wondering in disbelief what had come over the older man. Had he simply lost his head in temper? Would he really have raped her? Fear and revulsion curdled low in her stomach. He had tried to rip off her jeans, she recalled with a shudder. There could be no mistake about the motivation of his attack.

'His conduct is nothing to do with you,' Ella continued a little unevenly as her breathing began to settle back to normal levels. 'I was the one who kept up the friendship with Cyrus after Paul died. I used to talk about Paul with his uncle. I needed that outlet after the funeral.'

She fell silent, finally allowing herself to consider what Cyrus had told her about Paul. All the insecurities she had ever felt in her fiancé's radius briefly returned to haunt her. Paul had been a real extrovert and very popular and when she had first known him she had very quickly fallen for him and longed for more than friendship. But nothing had come of her hopes until Paul had fallen ill. That was when she had become important to Paul and when he had first told her that he loved her. Her eyes prickling and burning, she crushed the memory, which now seemed soiled.

There was no point in revisiting the past and allowing Cyrus's allegations to upset her. Paul was gone and her questions couldn't be answered now. But was it possible that she had been blind to the reality of a man's sexual lack of interest? Had she wasted four years of her life on a non-relationship? That was a very distressing thought.

'We should've called the police on Cyrus,' Nikolai breathed in a savage undertone. 'Had him arrested for what he did to you—'

'But thanks to you he didn't really *do* anything. He certainly scared me out of my wits for a few minutes but I wouldn't want to involve the police. He was incredibly generous to Paul while he was ill and, even though today he insisted that he only did all that for *my* benefit, I have to stay grateful for what he did do to help then,' she framed shakily.

'You're crying...' Nikolai registered belatedly as a solitary tear dropped on his hand.

Ella crammed a hand defensively against her wobbling mouth. 'Sorry—'

'No, let it out...you've had a very frightening experience,' Nikolai pointed out, furious that he had let her stand there ministering to his minor injuries when she herself had been through so much more. Without hesitation he bent and swept her up into his arms. 'You need to lie down for a while.'

'Do you really think he would have r-ripped off my clothes *and*...?'

'Yes, I do think that,' Nikolai admitted as he rested her down gently on the disordered bed and sat down beside her. 'Obviously he had wanted you for a very long time and your rejection would have hurt his ego. Make no mistake; Cyrus thinks he's a hell of a good catch.'

'To accept that all this time he's been thinking of me like that and I hadn't a clue...it's *horrible*!' Ella broke off with a sudden sob and Nikolai lifted her up into his arms, muttering what sounded like soothing things in Greek.

Ella let the tears fall against his shoulder, belatedly appreciating that he wasn't wearing a shirt, that indeed all he was wearing was his jeans. He felt so hot against her cheek, like a muscular furnace, but she felt so incredibly safe and protected in his arms. 'I'm sorry... so sorry about this.'

'What are you sorry for? Cyrus assaulted you.'

'He said that Paul had had a gay affair,' she confided jaggedly, her heart beating like a hammer inside her. 'And the awful thing is that it might be true and I'll never really know *why* Paul—'

Comprehension entered Nikolai and he breathed in slow and deep. 'It doesn't matter now.'

But it mattered to Ella, who had on several occasions felt humiliated by Paul's physical restraint with her. Even Gramma had been surprised when Paul hadn't asked Ella to move in with him. Had Paul *ever* wanted that kind of intimacy with her? His resistance had made her feel like less of a woman. The suspicion that that might have all been a front to hide his secret cut even deeper because she had believed that they were as close as two people could be without sex.

'Cyrus would have said anything to sully your memories of his nephew,' Nikolai opined. 'He must've been very jealous of him.'

'No, the worst thing is that I'm scared that Cyrus was telling the truth about Paul…a truth I was too stupid to see on my own!' Ella gasped against a smooth, tanned shoulder, marvelling that she could be that close with Nikolai without him making any kind of move on her even though she knew how much he wanted her. That, she conceded dizzily, was yet one more striking difference between Cyrus and Nikolai. Nikolai wasn't taking advantage, *wouldn't* take advantage of her while she was upset. A vague sense of frustration and regret trickled through her in response to that recognition.

Nikolai usually ran a mile from crying women and he was at a loss with Ella. He didn't hug but that was all right because she was the one doing the hugging. He didn't know what to say, though, particularly when she referred to a gay affair. He was definitely out of his element there. Changing the subject struck him as the only possible option and he breathed in deep. 'Desmond, the bar manager in the burns unit, died an hour after I left the hospital,' he told her. 'His son phoned to tell me.'

Ella froze and then jerked up her head to look at him. Her face was flushed and her little nose was red but her green eyes were wet and impossibly appealing, Nikolai registered helplessly. 'I'm so sorry, Nikolai.'

'He was a good guy,' Nikolai volunteered. 'I met him when I started working at the hotel. I was only eighteen. He trained me…'

'What were you like at eighteen?' she whispered, relieved to be sprung from her introspection.

It was yet another one of those occasions when Nikolai found a woman hard to comprehend. What did what *he* was like at eighteen have to do with anything? How was that relevant?

'Cocky...horny,' he murmured blankly, his mind elsewhere as he breathed in the scent of her hair. She smelt like strawberries. Was that her shampoo? He stroked long fingers down the back of her head, watching the bronze strands shimmer like silk in the light. He was hard as a rock below the jeans and that seriously bothered him because it was inappropriate after what Cyrus had done.

Ella tilted her head back and looked up into Nikolai's lean dark face. She saw the raw hunger tightening his spectacular bone structure and the burn in his melted caramel eyes below the black velvet fringe of his lashes. 'You have beautiful eyes,' she told him truthfully, every fibre of her body suddenly prickling with physical awareness.

She had travelled from gay affairs to what he was like as a teenager to his eyes and that only reminded Nikolai why he rarely had conversations with women. He had sex with them and kept the talking to the absolute minimum. His strong jawline clenched. 'I was telling you that Desmond had died...'

Ella felt the heat of shame suffuse her mortified face. 'Yes.'

'His family were with him at the end. He would've wanted that. He was very much a family man,' he breathed gruffly.

And that catch in his dark deep drawl and the anguish he was struggling to contain in his stunning eyes simply fuelled Ella's fascination with the male holding her. Nikolai Drakos was incredibly emotional. That great well of intense emotion was what he hid behind the cold front and he usually hid it well but just at that moment pretence was beyond him and she loved that too. He was being so open with her, so frank and natural. His attitude washed away the bad feelings Cyrus and his revelations had infused her with and she felt her own strength again.

'Not that I know much about how normal families operate,' Nikolai acknowledged thickly.

Her fingers slid over a bare tanned shoulder. His skin felt like satin and the physical heat he put out attracted her as potently as the sun on a cold day. She quivered, awesomely aware of the swelling fullness of her breasts and the prickling tightening of her nipples. She was in control, in full control of herself, yet when she looked at Nikolai it was hard to breathe or swallow because she was remembering what his mouth felt like on hers. And unlike Paul, Nikolai *wanted* her, she reminded herself with satisfaction. Beneath her thigh she could feel him primed and ready, something she had never felt with Paul. Paul hadn't wanted her the way she'd wanted him but Nikolai did and couldn't hide it. That knowledge clenched something deep down inside her and made her feel oddly giddy.

Her hand came up of its own volition and skated along the tempting fullness of his sensual lower lip. His eyes lit up like firecrackers when she met them boldly, wanting, craving, needing and for the very first time unashamed of her natural instincts.

'Was that an invitation?' Nikolai husked, a faint

shudder racking his big, powerful frame because every atom of pent-up energy imprisoned inside him longed for release.

'You need it gilt-edged and engraved?' Ella teased, alight with her own daring, her own decision. He wanted her, she wanted him and it was normal and natural, she told herself firmly, even though somewhere deep down inside herself she was secretly shocked that *she* was the one taking the initiative.

'Oh, no... I'm a much quicker study,' Nikolai told her, sliding her down against the pillows and leaning down to trace her lush smiling mouth with his. In truth he wanted to flatten her to the bed and claim her body and soul like a Neanderthal. It took immense control to remember that she was innocent and deserving of the very best he could deliver.

The aggressive stroke of his tongue between her lips extracted a whimper of sound from the back of Ella's throat. Her whole body pulsed with expectation. She wondered dimly when it had happened, when she had travelled from simply wanting him to the edge of an unbearable craving that she could no longer fight. And she didn't care because there was no later or tomorrow or any kind of future in her thoughts, there was only this one special moment when she was finally making her choice and stepping out beyond the grief that had weighed her down for so long. His mouth crashed down on hers and she welcomed it, tipping her head back, parting her lips, all woman, all welcome. His passion enthralled her as much as the emotion he concealed as though it was something to be ashamed of.

'I swear I could devour you,' Nikolai swore against her swollen mouth.

He gazed down as her dreamy green eyes darkened to emerald, her bronze hair fanning round her head in a halo of vibrant colour. Cyrus had hurt and frightened her yet she still wanted Nikolai. It was a strangely humbling acknowledgement because he knew it meant that she trusted him. And yet he knew that he wasn't worthy of her trust because he hadn't told her what he had done. He crushed that train of thought to attend to the fact that she was still wearing far too many clothes.

Ella watched Nikolai yank off her jeans from the ankles and colour ran up over her chest as her serviceable black knickers were revealed. Nikolai tossed the jeans down and peeled her top off over her head, tumbling tresses falling back on her white shoulders above sweet little breasts cradled in lace cups. He could see her uncertainty, the nervous tension building as if she had no idea that *his* hands were shaking and that he was burning up for her, no idea at all that she was a rare and perfect beauty. He couldn't take his eyes from her as he unclipped the bra and lifted his hands to explore the delicate little mounds he had bared.

'Gorgeous...' he said gruffly, the word torn from him because she looked as though one wrong word from him would send her into flight.

'Seriously?' she pressed, face hot with a heady combination of surprise, embarrassment and doubt.

'Serious as a heart attack.' A long tanned finger stroked a dainty swell crowned by a straining pink nipple and he bent his head to capture it with his mouth. 'I like your breasts. I could even go as far as saying that I *love* your breasts,' he framed, his warm breath fanning her skin as he blew on a straining pink bud.

'But there's nothing much there,' she mumbled almost argumentatively because she had always felt that her lack of endowment in the bosom department was her biggest physical flaw. She was tiny and she was skinny and she didn't have the curves so many men were said to prefer.

'More than enough to satisfy me,' Nikolai growled, long fingers curving to a ripe little mound, gently stroking the responsive flesh, smiling as her back arched, driving her breast into his palm. 'You're delicious.'

Some of her tension ebbed. He wanted her, she reminded herself with growing assurance, and being wanted like that, complimented like that, suddenly seemed like the most wonderful thing in the world. He was accepting her, flaws and all, and in the same way she would accept him, she promised herself. She wasn't going in expecting perfection and eternal love.

The brush of his fingers against a prominent nipple made her hiss and her hips performed a little shimmy all on their own. Her body was warming up at its own pace, warmth gathering in her pelvis, tingles of reaction ensuring that she was fiercely aware of that part of her. He yanked off her knickers with scant ceremony, taking her by surprise. Her eyes flew wide, startled, apprehensive.

Nikolai smiled down at her. 'It's all right. We won't do anything you don't want to do...'

'I want to do everything,' she admitted shakily as he freed her from his weight and slid off the bed. 'Where are you going?'

'Condoms,' he explained, striding into the bathroom. 'There may not be any because I've never used the house...no, there's nothing here.'

'You don't need to,' Ella muttered, shaking her head. 'I have a contraceptive implant in my arm.'

He frowned. 'But why do you have that?'

'When Paul and I were together, I thought...well, that I'd need contraception.' Ella struggled to think back to that period when everything had been shiny and new and untested between her and Paul. As far as she recalled the implant would keep her safe from pregnancy for four years, but try as she did she could not remember exactly when she had had the implant put in.

'I've never had sex without a condom and I've been tested... I'm clean,' Nikolai assured her.

Ella was already thinking about something else. 'A moment ago you said you'd never used this house. *Never?*'

'Never,' he repeated. 'It didn't feel like mine. The day I got the keys I walked over every inch of it and thought what a waste it was that I was never allowed to meet the old guy. There are all these ancient photos of people and I don't know who they are and I never will know now because there's nobody left to identify them. Yet some of them must be relatives.'

'That's sad,' she agreed.

He didn't know why he was talking to her like that because he had been on his own a long time and he liked it that way...didn't he? Once his sister was gone, he had not had a single living relative that he knew of. Of course, he hadn't looked, he acknowledged for the first time, and he was well aware that his grandfather had had sisters because they had contacted him. He had simply decided that it would be pointless at this stage in his life to take the connection any further. And why the hell was he even thinking about such a thing?

What did Ella do to his wits? Why was he confiding in her when she lay naked and beautiful on a bed in front of him? What kind of black magic was that? He was talking about private things that he never ever shared. *Thee mou*, it had to be those soft, sympathetic eyes of hers working a dangerous spell.

'I've never needed family,' he told her flatly.

Ella was wondering if it would be pathetic to slide below the duvet to hide her naked body and she was stiff as a post while she lay there wondering, colour creeping up across her nudity in a mottled flush of awful self-consciousness. It was daylight and the drapes weren't fully closed and everything was on display and she felt incredibly uncomfortable.

'Family's everything to me,' Ella admitted, finally giving up the fight and diving below the duvet with apology. 'I can't imagine life without them.'

'The duvet won't hide you from me for long,' Nikolai warned, the command gilt-edged with the desire clearly burning in his eyes.

He unzipped and dropped his jeans and her eyes rounded at the sight of him because in his haste to check on her earlier he had forgone underwear below the denim. With a sudden laugh, Nikolai pounced and flipped the duvet back off her. 'Was that look one of awe or horror?' he demanded.

Ella's faced burned red. 'No comment...'

Nikolai kissed her breathless and then nipped a line down the slope of her neck that seemed to hit every pulse point she possessed. She gasped beneath his mouth, gasped again when his wickedly clever fingers found her clitoris and lingered with devastating intent. Startled, she jerked, she moaned, lashes fluttering in dazed dismay as he slid down the bed to part her thighs and pay attention to a part of her she much preferred to ignore.

'No, Nik—'

'Is that an embarrassed no? Or an absolutely not?' Nikolai prompted.

Forbearance became the better part of valour and she closed her eyes, trying not to think about what he was planning to do but reluctant to prevent him when her only excuse was shyness. She wasn't that shy, was she? And then he did something that sent a current of red-hot tingles racing through her entire body and her hips executed a sensual shimmy and her lips parted on a long, low whimper and whether she was shy or not got lost in the process. The prickling awareness in her pelvis coalesced into a heavy throb at the heart of her that made her all hot and needy. Suddenly she couldn't worry any more about how she looked or what came next, suddenly she was just in the moment and the moment was so wildly, insanely exciting and primal that she was lost in it. The pulsing heat expanded, sucking in more and more of her and then rising until she couldn't hold it in any more. She gave a helpless cry, her spine arched and her body flailed as an explosive climax gripped her.

'You see, the absolutely not would have been a mistake, *glikia mou*,' Nikolai pointed out as he drew level with her again, eyes like dark melting chocolate caressing her flushed face.

Dumbly she nodded, heart leaping as he claimed her mouth and his tongue tangled with hers in a frank expression of all-male hunger that made her blood thunder through her veins. He was rearranging her limbs, tipping her back into a new position and, before she could even gather all her nerves again, he was there at her entrance and pushing in. At first it felt so strange to her, his body joining with hers, and the sensation of pressure, of stretching, was surprisingly pleasurable, as if her body had been lying in wait for years to experience that exact sensation and was now pouncing on it with joyful acceptance.

And then Ella jerked as a stinging burn marked his invasion. It didn't kill the pleasure but it did make her tense and draw in her breath in dismay.

'Want me to stop?' Nikolai husked, eyes pure, gleaming caramel seduction.

'No...don't you dare!' Ella warned, impatient on the brink of what she had waited so long to experience.

He eased out of her and drove in again and the burn intensified and then vanished. She blinked, expecting pain because she had always expected pain, but the pain didn't arrive. 'It's OK now,' she whispered in surprise.

'It's got to be better than OK for you the first time,' Nikolai told her.

'No expectations here,' she told him bravely and wrapped her arms round him because she recognised his patience, his care and concern and knew it could have been a much less pleasurable experience with someone else.

Her body sang with his every movement, madly stimulated by excitement. Within the space of a minute and a half she travelled from the aftershocks of satiated pleasure to heart-stopping, racing excitement. She angled up to receive him, hips rocking, body thrumming joyfully to the age-old beat of passion. It was good, it was better than good, it was truly amazing to slot helplessly into that fierce hypnotic climb to pleasure again. A kind of frenzy gripped her muscles and she shook, feeling ecstasy within her grasp and snatching at it. And it ran over and through her, a rolling white-hot wave of convulsive delight and fulfilment that left her drained and limp.

Ella was convinced that she would never move again, and then Nikolai moved when she didn't want him to and she rolled over and rested her head on his chest instead, her arm wrapping round his narrow waist.

He dropped a kiss on her damp brow. 'Thank you,' he rasped breathlessly. 'That was amazing.'

She wanted to thank him but she was tongue-tied, everything she had thought she knew about herself, everything she had ever believed, thrown into turmoil. And, quite literally, she couldn't think straight and he felt like the only stable being in an unstable world. A deep sense of peace washed over her in waves of emotional and physical exhaustion.

Nikolai lay still and ever so slightly stiff. Ella was snuggling up to him. He had never snuggled before, was usually straight into the shower, clothes back on, goodbyes said within minutes. Well, isn't this a new experience to be savoured? a sardonic voice sniped inside his head. She deserves *more*, that same little voice added. What sort of more? Nikolai lay there until the even sound of her breathing let him know that she had fallen asleep. Only then did he gently and carefully slide out of the bed.

More as in flowers? He almost smacked his head against the shower wall in frustration. He had never done flowers before. But then he had never had sex with a virgin before. He had never coerced a woman into his bed either while pretending that he was giving her a choice. That final blunt acknowledgement sliced through him as painfully as a knife in the gut. Nausea rising, he got out of the shower and dressed. He would call by his apartment to change into a suit on his way to see Desmond's family and the police. And then what?

Nikolai looked at Ella sleeping in the bed, bronze hair in a mad tangle, a narrow white shoulder and a loosely unfurled tiny hand lying on top of the bedding. She looked so small, so defenceless and he had taken advantage of her. His heart sank. And then what? The question tolled in his conscience like a giant bell and he felt sick again. He had to deal, had no choice really: he had gone too far to turn back.

He sent her a text to explain where he was, which was a serious break from his usual habits. Never apologise, never explain was his usual mantra with women. He sent flowers for the first time in his life. He was almost desperate enough to throw in a cuddly toy as well. By the time he had commiserated with the dead bar manager's family and spent several hours in the police station telling them that, no, he had no idea why anyone would risk the life of so many people by setting his hotel on fire, he was shattered. Of course, he had had to pass on the names of anyone he might deem to have a grudge against him and he had had to mention Cyrus's name in that context. He had been frank with the police, but he had also had to admit that he had not uncovered any actual physical evidence of Cyrus breaking the law and that arson didn't quite run true to form for the man whose sole focus had always been innocent women.

Nikolai returned to his apartment. It was silent and he stood in the low-lit lounge and marvelled at the undeniable truth that in his desire for revenge he had veered badly off course and injured innocents. How had that happened? What had happened to his sense of right and wrong? When had his once pure motivation become twisted? He poured himself a whiskey and sat down in his shirtsleeves, struggling to work out how Ella could ever have struck him as a pawn and as mere collateral damage to be written off.

How could he ever have been that arrogant? That selfish? That wrong? And failed to recognise it? At some stage he had developed a dangerous form of tunnel vision and, seeing only Cyrus in his sights, he had taken aim and fired. Ella was the fallout and, even worse, he might as well have painted a target on her back because Cyrus's violent rage at the town house had been deliberately provoked by Nikolai. He had set her up for that scene and she had been hurt and he was painfully aware that she could have been hurt a lot more.

But how much more would the whole ugly truth hurt Ella? Ella, who was soft enough to sacrifice everything for her family? Ella, who had been unjustly damaged by his pursuit of revenge? He couldn't tell her the truth because that would humiliate and hurt her, inflicting more harm. Another glass of whiskey went down Nikolai's throat as he ran uneasily through all the wounding, shocking blows that Ella had already suffered. The father who had had a stroke, the fiancé who had died, the veterinary career that had had to be put on ice. She had kept on picking herself up and bravely soldiering on and then Nikolai had come along and suddenly everything had taken a turn very much for the worse. He had taken her from her home and her family and her life and then he had taken her to bed. Wrong heaped on wrong heaped on wrong. He raked a trembling hand through his black hair.

How could he possibly tell her that he had set her up and used her as a weapon? What woman's self-esteem could overcome a truth like that? Particularly one who had already had a fiancé who might or might not have had a gay affair?

He owed her.

Somehow, he had to make it up to her. He would give her what he should have given her from the start. Trust, support, stability, respect. Could he fake love? He knew she'd want it, he just didn't know if he could deliver what he'd never felt. He could try though, couldn't he? How hard could it be to say, 'I love you'?

His mobile phone pinged and he looked in consternation at the text she had sent. A black brow slowly lifted in wonderment. She was asking if he was still at the police station and there was a nosy bunny rabbit emoji attached to it.

Thee mou, he was planning to marry a woman who used emoticons…

CHAPTER SEVEN

ELLA WAKENED WITH the sense that something was not quite right in her world. Her hand slid across the empty space beside her and she suppressed a groan because Nikolai had not returned as she had hoped.

One swallow did not a summer make, one of Gramma's favourite sayings. She was not in a relationship with rules where she could develop expectations and act accordingly. No, there were no rules and she felt frighteningly lost without them.

Yet Nikolai had been so different with her the day before. Shorn of his icy, controlled detachment he was a different man. Yesterday he had simmered with passion and emotion. She loved that he had that depth, that capacity for feeling, even though he assiduously hid it from the world. He had been protective, tender and a wonderful lover. In every respect he had been everything she could have wanted, so why was she fretting?

Nobody got to know what tomorrow would bring. She wasn't alone in that situation. Possibly it was Cyrus's revelations about Paul that had left her feeling so unsure of everything. She needed to put what Cyrus had told her away and tuck it back in the past where it belonged. She had genuinely loved and grieved for Paul

and nothing could change that. Deep ties of friendship
and caring had bound them. And that was the best way
to remember him and what they had shared. How he
lived before they met was irrelevant and it would be
foolish to doubt her own judgment over past events.

As a knock sounded on the door she pushed herself up against the pillows, smiling when Max came in
with the dogs trailing in his wake. 'I've set your breakfast out on the deck. It's through the conservatory on
the other side of the corridor,' he told her, vanishing
into the annexe off the bathroom and emerging with a
flowing aqua dressing gown almost too fancy for the
description and a pair of slippers.

'Those aren't mine,' she said blankly.

'The closets on the left-hand side in the annexe are
packed with your new clothes,' Max explained, snip-
ping off the labels still attached to the garment and settling it down at the foot of the bed for her use.

As Max departed Ella got up and went into the bathroom. She brushed her teeth and ran a brush through
her tangled hair before peering into the units she had
assumed Nikolai used. A line of female clothing hung
there above racks of shoes and the drawers below were
filled with separates and fancy lingerie. She sighed and
padded back into the bedroom to pull on the robe and
slide her feet into the sleek mules.

Rory and Butch awaited her and accompanied her
into the conservatory, which had been restored but
which was still sadly empty of plants. She walked out
onto the deck, which was drenched in sunlight and
overlooked the very private garden below. Max had
set a tray on the table and she poured herself tea and
buttered a piece of toast. She wasn't accustomed to lei-

sure or luxury and what was for her the equivalent of breakfast in bed felt ridiculously decadent and frivolous. The dogs got bored and negotiated the steep spiral staircase that led down to the garden.

Ella sipped her tea and thought about Nikolai. He had probably stayed at his apartment the night before while she had stayed up late wondering when he would return. That had been a mistake and no doubt not the last she would make if she went on trying to squeeze their relationship into a normal frame with potential and boundaries. Sadly it could never be normal; it was a purely temporary arrangement, wasn't it? Nikolai buying her clothes and jewellery would never feel right in such circumstances but she could handle it, couldn't she?

Her family were safe and content and that was what really mattered, she told herself firmly. In three months' time when she was done with Nikolai, she would still have a whole life stretching ahead of her. She shifted in her wrought-iron garden seat, wincing at the soreness at the heart of her, the reminder that she was not quite the same woman she had been yesterday.

Nikolai was amazing in bed. And that was it. It had been good for her because he had *known* how to make it good. It was sex, only sex, just as her relationship with Paul had been more or less only friendship, she acknowledged uncomfortably. Maybe she was destined to have odd one-sided relationships with men, but she was determined that she would protect herself from being hurt again. She was learning from Nikolai, possibly even growing up a little, she reflected ruefully. A year ago she had hated Nikolai for making her want him when she had felt she should still be mourning

Paul, but how could anyone impose a time frame on either the pain and duration of loss or the heat of desire? From the very first Nikolai had lit her up like a firestorm. Her response had been immediate, basic, and utterly instinctive. Trying to prevent it, trying to stamp out the fire, would have been like trying to turn the tide back from the shore.

And Nikolai hadn't tried to turn the tide back either, she ruminated with an abstracted little smile. No, Nikolai had come back for her and had fought to get her into his life and his bed. It gave her the most disturbing guilty kick to be so desired by Nikolai, because with Paul she had always been the one left wanting and feeling inadequate.

Steps rang on the conservatory tiles and she lifted her head.

'Ella…' Nikolai murmured, striding out into the sunlight.

Garbed in a charcoal-grey suit that was exquisitely tailored to his lean, powerful frame, Nikolai took her breath away. He was no longer clean-shaven and the dark stubble demarcating his strong jaw and wide mobile mouth merely added a rougher, more potent edge to his aggressive masculinity. Brilliant dark golden eyes fringed by ebony lashes inspected her.

Mouth running dry, Ella sucked in a sudden breath. He could plunge her into a sea of drowning sexual awareness simply with a look. Her nipples tightened, her body clenched, her slender thighs pressing together tightly. As always he looked spectacular but she did notice that a slightly haggard quality had dulled his usual healthy glow of vigour.

Nikolai stared down at Ella, enchanted by the picture she made. The floaty thing she was wearing was sea green and it pooled around her like a mermaid's tail. In the bright light her perfect skin glowed against her rich bronze hair. Feeling a little less like a man caged and about to hand over the key to his freedom, he dropped down into a seat. *Thee mou*, she was exquisite.

Max arrived with coffee and biscuits. Max, Nikolai ruminated, knowing that that was a problem still to be dealt with: Max had ushered Cyrus into Nikolai's house. The dogs came up the stairs to investigate. At least Butch tried but he was unable to climb the stairs with his three legs and in the end, when he sat whining pitifully on the bottom step, Nikolai took pity on the little animal and went down to lift him and carry him up.

'He'll learn. He's taught himself to go downstairs safely,' Ella commented, but even so she was hugely impressed by his kindness.

'We all learn from our mistakes.' Nikolai lounged back in his chair and rested an ankle across one knee, the fabric of his well-cut trousers pulling taut to delineate the powerful muscles in his thighs. 'For instance, I made a mistake specifying three months with you...'

'Oh...' Ella stilled, her facial muscles locking as if she was in shock. 'Did you?'

'Three months is nothing. I don't want a time limit. I want to keep you,' he advanced levelly, speaking as though what he was saying were not at all personal but simply a matter of business to be taken out and discussed.

'I'm not Butch. I don't think you can just *keep* me,' Ella countered in a slightly wobbly voice, caused by the shock of thinking he wanted to end their arrangement early and then being shot fast in the other direction, only to fail to understand what he was talking about.

'I hope I can if I ask you to marry me,' Nikolai breathed very quietly, assessing dark eyes fringed with black lashes trained to her intently.

'Marry me?' Ella parroted as she straightened up, her shoulders stiffening. 'I asked you to marry me first and *you* said that marriage was out of the question.'

'You were right… I was wrong. Do we have to make a production out of it?' Nikolai asked in the most suspiciously reasonable tone.

Ella was knocked right off balance. In her experience all men found it a challenge to admit to being in the wrong but the admission had just tripped effortlessly off Nikolai's tongue. 'You're asking me to marry you…*now*?'

'Yes. I think we fit together well,' Nikolai declared.

Her wide green eyes couldn't have got any wider. 'In what way?' And her voice lowered. 'In bed?'

'No, I wasn't even thinking about that,' Nikolai lied.

In fascination Ella watched the faintest hint of colour line his sculpted cheekbones and she was tickled pink by the discovery that he could blush. From his point of view the sex genuinely must have been as amazing as he said it was, was all she could initially think. Why else would he be talking about marriage when he had previously been so against the idea?

'So, you want to marry me and keep me,' Ella recounted, thinking that a marriage proposal could not get much more basic and medieval in tone than that.

'Your family will be pleased… I think.'

'Yes, you're right,' Ella conceded, knowing that a wedding ring would make all the difference to her family's concerns because it was a promise of commitment that they trusted.

Nikolai leant forward and closed a hand round hers. 'I intend to do everything within my power to make you happy.'

'That's quite an aspiration.'

'I like to aim high.'

'But I haven't agreed yet.' Ella stared down nervously at the lean tanned hand that had engulfed hers. She glanced up involuntarily and fell into his melted-caramel eyes. Those eyes were as dangerous as a weed-infested pond to a lone swimmer, she thought crazily. She looked into his eyes and butterflies went crazy in her tummy and reasoned thought became too much of a challenge. She was falling for him, she recognised in dismay, falling fast and falling hard for a deeply unscrupulous male, who broke rules and ignored all her boundaries.

'But I'm hoping you will...' His black lashes swept down on his expressive eyes.

Nikolai didn't do fake humility very well, Ella thought in sudden amusement. She wasn't convinced for a moment. He was rich and gorgeous and successful and she was convinced that he had traversed a school of hard knocks to reach his current level. Cyrus had claimed that Nikolai's parents were a drug dealer and a whore and Ella knew no polite or gentle way of asking if that was the truth. What she did know was that sometimes Nikolai made her just want to hug him, and when he wasn't around it was a little like the sun vanishing without warning. She didn't understand how he could possibly have come to mean so much to her so quickly but there it was: Nikolai Drakos was already of enormous importance to her.

'I would want children,' Ella declared abruptly.

His dark head whipped up, caramel eyes flashing with surprise.

'And why are you looking surprised?' Ella enquired. 'Most women want children. I'm not talking this year or next year because I have to finish my training first, but eventually I would want children... I believe in being honest.'

Eventually.

'I've never wanted children,' Nikolai confessed.

'Well, it's children and me or *no* me, I'm afraid. Plus you'd also probably have to share your home with a selection of stray dogs and cats. That's probably not negotiable either,' Ella volunteered, determined to give him all the bad news at once before she lost her nerve and started trying to be someone she wasn't.

None of those life-changing possibilities was going to happen overnight, Nikolai reminded himself. She was trampling all over his most cherished convictions because she assumed that they would stay married for ever. But, of course, it wouldn't be that way, he reflected wryly. She would return to uni and meet some animal-loving younger man in muddy wellington boots and realise that Nikolai wasn't, after all, what she wanted. And he would let her go. A hollow sensation formed inside him. He pictured her in a country house awash with dogs and children. Home and family would come first with her...*always*. He understood that about her without even thinking about it. He couldn't give those things to her because he didn't form attachments, but she still deserved to have those things as well as the love of a man who deserved her.

'Are kids really a deal-breaker?' Ella demanded, troubled by the shadowed look on his lean, darkly handsome features. 'What *are* you thinking about?'

Nikolai sprang upright, bent down and scooped her off her seat to hold in his lap. 'Private matters.'

'If you marry me, you won't get to be private,' she warned him.

'Children aren't a deal-breaker if you're talking a couple of years down the road,' Nikolai conceded.

'And what if we have an accident?'

'I'm careful.'

Ella rested back in the cradle of his arms, drinking in the scent of his expensive cologne and the unique aroma that was purely, sexily his own. 'You really want to keep me?'

Nikolai screened his eyes. He knew that if a younger man in wellington boots had presented himself at that moment, he would have kicked him down the stairs and jumped on his corpse. He wanted her. He wanted her far more than he was comfortable with but he was equally aware of his guilt and of what he ought to be feeling. He had to be unselfish for *her* sake. 'I'll make you happy, *glikia mou*,' he swore doggedly and he meant every word of it.

He would make her happy, whatever it took and regardless of what it cost him. He would walk away from the pursuit of revenge that had consumed his life for the past five years. He would turn his back on Cyrus and his crimes for ever. Ella would become his first, his *only* priority.

'I believe you could,' Ella admitted in a softer tone than usual.

She wanted more time with him. She wanted to *be* with him because her heart stuttered and almost stopped at the thought of being without Nikolai. It was a visceral feeling, a scarily powerful feeling and not something she understood. She only understood that she needed to be with Nikolai. And there was a lot to be said in favour of a man who simply wanted to get married quickly, she reflected ruefully. Ella, after all, had been engaged for years to a man who had always found an excuse for not setting a wedding date. Paul had liked to talk about getting married but talking was as far as they had got.

'Yes, I'll marry you,' Ella declared with a sudden radiant smile.

Nikolai kissed her and a sizzle of naked longing snaked through her, leaving her limp and breathless. He settled her back down into her chair and produced a ring box while she looked on in astonishment.

'You have a ring?'

'Can't propose without a ring,' Nikolai quipped, sliding a diamond cluster onto her finger.

'It's dazzling,' she whispered as the diamonds flashed with iridescence in the sunshine. 'Thank you...'

'I'll stay in my apartment until the wedding,' Nikolai told her.

Ella gave him a bemused appraisal. 'But why?'

'I want to draw a strong line between where we started out and how we will continue,' Nikolai admitted smoothly. 'Everything will be different when we're married.'

* * *

'Nik's arranging for me to meet an interior designer here at the house next week,' Ella told Max when he served her breakfast two days later. 'I want the family things like photographs and papers put away somewhere safe first so that none of it ends up accidentally binned. I do think that at some stage Nik will want to look through it all. Where do you think we should start?'

'The late Mr Drakos's desk in the library. He kept a lot of stuff where he worked,' he volunteered. 'I'll try to get round every room before I leave.'

Ella frowned. *'Leave?'* she queried. 'Where are you going? Are you off on holiday or something?'

Max's thin face stiffened. 'I'm being replaced, Miss Palmer. Quite understandably your future husband has little faith in the man who allowed Cyrus Makris to enter his home.'

Max had been sacked over that? Ella was aghast at the news and furious that Nikolai had not told her about that decision. 'But that wasn't your fault... I mean, what happened.'

'What happened *happened*,' the older man pointed out with wry emphasis. 'I made a bad decision and you got hurt. Let's not discuss this, Miss Palmer. I not only let the man in but also went out leaving you alone with him.'

Angry words and defences bubbled in Ella's chest but she swallowed them back, recognising that further comment would only embarrass the older man. No, this was a matter she needed to take up directly with Nikolai. 'Could you give me directions to Nikolai's office?' she asked without hesitation. 'And perhaps while I'm out you could make a start on boxing up the Drakos family things I mentioned. If there are any particular pieces of furniture or other items that you feel should be considered an heirloom, please show them to me.'

Having lost the appetite to eat any more, Ella stood up. 'I'll fetch my bag.'

'Your driver will be waiting outside for you.'

'My...*driver*?'

'Mr Drakos has put a car and driver at your disposal...as well as a bodyguard,' Max completed. 'He wants to be assured of your safety twenty-four-seven.'

Ella shook her head in wonderment and compressed her lips. A driver? A bodyguard? Had Nikolai lost his wits? She was an ordinary woman and she did not require anyone to either drive her or guard her. He should have discussed those arrangements with her long before he made them.

Nikolai's offices were in a towering glass and steel office building that bore a fancy Drakos logo that appeared to be a dragon. Or was it a winged goddess like Nikolai's tattoo? She hadn't had the opportunity to get a closer look at it. To do that she would have to get his shirt off again. A rueful light entered her green eyes and her face warmed as she stood in the lift flanked by her silent monolith of a bodyguard, John. John was quiet to the extent that had he not cast such a big shadow she might almost have been able to forget he was there.

In Reception she asked to see Nikolai and was told he was in a meeting. Ignoring the fact, she sat down to wait and sent him a text warning him that she *had* to speak to him. Thirty minutes passed slowly and then a svelte older woman approached her to take her to him.

'You can wait for me here,' she told her bodyguard.

She smoothed down her fine wool trousers and the cashmere jacket that, in concert with her stiletto-heeled boots, gave her a fashionable air. Now that she wore Nikolai's ring she had no qualms about wearing the clothes he had bought her. It felt right, just as it had felt right to call Gramma and her father and share her wedding news and smile at their happiness on her behalf. Yet below the smile lurked a deep well of insecurity, for there were certain facts she could not ignore. She hadn't known Nikolai for very long and she knew very little about him because he was not the kind of male who shared personal details. Yet here she was, preparing to confront him over what she deemed to be a very bad decision.

'I have a bone to pick with you,' she murmured the instant she stepped into his office.

Without visible reaction, Nikolai studied her with shrewd dark eyes. 'That doesn't sound promising. I like the boots though.'

'Of course you do,' Ella groaned. 'Men always like sexy boots. You're being predictable. But when you sacked Max, you were being a complete tyrant... I don't want to marry a tyrant, Nikolai!'

An angry frown slowly drew together his black brows. 'He complained to you?'

'No, he didn't. I found out...quite by accident actually,' she assured him defensively. 'Can't you see that you're being unjust? Did you ever tell Max not to let Cyrus into your home?'

'No,' Nikolai conceded grudgingly.

'Well, then, how can you blame Max for what happened? *I* greeted Cyrus. Max knew that he was my visitor and thought nothing of it,' Ella protested.

'Max put you at risk. I can't close my eyes to that and whether I hire or fire anyone I employ is not your business,' he completed in a tone of cold finality.

Ella was undaunted, her eyes gleaming like polished emeralds. 'Oh, I would think that the hiring or firing of staff in the marital home would be very much my business as your wife.'

'But at present it is not our marital home and you are not my wife as yet,' Nikolai pointed out in stubborn challenge. 'The responsibility remains mine.'

'If you want it to *be* our marital home and you want me to *be* your wife you will listen to me,' Ella told him in raw frustration. 'You're being unfair to Max. I hadn't the faintest idea that Cyrus was liable to turn violent like that, so how was Max supposed to know? How were any of us supposed to know that?'

And that was the crux of the matter, Nikolai reflected with bitter acceptance. Everything that had happened was *his* fault. Only he had known that Cyrus could be dangerous. He had never dreamt, though, that Cyrus would dare to approach Ella when she was staying with Nikolai. But then very probably Cyrus had heard about the hotel fire and had assumed that that particular morning Nikolai would be otherwise engaged. Nikolai knew that he should have warned Max never to let Cyrus Makris into his home but that possibility hadn't even crossed his mind. When he had realised that Cyrus was there, when he had found Cyrus attacking Ella, the world had turned blood red for Nikolai. He knew that if Ella had not intervened, he would have kept on hitting Cyrus and in the aftermath he had been looking for someone to blame for an untenable situation. Someone, *anyone* other than his own self, he acknowledged with a fierce regret that he could never have expressed.

In the smouldering silence, Ella studied Nikolai. She knew he was thinking hard and fast and deep but typically he was not sharing a single thought. 'You said you wanted to make me happy. I *like* Max. You were exhausted that day after the fire. That ghastly episode with Cyrus upset you more. Don't make Max carry the can for something that wasn't his fault.'

'If I'm in the wrong I will change my decision,' Nikolai declared in a driven undertone.

'And why have I suddenly got a driver and a body-guard the size of a mountain?'

Nikolai breathed in slow and deep and wondered if this was what marriage promised to be like. Would Ella challenge his every decision? He made his own choices and he always stood by them but suddenly he was being faced with the need to compromise, the need to defend or reconsider his black-and-white thinking processes. It would be a steep challenge to become less rigid and more flexible for her sake.

Making Ella happy and keeping her happy would be no cake walk.

'I won't apologise for hiring a bodyguard for your benefit. It is my responsibility to keep you safe and I take it very seriously,' Nikolai assured her confi-dently. 'I will not take the risk of Cyrus approaching you again.'

'Do you really think that is likely?' Ella pressed in astonishment.

'He was off his head with rage that day. I don't think that we can afford to assume that he will keep his distance. I prefer to ensure that you are protected when I'm not around.'

Ella searched his lean, hard features and the lack of compromise etched in his strong bone structure. She suppressed a sigh.

'I will consider retaining Max but I will not reconsider my decision to hire a driver and a bodyguard,' Nikolai admitted with flat emphasis. 'Quit while you're ahead, Ella.'

'We still have so much to learn about each other,' Ella whispered ruefully. 'Am I stressing you out?'

His dark golden eyes glittered. 'I have strong shoulders.'

Nikolai was all male as he stood there straight and tall and tough. He wasn't about to admit that he had made a mistake with Max but she knew she had won because Nikolai had a strong streak of fairness. But in pushing that issue, she had crossed a line with Nikolai and she recognised that as well. She had forced him to acknowledge her as an equal, not as a weak or lesser person, and he wouldn't forget that.

Nikolai surveyed her, his wide sensual lips set in a hard line. He would take no risks with her safety and he didn't care if that infringed her freedom. If anything happened to her he would never forgive himself. She was *his* to look after. Only a couple of weeks back he hadn't recognised the level of responsibility he was taking on by bringing her into his life but he did now.

Ella first, second and third...by the time she met a nice young man in welly boots he would probably be relieved to graciously step back and hand her over. At least that was supposed to be his real goal, Nikolai conceded with brooding ferocity. Familiarity was supposed to lead to contempt. Responsibility was supposed to make a man long for freedom. If she met another man, would he then return to normal?

He was grimly conscious that in some peculiar way he had changed from the moment he saw Ella again. His legendary cool control was under attack. His mind was no longer his own. Ella sneaked into his thoughts far more often than was reasonable and he was already regretting having loftily declared that they would live apart until the wedding.

Indeed, so disturbing were the changes that he recognised in himself that he felt almost at the mercy of reactions and thoughts and anxieties that he had suppressed for years. That slight hint of instability totally unnerved him and made him feel like a man on the edge of a precipice. Even worse, the threat of seeing Ella with another man clenched every muscle in his body with aggression. Right at this very moment he knew he couldn't face that possibility, but surely with time those responses would fade?

It would be so simple. He would get used to having her around. He would get bored; *she* would get bored. She would want her freedom back and he would let her go...*wouldn't he*?

CHAPTER EIGHT

'So, ARE YOU putting in a replacement now?' Ella prompted the nurse who was engaged in removing the old contraceptive implant from her arm.

'Dr Jenks only asked me to remove this one,' the older woman responded cagily.

Perhaps her doctor thought she was suffering side effects from the implant, Ella reasoned wryly. That would mean looking at other contraceptive methods. Hopefully one without side effects, she thought ruefully, because she had only come to see the doctor in the first place because she wasn't feeling herself. Not ill exactly, just not *right*. Her appetite had changed, her taste buds had gone awry and she was suddenly so blasted tired all the time! He had sent her for a battery of tests the day before and made a second appointment for her.

Ella was grateful she had come home, which had enabled her to see her usual doctor rather than having to find a new one in London. She had persuaded Nikolai that she wanted to be married from home, so that family and friends could easily attend, and tomorrow was the big day. She still couldn't quite believe it but there was something that felt very right about the reality that she literally couldn't wait to get down the aisle to become Nikolai's wife.

'It's called love,' Gramma had told her cheerfully. 'I'd have been worried if you weren't excited about getting married to him.'

Resisting the urge to rub her slightly sore arm with its neat little plaster, Ella returned to the doctor's surgery. She was thinking about her wedding dress, which she adored, when one of the doctor's measured words finally penetrated her wandering concentration. Conceived...*conceived*? Her mind went blank as though the word were foreign because the very unexpectedness of it threw rationality out of the window.

'But I had the implant!' she bleated, hands abruptly closing very tightly together on her lap.

'As I pointed out, the implant is only effective for three years and you missed your follow-up appointment and failed to respond to the letter that was sent out.'

'But it *is* only three years since—' she began heatedly.

Dr Jenks went through the dates with her. In fact, it turned out to be over four years since she had got the implant and she had the vaguest recollection of the reminder letter he mentioned. After Paul had passed away, contraception had been very low on the list of her priorities. But Ella was still stunned to appreciate that when she had lost her virginity with Nikolai she had not been protected as she had naively assumed. Her main mistake had been the assumption that the implant lasted for four years when in fact it only worked for three. And she *had* conceived. Nikolai was going to be shattered...but Ella was equally convinced that she would never recover from the shock either.

Until that moment Ella had believed that total honesty between partners was the only way to go. And then without the smallest warning, she found herself changing her mind. Floating down the aisle to Nikolai and announcing almost simultaneously that she was pregnant would absolutely ruin the day. He would be taken aback, unprepared, *stressed out* by the news because Nikolai was a planner, who liked everything in its place, everything clean and tidy. And there was nothing clean or tidy about an unplanned pregnancy when they would be only newly married and looking forward to the unfettered joys of coupledom. In addition he had been quite blunt about only wanting to become a parent in a few years' time.

They were flying to Crete after the wedding to stay at the house Nikolai owned there. She would tell him on the island, when he was relaxed and better able to handle an unforeseen development. *Pregnant!* Ella drove back home and reflected that her own mother must have suffered a similar shock when she realised that she was pregnant. Ella, after all, had not been a planned baby either and her arrival had threatened to derail her mother's career plans. Soon after her birth, however, her mother had flown off to take up her top job, leaving her infant daughter behind with her father and grandmother. To walk away had been her choice. What if Nikolai felt so strongly about not starting a family that he chose to walk away too? No, that was the absolute worst-case scenario, Ella told herself firmly. He had said that he was willing to have a family eventually and there was nothing wrong with holding back on telling him her news. It wasn't as though she would be telling him any lies, she was simply *delaying* telling him, she reasoned defensively.

Ella knew that once again her own plans would be forced back on hold because it would be incredibly difficult for her to adequately complete her training while she was pregnant. But she knew too that sometimes it was necessary to make the best one could of a life change that came as a surprise. It would only be a bad development if she allowed herself to think that it was. All right, she conceded, the timing wasn't what she would have chosen but she had always wanted children. She thought of all the worse things that could have happened, imagining how she would have felt had she had trouble conceiving, and before very long her dismay subsided entirely. As for Nikolai? She would wrap up her news like the gift she believed it to be and present it to him at the best possible moment.

'You look so beautiful,' Gramma enthused warmly as Ella twirled at the foot of the stairs.

Her father was misty-eyed at the picture his daughter made in her lace wedding gown. The gorgeous lace was her only adornment because Ella, conscious of her diminutive height, had opted for a plain design that bared only her back while encasing her arms and slender body in sleek lace. On her feet she rocked a considerably less conservative set of strappy, very high-heeled lace ankle boots, teamed with stockings and a garter. Nikolai liked boots and Ella was in the mood to give her bridegroom boots.

She hadn't breathed a word about her pregnancy since she left the surgery. She felt that announcement should first be heard by her baby's father. They travelled to the little local church in the limo Nikolai had sent, her bodyguard bringing up the rear in his own vehicle. The church was full and she walked down the aisle slowly on her father's arm, noting all the unfamiliar faces on Nikolai's side of the church and thinking it sad that he had not a single relative to grace those pews. She had, however, from the letters and cards she had found in the town house, discovered that Nikolai's grandfather had twin sisters still living on the island of Crete, where the Drakos family had originated, and she wondered if Nikolai would make use of that information.

Nikolai watched his bride approach with bated breath. His brain told him there was no such thing as perfection but he *saw* only perfection, from the sleek coil of Ella's bronze hair to the fine-tuned delicacy of her figure encased in exquisite lace. It had been less than a week since he had seen her but it felt like a lot longer. *Thee mou*, he couldn't sleep for wanting her and, as he had so frequently told himself, getting married meant an end to cold showers and wondering where she was, who she might be with and what she was doing. He watched her drift towards him with keenly appreciative eyes of possession and pride.

Ella smiled at the altar, looking up into those melted-caramel eyes, admiring the smooth angle of his strong jawline, the jut of his nose and the high cheekbones that lent his lean, darkly handsome features such electrifying magnetism. The ring went onto her finger and she thought about the baby with a deep inner sense of happiness. Since she had found out so early it would be ages until she started showing and she had plenty of time before she needed to worry about telling Nikolai that he was going to be a father.

They travelled to the hotel where the reception was being staged. 'You have a lot of friends,' she remarked.

'Mostly business acquaintances,' he corrected. 'While you seem to have hundreds of cousins.'

'Dad has five sisters,' she reminded him.

'My very best wishes. I'm Marika Makris, Cyrus's sister.' A middle-aged brunette wearing a superb diamond necklace introduced herself to Ella while the bridal couple circulated amongst their guests before the wedding breakfast was served. Nikolai had mentioned in passing that Marika would be attending and she knew that the older woman had been estranged from her brother for years, so there should be nothing uncomfortable about the meeting.

'Ella... Drakos,' Ella framed and laughed. 'It's so hard to say a different name but Nikolai very much wanted me to take his name.'

'Naturally, you *are* Nikolai's crowning triumph,' Marika informed her with a smug little smile.

'Well...thank you,' Ella responded after a blank pause in which no inspiration came to mind.

'Nikolai and Cyrus have been enemies for so long that my brother forgot to watch his back,' the brunette remarked sagely before drifting on at a regal pace.

Ella blinked in bewilderment. Enemies? Since when had Nikolai and Cyrus been enemies? She knew they didn't get on, but thought they were just business rivals. But enemies spoke of something much deeper between them. Both men were Greek, which she supposed was the connection. Resolving to ask Nikolai about that comment later, she took her seat for the meal.

After eating, she went to the cloakroom to repair her make-up. As she paused at a crowded corner to allow people to pass her by she heard a woman say loudly, 'What I want to know is what does *she* have that the rest of us don't? Nikolai is the original ice man and he ditched all of us in record time!'

Ella's brows rose. 'Ditched *all* of us?' Who was she eavesdropping on? The ex-girlfriends' club?

'She *is* beautiful,' another female voice opined regretfully.

'She's the size of a shrimp!' someone else objected. 'But she must have some very special quality for him to be marrying her.'

'Maybe she's a wildcat in bed,' the first voice suggested.

'Maybe he's finally fallen in love,' the kinder voice that had described Ella as beautiful remarked.

There was an outbreak of female voices at that point. 'If pigs could fly!' was one of the few repeatable opinions expressed.

Lifting her chin and gathering her pride, Ella rounded the corner and passed the small group of fashionably dressed women all waving glasses around and talking loudly. Even a cursory glance in their direction was sufficient to warn her that Nikolai had very good taste and while Nikolai had apparently dumped those women they were all attending the wedding with partners. How naive she had been not to be prepared for the reality that Nikolai was almost certain to have former lovers attending, she thought wryly.

She studied herself in the mirror. A shrimp? Well, compared to those tall, shapely ladies outside she was indeed a shrimp in size, she conceded ruefully. Seemingly Nikolai had once had a particular type he went for because all those women were blonde. So where did she fit in? And why had he married her? She could not help recalling Cyrus's claim that Nikolai was notoriously badly behaved with women. Possibly that had been true, Ella reasoned, but people could change... couldn't they?

'You're as stiff as a fence post,' Nikolai groaned as they opened the dancing, something Ella was not very confident about doing in front of an audience. 'And you're very quiet. Naturally I'm worried.'

'How many ex-girlfriends of yours are here today?'

His wide shoulders tensed. 'A couple, and only because they're now married to friends of mine. Why? Has someone said something they shouldn't?'

'Don't talk down to me like I'm a child!' Ella snapped into his chest, feeling distinctly shrimp-like in spite of her heels.

'If you won't tell me what's wrong there's nothing I can do about it.'

'There's nothing wrong,' Ella declared loftily, drinking in the scent of his cologne and the husky, intrinsic smell that was purely him and which warmed her somewhere down deep inside. There was no way on earth she was about to allow insecurity to drive her into arguing with him on their wedding day. 'But be warned. I'm the jealous type. And I may be small but I'm lethal.'

'I knew that already,' Nikolai confessed, long fingers splaying caressingly across her bare spine as he shifted his lithe hips against her. 'Lethally appealing and lethally sexy.'

'Wait until you see the boots,' she whispered teasingly, wildly aware of his arousal and flattered that he was in that state purely because he was close to her. 'And the garter and the stockings.'

'I'm getting you in stockings for my wedding night?' Nikolai murmured thickly. 'Bring it on, *khriso mou*!'

And Ella laughed and forgot about what she had overheard. Of course he had exes and a past but that was life and she had to live with it.

'I felt sad when I realised that you didn't have a single relative at our wedding,' Ella admitted during the flight in the private jet to Crete.

'I didn't feel sad,' Nikolai countered squarely, lounging back in his leather seat, very much in command. 'But then I didn't have a white-picket-fence childhood like yours.'

'It wasn't like that. I didn't have a mother,' Ella argued and shared her story.

'You had a father and a grandmother who loved you. You were lucky.'

But Ella would never forget how rejected she had felt when she had first met her mother as a teenager. Her mother had not regretted never having got to know her and, more hurtfully still, had had no ambition to foster an adult friendship with her long-lost daughter either. It had been a one-off meeting and a disappointment. In truth it had made Ella better appreciate the family she did have.

'Family can be toxic,' Nikolai remarked with rich cynicism.

'How...*toxic*?' she questioned uncertainly. 'Tell me about your childhood.'

'It's ugly.'

'I can handle ugly. Tell me about your father.'

Nikolai grimaced. 'He got into trouble from an early age. He was thrown out of several schools for dealing in drugs,' he divulged.

'How did you find that out?'

'My grandfather's solicitor told me what he knew about my background when he was trying to explain why the old man was so determined not to meet me,' Nikolai explained with a wry twist of his expressive mouth. 'Although my father was given every support to turn his life around and numerous second chances he continually chose to return to crime and violence.'

'Some people are just born with that tendency,' Ella imputed, sadness gripping her that Nikolai could not even respect his father's memory. No son would want such a father and nor would he want to grow up in such a man's image. 'What about your mother?'

'She was Russian…a lap dancer called Natalya.'

'You're half Russian?' Ella cut in, her surprise unhidden.

'When Natalya became pregnant with my sister, my father married her. Possibly the only conventional thing he ever did in his life. At some stage my grandfather disinherited him and cut off all contact with him. I have few memories before the age of five,' Nikolai admitted stiffly. 'I do remember chaos…shouts, screams, hiding behind a locked door with my sister begging me to keep quiet. My father was in and out of prison. We moved around a lot. There were frequent police raids, gang attacks. My sister looked after me.'

Ella was quietly appalled by what she was learning about his background and finally comprehending why

Nikolai would say that a family could be toxic. 'Why not your mother? Was she at work?'

'No, she didn't work. She was always in the background somewhere drunk or high. But for Sofia I would either have starved or been beaten to death. My father took his frustrations out on me,' Nikolai volunteered without any expression at all, watching her as though he was measuring her reactions to what he was telling her, which made her all the more careful not to reveal a sympathy, which could hurt his pride. 'He broke Sofia's nose once when she came between us in an effort to protect me... I was more her child than my mother's.'

'I'm really sorry it was so bad for you,' Ella whispered, green eyes luminous with a compassion she couldn't hide.

She wondered if anyone but his sister had ever loved Nikolai. And he had lost her as well. Was that why he kept himself so isolated? Why he was so determinedly detached?

'My parents died in a car crash when I was ten and my grandfather set up a trust to pay for my education. I was sent straight to boarding school in England.'

'He saved every one of your school reports,' Ella reminded him, because she had told him what she had found in his grandfather's desk. 'And yet he didn't want to meet you?'

'He was afraid of being disappointed. I think he'd already worked out by then that if you make an emotional investment in individuals you get hurt, and he was old and tired.'

'So, he kept you at arm's length.' Ella sighed. 'But he missed out on so much. Obviously you're not like your father.'

'I'm brighter but I don't know that I'm better,' Nikolai murmured with forbidding honesty, studying her in all her bridal finery. So appealing and beautiful, so vulnerable, so *clean*. She had probably never done a really mean thing in her life. Ella was too good for him. He knew that he didn't deserve her. He had seduced her with blackmail into his bed…no honour or decency there! And if she knew him now as he truly was and stripped of pretence, she would never have married him.

'Your troubled background was what made you… unsure about having a family, wasn't it?' Ella probed helplessly.

Nikolai shrugged a broad shoulder. 'Of course. What does a man like me know about being part of a normal family? How could I ever be a father when I wouldn't know where to begin?'

Ella paled. 'You could learn.'

'And what if I don't have the interest to learn? I've heard that children put a lot of pressure on a relationship. Why would you take that risk?' Nikolai enquired with sardonic bite.

Ella could only think of the tiny seed in her womb, which she would have protected with her life, and she turned her head away lest her face reveal too much. For the first time she was scared of what she had to tell Nikolai. It was true that, while he had no experience of family life, he could certainly learn. But would he *want* to learn? A baby coming so early in their marriage would definitely impose restrictions on them that he might well resent. Yet it was important to Ella that her baby have two loving parents, for she knew how much her own mother's indifference had hurt her even as a young adult.

'And I'm not *unsure* about whether or not to have children,' Nikolai contradicted. 'I have simply never felt the need to reproduce.'

'But you *agreed* that if I—' she began heatedly.

'Yes. I'm not that selfish. I will adapt to whatever the future brings.'

But how far would 'adapting' get him if he had a fundamental dislike of the idea of becoming a parent? Ella repressed the thought and breathed in deep and slow. She had to be patient and understanding, not critical and pushy. Honey was much more effective than vinegar.

She collided with hard dark eyes, finally noticing the rigidity of his sculpted bone structure. Nikolai's sheer tension leapt out at her. She had raised sensitive issues when she'd forced him to share the story of his dysfunctional childhood and family. Was it any wonder he was on the defensive? Still gorgeous though, no matter what mood he was in, she thought helplessly as she studied him, her guilty conscience assailing her until the germ of a wild idea struck her. The instant she thought of it she wanted to smash the mould of his undoubtedly low expectations and seduce him.

Could she? *Dared* she? Wasn't this the male who had moved heaven and earth to bring her into his life and his bed? With Nikolai she never needed to doubt her welcome. Nikolai always wanted her. Uplifted by that conviction, she felt bold but she also needed to be closer to him and she craved the soothing balm of the intense connection they shared when they made love. Unclipping her seat belt, she stood up before she could lose her nerve. 'Ask the cabin staff to stay out,' she told him tightly.

His brow indented as he lifted the phone at his elbow and spoke. He stared at her, watching the colour rise in her cheeks. 'Why?'

'Newly married? Do not disturb? Do I need to draw a picture?' she asked teasingly, feeling the wanton heat of anticipation coil at the heart of her.

'I think perhaps you do,' Nikolai murmured, still frowning, still not getting the message.

Ella tugged up the tight skirt of her gown and knelt very deliberately down at his feet and pressed his thighs apart. Only as she reached for his belt buckle did the extreme tension go out of him to be replaced by tension of an entirely different variety.

'You're kidding me?' Nikolai husked, black lashes rising over stunned dark eyes.

'Does this feel like a wind-up?' Ella enquired, running a caressing palm down over the revealing bulge at his groin.

He shivered, hard dark eyes flashing to pools of melted-caramel astonishment.

Face hot, Ella ran down his zip. Helpfully he lifted his hips to allow her to move his pants out of the way. She was determined to use all the things that she had learnt from the books she had read. Her tongue stole a long swipe along the length of him.

Nikolai swore in Greek and pushed back in his seat with a little groan. 'I never know what to expect from you but I adore the way you continually surprise me. Presumably you know what you're doing...'

'No, this technique is straight out of a book.'

'A *book*?' he repeated in disbelief.

'Shut up…you're distracting me,' she muttered shakily, settling down to practise everything she had learned with enthusiasm.

Nikolai very quickly decided that she must've read a humdinger of a text. Her tongue stroked and flicked and circled and her luscious lips engulfed. Her warm, wet mouth took him to paradise. His hands fisted in her hair and as she found her rhythm an earthy groan of satisfaction escaped him. She looked up at him once when he was right on the edge, little shudders travelling through his muscular thighs, eyes glowing gold.

Nikolai had never been so aroused and he knew he wouldn't last long. He tried to back off once he realised he was about to come but she wouldn't let him take control. He climaxed in a storm of raw excitement and threw his dark head back, watching in wonderment as his so recently virginal bride swallowed, zipped him back up, straightened her dress and returned to her seat as though nothing had happened.

'A book?' Nikolai queried raggedly as he shifted with voluptuous contentment in his seat.

'Why not a book? I don't like not knowing how to do things.'

'I'm willing to teach you anything you ask, *so* willing,' Nikolai savoured in a roughened undertone, still barely able to credit what she had just done. 'You are insanely sexy, *khriso mou*. I am a very lucky man.'

Ella was so pleased that she'd chased the shadows away. His eyes had been haunted because she had asked him to talk about his disturbing childhood, but she had sent his thoughts and his imagination racing in a far more positive direction. There was more she needed to know about Nikolai's past, but she had learnt enough for the present and she loved him. Loved him so much that she couldn't bear to see shadows in his lean dark face and listen to him insisting that he wasn't sensitive or upset when he *was*.

And she had learned from what he had told her as well. One person had rejected her but more than one had rejected Nikolai: his mother, his father, his grandfather. Of course he didn't know how a family operated. Of course he worried about being a father when his own had set such a bad example. But with her love and support his outlook would change so that when he found out about their baby he would feel very differently...wouldn't he?

CHAPTER NINE

'SO, WHERE ARE we staying?' Ella enquired after a car had collected them from Heraklion Airport and begun the drive along the coastal road in the fading light of dusk.

'The house where my grandfather was born.'

'I like a place with family connections,' Ella admitted. 'Did you inherit it?'

'Yes, but by the time I did it hadn't been occupied in years and it needed gutting. It started out as a simple farmhouse, which was gentrified when the family fortunes improved, but my grandfather never used it. I almost had it demolished,' he confided with a wry smile. 'And then I stood on the veranda in the sunlight and thought of all the generations who must have enjoyed that same view and I decided to try and retain the character of the place.'

'You see, you *do* have sentimental attachments,' Ella told him with an appreciative glance as the car turned off the main road onto a much more narrow one lined with trees.

'I also have a surprise for you,' Nikolai admitted. 'But you won't get it until later.'

The house was larger than she had expected, a

sprawling ranch-style villa with various offshoots and a large inviting veranda. Nikolai gave her a brief tour of the house, which was all cool tiled floors and contemporary furnishings. The beautifully carved staircase had been conserved, as had a turn-of-the-century stained-glass window of saints in the hall, but it remained first and foremost a luxurious and comfortable modern home.

At the foot of the stairs, Nikolai bent without warning and scooped her up into his arms.

'What on earth?' Ella gasped.

'I always wanted a woman small enough to carry up the stairs.'

'So why did you only get involved with very tall blondes?' Ella quipped, unimpressed, thinking about the women she had heard talking about him at the wedding.

'I was running scared,' Nikolai assured her, deadpan. 'I knew when I found a little one I'd have to marry her.'

Involuntarily, Ella laughed because he was so slick with that response. He pressed open the door on a spacious bedroom. A tall geometric vase of glorious flowers adorned a side table and beside it stood an ice bucket and two champagne flutes. He lowered her carefully to the polished wood floor and uncorked the champagne to fill the glasses. Ella put the glass to her lips, bubbles breaking beneath her nose as she pretended to sip as she had done all day while drinks were served and toasts were being made.

'You look fantastic in that dress,' he told her huskily, sincerity ringing from every syllable and empowering her.

Ella set her flute down and turned her back to him. 'Undo my hooks,' she urged.

'You're still determined to surprise me,' he said thickly, deftly dealing with the hooks at her nape and then running down the side zip over the swell of her hips.

Ella moved back a few steps, loosening her sleeves and slowly working the gown down and off, murderously conscious of the bareness of her breasts because the dress had had built-in support. And she was still shy with him, foolish she knew after the intimacy they had already shared but she was still afraid that he might be disappointed by what she had to offer.

Nikolai leant back against the ornate black iron footboard on the bed and stared at her. 'I think I've died and gone to heaven, *khriso mou*.'

Fiercely resisting the urge to cover her breasts with her hands, Ella stepped out of the gown and settled it over a chair.

Nikolai simply gloried in the view. She was wearing ridiculously cute lace ankle boots and stockings that stopped mid-thigh. One slender thigh sported a frilly blue garter and cream lace knickers encased her pert little derriere. Breasts with straining soft pink nipples seized his attention and that fast he was on sexual fire.

Ella loved that Nikolai was staring at her like a man in the grip of a holy vision. He made her feel like a sex goddess. Suddenly it didn't matter that she had tiny boobs and a rail-thin body. Nikolai looking at her like that was like a shot of power-packed adrenalin in her veins. He peeled off his jacket, wrenched almost clumsily at his shirt. A long delicious slice of bronzed muscular torso appeared.

'And the best thing of all, *khriso mou*,' he breathed in a roughened undertone as he reached for her. 'That ring on your finger says you're all mine.'

He fed on her mouth like a hungry wolf and that kiss was rough, uncompromising and absolutely dominant. It also set alight every nerve ending in her quivering body. He pushed her down on the bed and claimed a taut little nipple while long fingers toyed with its twin. It was as if an electrifying piece of elastic ran between her breasts and her pelvis as the heat surged through her. A finger skimmed aside her knickers and skated through her damp folds. As she gasped he groaned.

'You're so ready for me…' he savoured, claiming her succulent mouth again with driving hunger.

He spread her out on the bed like a pagan sacrifice and the burn at the heart of her tingled and seethed even before the stubble on his face grazed her inner thighs. She wanted him so much. She had never wanted anything or anybody so much that it literally hurt to wait. A finger teased her inner sheath and her hips wriggled, her spine arching as he found the tiny bundle of nerves with his expert mouth. And what happened after that, well, she wasn't quite sure because she was bucking and shifting and moaning and the pleasure kept on building and building until she couldn't contain it any more and a climax ripped through her lower body like a detonation, flaming through every limb and nerve ending with explosive effect. It was almost as though the world stopped for a moment and she held onto him as though he were a rock in a whirlwind.

'I love what you do to me,' she whispered breathlessly into a satin-smooth dark-skinned shoulder.

'That was a bit bull-in-a-china-shop,' Nikolai

growled, rolling free and springing off the bed, dark eyes volatile as a hot fire ready to rage out of control. 'This is our wedding night. It was supposed to be a slow, sweet seduction.'

'Stop talking,' Ella told him. 'Being thrown on the bed works for me. Seeing you a little out of control is more *real* than some plan of slow seduction.'

'Blame yourself. You've been wrecking my plans all day,' Nikolai asserted, swiping the package off the dressing table and returning to the bed. 'First you blew my mind on the flight and then you flaunted your gorgeous self in boots and stockings and a garter and I was *lost…*'

'Is that a complaint?'

'No.' A wicked charismatic grin slashed his lean, darkly handsome features. 'That was an "any time you want me, I'm yours" speech,' he teased.

'You can be yourself with me, you know,' she whispered feelingly. 'Just do what you feel like.'

'Can't,' Nikolai incised, passing her the package. 'I'd eat you alive. Happy wedding day, Mrs Drakos.'

'I didn't get you anything.'

'You gave me you…unforgettably,' Nikolai growled, flipping open the box for her in his impatience and lifting out a three-strand pearl necklace with an elaborate emerald and diamond clasp.

'My word…' Ella stroked a wondering finger over the gleaming iridescence of the perfect pearls. 'It's really beautiful.'

Nikolai clasped the necklace round her throat. 'Their purity reminded me of you.'

'I'm not pure… I'm not perfect…nobody needs to be perfect,' Ella declared in a rush, thinking of the secret she was holding within her body, fearing his reaction more than ever because, the happier she became, the more she feared a potential fall.

'You're a lot more pure and perfect than I will ever be.' Nikolai pushed the tangle of bronze-coloured hair back behind her small ears and tipped up her chin to kiss her again.

The heat inside her claimed her again faster than she could've believed. It was as though her body were programmed to his. A muscular, hair-roughened thigh slid between hers as he rested her back on the pillows again and everything below her waist tingled with awareness.

'I want you so much,' she whispered helplessly.

'And you're going to get me. Over and over and over again,' Nikolai husked hungrily against her swollen mouth.

Ella stroked the long, thick length of jutting virility against his stomach, no longer nervous, no longer unsure. He wanted her every bit as much as she wanted him and knowing that set her free and filled her with happiness.

'If you do that I won't last.'

Ella reared up and pushed him flat. 'Oh, stop with the threats, Mr Drakos!' she told him, laughing down at him.

Nikolai could never remember laughter along with sex but he liked it. He liked it even more when he pulled her back down again and reinstated supremacy because there was no way he would allow her to call the shots in bed. He felt strange, almost giddy, and he wanted to smile and he wondered what was wrong with him. His little hummingbird of a bride was changing him and he knew as he looked down into her hectically flushed, laughing face that there was no way he was ever going to willingly hand her over to another man.

'I want this night to last for ever,' she murmured against his chest, drunk on the smell of his skin.

'*For ever* is a big challenge,' he husked, rocking his hips against hers, letting her feel the hardness of him, sending a wanton thrill of naked hunger shooting through her veins.

'It wasn't a challenge,' she protested as he touched her where she most needed to be touched and she jerked and whimpered, defenceless against the surge of need controlling her.

He eased over her, rearranged her to his satisfaction, slowly surged in and she shut her eyes tight, every nerve screaming for the satisfaction only he could give. Inch by agonising inch he entered her and when he was finally fully seated she loosed a sound of pleasure she couldn't hold back. She could feel how damp, how ready she was and his sheer strength as he lifted her up to him, muscles bulging in his forearms, left her weak with longing. He slid back and then plunged, his speed picking up. Excitement detonated inside her and she wrapped her legs round him. As she bucked he pinned her to the mattress and thrust into her fiercely with a primal grunt of pleasure. It went on and on and on until she was sobbing with excitement and the band of tension at the centre of her body was tightening and tightening. Release came in a rush of feral fire, lighting up every nerve and skin cell, and she cried out, her nails raking down his back in an ecstasy of pleasure.

She was dizzy with lingering joy when she recovered enough to be aware of her surroundings again.

'I'm flattening you.' He dropped a gentle kiss on her brow and released her from his weight to turn over.

Flatten away, she almost told him, until her attention was grabbed by the tattoo on his shoulder. Yes, it was a winged goddess, but incongruously a tiny rainbow and the head of a unicorn peeked out from below one wing. 'A rainbow and a unicorn?' she queried, tracing the design with a curious fingertip.

Nikolai went rigid and flipped back to face her, dark eyes grim in his lean, strong face. 'To remember my sister...the fairy-tale things she liked,' he confided with a reluctance she could feel.

'That's sweet...when did she...?'

'Five years ago.' His rich, dark drawl had gone all gravelly. 'I don't want to discuss it.'

'OK,' Ella said lightly, although it wasn't OK in any way and his reserve hurt.

Did you really think being married to Nikolai was going to be all rainbows and unicorns? she asked herself irritably. He wasn't going to have a personality transplant overnight and suddenly begin sharing his every innermost thought and feeling. Obviously he still felt the loss of his sister deeply and he wasn't ready to talk about it yet. That was all right. She didn't have to blunder in where angels feared to tread, did she? She didn't have to know *everything* about him...did she?

Love was a hard taskmaster, she conceded then, running a tender fingertip over the hard line of his tense mouth before giving up on that approach and rolling away from him to climb off the bed. 'I'm still wearing my boots,' she noted in wonderment.

'I like them,' Nikolai told her in a driven undertone.

'I knew you would...but my feet are hurting now,'

she admitted, sitting down by the table with the flowers to take the boots off and noticing the envelope sitting there unopened. 'Oh, you haven't opened this yet. It must be from whoever sent the flowers.'

Sitting up in the bed, Nikolai tensed again as she dug out the card. 'Dido and Dorkas Drakos...the flowers are from your great-aunts!' Ella exclaimed with satisfaction. 'You'll have to go and look them up now.'

'I hate to rain on your parade but I met them years ago when I was having this place renovated,' Nikolai admitted abruptly.

'You didn't mention that,' she said in surprise. 'Were they friendly?'

'Very...but it seemed a bit too late in the day to get sucked into the family circle when I had spent most of my life alone,' he admitted stiffly.

'When did they first find out that you existed?' she pressed.

'When I inherited from my grandfather.'

'Then you can't blame them for not being around when you were younger,' Ella pointed out squarely. 'We should go and visit...see how it goes.'

Nikolai rolled his eyes and said nothing. Meeting his relatives would make her happy and it would cost him nothing. He knew she was keen to give him family roots on Crete. She couldn't grasp that he had lived most of his life without such ties and that they meant a great deal less to him than they did to her. He had learned a lot in his first ten years at the hands of totally detached parents.

A little hurt by his discouraging silence, Ella went for a shower. As she stepped out of the cubicle, however, he stepped in.

'Do you want some supper?' Nikolai enquired when he wandered back into the bedroom clad in the twin of the dark towelling robe she had found hanging in the bathroom.

'Is there anything available?' Ella asked, knowing that he wasn't much better at cooking than she was. At home she had looked after her father when he'd needed care and had generally taken over his jobs, keeping the garden and lighting the fire, while Gramma had presided over the kitchen. There had never been any need for Ella to learn how to cook.

Nikolai gave her an amused appraisal. 'I think you'll be pleasantly surprised.'

Ella was bemused when she heard dogs barking somewhere nearby. Nikolai opened the bedroom door and Rory and Butch charged in to careen round his feet. He moved the vase of flowers to allow Max to settle a laden tray down on the table.

'This was my surprise,' Nikolai told her wryly.

'I thought it was the pearls.'

'No, Max and the dogs flew out the day before yesterday to ensure our comfort while we're here. They're staying in the guest cottage down the lane.'

As the dogs romped around her, deliriously excited at the reunion, Ella could not have been more pleased by Nikolai's surprise. Although she had already been aware that Max was to continue working for them, the older man was a fabulous cook and organiser as well as being wonderfully pet friendly. His presence on the domestic front meant that Ella could totally relax.

Nikolai eyed the level in the wine glass and watched Ella reach for her water bottle. He knew the main rea-

son why women usually stopped drinking and it sent
a chill of dismay down his spine. But how could Ella
possibly be pregnant? One of the qualities he most admired about Ella was her unflinching honesty and in
his world that was rare indeed. Had she been pregnant
he knew she would have told him immediately.

'Why have you stopped drinking?' Nikolai asked
lazily.

Ella had been almost drugged by the sun-drenched
scene before her. They were lying on a rug in the shade
of a giant chestnut tree only a few yards from a deserted cove where unbelievably blue and clear water
washed a pale sand shore. Weeks of relaxation on Crete
had brought down most of Ella's defences and she only
stiffened a little in receipt of that awkward question,
relieved that she had an answer already prepared.

'I had a ghastly hangover a couple of months back
and I just lost my taste for alcohol.'

'But why pretend to still drink?' Nikolai broke in.

Her tension soared up the scale. 'It *can* make people
uncomfortable when you say you don't drink.'

'It doesn't make me uncomfortable.'

'Then I won't pretend any more,' she told him glibly
but she was shocked at herself. She was actually *lying*
to Nikolai and it was wrong. When had wrong begun
to seem right? She had had three perfect weeks with
Nikolai, without a doubt the happiest three weeks she
had ever enjoyed. Even flying back to the UK to attend the funeral of the bar manager who had died in
the hotel fire had not doused that happiness. Nikolai
had said that she didn't need to accompany him but
she had wanted to give him her support and she knew
he had appreciated her presence. She had not accom-

panied him though when he had had yet another interview with the police, but had shared his relief when the police had intimated that, although they were as yet nowhere near charging anyone for arson, they did have leads to follow.

Back on the island Nikolai and Ella had continued to make memories. They had visited fabled ancient Minoan sites, including the archaeological dig that was currently taking place on land Nikolai owned nearby. They had explored Chania after dark on several evenings, eating at lively *tavernas*, shopping for gifts and visiting clubs in the old harbour area. Ella preferred the seafront bars to the clubs once she saw how blatantly Nikolai was besieged by predatory women drawn by his looks and wealth. Returning from the cloakroom to find him surrounded had been unnerving and had ramped up her insecurity.

How attractive would Nikolai still find her once pregnancy changed her body? There were already little changes that only she was aware of. Her breasts were a little bit fuller and her nipples more tender. When they had visited the almost tropical lagoon at Elafonisi it had become very hot and she had felt dizzy for the first time. In a Byzantine monastery in the mountains that glowed with colourful frescos and icons, she had felt nauseous because they hadn't eaten in hours and Nikolai had fussed all the way down the hill to the village café, where they had stuffed themselves full of pizza.

She had already decided to tell him about the baby once they had returned to London. She had an almost superstitious fear of breaking the news on their idyllic honeymoon. He didn't love her. She was very, very conscious of that, because she had been the idiot who

had involuntarily shouted out her feelings in bed one
night and he had not reciprocated, although he had held
her close afterwards while probably fighting the desire
to apologise for not being able to return the sentiment.

And that was what she didn't want: a male who felt
guilty because he *didn't* love her, because eventually
that guilt would eat away at what he did feel. Even so, a
man in love with his wife would be much more accepting of an unplanned pregnancy than one who merely
suffered from insatiable desire. And Nikolai was insatiable with her, she conceded, a secretive smile tilting her lips as long fingers swept below the hem of
her dress to stroke her thigh in a way that sent tiny hot
tremors of helpless anticipation rippling through her.
That seemingly unquenchable hunger of his made her
feel safe. She was willing to admit that it wasn't the
fairy-tale relationship she had once dreamt of having,
but it was still a lot more real and passionate than anything she had ever known.

Nikolai kissed her, slow and deep, and then lifted his
tousled dark head again. 'My sister, Sofia...' he framed
with startling abruptness, 'committed suicide. She took
an overdose. That's why I find it hard to talk about.'

Emerging from a male as reserved as Nikolai, that
speech was a breakthrough and Ella gazed up at him
with warmly concerned eyes. 'That must've been very
tough for you to accept.'

'I didn't even know she was depressed. I hadn't seen
her in months,' he explained in a bitten-off, tight undertone. 'I kept on offering to fly her over to London
and she made excuses. I should've realised something
was wrong and flown to her in Athens, but that was
in the days before my private jet and I was working

night and day on getting my first hotel opened up. I neglected her. I put profit first.'

'You didn't know there was anything wrong. When you're busy time goes by and you don't notice.'

'Don't try to comfort me,' Nikolai interposed darkly. 'I let Sofia down when she needed me, the *only* time she ever needed me. I had all these ideas about what we would do together once I made some money, but I should've been concentrating on the present, not the future.'

Ella's eyes stung, for she could feel the guilty grief he had never managed to overcome. 'You didn't know, Nikolai, and obviously she didn't want you to know or she'd have told you how she was feeling.'

His lean, strong face froze. 'I found out by reading her diary. I felt bad about doing that but I needed so badly to know...*why*...' he completed jaggedly.

'Of course you did. That's human nature,' she murmured softly, touched that he had finally chosen to confide in her, her heart full to overflowing with love.

She still didn't know what it was about him that had made her fall so deeply in love at such speed, she only knew that the thought of life without him terrified her.

And in their differing ways that evening as they attended a party at Nikolai's great-aunts' house in Chania, both of them mulled over that conversation and reached certain conclusions.

After being widowed in their sixties, the twin sisters had set up home together again and as each of them had had several children, all of whom lived locally, they were rarely without visitors. From their very first visit, Nikolai and Ella had been made wonderfully welcome, long-lost members of the family being brought back into the fold. Ella had watched Nikolai slowly unfreeze and lose the cool distrustful front that he so often wore to the world. That particular evening, Ella saw him tripping up over one of the toddlers and pausing to pick him up and dry his tears.

'He'll make a good father, unlike his own,' Dorkas Drakos pronounced with satisfaction.

'Our brother was a misery all his life. His money never brought him happiness,' Dido piped up at her sister's elbow. 'Nikolai is very different.'

Guilt was nagging at Ella as she watched Nikolai with the little boy. Maybe she shouldn't wait until they returned to London to make her announcement...

Straightening, Nikolai met his bride's luminous green eyes. He *had* to tell her the truth. She had said she loved him but had she meant it? Nikolai had never seen himself as remotely loveable. When other women had told him they loved him he had known in his bones that the only thing they really loved was his wealth and generosity, but he knew that wasn't true of Ella, who thought he spent money far too freely on her and got embarrassed whenever he gave her anything.

But to tell her the truth would entail hurting her and he had never dreaded anything more than he dreaded that prospect. If she was too badly hurt would she fall out of love again? Would she walk away? Would she never again see him in the same light? Would he irrevocably damage all that was special between them?

The more those anxieties infiltrated Nikolai, the more determined he became to clear his conscience. He didn't want to keep secrets from Ella. How could he expect her to trust him when he had yet to trust her with the truth about himself? Nor would he ever forget Ella insisting that with her he could be his *real* self. Even so that was still a major challenge for a male who had never before shown a woman his real self...

Early the following morning, however, everything changed without warning. They were having breakfast when Nikolai dug his phone out to answer a call. Ella watched his lean, darkly handsome face freeze and then saw the colour steadily draining from below his bronzed skin. His eyes cloaked as he put the phone down.

'Cyrus Makris has been arrested and charged for paying two men to set my hotel on fire and for Desmond's death,' Nikolai relayed flatly.

With the air of a sleepwalker, Nikolai rose upright and walked back indoors.

Cyrus had organised that dreadful fire? Ella was appalled and disbelieving but she did not understand Nikolai's reaction and she raced after him. 'Nikolai... what Cyrus did was unspeakable but at least the police have nailed him for it!'

Nikolai spun back to her, his dark eyes tortured. 'You don't understand. How could you? This is *my* fault... Desmond's death is down to me, no one else.'

CHAPTER TEN

As Nikolai strode off to take refuge in the room he used as an office Ella froze in place in the hall, with the dogs wandering restively round her feet. How could the fire or the bar manager's tragic death be laid at Nikolai's door? How could he possibly be thinking that way?

Nikolai turned from the window as Ella appeared in the doorway to study him with frowning bemusement. He knew he wasn't making sense. He knew she didn't get it and a great sense of weight bowed down his wide shoulders.

'Cyrus and I have been bitter enemies for a very long time,' he told her flatly.

Belatedly Ella was recalling Cyrus's sister's comment at their wedding. She had intended to ask Nikolai for further clarification but had not got around to it because at the time it hadn't seemed that important. 'Why?' she asked simply.

Nikolai's spectacular bone structure went rigid. 'He raped my sister...'

Ella paled and moved forward.

Nikolai leant back against his desk and raked long, taut fingers through his black hair, expelling his breath in a hiss. 'It was all in the diary. That's what I found out five years ago.'

Ella was filled with horror, recalling Cyrus's violent assault on her. 'What a nightmare that must have been for you.'

'Cyrus has been accused of rape before but the accusations tend to be kicked out or withdrawn or they miraculously disappear,' Nikolai advanced in a harsh undertone. 'His father is an enormously powerful and wealthy man. I looked into the cases of Cyrus's previous accusers. One of them dropped the case and now has a seat at the directors' table. She rose up the ranks at meteoric speed and is now an affluent woman who flatly refuses to discuss the matter.'

'You think she was paid off,' Ella gathered.

'Police and members of the legal profession have been bribed. A couple of other victims went from poverty to prosperity. I would assume they were compensated. But Sofia *died*,' Nikolai emphasised with pained ferocity. 'She was poor and powerless and she couldn't bear to tell me what that bastard had done to her.'

'Tell me what happened,' Ella urged quietly.

She poured Nikolai a fresh coffee on the veranda. Her hand wasn't quite steady. She was in shock about what he was telling her about Cyrus. She was remembering the way Cyrus had attacked her and suddenly taking that assault a great deal more seriously. If Nikolai was to be believed it hadn't been a momentary loss of control, the case of a man losing his temper and barely knowing what he was doing.

Sofia, Ella learned, had not enjoyed Nikolai's educational advantages and had worked in a variety of dead-end jobs before equipping herself with secretarial skills at night class. She had then taken a position as a typist in Cyrus's Athens office and one day when she was on reception he had noticed her.

Ella scanned the photo that Nikolai removed from his wallet. His sister had been truly beautiful.

'Cyrus goes for virgins. My sister was older than his usual victims but she was innocent,' Nikolai gritted, perspiration beading his upper lip as he went on to tell her how Cyrus had invited his sister out for coffee a couple of times and once to lunch, while telling her to keep their meetings secret from the people she worked with.

'I suppose that's when she should've got suspicious.' Ella sighed.

'She was naïve; thrilled and flattered that a handsome, successful man was showing an interest in her, and when he asked her to come to his apartment one evening to do some private work for him she went,' Nikolai completed.

'And that's when…right.' Ella nodded in shaken acknowledgement. 'Did Sofia go to the police afterwards?'

'Only after she had showered but the medical did show that she had been badly bruised. She was told that there wasn't enough evidence. Cyrus insisted that they had had consensual sex and he was believed and she was more or less told that she was a lonely fantasist. She felt humiliated that the police didn't believe in or support her. That's what drove her to take her own life.'

'It must have been terrifying for her,' Ella acknowledged heavily. 'I can't begin to imagine what she must have gone through.'

Nikolai was very still. 'I've spent the past five years plotting my revenge against Cyrus.'

Her smooth brow furrowing, Ella gave him a bemused look. 'Revenge?'

'After what my sister suffered, I couldn't live with the idea of Cyrus walking around unpunished. I had him investigated and, the more I learned about him, the more disgusted I became that a sexual deviant like him has never been brought to justice,' Nikolai revealed. 'To be honest, I became *obsessed* with my desire to take revenge on Cyrus...'

Ella strove to look understanding because she really couldn't blame him for his feelings after hearing the tragic story of his sister's death. Even so, the concept of revenge was so foreign to her own nature that she really couldn't grasp it at all.

'And somewhere during that five years I forgot who I was supposed to be and the man my sister had tried to raise me to be,' Nikolai admitted gravely. 'I stole business deals off Cyrus—not very satisfying. However, that was really the only damage I was able to do until his sister, Marika, phoned me a couple of months ago and informed me that Cyrus was planning to marry *you.*'

'The sister he doesn't even speak to was aware that Cyrus wanted to marry me when even I didn't suspect it?' Ella gasped, more than a little disturbed by the bombshell of her own name and connection to Cyrus Makris entering Nikolai's explanations. 'How is that possible? And why would Marika go out of her way to contact you and tell you that about me?'

'Cyrus told his father that he was planning to marry his nephew Paul's former fiancée. His father had been pressuring him to marry for some time and, after Cyrus named you, his father confided in Marika and asked her if she had ever met you. Marika contacted me because she knew that I was her brother's biggest enemy and she hates him for reasons she has never shared with me.'

Ella shook her head dully. She was getting lost in the story while sixth sense was warning her that there was something very important for her to learn from what Nikolai was telling her. Unfortunately her brain was refusing to join up the dots and pick up the clues she needed.

'When I saw your photo I couldn't believe you were the same girl I met in that car park last year,' Nikolai told her tautly.

'*When* did you see my photo?' Ella pressed, frowning as she moved restively against the wooden support post she had braced a hand on, her simple turquoise sundress swirling round her slim legs.

'As soon as I had your name I had you checked out.'

Again Ella shook her head. 'But why would you *do* that? What could Cyrus's crazy belief that he could get me to marry him possibly have to do with you?'

'I wanted to *hurt* him, Ella!' Nikolai bit out in frustration. 'I wanted to ensure that his plans for you came to nothing and that meant I had to get to you first and make you mine instead! I knew that my taking you from him would hit him hardest.'

Ella could feel the blood below her skin draining away as she finally grasped the connection he was making. Wheels within wheels and secret plotting going on behind the scenes. She could never, ever have dreamt that she owed Nikolai's keen pursuit to such a cold, merciless motivation. Indeed his pursuit had been nothing to do with her at all, nothing personal, she thought sickly, nothing personal when she so badly needed it *all* to have been personal for him.

Nikolai could hear his own heart thumping out his tension in his ears as he watched her like a hawk. She looked sick, shocked. 'I had to tell you. You have the right to know the worst about me. You need to know what and who I am and what I'm capable of.'

'Not sure I *want* to know,' Ella forced out between teeth that suddenly wanted to chatter. Her brain was in a fog. She couldn't think. She was scared to think that the male she loved could have seen her merely as a means of revenge and a weapon with which to taunt Cyrus. Was that what Nikolai was saying? Or was she picking him up wrong? Oh, dear heaven, why couldn't she think and put it all together properly?

'You married me…' she whispered shakily. '*Why* did you marry me?'

'I wanted to make you happy. After what I'd done… the blackmail, the way I treated you…the very fact that rage pushed Cyrus into attacking you. I'm the one to blame for that… I owed you.'

Of all the sentiments a woman madly in love didn't want to hear, Ella thought numbly, those three little words had to be at the top of the least popular list. *I owed you!* What was she? A debt he had to pay off? A helpless child he had to comfort and compensate? Or was the light in which he saw her even worse?

Had he guessed even before she married him how she felt about him? Had he worked out that his weapon of choice was so stupid that she had fallen in love with the blackmailing, ruthless, seven-letter-word of a man who had used her to strike a blow against his enemy?

Ella cleared her dry throat with difficulty. 'So, you had second thoughts about what you had done.'

'I felt bloody guilty!' Nikolai fired back at her in a forceful rush. 'Of course, I did. It may have taken me a while but I did eventually come to my senses and appreciate that what I had done to you was absolutely wrong on every level.'

Ella was unimpressed by those strong words.

'And is that why you made the biggest sacrifice you could think of and *married* me?' she prompted, her distress threatening to break through the false composure of shock. 'Because you were way too smart for your own good! Presumably you never planned for this marriage to last either. Well, you shot yourself in the foot bedding a virgin, Nikolai!'

'What are you talking about?' It was Nikolai's turn to look bewildered.

'A virgin has to be more likely to make a mistake concerning the efficiency of her birth control,' Ella contended, her chin tilted at an aggressive angle because she definitely didn't want to him to get the impression that she was ashamed or embarrassed or even slightly apologetic. 'I made a mistake and I'm pregnant…so sorry that doesn't fit in with your cruel, nasty, callous plans!'

His luxuriant black lashes dipped and then slowly rose again, revealing the sudden glitter in his dark eyes. 'Pregnant?' Nikolai breathed in a driven undertone, a sudden inner tide of relief making him feel almost dizzy.

If she was pregnant, he had a whole new line of reasons to argue why she should stay with him. Pregnant, he thought again, only dimly recognising the level of his own astonishment. A baby. *His* baby. After all the hints his great-aunts had dropped and he had studiously ignored, Dido and Dorkas would be ecstatic at that information.

'And the good news *is*,' Ella suddenly spat at him without warning, while his brain was still wandering all over the place in a most unfamiliar way, 'you don't *owe* me anything! The way I see it, you married me under false pretences, so we're *not* married!'

Ella wrenched at the rings on her wedding finger and flung them at his feet with bitter satisfaction. Turning on her heel, she sped off. She could feel herself coming apart like wet shredded paper inside herself and she had no intention of coming apart in front of him. She wasn't a victim; she *refused* to be a victim; she was strong. There was nothing Nikolai Drakos could throw at her that she couldn't handle, she told herself staunchly as she walked fast down the hill towards the beach.

Nikolai crouched down and lifted up her wedding and engagement rings. He was taken aback to register that his hand was shaking. He dug the rings into the pocket of his tight faded jeans. *His* baby. His baby needed her the same way he needed her. But would she be better off without him? That was a deeply wounding thought for him and he shook it off. He could be what she wanted him to be; he could deliver what she wanted him to deliver for both her *and* the baby. He would fight to keep her but he just didn't know what to say to her. He genuinely didn't know how to persuade her to stay. Ironically Nikolai had much more experience at ditching women. After all, he had never wanted to keep one for ever before.

And unhappily for him, Ella had scruples and standards and he had stomped roughly over all of them. He didn't deserve a second chance. He knew that, but admitting that he didn't deserve a second chance to her would only reinforce the wrong, negative image, he reasoned painfully. The apology front didn't look very promising either because sorry could never begin to cover the damage he had done.

Ella kicked off her shoes when she reached the shore and sank her toes into the hot sand. But her soles burned and she took off in haste for the cooler sand at the water's edge. There the sea looked so temptingly cool that she walked out into it until the lapping water was right up to her knees. She was breathing as fast as a marathon runner and her heart was pounding like mad. Calm down, she urged herself, you're pregnant.

But there was a giant ball of pain ready to explode inside Ella. Nikolai had taken her dreams and torn them apart. Once again she had placed her faith and her hopes in the wrong man. What was it about her? Was she more naïve than other women? Fatally attracted to the wrong types? And yet there was not an iota of similarity between Paul and Nikolai, so how could she have known?

Well, of course she *should* have known, another, more negative voice told her. She had gone for the fairy-tale version, hadn't she? This idea that she was so irresistible to Nikolai Drakos that he would track her down after that single meeting in the car park and settle her father's debts simply to get her into his bed? *As if!* And what sort of woman fell for the kind of guy that would blackmail a woman into his bed? And how on earth *had* she fallen for him?

By the time, Ella reached that point in her attack of self-loathing she was sobbing and the tears of heart-break were coursing down her cheeks. Where had the love come from? He had been so distraught, so devastated by that fire, and everything warm and caring in her had loved that in him. She had suddenly seen that the cool, detached male he pretended to be existed no place except inside his own head and the façade he wore to the world.

Only, sadly, it had not occurred to her that behind his grief for the bar manager's death at his hotel lurked a male willing to break every rule of decency and wreck a perfectly innocent woman's life in an effort to destroy an admittedly very nasty man. And he had wrecked it, Ella reasoned bitterly. He had allowed her to think that she was special to him, that he cared about her even if he hadn't given her the actual words. Didn't everyone know that most men were wary of saying the fatal words that could lead to permanent commitment?

Even so, leave it to Nikolai to find a novel slant… *I want to keep you.*

I owed you. Dear heaven, the pain of hearing that sentiment would haunt her to her dying day. So, his guilty conscience had made him offer her a wedding, a ring and the luxury of his wealth. And now here she was standing out in the sea like an idiot, she thought with another sob. It was her moment of truth, she dimly recognised. Once again she wasn't going to get the fairy-tale happy ending. Had Nikolai faked absolutely everything?

Well, he hadn't faked the sex or the insatiability factor on that front but what was that worth? He had got cuddlier too. He was actually hugging now without prompting, reaching for her hand, touching her, *always* touching her just like a besotted new husband could be expected to do. Was that all a lie as well? Some sort of a convincing act? She wiped her face with trembling hands, suddenly cold in the sunlight. He didn't love her. He hadn't moved heaven and earth to find her again or to make her his and only his. He had pursued and entrapped her *only* to punish Cyrus. That was always going to be her bottom line.

Nikolai saw her standing in the sea and sheer panic controlled him. Later he didn't remember running down the hill, racing through the orange groves and taking a flying leap down onto the beach instead of following the path. He waded out into the water and snatched her up into his arms just as the sound of his splashing approach began to turn her head.

Bronze-coloured hair fell down over his arm. Slightly pink-edged green eyes gazed up at him in astonishment. 'What are you doing?'

Nikolai couldn't find his voice. He strode up the beach and sank down on the steep edge of the path with Ella still tightly cradled in his arms.

'Let me go!' she exclaimed.

'Not until I know for sure you're all right.'

Against her cheek she could feel his heart thumping very fast and he was breathing heavily. 'I don't know what you're talking about.'

'You were standing out in the sea. It scared me,' he acknowledged gruffly.

'You think I'd do something silly to myself and my

baby over what you've done?' Ella pelted back at him, going from tearful acquiescence to rage in the space of seconds as she finally understood his concern. 'Are you out of your mind? I spent years watching Paul struggle and fight to live. Life is a very precious thing!'

Nikolai breathed again but he still didn't want to let go of her. 'The baby…how long have you known?'

Ella stopped struggling to escape. 'The day before the wedding I discovered that my implant was old and inactive by the time we…had sex,' she framed with cold precision.

'It wasn't only sex. It was something rather more meaningful.'

'Says the man who wouldn't know meaningful from a slap in the face!'

'Why didn't you tell me you were pregnant?' Nikolai persisted, hitting her on her weakest flank. 'Why, in fact, did you come very close to lying in an effort to deflect my questions about why you weren't drinking alcohol?'

'No comment.' Ella buttoned her lips together.

'We can just sit here,' Nikolai conceded in a remarkably level voice.

'I'm all wet now—and you're even more wet!' she cried.

Silence fell, backed by the soft rush and retreat of the surf on the beach.

'I can't bear to lose you,' Nikolai volunteered gruffly. 'I'll do anything it takes to keep you.'

'My goodness, the sex must be stupendous,' Ella told him acidly, her attention involuntarily on his lean, dark, utterly gorgeous face while she scolded herself for even noticing.

He was beautiful but deceptive like a crisp, glossy apple with a rotten core, she told herself doggedly.

'It is,' Nikolai agreed. 'But we've got a lot more than that between us. You know we have.'

'I don't know anything about you any more.'

'I believe that if you stop and really think about it you'll realise that you know much more than you're prepared to admit right now. Obviously you know I'm not perfect.'

'Do you want a slow hand clap or a rousing cheer for that remarkably shrewd deduction?'

Glittering dark eyes assailed hers without warning. 'Do you want to be dropped back into the sea from a height?' Nikolai asked, his arms tightening suggestively round her slight body.

Ella closed her eyes tight, feeling a flush sting her tear-stung face and gritting her teeth. He had said he would do anything to keep her but he wasn't prepared to lie down and be kicked, which was all she wanted to do to him at that moment. She wasn't feeling forgiving or constructive or even like talking, she was simply feeling hurt. 'I want to go back up to the house if you won't leave me alone down here.'

Nikolai expelled his breath and slowly set her down on her own feet, almost as if he was afraid that without his support she might fall over. As he swept up the sandals she had abandoned earlier and painstakingly put them on for her an embittered laugh bubbled in Ella's throat. She held it in though, thinking she had to support herself, go forward, face the future as it was, not as she had wished and dreamt it might be. As she walked silently back to the house, she was conscious of her exhaustion and knew she needed to lie down. All that emotional turmoil had extracted a high cost in terms of her energy levels.

Nikolai followed Ella upstairs.

'Going to bed for a while,' she muttered limply, trying to slam the door in his face.

'Let me help you...'

Ella swallowed back the bitter comment that nothing he could do or say would help her state of mind. Some pain went too deep to be soothed by even the kindest gesture. He felt guilty and she knew that, recognised that, but she didn't want to have to deal with his guilt. That was *his* problem and she had enough to cope with. She pulled off her dress, letting it lie where it fell, shimmied out of her underwear and clambered into the bed naked.

'Do you want some tea?' Nikolai suggested, rearranging the duvet over her quite unnecessarily. 'I *can* make tea.'

Ella shut her eyes, fatigue dragging her down like a strong current in the sea. She wanted to sleep, she wanted to forget and she couldn't forget while he was around. 'No, thanks.'

Nikolai sank down silently on a chair in the corner of the bedroom. She was as white as a sheet and her eyes looked haunted, bruised, *hurt*. It was what he had most feared and it felt even worse than he had expected because he felt helpless and he wasn't used to being helpless. But he had had to tell her, he reminded himself heavily; she had deserved the truth rather than some fanciful fiction. It occurred to him that she hadn't yet heard the *whole* truth, but then she probably wouldn't believe him, would she?

Ella wakened to find Nikolai standing over her. 'You have to put these on.'

She surfaced from sleep and instantly remembered all that had happened but she had no idea why Nikolai was trying to induce her to put on a pair of winter pyjamas. 'Why?'

'The doctor is waiting downstairs to come up and check you over.'

'The doctor?' she gasped, sitting up and reaching for the ridiculous pyjamas in a rush. 'Why have you called a doctor?'

'Because you've had a major emotional upset and you're pregnant and you need to be careful,' Nikolai told her stubbornly. 'I'm doing what I'm supposed to do. I'm trying to look after you.'

'Yeah, push me down, walk over me, drag me up again,' Ella framed bitterly. 'That's great looking after on your part.'

'Mr Theodopoulos is the leading gynaecologist on the island. Dorkas and Dido recommended him.'

'So now they know I'm carrying a baby as well,' Ella mumbled resentfully.

'I'm proud that you are,' Nikolai declared, startling her as he plumped up the pillows behind her and twitched the duvet even higher. 'The doctor is young for his position. Perhaps you would prefer an older man or...even a woman?' he extended almost hopefully.

It was no surprise to Ella then that the gynaecologist who appeared enjoyed movie-star good looks and the kind of warm, soothing bedside manner that put a woman instantly at her ease while at the same time riling a possessive husband. Nikolai behaved like a dog with a juicy bone under threat. He insisted on staying and then paced grim-faced at the back of the room with folded arms, monitoring every smile the doctor won from his wife.

Of course, there was nothing to worry about where her health was concerned. Early pregnancy was tiring and that was all that was the matter with her.

Ella was in the shower when Nikolai came back upstairs after seeing the doctor off. She towelled herself dry in the cubicle and then stepped out, refusing to act self-conscious even though it no longer felt right to be naked around him.

'You don't look pregnant,' Nikolai observed.

'Of course I don't. I'm only a few weeks along. There won't be much sign of anything for a month or so yet. Don't you know that?' she asked, pulling clothing out of the closet while studiously ignoring him in the hope that he would recognise that his presence was inappropriate.

'No. I know absolutely nothing about pregnancy,' Nikolai admitted. 'But I can find out.'

'Don't push yourself on my account,' Ella flipped back drily.

'Why didn't you tell me sooner?' he pressed while she stood at the vanity combing through her wet hair.

'I was shocked. When we discussed us starting a family you weren't exactly enthusiastic about the concept of becoming a father,' Ella reminded him flatly. 'I assumed it would upset you and I didn't want that this early in our marriage. Of course, I didn't know that there was an even bigger elephant hiding in the room!'

Nikolai settled her rings down on the counter at her elbow. 'Please put your rings back on...'

'No,' Ella countered flatly, her lips compressed.

'After I first met you in that car park and you turned me down I ran like hell away from you,' Nikolai breathed, startling her. 'I think on some level I knew that if I got involved with you it was going to turn into something I wasn't ready for.'

'You have some imagination, Nikolai. Telling me that you ran like hell isn't exactly a compliment,' Ella pointed out.

'But it's the truth.'

'The truth is that you *only* looked me up again because Cyrus took a strange fancy to me,' Ella reminded him as she walked out of the bathroom back into the bedroom.

'I was obsessed by my need for revenge. I took no account of anything else. For five years I lived, breathed and slept revenge. I was very angry and bitter about Sofia and I think it was like poison in my brain.'

'And together we're toxic,' Ella slotted in, refusing to be persuaded.

'Max has lunch ready for us downstairs.' Nikolai pulled open the bedroom door.

The table on the veranda was beautifully set. The honeymoon couple's dream lunch served on exquisite china amid flowers and crystal. She breathed in deep, the dogs nudging a welcome against her ankles, and she paused for a moment to give them some attention.

Nikolai saw that having three or four legs, a shaggy coat and a tail bought advantages he couldn't dream of acquiring. He breathed in deep and slow, reminding himself of the positives. She hadn't gone for the suitcases yet, hadn't mentioned flying anywhere. He was terrified that she would want to leave Crete and him behind.

'We're not toxic,' he declared, pouring some water for her. 'And I wouldn't have got "upset" about the baby. Like you, I'm very practical. That's something we have in common. It is what it is and we can both adapt to suit a new situation.'

'I *loved* you!' Ella slung at him without the smallest warning.

Nikolai shrank from the past tense. 'The dynamic changed between us very fast. I had no plans beyond taking you to that charity function and moving you into the town house. Somewhere about there I lost control of everything...'

'Are you trying to excuse yourself for having sex with me?' Ella enquired in a glacial voice.

His dark deep-set eyes flashed gold. 'No. I'd be a complete liar if I said I had regrets about that. In fact you pretty much owned me from that day on.'

'*Owned* you?' Ella repeated emphatically. 'Because of the sex?'

Nikolai sank an entire glass of wine. It was *so* difficult. He had never done anything so difficult as trying to talk to Ella in the mood she was currently in. 'Hardly,' he deflected. 'I suspect that's when I fell in love with you. You snuggled up to me in bed and, although I didn't admit it to myself, I liked it. I still really like it when you do that and it's so peculiar for me to like something like that...'

Ella almost dropped the glass in her hand. She stared at him, colour rising in her cheeks. 'You're lying, of course you're lying. You're still in guilty-conscience mode and you know I love you, so you're telling me what you think I want to hear.'

'But you don't *want* to hear it,' Nikolai pointed out

helplessly. 'You only want to sit there judging me and deciding that I am a total bastard in every way. And I was a bastard before I met you.'

'*And* when you first met me *and* when you met me a second time,' Ella reminded him.

'But I changed. You changed me. Don't ask me how. It happened and here I am and I'm as obsessed with you now as I once was with Cyrus,' Nikolai completed fiercely. 'I don't do or plan anything without thinking about you. You're always inside my head.'

Ella was finally starting to listen. Even the dogs were listening because Nikolai had a piece of baguette in his hand and he was waving his hands around as he spoke and the dogs were very hopeful that that piece of bread would fall in their direction. *'Really?'*

'Yes, *really*,' Nikolai derided. 'I'm crazy about you.'

'You have a funny way of showing it.'

'I couldn't love you and not tell you the truth. That wouldn't have been fair.'

Ella studied him, slowly, almost painfully registering his sincerity, his certainty. He really believed that he loved her now. He really, truly believed that. 'When I told you that I loved you, you said nothing,' she reminded him.

'I had to tell you the truth first but I was… I was…'

'What?' she broke in impatiently.

'Scared… OK? Satisfied now?' Nikolai raked back at her angrily. 'I was scared I would lose you but I couldn't live with keeping a secret like that from you.'

Ella went pink and dropped her head. 'Oh,' she almost whispered, wondering why she was being so hard on him.

Yes, he had hurt her but she appreciated his respect

for the truth, his inability to stay quiet and pretend that everything was all right when it wasn't. She breathed in slow and deep. Nikolai Drakos loved her... Nikolai *loved* her. A tiny ping of happiness cut through her grey cloud of heartbroken misery and regret. She was scared to feel happy, scared to trust him. But Nikolai had pretty much felt the same way, she reasoned wryly. Love didn't come with guarantees any more than people did. And yes, he was far from perfect, but then she wasn't perfect either and she loved him so very much it hurt to have a table separating them. Slowly she rose to her feet.

Sensing a change in the atmosphere, Nikolai surveyed her warily. 'I can make this up to you. I do know I messed up really badly—'

'Shut up,' Ella told him, tipping herself down into his lap. 'It's done and dusted and when I told you that I loved you I meant it. I love you even when you mess things up. I may get angry and shout and throw my rings at you...but at the end of it all I will still love you very, very much. As long as the mess up doesn't involve another woman,' she qualified hastily, lest he think he could be forgiven for any sin.

Nikolai wrapped both arms round her very tightly and dropped a kiss on the top of her head. 'No other women,' he said gruffly, because he could hardly get breath into his deflated lungs. 'I need all my energy for you.'

Ella gazed up at him with a smile that was like the sun breaking through the clouds. 'So... I *own* you?'

His eyes were melted caramel. 'That's what it feels like sometimes.'

'No, that's being part of a couple,' she argued, hugging him back with all her strength, tears prickling in her eyes because she was experiencing the most enormous sense of relief. He had given her the fairy tale by falling in love with her and he didn't understand how it had happened any better than she did, but that didn't matter, did it?

'Are we hoping for a boy or a girl?' Nikolai asked, long fingers splaying across her defiantly flat stomach.

'We don't get to choose. I don't mind either way,' she muttered abstractedly as she brushed her lips back and forth very gently across his.

'Neither do I...' Nikolai growled, rising from the chair with her still gripped in his arms. 'You can have a dozen kids if I get to keep you.'

'Not thinking in terms of that many,' Ella declared, succumbing to a passionate kiss that sent tingles all the way to her toes. 'Are we going to bed?'

'Can't wait to make you mine again, *latria mou*,' Nikolai husked against her reddened lips. 'You gave me such a scare today. I need to know you're still my wife. You have to put your rings back on.'

'I'll think about it,' she teased, revelling in the sense of power he was giving her because it was wonderful to know and accept that she was so wanted, so loved, so valued.

'When I married you my only wish was to make you happy,' he admitted. 'And then *today*—'

'That's behind us now,' Ella interrupted. 'And you're about to make me incredibly happy by telling me that you love me again.'

'Do I really have to keep on saying it?' Nikolai groaned.

'Yes, that's your penance...' Ella whispered as he

laid her down on their bed and stared down at her with a fierce appreciation she could feel right down to the marrow of her bones. Yes, he loved her. She could see it, she could feel it and it felt amazing...

EPILOGUE

Tobias Drakos, five years old and a bundle of lively energy who was rarely still, raced downstairs in advance of his mother. Taking note that the front door of the country house, Tayford Hall, already stood wide with Max at the ready to greet his employer, Tobias crowed. 'I told you it was the helicopter, Mummy... I told you it was Daddy!'

Ella studied her son, the very image of his father with his above-average height, dark eyes and dark hair, and suppressed a groan because she knew that she would never get him to bed early now. That would have been acceptable any other night but it was Christmas Eve and she had loads of things she wanted to do while Tobias was upstairs and out of sight. Even so, he hadn't seen his father in a full week, which was a good enough excuse to loosen up on routine.

Ella knew that if she had a fault it was her tendency to stick too close to routine. But she and Nikolai led very busy lives, and without a routine someone or something got short-changed. Rory and Butch were already racing across the lawn in pursuit of their offspring, Maxie, the only one of Rory's litter of puppies they had kept. Maxie was an indiscriminate mixture of doggy genes and she had grown into a much leggier and larger dog than her diminutive parents. Before Ella could say a word, her son had raced out across the lawn in his pyjamas just as the helicopter landed.

Ella stayed circumspectly on the top step, although to tell the truth she would have been much happier pelting across the lawn with dogs and child because Nikolai rarely travelled these days and when he did she missed him terribly. And there he was, her for-ever-and-ever guy, tall and dark and handsome, striding towards her with over-excited dogs bouncing in his path and a son talking a mile a minute to him.

As Nikolai hitched Tobias up and hugged him, her heart constricted because she loved to see them together like that. Nikolai had had so many insecurities about becoming a parent but, like many goal-driven men, he had exceeded her expectations in that role. He tried to ensure that his son received everything he himself had been denied by neglectful parents. He gave Tobias his time, showed an interest and supported the little boy at every step of his development.

Ella smoothed down her scarlet knee-length dress and shifted in her very high-heeled shoe-boots, slender legs braced as Nikolai drew closer and his lean, darkly handsome features came into focus. Her whole body lit up like a firework display because just seeing Nikolai made her that happy and she had news to share that made her even happier.

Nikolai studied the picture Ella made at the front door and thought that he was an incredibly lucky man. Behind her the welcome of the house and the edge of the sparkling Christmas tree in the hall with its roaring log fire made him smile. He had bought the hall when Ella was pregnant and she adored country life. Once she had qualified as a veterinary surgeon, she had taken a job nearby and had become very popular in the local community. If he didn't watch over her she worked too hard, and now that she had her career and Tobias had started school if he went away on business he had to travel alone, which he disliked.

Nikolai swept Ella theatrically into his arms, melted-caramel eyes brimming with amusement. 'What have you done with my wife?' he teased. 'The last time I saw you, your hair was a mess, you were wearing a lab coat and wellies and now you look like a model.'

'And it took hours so appreciate it while you can,' Ella advised him while quietly revelling in the familiar scent of him and the feel of his lean, powerful body even briefly in contact with her own. A familiar burn sparked deep inside her, a burn and an ache that would have to go unsatisfied until much later in the evening because they had a houseful of guests to look after. Gramma and her father were staying for Christmas, as were Dido and Dorkas, Nikolai's great-aunts, and an array of other Greek family members, whom Nikolai and Ella had grown particularly friendly with during their frequent stays in the house on Crete.

'I find you sexy in anything. Naked, clothed, it doesn't matter, *latria mou*,' her husband assured her under cover of their son's chatter, lean fingers spreading caressingly on her hip. 'I'm shockingly lacking in standards in that line. I'll take you any way I can have you.'

Ella risked a quick kiss that smudged her lipstick and turned into something a little longer than either of them planned.

'That's not cool, Dad,' Tobias pronounced in disgust.

A highly amused grin slashed Nikolai's expressive mouth. 'I can assure you that it was very cool. We can catch up while I get changed,' he told his wife, grabbing her hand and only pausing on the stairs to greet his father-in-law and Gramma.

'I should be downstairs being a hostess,' Ella hissed guiltily.

'When you put Gramma with my great-aunts, we're coming down with hostesses who love to host. Anyway, I have something to tell you,' he announced, thrusting open their bedroom door. 'About Cyrus.'

'Cyrus?' Ella repeated in surprise, because she rarely thought now about the older man, who had received a lengthy prison sentence for his role in the hotel fire and the death of Nikolai's bar manager. While on bail for those crimes, Cyrus had also been accused of rape by a young woman in his employ and he had been found guilty of that offence as well.

'He's apparently in hospital after an attack by fellow inmates. He's not expected to survive,' Nikolai informed her flatly. 'Marika phoned me to tell me.'

'And how does that make you feel?' Ella prompted anxiously.

'As though it really is all over now and I can put it behind me,' Nikolai confessed. 'When his sentence was extended because of the rape, I felt that my sister was finally vindicated and I haven't really thought about Makris since then.'

'That's how it should be. *It's over.*' Ella wrapped her arms round him and rested her head against his chest, loving the reassuring beat of his heart and the heat of him on a cold wintry evening. 'We have more positive matters on our agenda.'

'Oh… I get it. You thought I only brought you up here to throw you on the bed? How could you think that?' Nikolai demanded, struggling to look offended.

'Because I know your sleek, sneaky ways, Mr Drakos,' Ella told him lovingly. 'No, I have other news. I'm pregnant again and this time around I'm telling you the same day I found out.'

Nikolai swung her up into his arms and kissed her with passionate satisfaction. They had waited to extend their family until their lives were more settled, but conception had taken several months longer than they had initially hoped. 'That's the best Christmas present yet!' he swore.

'No, that was our first Christmas when you brought me here to this house and told me it was ours,' Ella contradicted.

'And you were enraged that I'd picked a house and the furniture without getting you involved,' Nikolai reminded her.

'You did remarkably well on your own,' Ella said as she freed him of his tie and began to push his jacket off his shoulders. 'Take your clothes off, Mr Drakos.'

'I love it when you get domineering,' Nikolai teased, gazing down at his tiny wife with hotly appreciative dark eyes. 'I love you, *latria mou.*'

'I love you too…'

And they kissed, initially tenderly and then more

passionately. The three elderly ladies downstairs were terrific hostesses and ensured that dinner was put back until the owners of the house had reappeared with a noticeable glow of happy contentment surrounding them.

* * * * *

WEDDED, BEDDED, BETRAYED

MICHELLE SMART

This book is for Renata - thanks for feeding my
coffee addiction! xxx

CHAPTER ONE

THE SCREAM PIERCED through the silence of the Nutmeg Island chapel.

Gabriele Mantegna, having just climbed up the stairs from the basement, came to an abrupt halt.

Where the hell had that come from?

He switched off his torch, plunging the chapel into complete darkness, and listened hard.

Had that been a *woman's* scream? Surely not? Tonight, only the armed security crew inhabited the island.

Closing the basement door carefully, he walked to the one small window of the chapel not made of stained glass. It was too dark to see anything but after a moment a faint light appeared in the distance. It came from the Ricci house where at that moment an armed gang were helping themselves to all the priceless works of art and antiquities.

The island's security crew were blind to the gang, their monitors remotely tampered with and feeding them falsehoods.

Gabriele checked his watch and grimaced. He'd been on the island ten minutes longer than planned. Every extra minute increased his chances of getting caught. To reach the beach on the south side of the island, from where he would swim to safety, was a further ten-minute walk.

But he hadn't imagined the scream. He couldn't in good conscience make his escape without checking it out.

Swearing under his breath, Gabriele pushed open the heavy chapel door and stepped out into the warm Caribbean air. The next time Ignazio Ricci decided on a spot of peace and contemplation, he would find the code for the chapel alarm scrambled.

For a building designed for peaceable contemplation and worship, the Ricci chapel had been desecrated by Ignazio's real purpose.

It had all been there, directly beneath the chapel altar, in a basement stuffed with files dating back decades. A secret trail of blood money, the underbelly of the Ricci empire, hidden from the outside world. In the short time Gabriele had been in the basement he'd uncovered enough evidence of illegal dealings to have Ignazio spend the rest of his life in prison. He, Gabriele Mantegna, would personally hand the copied incriminating documents to the FBI. He would be there every day of the trial, seating himself so that Ignazio, the man who'd killed his father, would not be able to avoid seeing him.

When the judge's sentence was pronounced Ignazio would know that it was *he* who had sent him down.

But everything wasn't sunshine yet. The most important evidence for Gabriele, the documents that would have cleared his own name and exonerated his father once and for all, had not been found.

The evidence existed. He would find it if it took him the rest of his life.

Putting the missing evidence from his mind, Gabriele set out into the thick canopy of trees and, crouching low, made his way to the Ricci house, a huge villa set over three levels.

Lights shone from a downstairs window. Any subterfuge by the gang had been abandoned.

Something had gone wrong.

The men in the house were led by a criminal mastermind who went by the moniker of Carter. Carter's specialisation was in purloining high-end goods for order. Ming vases. Picassos. Caravaggios. Blue Diamonds. There wasn't a security system in the world, so the legend went, that Carter couldn't crack. He also had a knack of knowing where the shadier elements of high society kept their even shadier valuables, the type of valuables the owner most certainly would not report to the authorities. Carter took those items for himself.

The front door had been left ajar.

As he approached it, voices could be heard, muffled but undeniably angry.

Knowing he was taking a huge risk but unable to rid himself of the sound of the scream ringing in his ears, Gabriele pressed himself against the outside wall of the window nearest the front door, took a breath, and turned to look inside.

The main reception room was empty.

He pushed the door open a few more inches.

The muffled argument continued.

He crossed the threshold. The instant his neoprene dive slipper trod onto the hard lacquered wood flooring, a squeak rang out.

Swearing under his breath, Gabriele tried another step, placing his whole foot down in one tread. This time there was no squeak.

He took stock of his surroundings. The reception room had three doors. Only one, directly opposite him, was open.

He crossed cautiously, wishing there were at least a life-size statue to hide behind if needed. Reaching the door, he peered through it, taking in the wide cantilevered stairs to his right and craning his ears to the left in an attempt to determine what the men were arguing about. If it was a simple heist-gone-wrong scenario he would return to his plan and get the hell off this island.

But that scream…

It had definitely sounded feminine.

The arguing voices were all male. He still couldn't decipher what they were arguing about. He needed to get closer.

Before he could take another step, heavy footsteps treaded down the stairs. A huge figure dressed entirely in black strode past the door Gabriele was hiding behind and joined the others. He must have opened the door widely because now everything they said echoed off the great walls.

'The little cow bit me,' he said in an English accent, sounding incredulous.

'You didn't hurt her?' said another voice, this one American.

'Not as much as I'm going to when we get her out of here.'

'She's not going anywhere. We're leaving her here,' said the other voice sharply.

'She's seen my face.'

Much swearing ensued before the first man cut through the noise. 'I would still take her even if she couldn't identify me—whoever she is, she's got to be worth something and I want a slice of it.'

All the men started speaking at once, making it impossible to distinguish their words but the gist of it was clear enough. Upstairs was a woman, probably bound, and these men were arguing over what to do with her.

Suddenly the original man came storming back out, yelling over his shoulder, 'You pansies can debate it all you want. That bitch is mine and she's coming with us.'

The door was slammed shut behind him and the man hurried back up the stairs, taking a right turn at the top.

This was Gabriele's chance.

Not pausing to consider his options, he strode to the stairs then climbed them three at a time.

Half a dozen doors lined the hallway he found himself in but only one of them was open.

He peered cautiously inside.

The man stood in the middle of a pale blue bedroom, his back to him. Before him, her hands tied at the wrists to a headboard, her mouth gagged, her knees raised tightly to her chest, was a woman with terror-filled eyes.

Not giving the man time to respond, Gabriele stepped behind him and struck him in the neck, aiming for the spot that would bring instant unconsciousness. He aimed correctly. The man collapsed immediately, Gabriele only just catching him at the waist before he could fall in a thump to the floor and alert the men waiting below.

Laying him down carefully, he checked his pulse.

Satisfied he hadn't killed him, he unzipped the waterproof pouch and pulled out his penknife.

The woman's eyes widened further and she pulled her legs even closer to her chest, whimpers coming from behind the gag.

He crouched beside her.

'I'm not going to hurt you,' he said quietly, speaking in English. 'Do you understand what I'm saying?'

She whimpered some more but managed to nod.

There was something familiar about her...

'I need you to trust me. I am not with those men,' he said. 'If they hear you scream they will come up here and probably kill us both. I'm going to untie you and remove your gag and we're going to escape but I need your word you won't scream. Do I have your word?'

Another nod. The whimpering had stopped, the terror in her clear green eyes lessening a fraction. Now her eyes searched his, the familiarity he felt clearly reciprocated.

'We're going to escape,' he repeated. He sat on the side of the bed and lifted her head, enabling him to untie the cloth that had been wrapped around her mouth. As soon as it was freed, he placed a finger to her lips. 'We don't have much time,' he warned. 'We're going to have to escape through a window unless you know a way out that doesn't involve going downstairs?'

She jerked her head to an interconnecting door behind her. 'The dressing room is above a roof. We can slip out through the window in there.' Her husky voice was croaky. He guessed the scream she'd given had damaged her vocal cords. He could only hope she hadn't suffered damage of any other kind.

He admired the fact that through the abject terror she'd just experienced, she'd still had the foresight to plan an escape route in her head.

He thought of Paul, the captain of his yacht, who would soon be on the lookout for his return.

'Give me one moment,' he said, pulling his phone out of his pouch and pressing the emergency button that would connect him.

'Paul, I need the jet ski to be brought to the north harbour immediately.' It was one of the many contingency plans they had spent two days running through. Gabriele attempting one of these contingency plans with a woman in tow hadn't been in any of the blueprints.

His call done with, he sliced his penknife through the ropes binding the woman and quickly pulled the lengths away from her. Dark red welts encircled her wrists where the man had cruelly tied the rope so it bit into her tender flesh.

A groan came from the floor.

Gabriele ignored the urge to throw himself on the prostrate man and kick him in the ribs. Avenging this woman might give fleeting satisfaction but they could not afford to waste a single moment.

'Can you walk?' he asked, wrapping an arm around her waist and helping her sit up.

The woman was tiny. With white-blonde hair tied in a messy ponytail and those large green eyes, she reminded him of a porcelain doll. Breakable.

She nodded, but allowed him to help her to her feet. He wrinkled his nose. She smelt like a…bonfire? Studying her in more depth, he revised his porcelain doll opinion and altered it to grubby urchin.

Suddenly it came to him why she looked so familiar.

He recalled a small, doll-like girl from his youth, who had dressed like a boy and been able to climb a tree faster than anyone and then shimmy back down it as if a twenty-foot drop was nothing to worry about.

This was Ignazio's only daughter, Elena.

He was putting his life at risk for his enemy's daughter?

This woman was his enemy every bit as much as her father was. When Gabriele brought Ignazio's downfall he had every intention of bringing his entire family down with him.

The man on the floor's groans were becoming louder. Elena was eying him with a look that suggested she very much wanted to kick him in the ribs too.

'We need to leave now.' Gabriele grabbed her hand, having the presence of mind to avoid her wrists, and tugged her away and through to the dressing room she'd spoken of.

Whatever his personal feelings towards her and her family, and his plan to destroy them all, his destruction did not include allowing a vulnerable woman to be at the mercy of four armed men, one of whom he'd heard with his own ears wanted to hurt her.

He might hate Elena's family but he still wouldn't abandon her to such a fate.

He pulled the sash window up and looked out. As she'd said, a sloping roof ran under it.

Gabriele heaved himself out, dropping a couple of feet onto the roof.

'Come,' he said, righting himself when he was certain the roof was stable enough to hold his weight without crumbling beneath him.

Elena was already hoisting herself over the ledge. He put his hands to her tiny waist and helped her out, holding her tightly until he was sure she was secure on the roof. Apart from her bare feet, she was dressed in the perfect attire for escape, in long black shorts and a baggy khaki T-shirt.

Without exchanging a word, they both shimmied down to the edge of the roof.

'Rescue is coming from the north beach,' he said as he

tried to get his bearings as to where they were, exactly, in conjunction with said beach. 'We need to run to the right.'

She nodded, grim determination on her face, and then expertly swung over the edge so she was holding onto the rim of the roof with her fingers.

Being much larger, it took Gabriele a little longer to drop down. Before he could let go, she'd released her hold and fallen onto the wraparound veranda. Immediately she was back on her feet and jumping over the wooden rail and running to safety…except she was running to the left of the beach and not the right as they'd agreed.

He let go. He landed heavily but ignored the pain that shot up his leg and set off after her, calling as loudly as he dared, 'You're going the wrong way.'

She didn't look back. The band holding her hair back had come out, her long, straight white-blonde hair billowing behind her.

Run, Elena, run.

In her mind's eye she pictured the tree house her father's staff had built for her and her brothers when they'd been children. If she could only reach it undetected, she would be safe.

But no matter how quickly she ran along the beach, she could hear him gaining on her.

Gabriele Mantegna. A man she vaguely remembered from her childhood. A man who scared her as much as the armed men in her family's holiday home.

This was the man who had spent two years in an American federal prison and tried to implicate her father in his criminality.

In the distance ahead was the pathway that led into the forest and to her sanctuary.

She pushed on even harder but still he gained ground. His breaths were heavy behind her.

She wasn't going to make it.

A burst of fury rent through her, overriding her fear. She would not allow herself to be captured by this man.

Coming to an abrupt halt, she turned on the spot and charged, propelling her entire body at him. It was like charging at a brick wall.

But her ruse worked. Taken by surprise, Gabriele stumbled back onto the sand. Unfortunately he wasn't so off guard that he didn't immediately hook his foot around her ankle, sending her tumbling on top of him. Within seconds he had gained the upper hand, twisting her onto her back and pinioning her beneath him.

'Are you trying to get yourself killed?' he demanded, his angry breath hot on her face.

Bucking beneath him, she tried everything she could to throw him off but she was too tightly caught.

Gabriele swore and, panther-like, sprang back to his feet. There was no way for her to escape again for he unceremoniously pulled her up, hooked an arm around her waist, and slung her over his shoulder.

No sooner had he started running than shouts echoed from the house.

Terror as she had never experienced, not even when she'd unexpectedly stumbled upon the gang, careered through her.

Yet, even with the indignity of being carried like a naughty child and the pain in her stomach as it jostled against his shoulder, when the first gun shots rang out she squeezed her eyes shut and thanked God for Gabriele's strength, and prayed for the shots to fire wide.

She had no idea how long he ran with her thrown over his shoulder. It could have been one minute, it could have been an hour. All she knew was that the men were chasing and firing at them.

And then he was no longer running with her on the sand but wading through the sea. An engine ran close by. She hardly had time to register that a jet ski had appeared from nowhere before Gabriele had climbed onto it and shouted, 'Go!'

Whoever was driving didn't need telling twice. The jet ski shot off over the still waters.

Somehow Gabriele manipulated her body so she was no longer draped over his shoulder but secured on his lap, sandwiched between him and the man riding the jet ski.

Within minutes they approached an enormous yacht. To Elena's amazement, they steered straight into an opened hatch on the side and parked, exactly as if they were parking a car in a garage.

Gabriele and the man who'd ridden the jet ski helped her off.

'Are you all right?' Gabriele asked, looking at her closely.

She opened her mouth to retort defiantly that of course she was all right when the magnitude of everything she'd gone through that evening and the exhaustion that had brought her to Nutmeg Island hit her.

A hot fog formed in her brain, perspiration breaking out all over, her hands suddenly clammy.

And then it all went black.

CHAPTER TWO

ELENA AWOKE TO find herself cocooned in a heavy duvet on a bed so comfortable that for a moment the fact she didn't have a clue where she was didn't matter.

She stretched then sat bolt upright as memories flooded her.

She'd fainted. She remembered feeling all…wrong, remembered strong arms holding her, overriding her protests.

Gabriele Mantegna .

He'd kidnapped her. He'd given chase, thrown her over his shoulder and spirited her to his yacht via a jet ski.

Or had he saved her?

Yes, that was right. He'd certainly saved her from the criminal gang who'd done the unthinkable and overridden her father's state-of-the-art security system and broken onto their island.

But he was Gabriele Mantegna and instinct told her she'd be no safer with him than those men. The danger he carried was of a different kind.

He'd carried her away from the hail of bullets that had rained on them. God alone knew how they'd escaped without being shot.

What was he even doing there?

So many thoughts crammed in her brain it was a struggle to think straight.

Another memory came to her, of being placed on the bed and Gabriele's rich voice murmuring in their native Italian that she should sleep.

The only comfort she could take was that her clothes were still on.

Climbing out of bed, she held onto the frame until she

was certain her feet were steady, then drew the floor-length curtains.

Light flooded the cabin, almost blinding her with its brilliance. She opened the French doors and stepped out onto the balcony. The Caribbean Sea—at least she assumed they were still on the Caribbean—was calm, the yacht powering through it at a remarkable rate. If she closed her eyes she wouldn't know they were sailing.

Movement behind her made her turn and find a woman dressed in a maid's outfit standing at the door of her cabin.

The maid gave a tentative smile. 'Good morning Signorina Ricci,' she said in Italian. 'Can I get you some breakfast?'

The sea air had done a good job of clearing Elena's head and reinvigorating her. As much as she wanted food and a hot shower, what she needed was to see Gabriele and find out what the hell was going on.

'I would like you to take me to Signor Mantegna.'

The maid nodded her acquiescence and Elena followed her out of the cabin and into a wide corridor. A flight of steps led into a huge atrium where a white grand piano sat in the centre ringed by a circle of plush white sofas.

Gabriele was found on the third deck, sitting at a table overlooking a large, oval swimming pool, eating from a bowl of fruit.

He rose to his feet. He wore only a pair of canvas shorts. 'Good morning, Elena. How are you feeling?'

'Much better thank you,' she replied coolly, feeling her cheeks flame as she remembered basically falling into a dead faint at his feet.

Being eye level with his naked chest only caused the flames to burn harder. Quickly, she averted her gaze.

'You gave us quite a scare. Please, sit down. Coffee? Food?'

She took the seat opposite him. 'A *caffe e latte* would be nice.'

Turning to the maid, he said, 'Esmerelda, a *caffe e latte* and a tray of pastries for our guest, and a fresh pot of coffee for me please.'

While he spoke to the maid, Elena took the opportunity to flash her eyes over him.

Last night Gabriele had been dressed in a black wetsuit. It had been obvious then that he had a good body on him. However, nothing could have prepared her for seeing it in the flesh. Strong and defined, it was covered across the pecs with fine dark hair. This, coupled with his deep bronze colour, was testament to a man who enjoyed the outside life.

But there had been a couple of years when his outdoor recreation would have been severely limited...

'What's going on?' she asked abruptly.

It wasn't as if she hadn't seen a topless man before, she reminded herself. She had three older brothers. The male physique was hardly a mystery.

'I appreciate you saved me from those men last night but what were you doing on our island? If you had nothing to do with those men, how did you know to rescue me?'

It could only have been for nefarious purposes. Ever since Gabriele's release from prison he'd been conducting a subtle one-man vendetta against her family. The media intrusion had become intolerable.

The handsome, charismatic billionaire head of Mantegna Cars, a convicted fraudster and money-launderer, never missed an opportunity to make digs at her father. Gabriele had pleaded guilty to the charges and taken sole responsibility—though it was widely believed he'd only done so to save his own father—but many whispers had reached the media that Gabriele was fingering Ignazio Ricci as the real culprit.

Thoughtful eyes, such a dark brown colour they appeared black, met her gaze. With his strong nose and wide, sensuous lips, Gabriele's features had a soulful quality that was totally incongruous for a man such as him.

'I heard you scream. That's how I knew there was some-one in danger.'

Her throat still hurt from that scream.

'We'll wait until your refreshments have been served and then we can talk about the rest of it.' His gaze flickered over her, scrutinising her in a fashion that made her flush. Having not looked in a mirror, she could only imagine how awful she looked with her bed hair and the clothes she'd fished in, made a bonfire in and slept in.

'Can you at least tell me where we are?'

'We are currently in the Gulf of Mexico. All being well we should arrive at Tampa Bay by early evening.'

Since assuring himself that Elena's faint wasn't anything to worry about, Gabriele had done some research on the woman he hadn't set eyes on in over two decades. His mind had been so filled with revenge on Ignazio and, to a lesser extent, his three sons, he'd almost forgotten she existed.

From thinking a man like Ignazio didn't have the capacity to love anyone, Gabriele now knew that, in Elena, he had found his nemesis's Achilles heel.

Their fathers had been close friends since childhood. When Alfredo, Gabriele's father, had emigrated from Italy to the US with his wife and young son, their friendship had endured. Alfredo had passed on his new American contacts to Ignazio and vouched for him, enabling him to expand his own growing empire.

Their businesses had been complementary, with Ricci Components supplying many of the parts fitted in Mantegna Cars. Both men had subsequently diversified from their business origins and a decade ago had merged the overlapping aspects of their respective businesses, at Ignazio's suggestion. Gabriele had had some reservations about the merger but had kept them to himself—after all, Ignazio was practically family.

Despite their enduring closeness, Ignazio had kept his only daughter hidden away in Italy. Gabriele doubted he had seen Elena in the flesh more than a handful of times since she was a toddler. His only real memory of her was as an unabashed tomboy.

The light of her father's eye, she had been home educated and protected all her life. She'd joined her father's business at the age of eighteen and worked closely with him for a number of years before being given the role of running the European division of Ignazio's empire.

Unlike her brothers, who had all the subtlety of a trio of strutting peacocks, she still, as an adult, kept in the background. Media sightings of her were slim and those that existed were all business related.

One particular broadsheet interview with Ignazio had caught his attention. It had been conducted four years ago, when Gabriele's father had first been charged. Ignazio had slated Alfredo and spoken eloquently about how 'duped' he felt. The only sincere words Gabriele had sensed from the man had been about his daughter:

'Elena is the hardest worker of my staff and the best child a man could hope for. I know when I become infirm, she will be there to care for me.'

He allowed himself a smile.

Gabriele's visit to the Ricci chapel might not have provided the evidence to clear his name he so badly wanted but in Elena he had found a silver lining. He'd found a weapon that could hurt Ignazio much more than merely sending him to prison.

Oh, yes, as a weapon to hurt Ignazio, he had found none better.

But then his smile dropped.

There would be nothing to celebrate until he found the evidence that cleared his father's name—and his own—and would allow his mother whatever peace she was capable of finding.

'I should tell you that your presence here has presented me with something of a dilemma,' he said.

Her brows drew together, her startling green eyes holding his. 'What kind of dilemma?'

'You have provided me with options I hadn't considered before.' Seeing Esmerelda returning to them, he left it at that.

Elena's *caffe e latte,* a large fresh pot of coffee and a plate of pastries were placed between them, and Gabriele's coffee poured.

'Please, eat,' he instructed with a wave of a hand, as Esmerelda disappeared back inside.

'Tell me why I'm a dilemma.'

'I would prefer to have this conversation without worrying you're going to fall into another faint due to hunger.'

'I've never fainted before,' she stated matter-of-factly. 'It was the shock and adrenaline of everything, that's all. I've never been kidnapped before and then rescued, then chased, then thrown over a shoulder to a jet ski with live ammunition being fired at me.'

'Why did you run from me?' he asked curiously.

'Because you have a grudge against my father and hate my family. You appeared in the room like a dark phantom—I was scared.'

'I don't hold a grudge against your father,' he denied calmly. 'My loathing towards all you Riccis is much stronger than that.'

Her pretty, lightly golden face paled. 'Then why did you rescue me?'

'Because I'm not such a monster that I would leave you at the mercy of those men.'

A tiny, shaking hand took a cornetto. Instead of biting into it, she put it on the plate before her, then took a sip of her *caffe e latte*.

'I don't understand why you hate us all so much.'

'Really?' He allowed his disbelief to ring through the syllables. Elena was a child of Ignazio's loins. She worked closely with him. Gabriele doubted there was anything about Ignazio's business practices she was unaware of. She was as guilty as he. 'Then let me educate you.'

At the foot of the table sat his briefcase. He pulled it onto his lap, opened it, and took out a document file.

'I went to Nutmeg Island last night searching for evidence of your father's criminality. These are a few of the documents I copied from the basement of your family chapel last night. As you can see, I've had them printed off to make digesting them easier. These are irrefutable proof that Ricci Components is laundering money from its Brazilian base.'

'You're lying.' She bit into her cornetto. A small dollop of raspberry jam dripped down her chin. She wiped it away with a finger and licked it, all the while staring at him with eyes that had hardened.

'Read them for yourself,' he answered with a shrug. 'The proof is there. The US authorities will find it indisputable.'

Something flickered in her eyes.

'Your father's been running his business from Brazil for well over a decade. However, the accounts concerned use US dollars. That gives the US a jurisdictional right to launch an investigation. Trust me, should I give them these documents, they will be on your father and the rest of you like a pack of hyenas on a fresh carcass. Why do you think I spent only two years of a six-year sentence behind bars? They know your father's up to his neck in corruption but, until now, they've not had the evidence to charge him with anything.'

She swallowed her food and swiped a hand through her fringe, then snatched the file from him. Sipping her *caffe e latte*, she began reading through the papers.

Gabriele watched her closely. Her green eyes zoomed from left to right and back again, a concentration frown just noticeable beneath her fringe.

In the years since he'd last seen her, she'd gained a doll-like prettiness about her that, combined with her rather grubby appearance and boyish clothes, had the effect of making her appear younger than her twenty-five years. He had to remind himself that there was nothing doll-like or immature about her spine. She'd proved her tenacity last night: she'd had an escape route planned despite the terror that would have frozen any other person's brain, and not only had she run away from him but, when realising she couldn't outrun him, had fought back. If his own reflexes weren't so quick she would likely have escaped him.

But she would never have escaped the men. They would never have let her go. They couldn't have afforded to, not once she had seen her captor's face.

Whatever direction this conversation took, he could not afford to let those big green eyes beguile him into thinking she was something less than she truly was.

'Whoever created these documents is clearly a master forger,' she said tightly when she'd finished reading.

'Don't fool yourself. They're not forgeries. I took the pictures myself last night, in your chapel basement.'

'Which you broke into.' Her eyes narrowed, more suspicion and distrust ringing from them. 'Were you in league with those men?'

'No.'

'So it's coincidence you were there at the exact same time an armed gang raided our holiday island?'

'No coincidence at all.' He gave a nonchalant shrug. 'I knew they would be making their heist. I've waited a year for it.'

She stared at him with a clenched jaw.

He allowed himself a smile. 'The thing you have to understand about prison is that it's full of criminals. Not all prisoners are discreet. One liked to brag about how his brother was a member of Carter's gang. Have you heard of Carter?'

She shook her head.

'Carter steals to order. His price tag for a job is reputed to be ten million dollars.'

She let out a low whistle.

'He also does jobs for himself—heists where he knows illegal artefacts are kept. The kind of stuff no owner would dare report stolen to the police.' Gabriele rested his elbows on the table and leaned forward. 'It was a simple matter to tell my fellow prisoner of the island off the Cayman Isles packed full of illegal art worth tens of millions of dollars.'

'That's a lie,' she snapped, finally showing some animation.

He shrugged. 'Carter didn't believe it to be a lie and he does meticulous research. I knew it was only a matter of time before word reached him. I've been keeping close tabs on him and waiting for his gang to make their move—I have to give credit to your father, his security system is second to none. I knew it would take the best to break it and Carter is the best. All I had to do was wait for him to make his move and use his gang as cover to enter the island undetected.'

Her green eyes flashed with contempt. 'So *you* brought those men to my family's island?'

'All I did was plant the idea.' He rubbed at his jaw. 'You weren't supposed to be there. No one was. Carter's got away with it for so long because he doesn't take unnecessary risks.'

'If you're so convinced of my father's guilt, why didn't you take the risk yourself? Why use a bunch of criminals as cover?'

He smiled without humour. 'I've already spent two years in prison. Believe me, I have no wish to spend another day there. I let the experts take the risk.'

Without warning, she jumped up from her chair and hurried to the railing, whereby she threw the file overboard. The papers flew out, the breeze lifting them and scattering them in all directions.

'That's what I think of your evidence,' Elena said coldly, trying desperately to hide the fact her heart was thrumming madly and her blood felt as if ice had been injected directly into her bloodstream.

This was all a horrible lie. There was no other explanation.

Her father was *not* a criminal. It was possible some of his art might not be entirely legitimate but illegal art was a world away from fraud and money laundering. He was a good, loving man who had raised her and her three older brothers single-handedly after her mother's death when Elena had been a toddler.

She watched Gabriele's jaw clench. He gripped hold of his coffee and downed it.

She hoped it scorched him.

'There is plenty more evidence,' he said in a tone far more even than the brimstone firing from his now black eyes portrayed. 'One phone call will be enough to have the FBI and the local police obtain a search warrant. One call. Would you like me to make it?'

'Why would they believe you?' she sneered. 'You're a convicted criminal and that "evidence" is illegally gained. It wouldn't stand up in any court.'

'It's enough to get the ball rolling. The authorities are watching your father. They're watching your brothers...and they're watching you. Your family is like a collection of kindling. All the authorities are waiting on is the match to light it. If the worst happens and they judge they can't use the evidence, then copies of the documents will be emailed from an anonymous, untraceable email address to every major news outlet in the world. Either way he's finished, and you're finished too.'

Elena put a hand to her chest and blinked hard to clear the clouds swimming in her eyes.

Whoever Gabriele had paid to create the documents was

a master of the art. Anyone looking at them could be forgiven for thinking they had an air of legitimacy to them.

Her father—her entire family—had been living under a cloud of suspicion for a year, ever since Gabriele had been released from prison and begun his whispering campaign against them. He'd been clever about it, always making sure his comments were right on the cusp of slanderous.

There had been other incidents too, minor in the grand scheme of things; investors pulling out of deals at the last moment, the banks insisting on greater scrutiny of the books, all the little things that could be passed off as consequences of a turbulent global economy but as a whole were evidence of someone working against them.

She clung to the railing, her knuckles turning white. 'Do you hate us because my father never stood up for your father when the accusations first came out? Is that the reason for all this?'

He laughed. It was the bitterest sound she had ever heard.

'You're very good at the wide-eyed ingénue act, I'll give you that,' he said with a shake of his dark head. 'One could almost believe you're naïve about the fact that it was *your* father behind it all.'

She shook her head. 'You're lying. Everyone knows you and your father were in on it together. You took the rap to spare him. My father was questioned *once* and they found no evidence against him.'

'They found no evidence against *your* father because the trail he made was deliberately laid to lead to *my* father,' he snarled, showing the first real sign of anger, enough to make her recoil and tighten her hold on the rail. 'The FBI has been trying to pin something on him for years. Our fathers went into business together at your father's instigation so he could hide behind my father's respectability. He used my father's affection, good nature and loyalty to an old friend, and framed him.'

'Where's the evidence? You're making a lot of nasty insinuations and accusations here but where's a shred of evidence to back up the claims?'

'It's out there and I will find it.'

'Or forge it like you did those other documents you claim are from the chapel basement.'

Her father had stored business documents in the chapel basement for decades. There was nothing sinister about it— it was simply the most secure place for them. Or, rather, had been.

'Admit it, Elena, the documents I copied last night are the real deal. Their release is the smoking gun the FBI is waiting for.'

'They're forgeries.' But she could not deny that they were brilliantly constructed forgeries. As far as forgeries went, they were perfect.

'You know perfectly well they're not. You're up to your pretty neck in all this.'

'I'm not up to my neck in anything.' She wanted to scream. This entire conversation was like something from Dante.

'You are. But there is a way for you to save yourself. And your father. And that is what I mean about you posing a dilemma for me.'

'Go on.'

'The lack of documentary evidence to support mine and my father's innocence is a setback for me.'

'That's because it doesn't exist.'

'If I'm such a master forger don't you think I would fake it?' he demanded. 'Your father is a meticulous record keeper. It's out there somewhere and I will find it…or I could be persuaded to forget the whole thing. With the right incentive I could also be persuaded to destroy the evidence I copied last night rather than pass it on.'

'What incentive are you talking about?' she asked, the anger leeching out to be replaced with wariness.

'I've held back from sending the documents to the FBI because I have a proposition to make. You and you alone can save your father from financial ruin and a hefty prison sentence.'

'What does this proposition entail?'

A smile curved his handsome face. 'That, you will find, is the crucial question. To secure a healthy future for your father and the rest of your family, you will have to do one very simple thing—you'll have to marry me.'

CHAPTER THREE

GABRIELE WATCHED CLOSELY as the blood drained from Elena's face, the light golden colour turning white. The last thing he wanted was her falling into a faint again, especially as there was no possibility of him catching her as he'd done the night before.

It was the last thing he should have worried about. Instead of falling into a heap on the floor, she covered her mouth and burst into peals of laughter. And not just a short burst of it. Her body shook, the colour flooding back in her face.

'That's the funniest thing I've ever heard,' she said, wiping away tears of mirth with the back of her hand. 'You want to marry me?'

He didn't say anything, just folded his arms across his chest and stared at her implacably.

She must have seen something in his expression for all merriment came to an abrupt halt.

'You don't mean it? Do you? You want to marry me?'

'Marry me and all your father's financial and legal problems disappear.'

'But... But that's insane.' She ran her fingers through her messy hair. 'Tell me what your real proposition is.'

'That's it. I want my ring on your finger and my baby in your belly.'

'A baby? You want me to have a *baby* with you? You *are* insane—'

'Those are my conditions for not throwing your father and the rest of your family to the mercy of the authorities.'

She shook her head, visibly pulling herself together. Dragging herself away from the railing, she rejoined him at the table, finished her *caffe e latte*, then helped herself to the fresh pot of coffee.

Done, she leaned forward, her fingertips holding onto the table as if they were suction pads.

'Putting aside the fact your proposition is the most stupid idea in the history of humanity, and putting aside your monstrous idea of us having a baby together, what would you hope to achieve by marrying me? My humiliation? My subjugation? *What?*'

'I have one mission in my life and that's your father's destruction. You marrying me...' he allowed himself the luxury of imagining Ignazio's reaction to the news '...will destroy him emotionally. You're his special princess; the light of his life. Knowing you belong to me will cut right into what is left of his heart.'

Her eyes flashed pure hatred at him. 'I will never belong to you. And I am *not* having your child.'

'If you agree to my proposition you will take my name. You will have my child. A Ricci will become a Mantegna. Together we will make a new life.' Now Gabriele leaned forward to mimic her stance, placing his fingers on the table so they almost touched hers. 'Your father, your brothers, the whole world will believe you have fallen in love with me and that whatever heart you have in your body belongs to me.'

Now her eyes were wide with stark panic. 'I can't do it. No one would believe we're in love for a second.'

He shrugged. 'It will be your job to make them believe it.'

She rubbed at her eyes. He looked closely to see if there were tears but clearly Elena, despite her doll-like exterior and unfortunate fainting fit, was tough. It wasn't a thought that should make him glad but it did.

Knowing she was more than equipped to be his equal lessened a fraction of the guilt trying to eat at him.

He would not allow himself to feel guilt. After what her father had done, guilt and empathy had no place in his life.

Gabriele's father had worked hard all his life, had been a loyal and faithful husband, father, employer and friend. To see his reputation trashed and the anguish it had caused, along with his father's bewilderment that the man he'd considered a brother had been the root of it all…

'It's one thing wanting to hurt my father but why are you dragging me into it?' she asked, shaking her head. 'I've done nothing to you. I don't even know you.'

'Because I know you're as guilty as he is. Even if you didn't have a direct hand in the framing of my father, you did nothing to stop it. Your father is a monster yet you act as if he were a deity. You should consider yourself lucky that I'm giving you this chance. Be in no doubt, the FBI will find evidence against you and your brothers too.' Gabriele rose from the table. 'I appreciate it's a lot for you to take in so I shall give you some time to think things through.'

'How long? How long, damn you?'

He looked at his watch. 'I want your decision by the time we reach Tampa Bay.'

'I can't…' She swallowed, her face pinched and furious. 'I can't. It's impossible.'

'You can. The choice will ultimately be yours. Just bear in mind that should you choose the wrong option, your father will spend what's left of his miserable life in a prison cell. There might even be a cell with your name on it too.'

As he walked back indoors, the feel of her hate-filled eyes burning into his back, he took some deep breaths to dislodge the uncomfortable, cramp-like feeling that had settled in his chest.

A hot shower made Elena feel cleaner but not at all better.

She'd sat outside on the deck for almost an hour, trying hard to think but being unable to drag up a coherent thought.

She should never have taken the long weekend off work.

She'd hardly taken any time off in the past year: since Gabriele had started his whispering campaign she hadn't dared. She'd wanted her employees and the Ricci shareholders to see her relaxed and unworried. An average week would see her travel to a minimum of four countries. Yes, she travelled by private jet but even thirty thousand feet in the air there was no respite to be had. Always there was paperwork to catch up on, emails to send and reply to, daily conference calls with her father.

A fortnight ago she'd caught a cold that wouldn't shift. As the days had passed her energy levels had sapped. Getting out of bed had become a feat of endurance. Then, on Thursday, she'd sat through a board meeting in Oslo fighting to keep her eyes open. As soon as it had finished she'd dragged herself into her office, sank onto the sofa and promptly fallen asleep. While she'd slept she'd dreamt of the family Caribbean island, bought two decades ago, and had woken knowing she needed a break. She didn't need a doctor to tell her she was in danger of burnout.

Their home on the island was big enough that all the family could come and go as they pleased. As a rule, they notified the household staff so preparations could be made, but on this fateful occasion she'd decided what she needed more than anything was peace. Just the thought of being completely alone—obviously with the exception of the unobtrusive security guards—had lifted her spirits.

Three days of solitude and sunshine...

She'd arrived on the island late yesterday afternoon. She'd dumped her case in the house and then decided to do something she hadn't done since she was a child, and head to the south of the island where the clear shallow waters allowed her to wade far out, and catch a fish for her supper.

Her belly rumbled as she recalled how she'd never had a chance to eat her catch, a juvenile foot-long barracuda.

The sun had gone down and she'd built a small fire on

the beach. Her barracuda had been almost cooked to perfection when shouts had distracted her.

She'd assumed one of the security guards had injured himself and rushed off through the woods to help.

Luck had not been on her side. She'd stepped onto the main drive that cut through the woods at the exact moment the man clad head to foot in black had stepped out of the house. He couldn't miss her.

She'd been rooted to the ground, her shock so great she'd been unable to move more than a muscle. It was as if her brain had been incapable of comprehending that there was a stranger before her and that this stranger represented danger.

Then the adrenaline had kicked in and she'd turned to run but by then it had been too late—the man had already yelled for back-up and was powering towards her. So she'd done the only thing she could. She'd opened her throat and screamed, literally, for her life.

Thank the Lord that Gabriele had heard it. She couldn't bear to think of what would have happened if he hadn't, or if he'd ignored it.

Her wrists were still sore from where that man had tied her to the bed. He hadn't cared if he hurt her. Indeed, she would guess he got off on it.

It was this knowledge, that Gabriele had put himself in danger to rescue her, that tempered the fury ravaging her entire body. Even her *toes* were angry.

But he *had* saved her. He'd put himself in grave danger for her. When he'd slung her over his shoulder there had been an understandable impatience but not a roughness. Hurting her had been the last thing on his mind.

A bitter laugh flew from her mouth. She'd bet he wouldn't have bothered coming to her rescue if he'd known that it was *she* who was in danger.

Or maybe he would have.

Saving her had presented him with an opportunity and he was grabbing it with both enormous hands.

It felt as if needles were being pushed into her scalp and forehead.

She couldn't marry him. She'd never heard such a ridiculous notion in her life. Marrying a man she barely knew and who was intent on destroying her entire family?

And to have his child? To bring a child into such a hate-filled nest of poison?

Yet it was the only way to save her family. Those forged documents had the potential to destroy them all and she was the only one who could stop it happening.

No wonder her head hurt so much.

Forcing herself to gather her wits, Elena hunted around the cabin for something clean to wear as Esmerelda had whisked her filthy clothes away. All she found was a white silk robe hanging in the wardrobe. It felt beautiful on her skin but one look in the mirror made her whip it off. The material was practically transparent.

Esmerelda had brought some clothes for her to change into but judging by the size and quality of them, they belonged to Gabriele.

It was with great reluctance that she slipped a black T-shirt on. It fell to her knees and looked like a sack. Much better.

What wasn't better was the faint trace of cologne permeating through the fabric cleaner. It had to be Gabriele's. It smelt too much like him to belong to anyone else. She hated that it was a scent she found appealing.

As Esmerelda had whisked her underwear away with the rest of her clothes, Elena reluctantly donned the accompanying shorts. They swamped her.

Holding the shorts up to stop them falling down and trying to forget she had Gabriele's scent clinging to her, she set out to find him.

Retracing the route through the cavernous interior, she

found her way to the top deck. She stood at the rail that
overlooked the pool deck below, was about to turn back
when a figure in the pool made her do a double-take.

Instinct told her it was Gabriele powering his way
through the water.

For some incredibly strange reason her heart accelerated, her hold on the rail tightening.

Up and down he swam, his back muscles rippling with
the movement. No wonder he had such a fabulous physique...

He reached the end but instead of doing an immediate
about-turn and setting off again as he had done thus far,
he twisted round and looked up.

Mortified to have been caught...admiring him... Elena
went to step back but stopped herself in time. Hiding would
only confirm that she'd been spying.

Instead, she held her head high and walked down the
wide stairs to the pool deck. By the time she'd reached the
bottom Gabriele had hauled himself out of the pool and
was rubbing a towel over his face.

Dear Lord...

With the water dripping off his honed bronzed skin and
nothing but a pair of tight black swim shorts on with a definite bulge in them...

Feeling her cheeks turn scarlet, Elena hurried to take a
seat at a table where a jug of water and a couple of glasses
had been laid.

From the corner of her eye she saw him methodically
dry himself before slinging the towel over his shoulder
and joining her.

He flashed a quick smile and poured them both a drink.

'Do I assume your reappearance means you have come
to a decision?' he asked, placing her glass before her.

'Not quite.' She took a drink of the cold water, wiped
her mouth with her thumb and took a deep breath. 'There
are some things we need to discuss first.'

'Such as?'

'If I agree to marry you, I want a signed agreement that all the so-called evidence you have against my father will be destroyed.'

'The contract being drafted has that specified.'

'You're drafting one already?'

'Yes. It will set out in black and white exactly what this marriage will be so there is no room for doubt on either side.'

'Isn't that rather presumptuous? I haven't said yes.'

'You will,' he said with an arrogant shrug.

She sucked in air through her teeth and willed herself not to bite.

'Your father's liberty depends on it,' he added.

Growing up in an all-male household, Elena was well used to the male ego. Any man stupid enough to think she was inferior because of her gender or size soon learnt the error of his ways. It had delighted her father that his little princess was brainier than her brothers—admittedly not hard—and had never lost a physical fight against any of them either.

In the Ricci household you learnt to take care of yourself from a very young age.

Gabriele's arrogance—different from her brothers' and far more acute—was just another thing to add to the list of things to despise about him.

'Will I be expected to give up my job?'

'No, but I will expect you to make concessions on your workload as I will have to make concessions on mine. For our marriage to be believable we will have to marry our diaries as well as ourselves.'

She eyed him with a suspicious glare. 'And that will be in the contract?'

'Yes. Anything else?'

'Your demand for me to have your child is abhorrent and not something I can agree to.'

'Let me be clear about a couple of things.' Gabriele leaned forward, taking in the whiteness of her face. 'My only reason for marrying you is to hurt your father. You know as well as I do that our marriage will crush him. You carrying a Mantegna child will be the ultimate destruction for his pride.'

'You can't bring a child into a marriage like this,' she said hotly. 'It's immoral.'

'A Ricci lecturing me on morals?' He raised a brow and tutted.

'Why would you even want to have a child with me? You hate me. You could have a baby with anyone.'

'But I don't want *anyone*. I want you.'

Her slim shoulders rose. 'Why?'

'When my father and I were arrested four years ago, I was engaged to be married. I pleaded guilty to save my father's neck but Sophia, my fiancée, chose not to believe that or believe me. She couldn't handle the media scrutiny and the associated shame it brought on her and ended our relationship. Believe me, I will never trust another woman again. After what your father did I will not trust *anyone*. I am the last of my line. You having my child will mean the Mantegna name lives on.'

Merely thinking about Sophia made him feel sick. She'd broken their engagement in a clinical fashion that hadn't left him devastated for the loss of her love but furious that he had ever believed in it. He couldn't believe he'd been ready to commit his life to such a disloyal, spineless creature. Thankfully there had been no time to brood; his over-riding priorities at the time being to stop Mantegna Cars being pulled under and to protect his parents. That he'd only succeeded in the former was something he would live with for the rest of his life.

'And you could love a child with Ricci blood in it?' Elena challenged.

He shrugged. 'The child will be half Mantegna. That will dilute the impact.'

'What a disgusting thing to say.'

'I'm merely being honest. If you agree to this marriage then I don't want there to be any room for misunderstandings. Any child we have would be an innocent in all this and I do not hurt innocents.'

'You're hurting *me*.'

'You're not an innocent.'

She flinched and squeezed her eyes shut but he ignored her distress.

If she was anyone other than Ignazio's daughter and favourite, closest child, he would feel sorry for her.

Then again, if she was anyone else he wouldn't dream of the actions he was taking.

Elena was a special case.

Elena had watched his father be accused of a crime she knew damn well her own father had committed. She had seen Gabriele take the rap, had seen the worldwide media coverage, had likely seen the footage of him entering the federal prison system, and seen, mere days later, the coverage that his father's great heart had given up on him. And through it all, she'd said nothing.

She'd allowed his father to die with his only child imprisoned for a crime her own father had committed and his wife all alone in a country whose language she had never quite mastered. And she'd done nothing.

As far as he was concerned she was as guilty for his father's death as Ignazio, and he wouldn't rest until every single Ricci had paid the price for their heinous lies and betrayal.

If she wanted to know what real pain was she should walk in his shoes for an hour.

'Our marriage will last for as long as it takes to conceive and then we will go our separate ways.'

Her face went even whiter, her horror stark. 'You would take a child away from its mother?'

'I'm not the monster in this relationship,' he said. 'I'd be willing to have joint custody but the condition would be that it has no contact with any member of your family.'

'You *are* a monster,' she spat. 'How you can even think about bringing a child into the world under such conditions...'

'Nevertheless they *are* my conditions. Take it or leave it. I want a child. I want revenge. I can marry those two desires by marrying you. And look on the positives of having my child—as soon as you're pregnant you'll have outlived your usefulness and I will set you free. It is up to you. Or you can take your chances with the law.'

'Let's say for argument's sake that I do agree to have a baby with you.' Desperation laced her husky voice. 'How are you going to have...have...sex with a woman you hate?'

'Are you really that naïve about the workings of a man?' he mocked. 'Our libidos tend to work independently from our brains. You're not a bad-looking woman. I'm sure making a baby with you won't be too much of a hardship.'

If Elena had anything else to say she must have become incapable. Her eyes were wide and full of fury and outrage.

'It is best our cards are laid on the table,' he said. 'And now that you know where you stand on everything, have you come to a decision? Will you marry me?'

Her lips pulled together. He could hear her breathing.

'As long as that contract guarantees you will not take my baby away from me and as long as it guarantees you will destroy the alleged evidence and that you will stop the whispering campaign you've been conducting against my family then yes, I will marry you.'

He allowed himself the satisfaction of a smile.

But Elena wasn't finished.

Hands clenched into balls, she said, 'But you have to

buy me a house in Florence and one close to your home in New York.'

'What on earth for?'

'If we're sharing custody it means I can always be close to our child whenever it's with you and be there if it needs me.'

He was surprised to find she had some latent maternal genes in her.

'And I want it stipulated, in black and white, that you will never bad-mouth me or my family to our child.'

From the look on Elena's face, Gabriele judged this was the deal breaker. He had to admire her. She had spirit. And, despite being a Ricci, compassion for a child who hadn't yet been created.

'Okay,' he agreed with a lazy shrug. 'I can agree to that.'

'I want it written in the contract.'

'Consider it done.'

'Good. But just so you know, you're not the only one who can hold a grudge and wish for vengeance.' She rose from her chair and leaned forward so her furious eyes were mere inches from his. 'When this is over I will personally see that you pay. There will not be a minute of the day when you don't regret what you've done to me. I will see you burn in hell for this.'

Unexpectedly, something cold raced up his spine.

'I'm already in hell,' he said bitterly. 'Your father put me there.'

Her top lip curled. 'Then I will make it my mission in life to keep you there.'

CHAPTER FOUR

THE SOUND OF a helicopter flying overhead made Elena shade her eyes and look to the skies.

She was sitting on the balcony of her cabin, exactly where she'd been for the past two hours since she'd walked away from Gabriele, before she'd given into the temptation to punch him in the face.

Never in her entire life had she hated someone. Never in her entire life had she felt so, so, so...*much* towards another person.

Her early childhood had been spent rallying against the injustice of being the only female in a household of males. She had come to realise the only way to get their respect was to behave like them. She might have been home educated, unlike her brothers who were sent to smart schools, and she might have been sheltered from the outside world, but within the household she had turned her anger to her advantage and become one of the boys. She had forced her brothers' respect and at the same time gained her father's.

Now she felt as helpless and angry as she had at the age of ten when she'd finally comprehended that the education she dreamt of, one where she could be with other girls her age, had been denied her. Even now she still struggled with other women. She just couldn't relate to them. First kisses, first attempts at putting make-up on, everything that went with being a female adolescent had been denied her. She had learned to embrace it.

Well she wouldn't embrace this situation. Gabriele would pay for this. She didn't know how or when or... anything, but she would make him pay.

She couldn't even think about what it would mean to have his child.

A child. A baby. The one thing she'd never thought she would have.

Having intended to spend her life as a Vestal Virgin, Elena had reconciled herself to never having a child of her own. Her brothers had taken too much glee in sharing salacious stories of their conquests. She'd listened to all the sordid details and heard their obvious contempt for the women who were always, without exception, referred to as whores.

By the time she'd turned fifteen Elena had known she would rather stay a virgin than be subjected to that kind of disgusting treatment. She would never allow herself to be treated as a piece of meat. Yes, there were ways to conceive a child that didn't involve getting physical with a man, but they weren't ways she could bring herself to consider.

A knock on the cabin door brought her out of her reverie.

She unlocked it and found Gabriele standing there, a thin document file in one hand, the case she'd taken to Nutmeg Island in the other.

'Where did you get that?' she asked, amazed.

'I had it couriered to my assistant. She brought it on the helicopter.'

'But how?'

'A friendly police officer retrieved it.' He smiled a secret smile. 'Carter's gang disabled the security monitors before you arrived. All your security team saw on their screens was the feed from the day before. No one knows you were on the island and I would imagine the gang won't mention it unless they want to add assault and attempted kidnap to their list of charges.'

Immediately her blood pressure rose. 'So they get away with it?'

'Not at all.' A darkness crossed his features. 'They will pay for it. They were arrested before they could leave the island and can all look forward to a hefty sentence in a prison that will make the one I was incarcerated in look like a holiday camp.'

He threw a thin document file on her bed before she could argue any more about it. 'Here's the contract.'

'You don't waste time.'

'Read through it, sign it and we can leave.'

'Are we at Tampa Bay?' She hadn't seen any sign of land from her balcony.

'No. You've already reached your decision so my helicopter will take us inland to my jet. My assistant and lawyer are waiting in the saloon—they'll act as witnesses for the contract.'

'You can't expect me to sign it now?'

'It's written clearly and concisely. It won't take you more than five minutes to read it.'

Giving him a baleful glare, Elena leaned over the bed to grab the file and see for herself.

As she turned back again, pulling the elegantly bound papers out, something about him made her stop.

There was an expression on his face she'd never seen before. A look in his eyes…

Heat pooled in her stomach and spread through her, climbing up to crawl through the veins in her face.

She'd taken his oversized shorts off the second she'd arrived back in her cabin.

She'd leaned over to grab the file totally forgetting she had no underwear on.

He'd *seen* her.

Gabriele's breathing had become heavy, his eyes containing a blackness that was quite unlike the angry circles of ice he usually looked at her with.

Please, something, anything, swallow her up right now.

He'd *seen* her.

His throat moved and then he coughed and took a step back before pulling a small tube from his pocket. 'This is some lotion for you to put on your wrists—it should help with the bruising.

'I will leave you to dress and read through the contract.' He no longer looked at her, his voice even deeper than normal. 'I will send someone for you in thirty minutes.'

He didn't wait for a response, throwing the tube on the bed and leaving the cabin in three long strides.

Gabriele concentrated hard on the conversation with his lawyer, discussing the finer details of the contract Milo had drafted for him.

Milo knew better than to try and talk Gabriele from the route he was taking. He had been his family's lawyer for over two decades, and there was little about Gabriele that Milo didn't know. It was this familiarity that made him sense the lawyer didn't approve of this particular route.

Whether his lawyer approved was irrelevant. As for Anna Maria, his assistant, she was too well paid to have an opinion on anything.

His lawyer and assistant were the only people to know the truth and he intended to keep it that way. To the rest of the world, especially to Ignazio, his and Elena's marriage would be the real deal.

It was only when Milo and Anna Maria both rose that he knew Elena had arrived.

Straight away his mind flashed to the image he'd been fighting not to see for thirty minutes.

The base of her bottom.

The base of her white, peachy, perfect bottom. The way it darkened at the base of the curve to show the promise of her hidden femininity.

One look and his pulse had paused for a heartbeat then surged into life, heat throbbing through his bloodstream.

He hadn't had such a visceral reaction to a woman since his teenage years. Arranging his features into neutrality, he turned his head to see her standing by his chair. She'd changed into another pair of long, boyish shorts and a plain white T-shirt, her hair now neatly tied back.

Gabriele made the introductions.

She shook hands with them both before casting him with another of the baleful glares he was becoming accustomed to.

He waited until Milo and Anna Maria had left them alone before saying, 'That is not the kind of greeting a man expects from his fiancée when in public.'

'Get used to it.'

He fixed her with a stare. 'I do not expect you take pleasure in my company but when we are in the company of others I expect you to treat me with respect and adoration. That will begin immediately.'

'Adoration?' she snorted, taking the seat opposite him and crossing her legs.

'Have you read through the contract? It details it quite clearly.'

She met his eyes.

Colour flooded her cheeks and he knew that she knew what he had seen.

She snapped her gaze away and cleared her throat. 'As long as you only expect adoration in public. In private you can sing for it.'

'I wouldn't expect anything else,' he replied sardonically. 'Do you have any questions about the contract?'

'The sleeping arrangements...'

'Are non-negotiable,' he supplied before she could go any further. 'For as long as our marriage lasts, it will be a traditional marriage, one in which we make a child.'

'We can use insemination.' Elena knew she sounded desperate but she didn't care. How could she sleep with him? He might be a walking pack of gorgeous testosterone but she *hated* him.

He laughed. For once it sounded genuine. 'No. We will make a baby in the traditional way. The world will believe our marriage is for real. Given the history between our families, our marriage will generate media scrutiny like nothing you will have ever experienced. Our staff will be besieged and offered money which would tempt even the saintliest person. We sleep together and that's the end of the matter.'

Elena squeezed her eyes closed and wished herself away from this nightmare she had fallen into.

The contract had been as concise as Gabriele had promised but seeing the terms written so bluntly made her wish there had been some superfluous words to take the edge off.

Divorce proceedings shall be initiated by Party 2, Elena Ricci, only when conception has been achieved and subject to that Party 1, Gabriele Mantegna, shall initiate divorce proceedings without any encumbrances.

There were even long clauses regarding the custody of their mythical child, clauses that, while splitting custody evenly, gave Gabriele all rights with regards to education and *'moral upbringing'* whatever that meant. He'd included her demands but had also stipulated his stance that her family must not be allowed any contact with their child or else all custody rights would be revoked and he would become sole guardian.

That he would use an innocent child as a pawn in his game of vengeance made her blood fire with fury. What kind of despicable monster would do such a thing?

Yet a different kind of heat suffused her as she imagined sharing a bed with him.

She'd never shared a bed with anyone in her life. To think of sharing one with a man as overtly masculine as Gabriele, of being burrowed under the same sheets...

'The evidence against my father. I want it destroyed now, not when we divorce.'

He shook his head. 'If I destroy it now there will be nothing to stop you from backing out of our deal.'

'Isn't my word good enough?'

'You're a Ricci. Your word is as useful as a chocolate teapot.'

A choked laugh razed her throat and she coughed.

One day she would learn not to laugh at inappropriate moments. Unfortunately it wasn't something she had any control over and completely involuntary.

Finally daring to look at him, she found his quizzical gaze upon her.

'You're amused?' he asked with an arched eyebrow.

'I have a warped funny bone.'

A glimmer of light flashed in his eyes but it vanished as quickly as it came.

'Do you have any other issues with the contract?' he said.

'Other than the entire document itself?'

'Anything specific,' he clarified drily.

'I have issues with everything but no, not anything specific.'

'Excellent. Then let's get it signed and we can start our new life together.'

The helicopter took them straight to the airport where Gabriele's flight crew were waiting for them in his private jet. Before long they were in the air and on their way to New York.

'Why New York?' she asked. She'd assumed they would go straight to his home in Italy, what with them both being Italian.

'Because we can marry in a couple of days there.'

'That soon?'

'We'll get the paperwork sorted on Monday and marry on Tuesday.'

She swallowed.

Everything was moving so quickly it felt as if she'd filled up on rocket fuel.

'After we've married we'll go to Florence. I'm launching a new car at my headquarters there in a month's time so I need to be on site.'

'I thought Mantegna Cars were based in the US?' Despite herself, her curiosity was piqued. As a child she'd loved it when her father had taken her out for a drive in one of his new Mantegna Cars. They'd always been so glamorous and powerful, ahead of their time in the gadget department. She'd always been proud that so many of those gadgets had come from her father's factories.

'Florence is Mantegna Car's birthplace and it's always been our European headquarters.' There was a hardness in his face. 'My parents loved their time in America but with retirement around the corner, they wanted to go home. As you know, my father died before he could make it back. Being incarcerated solidified the decision for me. Florence is my main home now, and it's back to being the headquarters of our entire company.'

A gleam came into his eyes, dispelling the hardness. 'Just think, come the launch, you might have the seed of life growing inside you.'

'But the nightmare won't be over, will it?' She crossed her legs as an unexpected ripple of heat pulsed low in her. 'A child will tie me to you for the rest of my life.'

'As long as you keep to the contractual obligations you signed, there will be minimal contact between us when we part.'

'Zero contact would be preferable.'

Ignoring his low, mocking laughter, Elena clamped her lips together and turned her head to look out of the window, staring at the pillowy clouds beneath them.

To her chagrin, when she next looked at him, Gabriele had fallen asleep.

She was surprised his conscience allowed him to sleep.

But then, she supposed one must have a conscience in the first place, which he absolutely did not.

She ran her hand over her face then tilted her chair back and curled into it, breathing deeply to quell the rising nausea in her belly.

She could go and have a sleep in the bedroom as Gabriele had offered when they'd boarded but she wasn't yet prepared to get under the covers of any bed belonging to him. Not voluntarily. Not until she had to.

With the cabin crew undertaking their duties quietly, bringing her a fresh supply of coffee and a plate of delicious sandwiches, the most her ragged stomach could handle, she couldn't stop her gaze flitting to the sleeping form opposite her.

It was the first time she'd really had the chance to study him unobserved.

They said the devil took beguiling forms to trap people. In Gabriele's case this was true. He really was handsome. Sinfully handsome.

Sleeping, arms crossed loosely over his chest, his head tilted to the right, his dark hair touching his shoulder, his top lip covering the bottom, he looked as if he should be in a Caravaggio picture; a chiselled, handsome man emerging from an impenetrable darkness that not only surrounded him but lived within him.

Gabriele stepped into the penthouse apartment he'd bought a year ago on his release from prison. Spacious—for Manhattan proportions—and full of light, it was the perfect antidote to the cramped cell he'd slept in for two years. He considered himself lucky that Milo and his legal team had managed to get him into the minimum security camp and that his roommate had been an elderly 'white collar' criminal. Like himself.

But it had still been a prison. He'd still been locked away, his liberty taken from him.

Elena followed him inside, through the galley and into the living room, her head turning in all directions. She stood at the walled window that overlooked Central Park. 'This must have cost you a fortune.'

'It did.' Manhattan prices were extortionate by anyone's standards. Of all his properties this had cost him the most. He would pay it tenfold. New York had an energy to it he'd never found anywhere else, and here he was only an hour from his mother.

'Come, I'll show you around.'

With obvious reluctance, she stepped away from the window and followed him back into the galley.

'Kitchen,' he said, throwing open the door on the other side of the elevator. 'My housekeepers have the weekend off so you'll be able to settle in with privacy, but this is normally Michael and Lisa's domain. That room through there is their staff room.'

'You cook?' she asked.

'Badly. You?'

'Badly.'

Their eyes met and for a moment he was certain her lips were trying to smile.

'I've made reservations at Ramones for us, so we won't starve in their absence.'

'We're eating out tonight?'

'The sooner we're seen in public, the better. Ramones is the perfect place—there's always a paparazzo camped there.'

'I should call my father.'

'Call him tomorrow.'

'I don't want him to see the pictures before I've told him about…us.'

'You decided to take a last-minute trip to New York. We bumped into each other and decided to go for a meal to bury the hatchet,' he said, reminding her of the agreed script they had come to after signing the contract. 'You can tell him this tomorrow.'

'I can't believe I'm going to lie to my own father.'

'This has to be believable, Elena. Any hint that what we have isn't real then the deal is off and I take the evidence to the FBI.'

He led her out of the kitchen and back into the galley, ignoring the laser burn of her glare in his back.

'Guest room, guest room, guest room…our room.' He stepped inside and opened a door. 'En suite.' He opened another. 'My dressing room.' And another. 'Your dressing room.'

Elena peered inside and nodded, but didn't say anything.

'I'm going to take a shower. All the guest rooms have their own en suites if you want to freshen up. I'm afraid when I bought this property it wasn't with a future wife in mind or I would have had adjoining en suites put in. Can you be ready to leave in a couple of hours?'

She nodded curtly.

'Good. If you need anything, let me know.'

Her green eyes met his. 'The only thing I need is for you to admit you were wrong about me and wrong about my father and let me go.'

'You were right—you do have a warped sense of humour.'

Elena got ready in the guest room the furthest from the master suite, trying not to imagine that Gabriele was, at that very moment, naked in the shower.

Surely, any minute now, she would awake on her Oslo office sofa and find the past couple of days had been nothing but a bad dream.

She'd been tied up and threatened with kidnapping and, worse, rescued by the man who hated her entire family. She'd been forced to sign a contract for a marriage that would save her father from prison but would result in a baby, and been installed in a luxury Manhattan apartment. All in twenty-four hours.

Who knew what tomorrow would bring? Maybe she would wake up on the moon.

She was ready before Gabriele and took the opportunity to explore his apartment further.

Having grown up with wealth, she wasn't fazed by its opulence but had to admit he had exquisite taste. The high ceilings and floor-to-ceiling windows cried out for majestic furniture to match and he had stepped up to the mark. White walls, thick cream carpets her toes sank into and plush soft brown leather sofas that managed to be exquisite and comfortable all at the same time…it was like being in a homely art gallery with some very surreal paintings.

One particular framed painting caught her eye, a portrait of a man whose features were, upon closer inspection, painted entirely with fruits and vegetables; a pear for a nose, mange tout for the upper eyelids…and was that a husk of corn used as an ear…?

'Do you like it?'

So absorbed had she been in the painting that she hadn't heard Gabriele enter the room.

'It's brilliant. Is it a Giuseppe Arcimboldo?'

'You recognise it?' There was an approving tone in his voice.

She nodded. 'I love his work. It's mad and witty and so clever. I could look at it for hours.'

'This is only a reproduction but my home in Florence has a couple of his original pieces.'

A tiny shiver traced up her spine at the mention of Florence. Italy was her home. It was where Gabriele was from. Their respective families' lives had been turned into a soap opera there and she dreaded the reception that news of their marriage would bring in their home country.

'Are you going to change?' he asked. 'We need to leave soon.'

'I *have* changed.'

'You're not intending to go out like that?' The approval had gone.

Turning her gaze from the painting, she looked at him and saw disbelief on his face.

'What's wrong with it?' Having only packed for the weekend, she'd opted for the clothes she'd intended to travel back to Europe in: a navy-blue trouser suit with a high-necked white blouse and a pair of flat black shoes.

'You look like you're going to a business meeting. Have you anything else to wear? Anything remotely feminine?'

Bristling, she scowled. 'This is what I feel comfortable in. All my clothes are the same—trouser suits.'

'And when you're not working?'

She shrugged. 'Clothes don't interest me.'

'They do now,' he stated grimly. 'Stand still a minute.'

Burning under the weight of his scrutiny, she nonetheless held her head high, wondering what the big deal was. Clothes were clothes. They were worn to protect you from the elements and, in a business environment, to convey a professional approach. Everything else was superfluous.

'Untuck your blouse,' he ordered.

She did as he said, wondering what he was thinking.

'Now tie it into a knot around your waist.'

At her puzzled look, he sighed and reached for the base of her blouse, undoing the bottom two buttons.

'What are you doing?' she demanded, stepping back, unnerved.

'Unsmartening you. Now tie it into a knot and undo the top three buttons—unless you want me to do it for you?'

'Touch me again and I'll punch you in the nose.'

He raised his eyebrows but his tone remained civil. 'We're going out in public in a few minutes. You have to be comfortable with my touch if we're going to convince your father and the world that we've fallen madly in love.'

'I doubt a decade of marriage would make me comfortable with a man who wants to destroy my family.' And he absolutely could destroy them. It was the only reason she stood there taking this humiliation.

'Fake it.'

As he was looming so threateningly over her, she quickly did as he bid. Feeling like a complete fool, she unbuttoned her blouse. 'Anything else you want me to do? Get a face transplant?'

'You could do with a damn good haircut but seeing as we don't have time for that either tie it into a knot or wear it down. Ponytails are for schoolgirls. And tug your trousers down so they sit on your hips and not around your belly button.'

When she was done and had retied her hair into his requested knot, she put her hands on her hips. 'Am I presentable now?'

'Roll your trousers up a couple of inches.'

If she glared at him any more there was a good chance the wind would change direction and her face would stay that way.

Crouching down, she rolled her trousers up so they hung above her ankles.

'Have you any other shoes?' he asked when she was upright again.

'I have a pair of running shoes.'

He pulled a face. 'Then you will have to do as you are but first thing in the morning, we're going clothes shopping.'

'You do not get to choose my wardrobe.'

'I wouldn't think it necessary if you didn't have such dire taste. You dress like a straitjacketed man.'

'I do not.'

'You don't dress like a woman. Personally I couldn't care less what you wear,' he continued, speaking over her indignant yelp of protest, 'but the fact is you're supposed to be a woman in love. Women in love take pride in their appearance and the clothes they wear.'

'Do they?'

'They do.' A look of suspicion crossed his features. When he next spoke, it was with a hint of hesitation. 'You *have* been in a relationship before?'

'I'm twenty-five,' she scoffed, evading the question, damned if she was going to admit she hadn't even been on a date before. It was none of his business.

Even if she had been so inclined, there hadn't been any chance of boyfriends growing up, what with a solo education and three ready-made chaperones in the form of her brothers. By the time she was old enough to ditch the chaperones, she'd sworn off men for life. She knew everything there was to know about them and how they and their friends treated the women in their lives and spoke behind their backs. They were pigs. All men were.

Maybe she was being unkind to pigs.

'If I don't feel comfortable in what I'm wearing it will be harder for me to pretend to be in love,' she pointed out.

She was glad she'd thought of her brothers and the idiots they called friends. If she pretended Gabriele was one of them she could handle him without any problem whatsoever. *They* didn't unnerve her or threaten to overwhelm her with their latent masculinity as Gabriele did.

'You can choose your clothes but you *will* burn your existing wardrobe.'

'I'll put it in storage for the day we go our separate ways.'

'You know what you'll have to do to make that day come closer.'

More colour crept over her face but she didn't drop her gaze. 'Or maybe you'll get so sick of living with me that *you* end it before a baby's conceived.'

He shrugged a hefty shoulder and leaned forward, his eyes drilling into her. 'I spent two years in prison for a crime I didn't commit. In that time my father died and my mother's health deteriorated. Every day we spend together is another day of purgatory for your father. I have no time limit.'

For the first time a whisper of doubt blew at her.

Could he be telling the truth?

She discounted it as soon as she thought it. Her brothers might be pigs but her father was nothing like them. Her father would never have set Alfredo up. They'd been lifelong *friends*.

All the same, an unsettled feeling lay in her as they left the apartment a short while later, quite unlike the nausea she felt at the deal she was striking with the devil himself.

CHAPTER FIVE

RAMONES WAS A tiny restaurant in Times Square, bursting to the brim with diners. As Gabriele had promised, the paparazzi were stationed outside.

Once inside, Elena understood why.

'Is that Gary Milwake?' she whispered as they were led past a couple chatting happily in a booth by the window.

'It is,' he confirmed. 'And that's Serafina de Angelo with him.'

Gary Milwake was the breakthrough movie star of the year, his dining partner the star of the biggest-selling box set of the decade.

'They're waving at you.' She tried not to screech.

'That's because Gary's an acquaintance. He drove a Mantegna supercar in *The Long Drive By*. I took him for his original test drive.'

She took her seat, trying in vain not to look too excited at all the other familiar faces. While Gabriele ordered a bottle of wine for them, she couldn't stop herself staring. There was a pop star dining with a man who she didn't recognise but was definitely not the man she was reported to be dating, and she said as much.

'Eating here guarantees publicity,' Gabriele said, opening his menu. 'Tomorrow the Internet will be abuzz with gossip about her. That's all that matters—publicity.'

She wrinkled her nose. 'How sordid.'

He shrugged. 'It's business for them. Column inches matter. Now stop staring at everyone and look adoringly at me.'

'If this is our first date then I wouldn't look at you adoringly,' she contradicted, speaking off the top of her head.

Never mind looking at him with adoration, every time she looked at him she felt a snake uncoil itself within her and want to launch at him. 'This is the evening we play "getting to know you".'

'A fair point. However, even on a first date people who are attracted to each other lean in closely together and speak intimately. They do not spend their time star spotting.'

She smiled and tried fluttering her eyelashes. 'I've never met a star before.'

'Your family has always mingled with celebrities. And you look like you have something in your eye.'

'I'm trying to look adoring.'

'Just lean towards me and remember, whatever you say, say it with a smile on your face.'

She rested her arms on the table and leaned closer to the face she found more handsome every time she looked. Smiling brightly, she said, 'Is that better, you savage bastard?'

Mimicking her actions and with a full-wattage beam, he replied, 'It's a start, you poisonous viper.'

'Is that the best you can do? My brothers have much better derogatory names for me than that.'

'They've had many more years of practice. Look at *me*,' he added when her attention was taken by another passing film star.

'Sorry.'

'How can you be so star struck when your family have partied with celebrities for years?'

'My father and my brothers have. You forget, I run the European division. I have nothing to do with what happens in the US and the rest of the world.'

'By choice?'

'I started off working in Rome then gradually progressed to take over Italy, then the rest of Europe.'

'Nepotism at its finest.'

'That's rich coming from a man who took the same route through *his* family firm.'

'The difference is I've enhanced what we already had. When I joined Mantegna Cars we had a turnover of half a billion dollars. Within five years of me joining that figure had tripled because of the diversifications I put in to trade on our name.'

Her smile dropped a fraction as she tried to think of what she'd personally done to enhance her division and boost Ricci Components' profits. Nothing sprang to mind.

'Now we are one of the top car manufacturers in the world,' he continued, 'even with the battering we took at the hands of your father's fraud and lies.'

She couldn't stop the glare from forming and had to fight hard to paste another smile on her face.

Thankfully, the waiter returned with their wine. After a glass had been poured for them both and they'd given their food orders, Gabriele raised his glass to her.

'To the start of a wonderful new relationship and to the best of nepotism.'

She chinked hers to it and smiled as she said, 'And here's to revenge, which everyone knows is best served cold.'

'I prefer my revenge to be scalding hot but cold serves my needs equally well.'

With mutual antipathy, they both sipped their drinks, both smiling, both firing ice and loathing from their eyes.

As a way to toast their new relationship, Elena thought it very apt.

Gabriele surprised himself by enjoying their meal out. There had been more than a few occasions when he had laughed out loud at the barbs coming from Elena's tongue, all of them dressed with a sweet smile.

Now they were back at his apartment and the slight relaxing of her demeanour in the restaurant might never have been. Elena was back to being as tight as a coiled spring. She'd even stopped throwing barbs at him.

As soon as they'd left the car, thanked his driver, and taken the lift to his apartment and were alone for the first time since leaving, she'd turned to him.

'I'm not sharing a bed with you tonight. The contract stated we share a bed and...' her cheeks turned scarlet but she carried on regardless '...and, do what needs to be done when we're married. We're not married yet. Your house-keepers have the weekend off so there is no one for us to convince of our blossoming romance.'

'They will know if a guest bed has been slept in.'

'I don't care. Not everyone jumps into bed on a first date. They'll assume one of us has some morals.'

He arched a brow. 'Meaning?'

'Meaning they work for *you* so it's doubtful they associate morals with you or the people you call friends. You're a convicted criminal, remember?'

'Are you deliberately trying to anger me?' he asked slowly, holding onto his temper by a whisker.

'What, by speaking the truth? Oh, sorry, I forgot, you believe *my father* to be the criminal.'

Gabriele silently counted to ten, breathing heavily as he did so, staring at this woman who dared speak to him of morals when she came from a family of conscience-less snakes.

She didn't drop her stare, holding her ground with a raised chin and a pursed mouth.

Only her eyes showed vulnerability. It was there, ringing out from them, mingled with the defiance and it tempered the fury that had shot through him.

There was no room in this relationship for pity but as much as he didn't want to put himself in her shoes he could understand why she would feel vulnerable.

'Tonight you can sleep in a guest room,' he agreed, rolling his neck to loosen the knots that had formed in it. 'It's been a long day for both of us. But from tomorrow you sleep with me.'

'There will be no *sex*...' she spat the word as if it were an oath '...until we're married.'

He gave a slow, deliberate smile. 'Which is only three days away. Three days until you're Mrs Mantegna and welcome me into the warmth of your delightful body with open arms.'

'Welcoming? I think not.'

'You expect me to believe that when I've seen the way you undress me with your eyes? Admit it, there's an attraction between us. Inexplicable, I admit, but there all the same.'

Her cheeks flamed with colour, letting him know he'd scored a direct hit.

When he'd made the demand that she have his baby it had been a logical progression to his thoughts on marrying her. He wanted a child but he didn't want the commitment to a woman that went with it. To his mind, Elena having his child was the perfect solution. It would make his revenge on her father almost complete—until he found the evidence to clear his name it would *never* be complete—and give him the heir he so wanted.

She was dressed in the most hideous outfit he'd ever seen on a woman, even with the improvements he'd made to it. But still his imagination ran amok wondering what lay beneath; the image of her naked bottom never far from his thoughts. All that, and the way she fought fire with fire... it all conspired to make his loins tighten in a way he'd almost forgotten.

Elena Ricci was the complete reverse of what he usually found attractive in a woman but there was something about her his senses responded to.

She stared at him, her eyes flashing, but then gave a slow, deliberate smile of her own. 'The only thing I will welcome is the blow to your ego every time you remember that you could only have me by blackmail.'

'Then I will be sure to take extra special enjoyment every time I make you come.'

Colour heightened not only her face but her neck too.

'You're crude and you are not a gentleman.' Turning on her heel, she marched from the living room, saying over her shoulder, 'I'm going to bed. Goodnight. Hope the bed-bugs bite.'

'Elena,' he called after her.

'What?'

'Next time you try and rouse my anger to keep me out of your bed, know your efforts will be wasted. Any more excuses and I rip our contract up and throw your entire family to the wolves.'

She left the living room without looking back.

Elena awoke early after a night of fitful sleep, rising shortly after the sun.

With nothing but a pair of pyjamas on, she padded to the kitchen in search of coffee only to find Gabriele had beaten her to it, already showered, shaved and dressed. He'd even been out and bought bagels for them both.

'Bagels, for breakfast?' she mumbled, shuffling onto a chair at the kitchen table, feeling awkward with her sleep-crumpled face and mussed hair.

'You don't visit New York often?'

She shook her head and opened the box hers was in. 'This is only my second time here.'

He stared at her, making her feel even more self-conscious. When he looked at her like that it felt as if he were trying to pry open her thoughts.

No one had ever looked at her like that before.

After a long bout of silence broken only by her nibbling as quietly as she could at the bacon and cream cheese bagel, which turned out to be delicious, she excused herself to take a shower.

'We'll make a move when you're ready,' he said to her retreating figure. 'We're going to get you a new wardrobe and have you made over. I've booked you in with a stylist.'

'You're not going to police my purchases?'

'No. Your stylist will guide you in selecting clothes you feel comfortable in. I'm going to the office.'

'It's Sunday.' Even she, a self-admitted workaholic, didn't go to the office on a Sunday. That didn't mean she didn't work on the supposed day of rest, only that she didn't expect anyone else to.

'We've a busy time coming up,' he answered with a shrug. 'There's some stuff I need to get done before we head off to Florence and I won't have many opportunities after today.'

Two hours later, they entered an exclusive store on Fifth Avenue.

Having had such a rubbish night's sleep, Elena was well aware of how drained she looked. Even her hair, thin as it was at the best of times, was lank.

When the stylist, a tall, immaculately dressed woman in her forties, strode towards her with an outstretched hand, she felt even more conspicuous.

Gabriele greeted her as if she were an old friend, kissing her on each cheek.

'I will leave you in Liana's capable hands, *tesoro*,' he said to Elena, his tone affectionate.

Had he brought other women here?

The strange pang that twisted her stomach was smothered when he caught her off guard, wrapping his arms around her and placing a brief kiss to her lips.

The briefest of kisses. Tiny. Insubstantial. And yet enough to set her heart fluttering.

He pulled away, rubbing her arms for good measure.

'My phone will be on if you need me, otherwise, if I don't hear from you I'll pick you up at four.'

Too shell-shocked by the unexpected heat of his mouth on hers and his fruity, masculine scent playing in her senses to respond with anything but a weak, 'Okay,' she watched him stroll out, her eyes drifting to the tight buttocks wrapped in a pair of snug-fitting black jeans, which also emphasised the length and muscularity of his thighs.

She dug the nail of her middle finger into the flesh of her thumb.

That was what happened when you didn't get a good night's sleep. Your body reacted in unpredictable ways when the monster you were being forced to marry kissed you.

It was only because she hadn't been prepared for it. Next time she would be, and would bite his lip for good measure.

Liana bore her off to an elevator, asking questions about her taste in music and books and films that sounded innocuous but which Elena was certain had meaning. The stylist was trying to figure her out.

Before they'd reached the floor they were heading to, she could hold it back no longer. 'Have you dressed many of Gabriele's lady friends?'

'He brought his mother here at Christmas.' Liana used such a sympathetic tone that a ripple of unease ran through her, making Elena wonder what it was about Gabriele's mother that elicited such a tone.

When they reached the intended floor, Liana knew exactly where she wanted to take her.

Following in her wake, she passed two women, one of whom was holding a small baby.

She turned back for a second look, her heart thundering.

She was going to have one. She was going to have a baby.

The one thing she had never allowed herself to dream of having.

But to get one she would have to have sex with Gabriele.
God help her.

And God help her that a thrill of heat pooled in her abdomen every time she imagined it.

Liana whisked her into a private dressing room and brought armfuls of clothes in a steady stream, from elegant business outfits to cocktail dresses, to everything in between.

Although reluctant to try them on, feeling that to do so would in itself be a victory for Gabriele, to her surprise Elena soon found she was enjoying herself. Even more surprisingly, the clothes Liana selected were items she would have chosen for herself if she'd ever given it more than a few seconds' thought. Nothing too girly, which she would have rejected on the spot, yet definitely feminine.

The only time she truly wanted to put her foot down was when Liana measured her bra size and brought in sexy little items of lingerie. She could hardly say, 'No thank you, it would be a waste as I couldn't care less what Gabriele thinks of my underwear,' because that hardly fitted the image of a woman newly in love. Elena did manage to dissuade the stylist from checking the fit of them for herself, which she considered to be a personal victory.

Left alone with a pile of bras, she gazed at her reflection in the three full-length mirrors. And gazed again.

She looked different. And all she'd done was try on some clothes.

Peering closer, she studied her face, certain something had changed.

Her skin appeared to glow. Her eyes seemed brighter, the green more vivid. Her lips looked fuller.

It had to be the lighting, she told herself, slipping one of the bras on. The owners must have done it to enhance their customers' reflections.

But even her breasts looked fuller, the lacy bra pushing them up and giving her an actual cleavage. Giving her shape.

She couldn't help her mind from flitting, as it had done seemingly every minute since they'd made their agreement, to being in bed with Gabriele.

The thought *terrified* her.

It should repulse her too. After everything he was doing, everything he was demanding, the thought of sharing a bed with him should have her crammed full of revulsion.

The butterflies in her belly shouldn't feel like the flutters of excitement.

An image drifted into her mind of Gabriele peeling the bra from her body...

She shouldn't have these thoughts. Not of him.

When she gave him her body it would be with the minimum of interaction on her part. She would do what she had to do and nothing more. She would not enjoy it.

Her phone went off, a distraction she welcomed until she clicked on the link Gabriele had emailed to her.

A picture of them outside Ramones had been published online. Elena had been dubbed 'The Convicted Italian Stallion's Mystery Date'.

The first seeds of them as a couple had been planted.

Her identity would be revealed sooner rather than later. Her profile in America was non-existent but all it would take was one Italian to read the article and the world would know who she was.

She'd have to phone her dad as soon as they got back to Gabriele's apartment, a thought that made her already tender stomach lurch some more.

There was no time to worry about it though, as it was time for her makeover. Liana gently persuaded her to change into one of her new outfits rather than slip back into her boyish shorts and T-shirt.

In the beauty department she was taken into a private room. There, a flamboyant man named Adrian, who had the most perfectly plucked eyebrows, sat her onto a high stool and studied her face.

'Your eyes!' he exclaimed. 'They are to die for. And your lips…are they natural?'

At her puzzled expression he said, 'No fillers?'

'No.'

'No work at all?'

'No.'

He sighed. 'A natural beauty. Your face is a blank canvas for me to enhance. But first…' He lifted the lank strands of her hair. 'First we do something to this.'

For the next hour her hair was washed, snipped and dried by yet another stylist, all the while Adrian and Liana chatted to her and plied her with coffee. They refused to let her see the end result, Adrian explaining that they 'wanted her to see the whole effect in one go'.

As he got to work on her face, he gently gave details of what he was doing so she could replicate it for herself.

When he was done, he took her hand and helped her down, then led her to a floor-length mirror so she could see the final results.

'What do you think?' he asked, smiling widely.

As she gazed at her reflection, a lump formed in her throat.

It was her but…not.

Her hair had never looked so voluminous. The severe fringe she chopped herself when it got too long had been feathered. Layers had been cut into the length, which still fell across her shoulders, but instead of just hanging there now became a frame for a face that belonged to her but one she had never seen before.

Far from making her look like a clown as she had feared, Adrian's makeover was surprisingly understated.

Her eyes, darkened around the rims, gleamed, the black mascara making them appear rounder. Her cheeks had a subtle hint of blush on them, defining her bone structure.

Peach lipstick had been applied that made her naturally full lips look even plumper.

It was hard to believe...

'Is that really me?' she whispered, her eyes filling. She'd never imagined she could look so feminine. She'd never imagined she could *feel* so feminine. Not her, the little tomboy.

Adrian put an arm around her and hugged her to him. 'Don't cry. If you don't like it we can take it off and try another—'

'No,' she cut him off with a choked laugh. 'I *do* like it. I love it. You're a miracle worker. All of you.'

He shook his head. 'Elena, you are exquisite. Now promise me one thing.'

'If I can.'

'Always use blush.'

Laughing, she threw her arms around him. 'Thank you.'

Bags of cosmetics and face creams had been packaged for her, along with her new wardrobe of clothes. Her shopping trip was over and it was time to pay the bill.

Elena got her credit card out.

Liana shook her head. 'Mr Mantegna has made arrangements to pay.'

About to protest—after all, she was an independent woman, no matter what charge of nepotism Gabriele laid at her door—she had a nice vision of Gabriele receiving the bill. *He* was the one who insisted she get remodelled. *He* could foot it.

And speaking of *he*...

Now it was time to face him.

The heels of the ankle boots she wore gave her a lift in more sense than one. Never mind being two inches taller, she found she held herself taller too as she strode through the main beauty floor with Liana at her side. She didn't know if she was imagining it but she could feel eyes upon her and had to force herself not to stare at the floor in embarrassment. People *never* looked twice at her.

'One more thing,' Liana said suddenly, coming to a halt by the sunglasses section. She considered them for a while before going behind the counter and handing Elena a Cartier box. 'For when you have to deal with the paparazzi,' she said with a knowing smile.

Elena thanked her and put the box in one of the bags containing the cosmetics she was already looking forward to experimenting with.

As much as she told herself that she couldn't care less what Gabriele thought of her makeover, her heart galloped when Liana opened the door to the private waiting room and Gabriele looked up from the laptop he was working on.

His brown-black eyes widened, and he half rose, the laptop almost falling onto the floor in the process.

After six hours in the department store, Gabriele had been prepared for Elena to come out looking better than she had before. After all, she could hardly present herself any worse. He would have had to be blind not to see her innate prettiness, even though she clearly couldn't be bothered to do anything with it, but nothing could have prepared him for the beauty that walked into the room.

Dio, it was like one of those before and after television programmes his mother had liked to watch.

A pair of tight pale blue jeans that came halfway up her calves was topped with a long shimmering silver off-the-shoulder top under which were the straps of a purple bra. The clothes themselves were nothing to shout about but put together with clever plum costume jewellery, black ankle boots and a haircut that screamed *just got out of bed* without having actually just got out of bed...

It was still Elena the tomboy, but with a very sexy, feminine difference.

The pretty shell had been burst open and the intrinsic beauty had emerged.

This was the sexy, beautiful woman he would be marrying in two days.

Aware of Elena and Liana both waiting expectantly for his reaction, he closed his laptop and got to his feet.

'*Tesoro*, you look wonderful,' he said. 'Did you have a good day?'

'Lovely thank you,' she replied with a sweet smile that didn't fool him for a second.

'You deserve it, you work so hard.'

After satisfying himself that all her purchases were being sent to his apartment, Gabriele led Elena out of the store and to his waiting car at the back.

Once they were settled and the driver was making his way through the heavy Manhattan traffic, Gabriele twisted round to look again at Elena.

The unexpected but very welcome news he'd received that afternoon that a senior member of Ignazio's closest team could possibly be bought now took second place to the woman beside him.

Her cheeks were flushed, her eyes bright and there was an air about her he couldn't put his finger on.

'You did enjoy it,' he stated shrewdly. Now they were alone they could go back to being honest with each other.

'Yes,' she admitted. 'I hadn't realised shopping could be fun.'

'How do you normally buy clothes?'

'I dive in and out of the shop and hope whatever I've chosen fits.'

'You're the only daughter from a family with three sons. Why weren't you dressed as a princess?'

She shrugged. 'I always wanted to be a boy like my brothers. I hated that being a girl made me different.'

'Why did it make you different?'

She pulled a face that conveyed she thought he was an idiot for asking.

'I don't have siblings,' he reminded her. 'All my cousins

are boys. Those kind of family dynamics are not something I've experienced.'

'Girls are considered more delicate than boys. Weaker. More prone to tears.'

He considered this. 'I think the tears thing is true…'

She sucked in an outraged breath.

'But as for being more delicate, that's bull,' he finished. 'Women *are* different from men, that's a biological fact but the kind of delicacy you're talking about doesn't exist.'

'I know that. I've spent my entire life proving it.'

'How? By acting like a man?'

'How else could I be taken seriously?' she demanded. 'The only way I was able to gain my brothers' respect was by being one of the boys.'

'So it wasn't through choice?'

'I *wanted* to be like them. I didn't know how to be a girl and had no interest in learning.'

'Do you think it would have made any difference if your mother had lived and been there to guide you?'

Her eyes met his. 'I wouldn't know. I don't remember her.'

'That's a real shame,' he eventually replied, remembering the Swedish woman who'd always had a ready smile on her face and a batch of meatballs on the go. Elena could only have been two when she died. 'She was a nice woman.'

Her brows drew together. 'You knew her?'

'Of course. Our families were friends. Our mothers were very close.'

'I didn't know that.' A burst of fire sparked in her eyes and she leaned towards him fiercely. 'If they were such good friends I would imagine your mother will be very disappointed with you when she learns that you're forcing me to marry you.'

'We will never know. She has dementia. My father's death accelerated the process. There are days she doesn't even know who I am.' Something else he absolutely blamed her father for and, by extension, Elena herself.

Her latent beauty might now have pushed to the surface but that was all it was: surface.

Beneath the skin she was a Ricci to her core and he would never allow himself to forget it.

CHAPTER SIX

ELENA WAS MIGHTILY relieved to go straight to her father's voicemail.

'Hi, Papà, it's me. I'm in New York, finally taking that holiday you keep nagging me about.' She injected a false laugh, meeting Gabriele's eye.

He was watching her from the dining room table, his expression inscrutable.

'You'll never believe who I bumped into last night—Alfredo Mantegna's son.' She cleared her throat before ploughing on. 'I've decided to stay in New York for the week and do some sightseeing. Christie will be running things for me. Hope you're well. *Ciao.*'

Done, she disconnected the call, then, for good measure, turned the phone off and stuffed it in her favourite of the designer handbags Liana had selected for her, then faced him with her chin up.

'Well? Was that convincing enough?'

'On a scale of one to ten I'd give it a five,' he drawled, rising to his feet. 'Let's see how you perform this evening—see if we can get it to an eight.'

Tonight they were going to dine at another paparazzi-encamped restaurant, a thought that thrilled her as much as swimming in a shark-infested pool. Since their return from shopping, she'd checked the Internet a dozen times to see if her name was out there but so far, nothing.

Throwing him a brittle smile, which more than spoke the caustic response she wanted to give, Elena slung her handbag over her shoulder and headed to the elevator.

Inside, she surreptitiously checked her appearance.

She was pleased to see the magic Adrian had done to her

face was mostly still intact. Scared of damaging his work, all she'd done for their evening out was apply some more of the lipstick she had taken the lid off a dozen times to smell—who knew cosmetics smelt so good?—and spritzed some perfume onto her neck and wrists. She'd changed out of the jeans into a pair of bright red straight-legged trousers and a pair of silver sandals with a low pointy heel, but had opted to keep on the shimmering top she loved so much.

Gabriele's only remark had been to say, 'That is a definite improvement on last night.'

Except the look in his eyes had said something else.

For the first time she wished she had some experience with men, something that would allow her to translate Gabriele's unspoken expressions. All she had was gut instinct but that was becoming unreliable. All she felt when he looked at her was a feeling she couldn't quite interpret but which she was terrified meant nothing but trouble.

Her response had been a glare and a, 'I'm delighted I meet your approval.'

She didn't believe for a second that he was attracted to her.

All Gabriele wanted was what she could give him. He wanted her body. Not her core. Not her soul. He wanted Ignazio's daughter. If she'd had sisters, any of them would have served his purpose equally well.

Now, catching his eye in the mirror, she quickly looked away, but not before she caught the expression she'd seen earlier, when she'd been presented to him like a fully made-over doll.

That strange feeling stirred in her stomach again.

He doesn't want you.

And neither did she want him. She could never want someone so cruel.

When they reached the ground floor, he turned to her. 'Ready?'

'No.'

'Good.' Smiling broadly, he took her hand and led her out into the Manhattan night for the second time.

Her pulse kicked into life.

This was the first time he'd properly touched her skin other than that fleeting kiss earlier.

His hand was enormous, swallowing hers like a giant paw.

His driver was ready for them.

Thankful to be able to shake her hand out of Gabriele's so she could get into the open back door, she sat down and pressed her hands between her thighs, wiping away the moisture that had sprung on her palms.

They rode in silence, the darkened glass dividing them from his driver meaning they didn't have to fake conversation or adoration.

Traffic was lighter than the night before but it still took them twenty minutes to arrive at the restaurant Gabriele had chosen for them.

The second the driver opened her door, Elena knew her identity had been discovered.

Lights flashed in her face, blinding her with their brilliance.

Gabriele took charge, getting out first and marching through the waiting paparazzi, to take her hand. Placing a protective arm around her waist, he led her inside.

Totally unprepared for a siege, she shrank into him, horrified at such behaviour and the shouts being called out as the horde yelled questions about their relationship.

They were led straight to their table. When they were sitting down and facing each other, she was astonished to see a look of satisfaction on Gabriele's face.

'You *enjoyed* that?' she asked.

His eyes gleamed but there was a fury contained within them.

'I've dealt with much worse. And their presence here— they were waiting for us, in case you hadn't realised—guarantees that your father will have his morning coffee seeing pictures of you held in my arms.'

It was at that precise moment she understood Gabriele genuinely believed her father had set Alfredo up.

The hate he had for her family was built, at least in his own mind, on solid foundations.

He'd taken the rap to protect Alfredo but could not allow himself to believe in his father's guilt. He was in denial. Rather than accept the truth he'd pointed the finger at her father.

Which meant that Gabriele himself was innocent of the crimes he'd spent two years in prison for.

Was it possible he was right about Alfredo's innocence too…?

No, she couldn't believe that. Because that would mean he was right about her own father and she just could not believe her father would commit fraud and set his oldest friend up to take the fall.

She wasn't naïve enough to think her father had never cut corners in his life but what Gabriele was accusing him of?

No. It just couldn't be.

'Elena?'

His voice broke her out of her trance.

He leaned forward and murmured, 'Adoration, *tesoro*, adoration.'

Taking a deep breath to clear the unwarranted thoughts, she rested her chin on her hand and gazed at him.

And, as she stared into those soulful dark eyes, she couldn't help but think that should he be anyone other than he was—a vengeful blackmailer—looking at him with adoration would be no hardship at all.

Elena had been locked in the bathroom for so long Gabriele wondered if she'd drowned in the shower.

He had to give it to her; she'd performed admirably that night.

All evening she'd kept her eyes on his, fluttering her lashes, laughing and smiling. She'd even managed not to flinch too overtly whenever he'd taken her hand. No other diner in the restaurant would be in any doubt that they were a couple very much enjoying each other's company.

When Elena finally came out of the bathroom he wasn't surprised to find her wearing her oversized pyjamas rather than the sexy sleepwear Liana had selected for her and which she'd put away in her dressing room earlier with her other purchases.

'Do you have a preference to which side you like to sleep?' he asked from his vantage point in the middle of the bed.

She shook her head, shuffling with obvious trepidation to him.

'I'll take the right side, then.' He moved over.

Gingerly, she lifted the sheets and climbed in. As she did so he caught a whiff of minty toothpaste and a delicate floral scent.

There was an immediate thickening of his blood. And a thickening of another part of his anatomy.

She turned her back to him and burrowed under the sheets so only the top of her white-blonde hair showed.

Gabriele switched the bedside light off, plunging the room into darkness.

He gazed up at the ceiling, a hand resting above his head, and tried to empty his mind of clutter and not pay too much attention to the fact that Elena lay beside him.

Soon the stiffness in his loins would subside.

These were natural reactions for a man to have.

Sharing a bed with a pretty woman, even one clad in the most disgusting nightclothes he'd ever had the misfortune to see, would be enough to make any man hard, especially when that man had been celibate for the best part of four years.

After Sophia had ended their engagement, he'd smarted for a while but had been too caught up in the legal battle to allow himself to dwell on it for any length of time. Prison itself had been about getting through each day. Even with his work detail he'd had plenty of time to think and all that thinking had been spent on one thing—revenge. Sophia had hardly crossed his mind.

Since his release, the part of his brain not plotting his revenge had been spent rebuilding his and Mantegna Cars' reputation. This rebuilding would culminate in the car being launched to honour his father's memory. There simply hadn't been the space for a woman, not in any capacity.

So it was no wonder that lying in the dark next to Elena had made his libido jump-start itself.

They were on the front page of every major paper in the US and Europe.

The Burying of the Hatchet? screamed the most common variety of headline.

They were also the headliners of all the major news outlets on the Web and the top trending story on social media. The picture most commonly used in them had Gabriele's arm wrapped protectively around her and Elena's head resting against his chest.

While she'd been sleeping, her phone, put on silent for the night, had gone berserk. She awoke to eleven missed calls from her father and brothers. All their texts and emails were variants of 'call me now'.

There were also dozens of messages and missed calls from journalists and bloggers wanting comments on her relationship with Gabriele.

She couldn't bring herself to listen to the voicemails.

Turning her phone off, she climbed out of the empty bed

and headed to the bathroom, splashing some water on her face and brushing her teeth.

As with the day before, Gabriele was already showered and dressed. She found him in the dining room sipping a cup of coffee. He was casually dressed again, wearing black chinos and a grey T-shirt under an unbuttoned checked shirt with the sleeves rolled up.

An empty plate had been pushed to one side, half a dozen newspapers strewn before him.

'Good morning, *tesoro*.' He rose to his feet, a smile playing on his lips, one she was coming to recognise as the smile of satisfaction he gave when he was pleased with a plan coming to fruition.

To her shock, he stepped to her, pulled her into his arms and briefly covered her mouth with his own.

She reared her head back but couldn't break free from his hold. 'What are…?'

'We have company,' he interrupted in a low voice, dragging his lips across her cheek and dipping into her neck, his hand rubbing across her back.

'Come, have some breakfast,' he said in a normal tone, pulling the seat out from beside his own and virtually pressing her into it.

It was then that she saw the small man standing at the door separating the dining room from the kitchen.

'Michael, this is Elena,' Gabriele said by way of introduction, smiling affectionately at her as he took her stiff hand in his.

Michael bustled into the room, beaming widely. 'It's a pleasure to meet you, Miss Ricci.' He spoke with a strong New York drawl. 'What can I get you for breakfast?'

'Erm…'

'I can recommend his poached eggs.' Gabriele smoothed a strand of hair away from her cheek.

As soon as Michael had disappeared back into the kitchen, Elena snatched her hand from Gabriele's hold.

'There was no need for that,' she hissed.

'There was every need,' he answered, taking her hand back. 'You are like a cat on hot coals around me. We're going to the city clerk's office later to arrange our wedding licence. Tomorrow we marry. You need to be comfortable with me holding you and touching you.'

'I did all that last night,' she said indignantly, though making an effort to keep her voice down.

'No, you made a start last night,' he corrected. 'You were as stiff as a board under my touch but anyone would excuse that because of the paparazzi's presence. When we see the clerk, you have to keep in mind they deal with couples in love all the time. They will know a fake when they see it.'

'I am *trying*.'

'And I'm going to help you.'

'How?'

'By kissing you. Properly.'

Any objection she would have made was swept away when he placed his giant palms to her cheeks and brought his mouth to hers.

The couple of times he'd kissed her before had been the briefest of touches, a flash of warmth and then done, leaving nothing but the faintest impression on her lips and a trace of his masculine body heat.

This time...

His lips caressed hers, moving softly. His long fingers traced her cheeks then spread out to thread into her hair and massage into her scalp.

Gently but authoritatively his tongue slid out to probe and caress her lips, which were still clamped tightly together.

But she was fighting a losing battle.

As hard as she tried to keep a hold of herself, to stop this subtle erotic assault from seeping into her, all the tiny atoms inside her were awakening, sensation spreading through her.

What was happening to her?

And then her lips made the tiniest of partings that was enough for him to sweep his tongue into her mouth.

Deep, dark heat suffused her, his taste seeping into her. Coffee, the faint trace of mint and a taste she didn't recognise but she knew was his and his alone.

With shock, she suddenly realised her hand had moved of its own accord to rest on his shoulder, her fingers gripping it tightly.

And she was kissing him back. Her tongue had slipped into his mouth and was mimicking the explorations he was making in her own.

She flexed her fingers and let go, then reared her head back enough to break the kiss.

'That's enough,' she muttered in a voice that sounded distant. The only sound she could make out was the ringing in her ears.

Gabriele didn't say anything, his hold on her head still firm as he gazed intently into her eyes, the expression on his face making her stomach contract in on itself and her thundering heart crash painfully against her ribs.

Thank God Michael chose that moment to come back into the room with a pot of coffee, clearing his throat loudly to announce his presence.

Gabriele moved his hands from her hair and straightened.

'Your breakfast will be with you in five minutes,' Michael said, pouring her a cup and then leaving as quickly as he'd come.

Shaken, her body still singing, heat still swirling, she added a spoonful of sugar with a trembling hand.

Gabriele was her sworn enemy. She had no right to take such pleasure from his kiss.

She had no right to want more.

'That's much better,' he said with approval.

'Don't ever do that again.' She couldn't look at him.

'Don't pretend you didn't enjoy it.'

'Don't pretend that I did.' She hadn't *enjoyed* it. What she had felt—what she still felt—was something she hadn't known she *could* feel.

His voice dropped and he spoke into her ear, blowing more of that gorgeous heat over her sensitised skin. 'You taste like nectar. Soon, I will taste all of you.'

She wrapped her hands around her cup, breathing deeply, trying in vain to take control of herself.

His gaze stayed locked on her, penetrating her skin.

This man was her sworn enemy.

'What's the matter, *tesoro*? Does your desire for me scare you?'

'There is no desire. All I feel for you is loathing. All I want is for you to release me from this nightmare.'

Instead of being angry, he laughed. 'There is no shame in attraction. It is natural.'

Not for *her* it wasn't.

But she had no intention of sharing that with him. The contract she'd signed stipulated she gave him her body, not her thoughts. The only intimacies they would share would be in the bedroom and they would be as brief as humanly possible.

Gabriele got to his feet. 'I have some calls to make. Can you be ready to leave in an hour?'

Thrown at his abrupt change of conversation, she looked at him.

And immediately wished she hadn't.

Every time she looked at him her chest tightened some more.

Tomorrow she would marry this man.

She would belong to him.

And the only way to cut the bonds that would bind them was to give him the one thing she'd never given to anyone. Her body.

But the one thing she now knew above all else was that

she would never allow him to kiss her again. Not as he'd just done.

It made her feel too much.

Somehow Elena made it through their meeting with the official at the city clerk's office without incident. She'd held Gabriele's hand and smiled adoringly every time their eyes met. She'd even managed a simper.

The only time she'd come close to crumbling that day was when Gabriele had taken her to a boutique, leaving her with the instructions, 'You need to choose a dress to marry in. White. Nothing subversive.'

She'd thumbed through the many and varied beautiful dresses with a deep ache inside her.

She might never have expected to marry, but this...

This was an abomination. A mockery of everything marriage was supposed to stand for. She was marrying a man she despised and who loathed her with equal intensity.

You have to do it. If you don't, he'll destroy you all.

It was this thought that had sustained her through her chat with her father that evening, before she and Gabriele had sat down for a quiet meal prepared for them by the housekeepers.

Elena refused to give credence to Gabriele's belief that her father had framed Alfredo, yet it echoed in her head with every word exchanged between them. But she would not ask for her father's side. He had nothing to answer for.

It hurt so much to hear the strain in her father's voice, knowing his fears of his only daughter seeing a convicted criminal. He'd casually asked if she'd any plans to see 'Mantegna' again. She'd crossed her fingers and said in as cheerful a voice as she could muster, 'Oh, yes, Papà, he's such a lovely man.'

Now she lay beside that 'lovely man' feigning sleep.

This time tomorrow they would be married.

This time tomorrow she would no longer be a virgin.

Gabriele turned in his sleep. A warm leg brushed against her.

She stopped breathing.

Sensation spread throughout her, a low ache pulsing deep in her pelvis.

She gritted her teeth and exhaled through her mouth.

How could she be so aware of him? Why could her body not hate him with the same passion as her brain?

If she could only switch her body off she would be able to ignore the fact that sleeping beside her was the most physically attractive man she'd ever met.

She could pretend the heat suffusing her at his nearness meant nothing.

'Elena, are you ready?' Gabriele banged on the bedroom door, where she'd been holed up for the best part of an hour, telling him she wanted to be alone as she prepared.

The door swung open.

All she had on was a mauve robe. A towel was wrapped around her hair.

'I can't do it,' she said, panic in her voice.

'Do what?' He looked at his watch. His driver would be here any minute to take them to the Manhattan Marriage Bureau. Everything was set. All they had to do was turn up. If she was about to renege on their contract...

'My make-up,' she screeched. 'I can't remember what Adrian told me to do.'

Not only was there panic in her voice but in her eyes too.

She was so highly strung at that moment she could snap like a too taut piece of elastic.

'I'll be back in a minute,' he said.

'Where are you going?'

'One minute.' He went to his drinks cabinet and poured

two hefty measures of brandy, then carried the glasses back to the bedroom and pressed one in her hand.

'Drink it,' he commanded. 'It will calm your...'

She'd downed it before he could finish his sentence.

'Can I have another?'

'Sure.'

He went off and poured them both another. She drank it as quickly as the first and wiped her mouth with the back of her hand.

'Better?'

She nodded.

'Elena...' Her robe had opened a touch, enough for him to catch a glimpse of a small breast.

He blinked and refocused his attention on her face.

'Elena, we have plenty of time,' he lied. 'Just do your best. Everyone will be too busy looking at your dress to pay attention to your face.'

He'd waited in a nearby coffee shop while she'd bought it. He'd spent the time trying not to think of their breakfast kiss, the remnants of which had still lingered in his blood-stream. It *still* lingered.

Before his engagement to Sophia he'd had a steady stream of regular girlfriends. He would never have considered himself a playboy but he'd had a lot of fun. Then he'd turned thirty and decided it was time to settle down. It was what people did when they still had trust in human decency.

Now, there was no one alive he trusted and he never would again.

His father had trusted Ignazio. He'd never dreamed his oldest, closest friend would betray him in such a manner.

Gabriele had trusted Ignazio too. Why on earth would he not? But where had this trust got him? A prison sentence, a dead father and a severely incapacitated mother.

He'd trusted Sophia. She hadn't cared to believe in him, her only concern saving her reputation.

That was what trusting someone who wasn't your own blood got you. Pain.

When his time with Elena came to an end, he was sure he would date again—he wasn't *dead*—but sharing a life with anyone? Not a chance in hell.

At the time, Sophia had, on paper, seemed the perfect wifely candidate. They'd agreed on all the major things like religion and politics. It was the perfect meeting of minds. Plus she was from an old wealthy family so there was no question of her being a gold-digger. And she was beautiful. Properly beautiful. The kind of beauty that men and women alike would turn their heads to look at twice.

In the year he'd been with her, not one single kiss had elicited the reaction kissing Elena had evoked. He couldn't remember a single kiss that had ever provoked such a strong surge of heat not just through his loins but through his blood, his bones, his very flesh.

He'd sat in that coffee shop, talking quietly on the phone to the man who could clear his name, trying to think of the words to induce him into switching sides, but his concentration had hung by a thread. His blood had thrummed too deeply from his kiss with Elena to think clearly.

The desire it had provoked in him had been inexplicable. It still was. As he looked at her now, standing before him with nothing but a robe covering her, the urge to take her into his arms and carry her to the bed was strong.

But, as he told himself grimly, desire meant nothing. It didn't change anything.

But it would certainly make marriage to her more pleasurable.

She nodded, her lips pursed, determination etched on her face. 'I can do this.'

'Good. I'll leave you to get on.'

Closing the door behind him, he wondered what kind of woman made it to the age of twenty-five without knowing how to apply make-up. He'd always assumed it was something inbuilt in them, like their ability to multitask without breaking a sweat.

How sheltered *had* her life been?

He knew Ignazio had kept her in the home for much of her childhood. His own father had often commented on it, saying how sad it was that his friend was hiding his only daughter away while his sons roamed free. No wonder she had aspired to be as much like her brothers as she could.

She was a strong, confident woman now, he assured himself. Whatever kind of childhood she'd had, it didn't change who she had become.

Forty minutes later she finally appeared.

The dress she'd chosen to marry him in was white, as he'd stipulated, but that was the only truly traditional aspect. Sleeveless, it had a high lace neckline and fell like a fan above her knees. On her feet were simple white shoes with the tiniest of heels.

Her newly feathered fringe had been swept to one side, the rest of it gathered in her newly favoured knot at the back of her neck. She'd kept her make-up simple but effective.

'Well?' she demanded.

'It's perfect.' He nodded his approval. 'You've chosen well.'

'I couldn't bring myself to buy a floor-length traditional dress. It would have made this whole farce an even bigger mockery.'

'Quite,' he said sardonically, not liking the cramp of guilt that seized his gut.

Had Elena *wanted* a traditional marriage?

It wasn't something he'd cared to consider.

And now was not the moment to consider it. Whatever she'd hoped for was none of his concern.

Besides, if a large, cherub-filled church wedding rather than what was regarded as an *intimate elopement* was something she wanted, she could always do it with someone else once they were divorced.

Remembering the delivery that had come earlier, he strode to the table and removed the delicately tied white roses from the box.

'What are they for?' she asked with a puzzled frown, taking them from him and sniffing them.

'They're your bridal bouquet to hold as we exchange our vows.' As he spoke, he pinned a single white rose to the lapel of the blazer of his navy pinstriped suit. 'You didn't think your loving fiancé would forget such an important detail, did you?'

She smiled with poison-laced sweetness. 'As we're not bothering with an engagement ring, guests or a reception, I'm surprised you bothered.'

'But, my love, there will be photographers there to witness our joy when we leave the civic hall.'

'Let's hope they don't learn we spent the night before our wedding together, and that you saw me before we exchanged our vows. It would be dreadful if they were to say our wedding is doomed by bad luck before it's even started.'

'Then we must put on a worthy display of our love so those doubts never rear up. Don't you think?'

She tilted her head coquettishly and fluttered her eyelashes. 'But of course, my mouldy little acorn. Our love will shine through.'

'A mouldy little acorn?' God, she amused him. He had no idea why but she did.

And he had no idea why he experienced a pang to wonder what it would be like between them if they had met under entirely different circumstances...

CHAPTER SEVEN

THE THREE OTHER couples in the waiting room were bouncing with excitement.

Elena tried not to study them too overtly but their body language fascinated her. And saddened her.

These couples were happy. They were marrying with the best of intentions—for love. She was marrying to stop Gabriele from destroying her family.

She'd made her daily call to her father and had been utterly relieved when it had gone to voicemail. She'd left a message saying she would call tomorrow then switched her phone off.

It hurt to think how upset he would be to learn she'd married the man subtly poisoning minds against him.

Gabriele's enormous arm was around her, her head nestled carefully in its crook.

She could feel the thud of his heartbeat. She could smell that masculine fruity scent.

It felt far too good to allow herself—for the sake of their audience—to sink into his strength.

Michael and his wife, Lisa, were sitting beside them, the pair beaming, clearly delighted their boss was getting married.

Romantic was the word Lisa had used when they'd met them there.

An elopement to a register office was romantic?

Elena's parents had married in an old Tuscan church surrounded by hundreds of loved ones. The pictures in their official album had shown her father beaming with pride and her mother, dressed in a traditional floor-length white dress, glowing with happiness. Their love had shone through.

She had never expected to marry but in the back of her mind had always been the wistful imaginings of a big traditional wedding surrounded by people who loved her, and with happiness in her heart.

Not this. Nothing like this.

An official appeared, ready to lead the next couple to the room in which they would legitimise their relationship.

It was *their* turn.

Ice filtered through her veins, freezing her bottom to her seat.

Gabriele helped her to her feet and pulled her to him.

'Ready to become Mrs Mantegna?' he murmured, rubbing his nose against hers, a warning in his eyes.

Aware of happy gazes upon them drinking in their devotion, she pressed her lips lightly to his.

'I hate you so much,' she breathed.

She could only assume it was a form of punishment that made him dart his tongue into her mouth and kiss her with such possessiveness that she had to cling to him to keep herself upright.

Her legs turned to jelly, her stomach to goo and she had to fight with everything she had not to take pleasure from it... Except she did. Every part of her body took pleasure from it.

Done; his eyes gleamed before he turned to the official and said, 'Lead the way.'

Five minutes later they were husband and wife.

They left the building into a blaze of afternoon sunlight, the rays bouncing off the elegant gold band now firmly placed on Elena's wedding finger. It had surprised her that Gabriele had chosen to wear one too.

The handful of photographers who pitched themselves outside the building in the hope of business from those marrying on the spur of the moment had tripled in numbers.

The paparazzi had arrived.

No guessing who had tipped them off.

Hands clasped, they posed but refused to make any comment.

A crowd of curious well-wishers began to surround them, snaps from phones being taken at all angles and directions.

Michael and Lisa, trailing behind, spoke only to say of their happiness for them, then left in a cab, en route to the airport, where they would be taking a two-week holiday courtesy of Gabriele.

When enough pictures had been taken, they fought their way through the crowd that had grown to epic proportions and got into the back of Gabriele's waiting car.

Elena would bet anything the snaps of them had been beamed around the world before they'd turned the corner of the block.

'Don't you want to go out and celebrate?' she asked with only a small amount of sarcasm. 'I've never known of a marriage without a big feast and party afterwards.'

'This is New York. Marriages here come in many different flavours.' He grinned, his eyes glittering. 'We will return to my apartment and celebrate privately.'

She didn't answer. She couldn't.

What was the point in arguing? It would only delay the inevitable.

There was no backing out. That avenue was closed. She'd married Gabriele knowing full well that when she signed the marriage licence it cemented her commitment to sleep with him.

The worst of it all was knowing that she *wanted* it to happen.

Her fear was enormous but the thrill of anticipation equalled it.

There had been a moment in the night when she'd awoken from one of her intermittent dozes to find her face close enough to feel his breath on her skin. The *longing* she had experienced in those few semi-conscious moments...

She'd wanted to kiss him.

It had shocked her. It still did.

She cleared her throat before speaking. 'I assumed you would want to throw a big party to show the world you own me now.'

'I thought you said I would never own you?' he said, his tone lightly mocking. 'But yes, I am ahead of you on that—Anna Maria is organising a party in Florence for all our family and friends to attend two weeks on Saturday. The invites will be sent tomorrow.'

'Will my family be invited?'

'*Our* family,' he corrected. 'We're married now so your family is mine and mine is yours and they will all be invited.' His grin remained fixed but his eyes were hard. 'I'm very much looking forward to seeing them again.'

'I'll bet you are.'

He leaned closer to her and took her hand, bringing it to his lips. 'It will be an evening of celebration but that is for another day. Right now my attention is on an altogether more pleasurable occurrence.'

Elena had stopped breathing, her fingers tingling with sensation where his breath whispered against it.

How could she respond so physically to him? By any law of logic and decency, it shouldn't be possible.

And how could her body buzz with the thought of what the night would bring?

They'd arrived back at his apartment.

Gabriele let go of her hand but instead of getting out, he brushed his lips against hers, catching her unawares, not giving her time to turn her face away. 'Come, Mrs Mantegna, let us celebrate our new union.'

The atmosphere in the elevator to Gabriele's apartment was as charged as he'd ever known it, as if an electrical current had been looped around them, pulling them ever closer together.

'Let's get a drink,' he said, leading her into the dining room.

She stepped through the door and came to an abrupt halt.

'Did you do this?' she asked.

On the table were two bottles of pink champagne in a bucket and two flutes. Next to them were silver trays of Italian and American canapés and sweet treats, from asparagus wrapped in Parma ham, to delicate pastry bites to heart-shaped chocolate truffles. Somewhere in those delicious-looking trays of food lurked a bite or two laced with real truffles—he could smell the distinct musky, nutty scent, an aroma that brought to mind memories of his childhood before they'd emigrated, when he and his father had spent a day truffle detecting.

He had so many happy memories of his father. A childhood filled with happiness. But that was all he had left. Memories.

'A private feast for two,' he murmured, slipping an arm around her waist and pressing into her back.

There was the lightest of pressure returned to him before she jolted forward to the table. 'Well, thank you for this because I am starving.'

'That'll teach you to skip breakfast.'

She met his eyes. Her cheeks coloured and she looked away.

Gabriele hid a smile.

The anticipation of the consummation of their vows had given an added piquancy to their mutual loathing. He could almost taste it.

There wasn't the slightest doubt in his mind that the attraction was reciprocated. None at all. He could see it in her colouring, hear it in the deepening of her breaths. And, most of all, he could still feel the kisses they'd shared. And they *had* shared them. She'd kissed him right back.

'Take a seat,' he said, pulling a chair out for her. While she sat and began unwrapping the trays of food, he took a bottle of the champagne, aimed it at the wall, and uncorked it.

He poured them both a glass and passed one to her.

Raising his glass in the air, he said, 'To us.'

She chinked her glass to his.

'To us,' she echoed, before adding, 'And here's to as short a marriage as it's possible to have.'

'And may all those short days be as pleasurable as they can be,' he retorted, enjoying watching the colour rise back up her cheeks again.

For all her words of being starving, Elena only nibbled at the spread before her.

Gabriele, never one to turn down food, found his own appetite strangely diminished too.

It had been a long time since he'd been with a woman, he reasoned. The expectation must be affecting him more than he'd expected. All the same, he ate over half the available food and a handful of the truffles.

He was content to let the meal drag out and make idle chit-chat. There was no rush. They had all night.

He almost laughed. A piece of paper they'd both signed that day said they had the rest of their lives.

When the first bottle of champagne was empty, he reached for the one sitting in the ice bucket.

'I don't want another drink,' Elena said suddenly, her eyes on him. 'I'm ready to go to bed.'

He raised a brow, a thrill racing through him at her admission.

Colour crept over her cheeks but she held his gaze, searching his eyes as intently as he searched hers. He brushed his thumb down the length of her cheekbone, marvelling at the softness of her skin. Her eyes closed and when she opened them the green darkened and a spark flashed from them.

'I'm ready for bed,' she repeated in a whisper.

* * *

Elena felt so tightly wound that she fleetingly wondered if she would be sick.

She'd hardly eaten a thing, the butterflies in her stomach fluttering too madly to let anything else in. With every passing minute of their shared meal she'd expected Gabriele to take charge, declare their meal over, and lead her into the bedroom. That he had been happy to linger had only added to the fear and anticipation rioting together in her. It had been like a ticking clock, the pendulum swinging louder and louder with every beat until it had become too much to bear.

She hadn't been able to take the suspense a moment longer.

Being the one to vocalise it had felt, strangely, empowering. She had made the first move. She'd taken the power out of his hands and claimed it for herself.

And now the butterflies had gone berserk, the fear being crowded out.

God forgive her, she *wanted* him. She wanted this to happen.

But she would only give him her body. Her head and emotions belonged only to her and she would keep them firmly detached. Men did it all the time so why should she be any different?

All the same, it took a few moments to get her feet moving out of the bathroom.

Gabriele was already propped up in bed, waiting for her, his broad chest bare.

His eyes shimmered to see her. He turned the sheets over beside him.

Under those same sheets she knew the rest of him was naked too. Just as she was naked beneath her silk robe.

The summer sun was still making its late descent, casting the room with a dusky hue. She wished it were fully dark; was certain it would make her feel a little less vulnerable.

She got under the sheets and lay on her back, pulling the sheets up to her shoulders.

Gabriele propped himself on an elbow and stared down at her. Unable to help herself, she gazed back.

Those soulful dark eyes swirled as if magma had been poured into them, an intensity there that made her heart skip and her nerves tauten painfully. Excitement and fear collided but she couldn't look away.

A large, warm hand rested on her collarbone, fingers tracing across to dip under her robe and begin the trail down to her belly, peeling the fabric back until he reached the knotted sash.

His eyes holding hers, still propped up on his elbow, he untied it.

Elena's heart hammered so hard its beats echoed in her ears. Breathing had become difficult, the air sticking in her throat. The line on her skin where his fingers had traced had been marked by his touch, the tingles spreading out through her flesh.

When Gabriele dipped his head and moved his mouth to hers, she only just turned her head away in time.

He stilled and gazed at her with questioning eyes before a half smile formed on his face.

'Ah,' he murmured softly, kissing her neck. 'This is where you make a show of doing your duty and nothing more.' He caught her earlobe in his teeth while he pulled her robe apart, exposing her breasts to him.

He gazed at them then looked back in her eyes, the magma in his pulsing. Gently he cupped her breast and stroked the puckered nipple with his thumb.

She closed her eyes as sensation rippled through her.

'We both know your desire for me is as strong as my desire for you,' he whispered, his mouth back at her ear, more sweet, sweet sensation skittering on her skin, under her skin, everywhere…

Gabriele shifted off his elbow and raised himself to kneel over her thigh. The movement shrugged the sheets off him, exposing more of the dark hair that covered his chest, down to his abdomen, thickening at his groin, where…

She blinked in shock.

She might have zero experience in this but even she could tell he was fully erect and hugely so.

A dull throb set off low within her, becoming altogether heavier and more heated when he pressed another kiss into her neck. And another. And another, drifting lower, down the valley of her breasts and over to capture a nipple in his mouth.

She couldn't contain the gasp that flew from her mouth.

The urge to touch him back grew from nowhere, and she grabbed at the ends of her pillow, clumping them in her fists.

This was too much. And yet, not enough.

Lightly, he traced his fingers over her skin, making swirls over her belly, his movement unhurried; lazy. Sensation was everywhere.

When he trailed a hand down her body and dipped a finger into her most intimate area, she clenched her teeth, still determined not to react. But *this*…in a place she'd never even touched herself…

Now he was the one to groan, a deep sound that came from the base of his throat, more like a growl from a wild animal than anything human.

'You really are exquisite.' He rested the palm of his hand so it covered the heart of her pleasure and slid another finger inside her.

Her breaths shortened.

The friction of his palm on her and the wholly unknown sensations being set off by the magic of his fingers…the battle to keep her head was being lost and she held the pillow even more tightly lest she give in and flatten her hands onto his back and feel the skin for herself and see if it felt as smooth beneath her fingertips as it seemed to her eye.

She would not give in. No matter how desperate a fight it would be.

But she was helpless to prevent the moan that left her mouth like a whimper.

'Admit that you want me,' Gabriele said hoarsely into her throat, his breath sending more sensation over her skin. 'I need to hear it.'

How could she deny it? Her body betrayed how much she desired him, reacting to his touch as if it were heaven-sent.

'Yes, I want you,' she whispered fiercely.

He groaned at her whispered admittance and moved fully between her thighs and took hold of himself, guiding himself to the place he'd just been touching her.

His erection pressed into her opening and then there was a sharp lance of pain as he drove inside her with one long, determined thrust.

Elena sucked in air and froze, so stunned at the sudden feel of him inside—fully, massively inside her—that she couldn't move.

Gabriele stopped moving too.

'Elena?'

His eyes, which hadn't left her face, now reflected stark shock.

After long moments passed in which nothing more was said but understanding flowed, he lowered himself to rest his weight on her, not enough to crush but enough that his entire upper body rested upon her, the darks hairs on his chest bristling against her breasts, his groin now resting against hers.

And, God, he was still inside her.

He was a part of her.

'Put your arms around me,' he said quietly.

The shock had gone from his eyes. Now there was something else there, a tenderness that made her lungs close even tighter.

Her fingers uncurled from the pillow of their own accord. At that moment Elena wasn't capable of rational thought. She wrapped her arms lightly around his back.

His skin felt so *smooth*.

'Breathe,' he whispered. He placed his forearms either side of her head and captured locks of her hair in his fingers. 'Breathe.'

She tried, drawing in choked air.

'Breathe.'

He moved inside her gently, his eyes holding hers, his hands stroking her hair.

'Move with me,' he said in that same low tone.

'I...' She didn't know how.

He must have understood.

A thumb brushed along her cheekbone. 'Do whatever feels good for you.'

He moved again, pulling out a little then pushing slowly back. 'Move with me,' he urged.

She raised her thighs a little and immediately the friction deepened.

His jaw clenched but his eyes were open, feeding her messages that there was nothing to be afraid of. Slowly, very slowly, he increased the movements.

From all Elena knew of sex, it was something to be hurried, a carnal event for the man to take his pleasure and for the woman to endure.

She had never known it could be tender.

She had never imagined *Gabriele* could be tender. But he was. His only concern was her pleasure and making this as good for her as it could be.

A swell of something she couldn't discern grew inside her chest and her fingers dug into the planes on his back, feeling the muscles beneath the smoothness.

Instinct took over and she found herself moving with him, hesitantly at first but with slow-increasing confidence, meeting his still-restrained thrusts as her body adjusted to these wonderful sensations spreading through her.

And they were wonderful. Like nothing she could ever have imagined.

The pulsations that had been building in her core grew stronger. Gabriele rocked gently in her, letting her have control of the tempo and strength. She raised her thighs a touch more, deepening the effect, and pressed herself tightly against him, locking her cheek next to his, feeling his hot breath on her skin.

And then she was crying out as the swelling exploded within her, rippling through every part of her with a strength that made her cling even tighter to him for support.

Through the heavenly yet shocking delight of what she was experiencing, Elena heard Gabriele's breathing deepen.

He whispered endearments, coaxing her to ride the waves until he let out a ragged groan and gave one last, lengthy thrust.

And then he collapsed on her.

With his face in her neck, his hands still running through her hair and the thunder of his heart echoing through her skin, Elena gazed at the ceiling, too shocked at what she had just experienced to think coherently or attempt to wriggle out from beneath him. The weight of his body on her and the heat of his breath in her neck…

Had that really just happened?

A strange lethargy crept through her sensitised body and a lump formed in her throat.

A lifetime of listening to her brothers and their friends discuss women with what amounted to contempt, and witnessing them treat the women in their lives as mere possessions, had convinced her that sex was a tool for men to assert their dominance. She'd assumed the phrase *making love* was from the realm of movies.

She hadn't been prepared for Gabriele to be so tender and gentle with her.

Even now that it was over, she would have assumed he would roll off her, let out a snore and, job done, go to sleep. She hadn't thought he would continue to caress her as if she mattered in any way; and this man was her enemy.

She hadn't expected to feel so *close* to him.

She could only imagine how he would make love if he was actually in love with the woman in his bed.

With that bitter thought, she finally psyched herself to move out from beneath him. He obliged, shifting his weight off her so she could roll onto her side and turn her back to him.

She could feel his eyes upon her, and waited for the dissection of what had just occurred to begin.

Instead, he hooked an arm around her waist and pulled her back so she was spooned against him.

Inexplicably, her eyes filled with tears. She blinked them away.

This was what she'd signed up for, she reminded herself for the umpteenth time.

Just because having sex with Gabriele had been the most incredible, fulfilling experience of her life didn't change any of the facts about him or them.

Yet, with his warmth permeating through her and his strength cocooning her, she drifted into sleep with a contentment in her limbs she had never known she could have.

CHAPTER EIGHT

GABRIELE PAUSED IN the doorway of the bedroom and peered at Elena's sleeping form.

The sheets looked as if she'd been wrestling them, a leg hooked around them, her arms thrown outwards.

He'd slept fitfully, waking half a dozen times, not touching her, just gazing at her with a chest so tight breathing was painful.

Staring at her now, he still couldn't comprehend that she'd been a virgin.

A virgin.

She shuffled and then raised her head. Opening a bleary eye, she stared at him for a moment before saying, 'What time is it?'

He looked at his watch. 'Six o'clock.'

Sitting up, she brushed her hair away from her face and hugged the sheets to her. 'Have you been working out?'

He looked down at his shorts and T-shirt and the training shoes still on his feet. 'What gave it away?'

The glimmer of a smile played on her lips.

'I went for a jog around Central Park.' Always up before the birds, that morning he'd risen even earlier, which was hardly surprising as they'd both fallen asleep in the early evening. 'Are you hungry?'

She rested her chin on her knees and nodded, almost shyly.

'I'm going to take a quick shower then I'll get some breakfast for us. Any requests?'

She shook her head.

She was so clearly ill at ease that for a moment his chest

constricted. He took a deep breath. 'Go back to sleep. I'll wake you when breakfast's ready.'

Not answering, she lay back down and curled the sheets around her.

Gabriele showered and dressed quickly, then went back out into the early Manhattan sun.

This was his favourite time of the day. In prison, early mornings had been filled with noise and activity. Here, in the open city streets, he could be on a different planet. There were people around—of course there were, this city never slept—but there was a stillness about them, as if they were robots charging themselves to alertness.

The welcoming scent of fresh donuts greeted him in his favourite deli one block from his apartment.

While he waited for his order to be done, he found his mind replaying everything from last night with Elena, just as it had while he'd jogged. Normally jogging cleared his mind of everything, allowing him to start the day afresh. Today...

One thing he had determined during his run was that he couldn't allow Elena's virginity to cloud his opinions or the route they were taking. She was still Ignazio's daughter. She was still up to her neck in his criminal doings and had played a hand in setting his father up. It was inconceivable that she wasn't involved.

Just because she'd been an innocent in one respect did not mean she was innocent in any other.

He would not allow himself to be derailed from his ultimate mission: the exoneration of his and his father's good names.

With that thought fortifying him, Gabriele took their breakfast and strolled back to the apartment block. While he waited for the elevator, his phone buzzed. It was a number he didn't recognise.

Putting the bag of food and coffee on a marble table in

the foyer, he hit the reply button and pressed the phone to his ear. *'Ciao?'*

'Mantegna?'

The voice on the other end was music to his ears. It was the voice he'd been waiting for.

'Ricci?'

'Is it true? Have you married my daughter?'

'Elena and I married yesterday afternoon—'

'You son-of-a—'

'It was a spur-of-the-moment thing,' Gabriele continued cordially as if Ignazio hadn't interrupted him, raising his hand to wave at the familiar face of a neighbour. 'We'll be having a party in a couple of weeks to celebrate. Your invitation will be posted today.'

The invitations would have the words 'Mr and Mrs Mantegna' emblazoned in large italics on them.

'What the hell are you playing at messing around with her?' Ignazio demanded, his tone full of menace.

Good. This was the reaction he wanted. Ignazio was wounded. He was also under threat. People under threat were more likely to make mistakes.

If Ignazio had any idea Gabriele was attempting to lure one of his most trusted aides away too...

'Elena and I are not playing at anything.' He didn't care if Ignazio believed in his love. All Gabriele cared was that Ignazio believed Elena had fallen in love with him. 'Elena loves me.'

He could hear heavy breathing down the phone, the sound of a man who'd smoked far too many cigarettes in his life fighting to control his temper.

'If you hurt her, I'll kill you.'

'Why would I hurt her?' He thought back to the shyness in her eyes when she'd awoken a short while ago. He remembered the breathlessness of her cries as she'd come in his arms.

'I mean it.' The voice was threatening but Gabriele detected an underlying tinge of panic.

Oh, this was *very* good.

Was this concern for his daughter or concern that Gabriele's access in the family had made Ignazio vulnerable?

He put him on the spot. 'Why do you think I would hurt your daughter?'

Ignazio didn't answer for the longest time. Gabriele could almost hear his brain ticking as he thought up an answer that wouldn't incriminate him.

When he finally answered, all he said was, 'Elena is nothing to do with anything.'

'Elena is my wife. She belongs to me now and I don't hurt what's mine.'

Terminating the call, he switched the phone to silent and stuck it in his back pocket.

Grabbing their breakfast, he got into the elevator and pressed the button for his floor, waiting for some form of euphoria to strike.

Ignazio was wounded. In the grand scheme of things it was a minor victory but one he had fully expected to relish.

Instead, he felt flat.

Back in the apartment he found Elena in the kitchen emptying the trays of food from the day before into a bin. As she leaned forward, her pert bottom, clad in black cropped trousers, curved for his eyes to appreciate.

After four years of celibacy he wasn't surprised to find that one bout of lovemaking had reignited his libido. What he hadn't expected was the strength.

She cast him a quick glance before tipping the remnants of the last tray in the bin. With a round-necked black and white striped fitted T-shirt, her damp hair loose around her shoulders and her face free from make-up, she looked as innocent as he knew she'd physically been only the day before.

'I've brought bagels and coffee.' He placed his wares on the kitchen table.

'Go ahead. I'll just be a minute.' She didn't look at him, intent on her clean-up mission. She moved to the sink, which she'd filled with soapy water, and dunked their champagne flutes into it.

'There's no need to do that. There's a cleaner coming in later.'

'It's therapeutic.'

'Elena, sit down and eat.'

She stood rigid at the sink then turned to join him, taking a seat at the far end of the table from him.

He watched as she ate, chewing slowly with each mouthful as if it were a chore that needed to be fulfilled.

'Did it not cross your mind to tell me you were a virgin?' he asked casually.

Her hand hovered in mid-air before she put her half-eaten bagel down. 'No.'

'You didn't think I had a right to know?'

'No.'

'Why not?'

She fixed cold eyes on him, so different from the shock that had reflected from them when he'd thrust into her that first time and so different from the wonder that had resonated when she'd come in his arms.

To discover the woman in his arms had been a virgin, that it was her first time...

The desire that had brimmed inside him, on the brink of boiling point as he'd plunged inside her, had notched down to an immediate simmer. The significance of what he had just done had hit him with full force.

From feeling as if he would explode, his only concern had been that she was okay, to soothe her, to wipe away the discomfort he knew that first thrust had given her.

Her response had been mind-blowing. Slowly, shyly, she had come alive in his arms.

'Did I hurt you?'

She shrugged. 'A little.'

'I'm sorry.' Sorrier than he could ever express.

Another shrug.

'If you'd told me, I would have been gentle.'

Something softened in her gaze before she looked away and said quietly, 'You *were* gentle.'

'I would have been gentle from the outset.' He took a drink from his coffee. 'I'm not going to lie to you, you are a very sexy woman. I haven't been with anyone in four years…'

Her eyes snapped back to him.

'…and I was like an over-eager panther. You should have told me.' He shook his head, still incredulous. 'Why?'

The softening of her features hardened again. 'Why was I a virgin?'

'Yes.'

'Honestly? If I'd had my way I would have remained a virgin until I died. Men are pigs and I knew I would never meet one who didn't conform to that opinion.'

He winced, wishing he could stick up for his gender but knowing he was in no position to offer a defence, not after he'd effectively blackmailed her into giving her virginity to him.

She drained her coffee and pushed her plate to one side. 'For all that, I do need to thank you.'

'For what?'

'For showing me that just because a man is a pig out of the bedroom doesn't mean he isn't capable of tenderness in it. I *should* have told you but I didn't think it would make any difference to how you treated me. I can see now that I was wrong.' The faintest trace of colour covered her cheeks but she carried on. 'It wasn't as bad as I thought it would be.'

Something swelled inside him that, for once, wasn't in his groin. 'Are you paying me a compliment?'

A smile ghosted her lips. 'Let's not get carried away. You can call it faint praise.'

'Then this afternoon it will be my mission to move on from faint praise to full-blown applause.' He didn't add that right at that moment he would happily pull her onto his lap and take her again.

Elena being a virgin put a whole new level of complexity on their physical relationship and he had to respect that sex and everything that went with it was new for her.

A thrill raced through him to think that *he* would be the one to teach her the art of pleasure.

'This afternoon?' Her eyes flashed. 'Won't we be travelling?'

'Our flight is scheduled for two p.m. We'll have ten whole hours to keep ourselves amused before we land in Florence.'

'I'll be sure to bring a good book with me, then,' she said with a husky catch in her voice.

The temptation to just pull her into his arms and take her grew stronger but he tempered it.

'We'll be leaving in an hour,' he said. 'Will you be ready?'

She nodded.

'Good. We're making a detour on the way to the airport.'

'Oh?'

'We're going to visit my mother. It's time for her to meet her new daughter-in-law.'

Elena gazed at the sprawling white ranch-type house on the fringe of New Jersey's Somerset County.

'What a pretty house,' she said, stepping out of the car and shielding her eyes from the brilliance of the sun. After the bustle of Manhattan the silence was stark. 'Did you live here?'

He nodded. 'My parents bought it when we first emigrated.'

'How old were you?'

'Ten.'

'What was that like for you? Was it hard moving to a new country?' The gravelled pathway crunched beneath her leather Roman-style sandals.

'It was fun.' He grinned but the apprehension that had lined his face on the long car journey was still there. 'My parents made it into a big adventure for me.'

They'd reached the steps to the front porch. Gabriele paused before climbing them. 'You remember I told you my mother has dementia?'

She nodded warily. She hadn't broached the subject on the drive over because she still smarted that he held her partly responsible for his mother's condition.

There was no way to prove a negative and, with his opinion of her so deeply entrenched, she knew that mere words would never convince him of her innocence.

In Gabriele's eyes, his father was Snow White to her father's Evil Queen.

'Just...' He sighed, shook his head and opened the door. 'Hello?' he called out, walking through a large reception room.

A large woman wearing jeans and a plain white top came out of a door. She beamed to see him.

'Gabriele, how lovely to see you,' she said in Italian. She looked at Elena, who was trying to hide behind him. 'And this must be your wife.'

There was a quizzical expression on her face that told Elena this woman knew exactly who she was.

'She is,' he said, stepping aside and taking Elena's hand. 'This is Elena. Elena, this is Loretta, my mother's nurse. How is she today?'

'Not too bad. I'd say this is a medium day.' Loretta opened a door for them and walked up a wide corridor with stained-wood flooring.

They were taken into a spacious and airy living room.

Sitting in a reclining chair by the window watching television sat a frail-looking woman with white hair.

Loretta went to her and crouched down. 'Silvia, look, you have guests.'

The white hair turned slowly and a pale wrinkled face stared at them blankly.

Elena swallowed back her shock. She knew Gabriele's mother could be no older than mid-sixties but she looked decades older.

Then a spark of recognition flashed on the too-old face and Silvia got to her feet.

Loretta was there to take her arm and assist as she shuffled over to them.

To Elena's alarm, the recognition on Silvia's face wasn't directed at Gabriele but at herself.

'Hilde,' she cried. 'I knew you would come.'

Hilde?

Elena's blood stopped flowing.

Dimly she was aware of Gabriele and Loretta exchanging glances.

'I've made a room up for you,' Silvia continued. 'And Ginny... Jenny... Oh, what's her name? She has made us meatballs. Italian, not Swedish,' she added with a cackle.

With a start Elena understood.

Hadn't Gabriele said their mothers had been good friends?

Silvia thought she was her mother.

Having only photographs to go on, Elena knew she had a strong resemblance to her mother. She hadn't realised how stark the resemblance actually was.

Silvia now seemed to notice Gabriele. 'Hilde, you've brought a friend.'

What did she do? Did she tell this elderly woman who thought she was living in a time over two decades before that she was wrong?

But looking in those large brown eyes, so like her son's,

and the happiness emanating from them, she knew to tell the truth would be a cruelty she couldn't inflict.

Elena swallowed before reaching out to take Silvia's hand.

'This is Gabriele,' she said quietly. 'Do you remember him?'

Silvia scrunched her eyes to peer closely at him. 'No.' Something clouded in her eyes and she dropped her voice to a whisper. 'Does Ignazio know you've brought a man here?'

Something in her tone set Elena's heart thumping. 'He knows.'

'Good.' Silvia's fingers closed around her hand. She could feel the tremors in them.

'Shall we sit down?' Elena suggested. 'I'm very tired from the drive here.'

'I'll get us refreshments. Wine? I've got a bottle of that… oh, what's it called?…that red wine you like?'

'Coffee will be fine.'

'I'll sort refreshments out,' Loretta cut in with a smile.

Silvia peered at the nurse. 'Do I know you?'

Between them, they got Silvia back in her seat and pulled an armchair close to her for Elena to sit on.

Gabriele sat on the sofa, elbows on his knees, watching them.

'Alfredo never said you were coming,' Silvia now said, leaning towards Elena.

'It must have slipped his mind.'

Somehow they managed to talk, not an easy task what with Elena pretending to be her long-dead mother and Silvia forgetting words and losing threads of the conversation.

Loretta had brought coffee and biscuits in to them and then disappeared.

Gabriele made no attempt to join in their muddled talk but she could feel him sitting there, observing them.

She could only imagine how he must feel, his mother

talking animatedly to a complete stranger while failing to recognise her own son.

The only moment when Elena thought she might crack was when Silvia suddenly said, 'They told me you were dead.'

She swallowed back the shock and answered weakly, 'I was ill.'

'What was it again? Not the breast thing?'

'No. Not cancer. Septicaemia.' Her mother had cut her finger while gardening. The wound had become infected. After five days in hospital being pumped with every anti-biotic known to man, her organs had failed and she'd died.

'I told Alfredo; Hilde would never be dead. She wouldn't leave her boys and that little girl. What's her name again?'

'Elena.'

'That's it. Elena. Such a pretty name. Did you get the dress we sent to her?'

'It's beautiful,' she said by way of an answer.

'Oh, yes. You sent a picture.' She craned her neck around the room before fixing on Gabriele. 'Alfredo, can you get the book for me? Hilde wants to see the pictures.'

Not by a word or expression did he react to being ad-dressed by his dead father's name, quietly leaving the room as she'd asked.

When he returned it was with a thick, old-fashioned leather-bound photo album.

'Here's the book you wanted,' he said gently, placing it on the small table beside her.

'Did I? We wanted wine, didn't we, Hilde? That nice red wine you like.'

'I'll see if I can find a bottle.' He threw a quick wink at Elena that was tinged with sadness.

Elena gave him a sympathetic smile, then looked at the album. Her heart thumped. 'May I?'

He nodded.

With Silvia now off on a tangent discussing swimming pools, Elena opened the album.

It looked as if the photos had been taken shortly after the Mantegnas emigrated. Gabriele couldn't have been much older than ten in them. There he was, sitting on an old sofa with his father in this very room. Identical grins beamed for the camera.

She went through it all discreetly, still keeping up the conversation with Silvia, who had now moved on to talking about a programme Elena had never heard of but which she tried her hardest to pretend was a favourite.

More pictures. A summer barbecue. Gabriele's eleventh birthday.

And then she turned the page and her heart stopped.

That was her father, sitting next to Alfredo, arms around each other, at a large dining table strewn with empty wine bottles.

There were her three older brothers, all sitting under a Christmas tree opening presents. Gabriele was sitting with them. All four were wearing oversized Santa hats.

And there was her mother, laughing. A white-blonde toddler sat upon her lap with her own oversized Santa hat covering half her face.

Another of her mother, this time with a woman who had to be Silvia. They were in the kitchen, glasses of wine in hand.

A group picture of the five Mantegna and Ricci children huddled together on the sofa. She peered even harder. That was Gabriele whose lap she had been sat upon…

Elena thought she might faint.

She had been in this house before. She had eaten and slept under this roof.

When she could finally tear her eyes away from the pictures, Gabriele was watching her, his brow knotted in a question.

All she could do was shake her head.

Gabriele took control and got to his knees before his mother. He took her hands in his. 'Hilde and I need to leave now.'

'Are you taking her home?'

'Yes. I will bring her back soon.'

'Does Ignazio know?' This time, as Silvia said the name, something clouded on her face. Her voice was confused as she asked, 'Is he in prison?'

'No.'

'But soon,' she said decisively. She placed a shaking hand to her son's cheek. 'He will go there soon, Gabriele. You promised me.'

He kissed the hand then kissed her on both cheeks and her forehead. 'I promise you, Ignazio Ricci is paying for his sins.'

Silvia insisted on seeing them out. Leaning heavily on her nurse's arm, she waved and said, 'Goodbye, Veronica.'

She didn't say goodbye to Gabriele.

Shaken to her core and feeling as if she'd just spent two hours on an emotional roller coaster with no brakes, Elena walked like a zombie with Gabriele back to his car, where his driver was waiting for them, leaning against the car smoking a cigarette.

Nothing was said until they crossed the county line and she quietly asked, 'Who's Veronica?'

'My mother's sister. She died ten years ago.'

'Is she always like this?'

'Yes. Some days are better than others but she rarely knows who I am any more.' He gave a deep sigh. 'She's lost to me now. Sometimes I struggle to remember how she was before.'

Impulse made her take his hand and squeeze it. However difficult she'd found it, she could only imagine how hard it had been for him. This was his mother regarding the man she'd given birth to as a stranger. It had only been at the end of their visit that she'd been able to grasp who he was for a few fleeting moments. And their talk of prison…that had been about her father. Silvia, in her one lucid moment, had asked if Ignazio was in prison.

Gabriele's eyes were dull but his lips curved a little as he said a quiet, 'Thank you for being so kind to her.'

A lump formed in her throat. 'I'm just so sorry that she is the way she is.'

His smile was rueful. 'Until the dementia set in she was the liveliest woman you could meet. She had an opinion about everything.'

'Do you see her much?'

'As much as I can. When I was released from prison I wanted to bring her back to Italy to live with me there but the doctors said it would be too distressing for her.' He shrugged a massive shoulder. 'I visit every couple of weeks and make sure to stay a weekend every month.'

'Don't feel guilty,' she said, picking up on his tone. 'You've got a global business to run. It can't be easy juggling it all.'

'It would be easier if I had siblings—there would be more of us to pitch in and spend time with her. But she has Loretta who lives in during the week and a weekend nurse. And she has many friends who take it in turns to visit and keep her company. I'm lucky that I can afford to bring the help to her rather than put her in a home.'

'And she's very lucky to have you.'

Feeling a growing tightness in her chest, she carefully moved her hand away and placed it on her lap.

She didn't want to feel empathy for him but how could she not? When all was said and done, Gabriele was human and this was his mother trapped in a past that had long gone.

But she shouldn't feel that she wanted to wrap him in her arms and hold him close, to smooth his hair and stroke his skin.

'It was good of you to pretend to be your mother. That couldn't have been easy.'

She gave a jerk of her head. 'When you said they'd been close friends... I hadn't realised how close they were. And I had no idea I'd been to your family home—I didn't know I'd even been to America. I thought the first time I came here was a few years ago.'

'Before we moved to America our mothers were inseparable. Our two families were incredibly close.' A smile tugged at his lips. 'I remember your christening.'

'You were *there*?'

'I think I was nine or ten. It was shortly before we emigrated, which is probably why I remember it. Did you know your father is my godfather?'

'No!' The word came out as a gasp.

'And my father is Marco's godfather, and my mother godmother to Franco,' he said, referring to Elena's two eldest brothers. His eyes were curious. 'Did you really not know this?'

She bit into her lip. 'It seems there's a lot I don't know.'

Gabriele stared closely, certain he could see tears brimming in her eyes. 'Are you feeling all right?'

She nodded then shook her head. 'Your mother...her mistaking me for *my* mother... That's the first time I've heard anyone refer to my mother as anything but an angel in heaven. In the Ricci world a woman is either a whore or a Madonna. To my father and my brothers, she's a Madonna without flaws *but she liked red wine*!'

A tear rolled down her cheek. She wiped it away.

'I didn't know she liked red wine. I knew our fathers were friends but I didn't know our families were such good friends too. We spent *Christmas* with you.'

Now it was his turn to take her hand and hold it tight. It felt cold. 'Our two families were like a real family from before even I was born, but everything changed when your mother died.'

'In what way?'

'It all stopped. When we first moved to America you and your family made plenty of visits. Your father was establishing his business here and I know your parents seriously considered emigrating too. But then your mother died and all the closeness was lost. All talk of emigrating stopped. Your father still visited us when he was in the country but the coming together of the two families...it just didn't happen anymore.'

'You visited us,' she said dully, shaking her head. 'I remember you and your dad staying at our house a couple of times. But that was so long ago.'

'Elena?' he asked when she drifted into silence.

She blinked. 'What you just said, I didn't know any of it.'

He reached out to finger a lock of her hair. 'Do you see why I loathe your father so much? We were family. I loved him. He didn't just set up my father, his oldest and closest friend, but he set up the man who had been like a brother to him. He let me, his own godson, go to prison. He knew my father had a heart condition but he didn't care. He let my father die.'

Her head shook slowly from side to side. 'He didn't,' she whispered. 'He wouldn't.'

'He did. And you *know* he did. You've seen for yourself the consequences of your father's actions—your father's betrayal, the shock of my imprisonment and the death of my father accelerated my mother's dementia.'

Quickly she wiped another fallen tear away and screwed her face, her lips trembling. Then she took an unsteady breath and sniffed lightly, swallowing as she visibly controlled herself.

'I'm sorry about your family and what you've all been through,' she said steadily, 'but I swear to you my family had nothing to do with it. My father is not that kind of man.'

She was lying. He could smell the lie falling from her tongue.

Was she lying to him or to herself? Because for the first time he truly considered whether Elena had been involved in her father's money-laundering racket and the cover-up that had led to Gabriele's father's door. Everything pointed to her having been purposefully kept aside by Ignazio.

But he knew better than anyone how Ignazio could form the most believable of trails.

'You said yourself that there were things about your life you didn't know; things your father and brothers kept from you. Is it not then conceivable that they would keep other things from you too?'

'No.' An obstinate look came on her face.

'Either you're in on it with them or you're in denial. Open your eyes. The truth is there waiting for you to find it.'

CHAPTER NINE

WAKING ALONE IN Gabriele's Florence home, a penthouse apartment spread over two floors overlooking Palazzo Tornabuoni, Elena wandered from the bedroom in search of coffee.

Even larger than his Manhattan apartment, it managed to be lavishly decorated and adorned yet remain homely. It had touched her to find he'd hung a Giuseppe Arcimboldo painting in the room he'd designated as her office.

Since their visit to his mother there had been a definite shift in their attitudes to each other. *Family* was a word no longer uttered between them. But it was constantly on Elena's mind.

How had her father been able to denounce Alfredo in such a way? And Gabriele, his own godson too. Why hadn't he helped their defence? *Of course* he hadn't been involved himself, but loyalty should have counted for something. Family loyalty was the crux of her father's personal philosophy and the Mantegnas *had* been family to him. She'd seen the photographic evidence with her own eyes.

And how could she not have known the full extent of their families' ties?

These were all questions she could not bring herself to ask him.

She had just settled on the balcony with a *caffe e latte* and fresh pastries made for her by Gabriele's housekeeper when he walked through the open French doors.

Her heart did that familiar little skip to see him.

'Good morning, *tesoro*,' he said, putting his hands on her shoulder as he leaned down to brush his lips against hers. 'You're up early.'

'Not as early as you.' She turned her cheek so he couldn't kiss her mouth.

In the ten days since they'd married her refusal to kiss him had become an unspoken rule. She would only allow him to kiss her when there were people around to witness it.

It was the only measure of control she had to hold on to. He never said anything to the contrary but she knew it got under his skin.

He hadn't been joking when he'd said they would spend the flight from New York getting to know each other better. Half an hour after take-off and they'd been locked in his jet's private bedroom. By the time they'd landed he'd made love to her so thoroughly and so often her legs had struggled to remain upright.

He'd kissed every part of her. He'd discovered erogenous zones on her body she hadn't known could *be* erogenous zones.

Every touch, every kiss, every murmur, every breath against her skin sent her senses into orbit and she had to fight to keep her responses contained.

As this was their so-called honeymoon period they spent nearly every waking minute together. They'd settled into a rhythm where the first hours of the day were spent working on issues for their respective businesses, then they would head out into Florence, or take a drive through the Tuscan hills. They'd visited museums, galleries and vineyards, eaten at a variety of restaurants and simple cafés, all the things Elena had never done before.

Growing up in the Ricci household, culture and days out were things people did on the television. Her father's idea of culture was a night out at the greyhound races.

While she and Gabriele didn't always agree on what made great art, often their views did concur. Arcimboldo wasn't the only artist they both admired.

She had to admit, she enjoyed his company. Their debates were always lively when they disagreed. He was opin-

ionated and arrogant but he *listened* to her without the smug
'humouring you' look she was so used to seeing from her
male family.

And they spent more time in bed than she had dreamed
it was possible to spend. Only a fraction of that time was
spent sleeping.

Gabriele was insatiable and, though she wouldn't give
him the satisfaction of vocalising it, her desire for him was
equally acute.

The only thing she wouldn't allow him to do in the privacy of their bedroom was kiss her on the mouth. That
would be a betrayal to her family too far.

Because she had to remind herself frequently that the
only reason she was there with him was to save her family. She was not with Gabriele for herself. Gabriele was
her enemy and she would not allow herself to forget it, no
matter how much she might enjoy his company or how
much she secretly looked forward to going to bed with
him every night.

Now he flashed her with a gleam of white teeth and
helped himself to a banana.

'Have you been for a run?' she asked, taking in his work-
out attire. The apartment had a gym but neither of them
had used it in the time she'd been there.

He nodded. 'I went down the Arno and up to Ponte
Vecchio.'

'Sounds nice. When I'm at home in Rome I like to jog
along the Tiber.'

'You're welcome to join me.'

An automatic refusal formed on her lips but she found
herself saying, 'I might take you up on that.'

'I run every morning. Name your day.'

'I'll get back to you on that.'

He grinned. 'Don't worry—I'll slow down enough so
you can keep up with me.'

'You don't think I can keep up with you?'

'You're half my size,' he pointed out, amusement lurking in his eyes, 'and I run every day. There's no question I'll have more stamina than you.'

If there was one thing Elena never backed away from it was a physical challenge. 'Tomorrow morning. What time do you want to leave?'

'I normally go as soon as I wake but I'm happy to wait until you get up.'

'No, no, you can wake me when you're ready.'

He fixed her with a wolfish grin and swallowed the last of his banana. 'It will be my pleasure to wake you up.'

Gabriele had known exactly what to say to get Elena out running with him. From everything she'd said about her childhood, the competition between her and her brothers had been fierce. Tell Elena she couldn't do something on account of being a woman and she would work twice as hard to prove she could.

It was a quality he admired.

He'd woken her at five, knowing to leave it much longer would mean losing the tranquillity of the early morning sunrise. While he loved Manhattan in the early hours, no city on earth could match Florence for beauty.

Apart from a tiny yelp when she'd seen the time, she'd thrown a pair of running shorts and a plain white T-shirt on without speaking. They'd set out at a gentle pace, jogging down Via degli Strozzi and on to Via della Vigna Nuova. Now, as they crossed Ponte alla Carraia, one of the bridges over the Arno River, she finally seemed to be waking up, continually scanning the skies to watch the sun make its first peeks.

'The best view to watch the sunrise is Piazzale Michelangelo,' he said.

'Can we go there now?'

'There isn't time—we'd need to leave at least an hour earlier than we did today.'

She made a noise under her breath that sounded remarkably like a curse.

'Early mornings not your thing?'

'Not that early.' Suddenly she turned to look at him, still keeping her stride. 'Have you been running every morning since we arrived here?'

'I told you, I run every day.'

'So you go for a run, get home and have a shower, all before I'm up?'

'Yes.'

'Are you a masochist?'

He laughed. 'The prison day starts early—I spent two years waking at four a.m. for the four-thirty cell-check. It became a habit.'

'That's barbaric,' she said with a shudder.

'You get used to it. Lights out was at ten-thirty so there was plenty of time to sleep.'

Elena fell silent, the only sound her breathing as she continued at the pace he'd set.

'How did you cope?' she finally asked.

'Prison?'

She nodded.

'I was fortunate that my lawyers were able to negotiate getting me into a minimum security prison so it could have been a lot worse. I won't lie; when I first walked through the doors I was sick with fear of the unknown but you adapt and it becomes…normal. But you know what kept me going?'

She didn't answer. Probably she knew what he was about to say.

'It was the thought of getting my revenge on your father. That's what got me through each day.

'But let's not spoil our time together on a subject we'll never agree on,' he continued, suddenly feeling like a heel for spoiling the peace that had settled between them. 'How are you finding the pace? Do you want to go slower? Faster? As we are?'

In reply, she accelerated, running ahead, her ponytail swishing behind her, her bottom swaying beautifully.

He laughed and increased his own pace to catch her. 'One day we'll have to have a proper race.'

'You'll beat me,' she said with certainty.

'That's not like you to be so defeatist.'

'It's called realism. I'm as fit as you are but you're more powerful. The only way I could beat you is if you were ill, which would make competing pointless.' She threw him a sly look. 'I'm certain I could beat you in a straight fight though.'

'I thought you were being realistic.'

'Wrestling and boxing were staples of our television viewing when I was a child. I copied their moves and used them on my brothers. They haven't beaten me in a one-on-one fight since I was eight.'

'You don't think they were going easy on you?'

'Not since the first time I beat them.' She flashed an evil grin. 'I wasn't averse to using pinches and scratches in sensitive places when it suited me. In that respect I had an advantage—my father would have killed them if they'd used the same tactics back at me.'

He grinned at the image. 'Didn't your father mind you fighting?'

'He thought it was funny to see his macho boys beaten by a girl. It's how I gained his respect.'

'You had to act like a boy to get it?'

By now they were crossing the Ponte Santa Trinita, back across to their side of the river.

'It was all of them,' she surprised him by saying. 'Not just my father. My earliest memories are of my brothers treating me like a doll. It *infuriated* me. My father thought it was funny to see his little girl pounding her fist into his youngest son's face. But it worked to his advantage.'

'How?'

'It gave him a legitimate reason to home educate me—

he couldn't send me to an all-girls private school if I was going to beat everyone up. My brothers went to school and had healthy social lives while I was kept locked away.'

'Do you think I'm exaggerating?' she asked into his silence.

'No. I'd already guessed as much.'

'It was the excuse he needed. He wouldn't have let me go to school however I behaved. I was still a female and even though I had proven myself physically, I needed protection from the big wide world.'

'He wasn't disappointed his princess turned into such a tomboy?'

'Not in the slightest. There was no chance of me catching any boy's eye if I was dressed in filthy ripped jeans and exchanging punches with them every five minutes.'

Gabriele laughed but he didn't find it in the slightest bit funny.

'If he kept you hidden away so much, why did he let you join the company?'

'To keep me close and under his wing. My brothers and I always knew we would join the family company in one capacity or another and my father always knew he couldn't wrap me up in cotton wool once I'd come of age.' She stopped running and held a hand to her waist, kneading at a stitch with a pained face. 'He does love me, you know.'

'I know.'

'And he's changed a lot in his attitude towards me since I started working for him.'

'That's because he'd assumed you're immune to men seeing as you hadn't even had a boyfriend in twenty-five years,' Gabriele said astutely. 'Your father assumed his tomboy would be his princess for the rest of his life.'

'It's not like that.'

'Isn't it? Your mother died when you were a toddler. Your father closed ranks on all his children but especially with you. He kept you protected far beyond what any normal person would consider to be appropriate and all because you were a girl. If you'd been a boy your childhood would have been different and you knew it, so you became a boy to please him because you thought that's what he wanted.'

She shrugged, gave the side of her belly one last massage and set off again.

'Not quite. I saw that men were considered better than women and I would never be respected unless I made sure I never behaved like a girl. I didn't want to be a whore and I knew I could never be a Madonna so I became something entirely different that could never be interpreted as one or the other.'

'You do know that being a woman doesn't make you subhuman?' he said. He hated to think Elena had grown up believing that the only way she could have any respect was by being other than she was.

Did she even *know* who she was?

'Of course I know that.'

'Women are no more whores or Madonnas than men are misogynists or feminists. We all have our own capabilities and desires that are ours alone.'

She didn't answer, seemingly concentrating on the pathway ahead of them.

Now that the sun was up, the streets were getting busier with workers bustling to their places of employment, dog walkers and other early birds.

'We're nearly home,' he said, spotting a trattoria that was open for business. 'Let's get a coffee.'

They took a seat on an outside table and gave their order, both ordering a cappuccino and a chocolate pastry twist. The owner brought them a glass of water each with a, 'You look like you need it.'

Elena wiped her forehead with the back of her wrist. As far as Gabriele could tell, it was the only sign of perspiration on her, whereas his T-shirt was damp.

'How often do you see your father?' he asked conversationally. She'd spoken to him daily since their first morning in Florence when Ignazio had offered to fly his jet to Florence and rescue her.

She'd played her part beautifully, insisting she didn't need rescuing and that she was blissfully happy with her new husband.

When she'd hung up the phone, she'd looked at Gabriele and said, 'I really hate you.'

'I hope one day you understand that I'm not the monster you think I am,' had been his entire response.

Other than that, for a couple who considered each other criminals, they got along surprisingly well.

Now she said, 'I see my father about as much as you see your mother. I take care of Europe while he deals with Asia and South America with my brothers.'

'Who runs the North American division?'

'That's only a minor aspect of the business now. We sell components to car manufacturers there but our design and manufacturing teams are based in other countries.'

'They never used to be. When we emigrated your father created many divisions in the US. They've all been closed down and moved elsewhere—Brazil's his favoured place of business now.'

'And your point is?'

'How often does your father visit the US? When was the last time he set foot on US soil? When did any of your brothers last visit?'

'I don't know. I don't keep tabs on them.'

Their cappuccinos and pastries were brought out to them. As soon as they were alone again, Gabriele continued with the conversation.

'Does your father ever mention visiting the US?'

'No.' She swallowed a bite of her pastry and fixed narrowed eyes on him. 'What is it with all the questions?'

'Has it never occurred to you that there may be a reason your father doesn't visit the US any more?'

'No, and I would appreciate it if you would stop trying to poison my mind against him.'

'I don't want to poison your mind,' he said quietly. 'All I want to do is open it.'

Her green eyes suddenly fixed on him. 'Does this mean you believe that, whatever happened between our fathers, I had nothing to do with it?'

Her words resonated. 'Does this mean you accept that *I* was innocent?'

'I asked first.'

He took a long sip of his cappuccino, staring at the face that was becoming as familiar to him as his own.

'I don't know,' he answered heavily. 'It's inconceivable to me that you could not know of your father's criminality…'

She closed her eyes slowly, her shoulders slumping.

'But,' he continued, 'the more I get to know you, the harder I find it.'

'You have doubts?'

'Many of them.'

'I can't persuade you either way, can I?' she said sadly, then shook her head and looked back at him. 'I believe in *your* innocence.'

He found his throat closing, making a response hard. 'Why?'

'The more I get to know you, the more I know you wouldn't go on a vendetta for no good reason. You believe my father to be the guilty party and a part of you still thinks I'm involved too.' Her eyes were steady as she said, 'But it doesn't excuse what you've forced me to do. Nothing will ever excuse that. I might believe in your innocence but don't think for a minute that I forgive you because that will never happen.'

'I haven't asked for your forgiveness. If your innocence

is proven then I will apologise and hope for it,' he answered evenly. 'But let us not get carried away—you yourself admit the proof of your innocence doesn't exist.'

Elena stood under the hot stream of the shower and waited for the heavy pour to soothe her wounded heart. Until that morning, they'd both studiously avoided any conversation about her father or family in general and she wished she hadn't risen to the bait. She didn't want to spend their marriage at loggerheads and discussion simply opened raw wounds.

What she hated Gabriele for the most was the doubts he put in her mind.

The daily calls to her father had become excruciating. It didn't matter how often she told him everything was great, he didn't sound convinced.

What she hated hearing in his voice was the underlying panic. Because she couldn't trust it. She appreciated her marriage had been a shock to him but she definitely had the impression it was more than that; that her marriage to Gabriele scared him.

And try as she might to think otherwise, she couldn't help but wonder if he *had* been involved in Alfredo's fraud.

He wouldn't have set him up. She was certain of that. Not her father.

But what did she *really* know of his business dealings in South America and Asia? They were kept separate from the division she ran.

And Gabriele's question of when her father had last visited the US…

She truly couldn't remember. When she'd been a child he'd made regular trips there, often accompanied by one or other of her brothers, but she could not remember the last time any of them had mentioned a visit there for whatever reason.

Were they afraid to step foot on US soil? And if so, why?

Surely, she reasoned, if the US authorities suspected him of anything they could get an international arrest warrant?

But according to Gabriele, all the evidence was in the basement of the Nutmeg Island chapel, which the authorities couldn't touch without hard evidence.

How would her father react if she were to ask him for the chapel code…?

God, she loathed herself for doubting him. Hated that she had to bite back the question every time she spoke to him. Hated that she feared his answers.

And she hated that the images of those photos played so greatly in her mind.

There was a whole history between the two families that had been all but erased. All she'd ever seen of it was a blurred outline; all the colour and vitality within the outlines faded into darkness.

And she really hated that it made her wonder what else she'd been kept in the dark about.

CHAPTER TEN

MANTEGNA'S HEADQUARTERS WERE located on the outskirts of Florence, in a sprawling complex that covered two square miles of land set in a basin in the Tuscan hills. Elena's first glimpse was as they drove over the crest of a hill. There it lay beneath them, gleaming in the midday sun.

Gabriele had decided to drive, and he brought the small sports car to a stop so she could admire the view.

Dozens upon dozens of futuristic buildings and hangars were encircled by a testing track. In the centre of it all was the famous electric-blue main building itself, shaped in the diamond Mantegna logo with the silver M dashed across it, its roof shining and glossy under the sun.

Mantegna Cars had manufacturing plants the world over but here was its heart.

'Have the renovations finished now?' she asked.

When Gabriele had been halfway through his prison sentence, work had begun, to much fanfare, on expanding Mantegna's European headquarters to make them his worldwide HQ. It had been a defiant gesture that had told the world Gabriele would not be skulking away and his business would continue to thrive and innovate. Having been unaware of her own father's involvement—*supposed* involvement—in the fraud, believing her father to be an innocent bystander in the Mantegnas' criminality, she'd thought it showed a lack of class.

But you never thought your father was completely innocent, did you? That twisting you experienced in the pit of your belly whenever you heard details of the investigation and the trial were testament to that.

Coldness ran up her spine and she clasped her hands tightly together.

What kind of daughter was she to even consider her father being capable of such a thing?

'The bulk of it was completed a month ago,' he said, oblivious to her inner turmoil. 'We've had a few teething problems but nothing major. When we launch the Alfredo next month, everything will work perfectly.'

The supercar that would be a tribute to Gabriele's father and an event that had the world's motor press salivating with anticipation.

'How did you do it?' she asked in wonder. 'The boss of one of the world's greatest car manufacturers goes to prison for fraud and money laundering but instead of your business collapsing around you, it thrives and comes back stronger than ever.'

Gabriele stared out of the window as she spoke. It was a long time before he answered.

'It helped that my staff believed in me,' he said quietly. 'They carried the business during my incarceration. We were all determined to fight back and so were the majority of my financial backers. They believed in my innocence.'

He spread out his hands and nodded at the Mantegna building in the distance. 'The expansion sent out a message of intent to the world. The launch of the Alfredo will be the pinnacle; proof positive that our cars are the best in the world and that nothing will be allowed to destroy us.'

Elena stared at him with her heart in her mouth.

How did someone inspire such blind loyalty? She had no illusions about her own staff—their loyalty was to their pay cheques. All it had taken was a couple of unfounded whispers from Gabriele for a handful of her father's banks to call in their overdrafts.

Yet Gabriele's staff and backers had fought for him.

He set the car in motion again and soon they were walking into the foyer of the headquarters of Mantegna Cars.

The interior of the main building was as futuristic as the exterior, all glass walls and electric-blue furnishings.

Gabriele insisted on giving her a tour of the entire facility, introducing her to scores of people as they made their way through it all. Nothing was off-limits. All of Mantegna Cars' intellectual secrets were opened up to her in a display of trust she found astounding and also incredibly touching.

Since their jog together, they had found a relative harmony, but, with their wedding celebration party only a day away, her nerves were a tangled mess knowing her father and brothers would be attending.

This was the perfect way for her to forget what the next day would bring.

As Ricci Components made parts for cars, everything was familiar to Elena, and yet refreshingly different, as if she'd been beamed to the twenty-third century. There was little hierarchy either that she could discern, everyone treating each other with mutual respect. There was less of a gender divide than she'd expected too. In the main manufacturing plant there were a handful of women working who clearly weren't there for decoration or to make tea. It was a nice culture shock to have, especially as Ricci Components tended only to employ women for clerical roles.

She had come to accept that even her own job was clerical. Everything Ricci Components made was manufactured in Asia or South America. The closest she came to the manufacturing process was through imports.

'Your deputy Chief Engineer is a woman,' she commented with a shake of her head when they were walking back to the main building.

'Yes,' was Gabriele's reply, as if the matter were so inconsequential it didn't need discussing.

She wondered if the deputy Chief Engineer had had to fight misogyny to get where she was, both within her family and the world at large. Or had she a family that was supportive to all her dreams?

Back in the main building, Gabriele took her up to the media suite, where a group of executives was waiting for them, trays of food and coffee laid out.

A wall-length flat-screen television played a montage of the new Alfredo supercar driving through the Tuscan hills.

'It's stunning,' Elena marvelled as the screen changed to show the Alfredo powering up the German Autobahn.

'I'm pleased you like it,' he said with a grin.

'Is this the advert you'll be using?' she asked.

'This is only for the press launch. We don't need to advertise.' Gabriele took a bite of a mini cheesecake, noting the sparkle in Elena's eyes. She really was in her element here. 'We advertise heavily for our more family-oriented cars but our supercars are niche—only five hundred Alfredos will be manufactured and they're sold out already.'

'So why do any press for it?'

'This car is a tribute to my father. I want the world to see it. I want to remind the world of his innocence.' The dimming of her eyes made him feel like a heel. Wanting the light to come back into them, he added, 'The launch also gives publicity for the Mantegna name, and prestige for our buyers. They like belonging to an exclusive club that everyone knows about but can't join.'

Gratitude flashed in her eyes. 'I'm tempted to ask you to produce one more just for me.'

He laughed. 'A wedding present?'

'A divorce present,' she retorted drily.

He hooked an arm around her and kissed her temple. He liked that she didn't automatically freeze when he touched her now. He liked it a lot. 'I'll see what can be done.'

It was amazing, he reflected, that a month ago the thought of a Ricci—any Ricci—driving the car named after his father would have been a dagger through his heart.

'At the very least I can offer you a test drive,' he said. 'I'll arrange for Monty, our resident test driver, to take you out on the track next week.'

Her eyes widened with enthusiasm. 'That would be fantastic. Incredible.'

'Am I right in thinking Mrs Mantegna is a petrol head?'

'A what?'

'It's what they call car enthusiasts in the UK,' he laughed.

'I suppose I am.' She sounded surprised at her agreement.

'Many women are, you know. They don't have to pretend to be just to be accepted as one of the boys.'

'If that's the case, why don't you manufacture a super-car *for* women?'

'We do.' He grinned. 'You like the Alfredo, don't you? When you consider women have as much purchasing power as men, it's ludicrous not to cater for their tastes too. For the past decade we've made sure all our cars, from every range, have gadgets that appeal to women as well as those that traditionally appeal to men.'

She gave an approving, if puzzled, smile and he thought of her obvious surprise about his deputy Chief Engineer being a woman.

He looked more carefully at her. Today she was dressed in her usual uniform of slim-fitting dark trousers matched with a mauve blouse, her hair loose around her shoulders. She seemed to enjoy her new wardrobe but was still unsure about wearing make-up or doing anything with her hair other than a knot or ponytail.

For Elena, being a woman was something she had fought her entire life. A new wardrobe and one make-up lesson could not overturn a lifetime of learned behaviour, no matter how much she secretly wished it could. He'd seen her watch Internet videos on make-up tips and hairstyles, her face screwed in concentration, but she never attempted them herself. He was certain she did want to embrace her femininity but something held her back.

There were times he'd be watching her and he'd feel

such a heavy compression in his chest that his lungs would shrink and he would struggle to breathe.

It should be of no consequence to him whatever was going on in her head but it was there all the same. He wanted to scoop her thoughts out and throw away the ones that hurt her; the ones that told her she wasn't good enough as she was.

There were times he could almost understand why Ignazio had gone to such lengths to protect her. There was something about Elena that made a man discover his inner Neanderthal. She was such a strange mixture of vulnerability and fieriness; so capable and determined yet so fragile too.

He smiled ruefully. One thing Ignazio had failed to learn but had taken Gabriele all of five minutes in her company to discover was that Elena didn't need protection. She was more than capable of taking care of herself.

All she needed and all she wanted was respect.

Anna Maria came into the media room and caught his eye.

Excusing himself, he went to join her by the door.

There was an air of calm excitement about her.

'We've got the proof,' she said in an undertone.

Automatically, his gaze turned to Elena. She was now talking to the director of the promo that had been recorded.

'Are you certain?'

'Yes. Carlos came through. He's emailed the proof.'

Gabriele closed his eyes.

At last.

Carlos was one of Ignazio's closest aides. He'd worked with him for decades. Other than his children, there was no one Ignazio trusted more.

It had bitten at his craw to reach out to a man who had effectively betrayed his father as much as Ignazio had but desperate times called for desperate measures. He'd spent a lot of money buying Carlos's loyalty and now it appeared to be paying off.

'I need the originals.' He wanted the proof of his innocence to be cast iron. As he spoke, Elena turned her head, saw his eyes upon her, and gave a small, shy smile.

How would she react when she learned what he'd been doing behind her back?

How would she react when she learned he had the proof?

And how would she react when she discovered what he planned to do with it?

He hadn't lied to her. Their contract had been clear. Marriage and a baby in exchange for him destroying the documents he'd copied from the chapel basement.

Nowhere on the contract did it stipulate he couldn't continue digging for evidence to clear his father's name and have his own criminal record expunged.

That Elena had assumed this would be covered by the original verbal agreement was not his problem.

All the same…

His guts felt very heavy when he imagined what her reaction would be.

'How much did you miss having a mother when you were growing up?' Gabriele asked once they were driving back home.

He felt her eyes rest on him and knew she was reading his face before deciding whether to answer. They had learned to read each other well.

She was silent for a long while before replying. 'Not my childhood so much as my adolescence. That's when I really missed having her there.'

'No counterbalance for all the testosterone?' He changed gear and tapped the brake as they approached a small town.

She smiled faintly. 'None at all. I hardly ever met any women. I was home educated with male tutors—our household staff were all men too, as were all the cousins from my father's side.'

'What about the rest of your family? Did you ever see anyone from your mother's side? Aunts? Cousins?'

'My mother was Swedish and all her family live there. I saw them a handful of times when I was growing up.'

'And now? You spend a lot of time in Scandinavia working. That must make it easier to be in contact with them.'

'They're strangers to me. I was twelve the last time I saw any of them.'

'They don't have to be strangers any more.'

He felt green eyes upon him.

'I've got a couple of female cousins around my age who wanted to be friends but I snubbed them. It's too late for me to expect a relationship now.'

'Why did you snub them?'

A dry laugh. 'Because they were girls. And they were beautiful and poised and wore the most beautiful dresses, whereas I was a tomboy dressed for a party in boys' clothes.'

'Did you want to be like them?'

'I don't know.' She took a breath. 'I suppose I did want to be a little like them but I didn't know where to begin. And I didn't want to give my brothers any ammunition to remember *I* was a girl. Girls were cheap meat to be made fun of, remember?'

'I'm very sorry you grew up believing that.'

It was with a heavy heart that Gabriele locked his car and went into the apartment with Elena.

When she excused herself to take a shower, he took the opportunity to catch up on emails with some privacy.

Carlos had agreed to meet him in person. For an extra one hundred thousand dollars he would bring the originals with him.

Gabriele didn't quibble over it. He would spend any

amount of money to exonerate his father and clear his own name. Whatever it took.

Anna Maria was convinced that, for an even larger sum, Carlos could be persuaded to defect and testify in person. It would be Gabriele's job to persuade him.

The end game was coming. If he could convince Carlos to testify—and that was by no means a given—then Ignazio Ricci was finished.

But the gratification of a game plan coming to fruition was nowhere to be found.

When he and Elena went their separate ways she would be all alone. He knew her father's arrest would be painful for her; he couldn't bring himself to imagine *how* painful. Who would she turn to? Her brothers?

He almost laughed out loud at the thought of those idiots attempting to comfort her.

She had family in Sweden though...

He straightened, an idea formulating.

He put a quick call through to Anna Maria. 'I need you to track down Hilde Ricci's family in Sweden,' he said. 'Call me as soon as you have anything.'

Tomorrow night he and Elena would celebrate their wedding. *They* might know it was all for show but no one else did. He had a decent-sized family and numerous friends. The only people attending from her side were her father and brothers. If his idea paid off, he might be able to even it out a little for her.

Feeling moderately better in himself, Gabriele headed to the bedroom, certain she would have finished showering by now. Elena spent more time in the shower than anyone he'd ever known. With anyone else he'd see it as an invitation to join them but with Elena he knew it was her way of destressing away from him when her thoughts became too much.

She was bent over, a large towel wrapped around her, rubbing at her hair with a smaller one.

She spotted him, straightened, tightened the towel and scurried back into the bathroom.

After three weeks spending virtually every waking—and sleeping—moment together it was hard to believe she could still be so shy around him.

Inhaling deeply, he undressed.

Moments later she returned wearing her robe, the sash knotted so tightly he was surprised she could breathe.

Her eyes widened to see he'd stripped off to just his boxers.

'Are you going to shower now?' she asked, averting her gaze, colour creeping up her cheeks.

'Soon.'

When would she have the courage to be naked around him outside the bed itself?

'Are we still eating out?'

'Yes.' As neither of them could cook and it suited him not to have his housekeeping staff around too much—he'd noticed Elena was much less inhibited when it was just the two of them even if the needed privacy meant she wouldn't kiss him—they ate out most days.

Stepping over to her, he took her by the arms and gently swivelled her round to stand before the full-length mirror. He undid the knot of the robe, and smoothed the silk away from her shoulders, letting it pool at her feet.

'What do you see?' he asked.

She met his eyes in the reflection, a question in them. 'You and me?'

'Forget about me. Look at your reflection and tell me what you see.'

'I see...' she lifted a shoulder '...me.'

'And who are you?'

'Elena.'

'And who is Elena?'

Her lips clamped together.

Stepping behind her, he placed his hands to her jaw and

rubbed his fingers against her soft skin, then gathered her hair together and kissed the swan of her neck.

'When I look at you, I see a woman. A beautiful...' he kissed her shoulder '...intelligent...' he kissed the top of her spine '...passionate woman.'

Snaking his tongue down her back, he dropped to his knees and kissed her bottom.

'You are neither a whore nor a Madonna. You are a woman with desires and needs that are all your own.'

She stood still but he could feel little quivers emanating from her.

He inched himself around so her abdomen was level with his mouth. He placed his lips to it then looked up at her.

She was gazing down at him, her eyes apprehensive and confused but her colour raised.

'You are not a woman pretending to be a man, you *are* a woman. You have a spine of steel and a mouth tender enough to heal a wound with a kiss.'

He kissed into the dip of her side and trailed his tongue to her hip and zagged it slowly across to her pretty blonde mound.

Scenting her excitement, he pressed his nose into the fine hair and inhaled.

'You have the scent of a woman, not a man.' He flicked his tongue out and encircled her swollen nub.

A tiny moan came from her throat.

'You have the silkiest skin of *any* woman.'

Now her eyes were dark and hooded.

'Look in the mirror,' he whispered, 'and tell me what you see.'

She stared at herself.

'I see...' Her words were heavy, laboured.

'Do you see the woman with the power to be whoever she wants to be? Do you see the woman who can embrace the passionate core beating inside her? Because that's the woman I see when I look at you, Elena.'

Her hands reached down to take his head in her grasp, her fingers digging into his scalp.

Her desire, unspoken, was given as an invitation.

Burying his face in her heat and sliding a hand up her back to steady her, Gabriele gently used his tongue to bring her to the heights he knew gave her so much pleasure.

He doubted he would ever tire of watching her orgasm.

That first time had been special. Discovering her virginity in such a manner had been as much a shock to him as the feel of him inside her had shocked Elena. Watching that shock slowly turn into bliss and then wonderment, knowing it was his arms she was coming undone in... It had been more than special. He'd thought nothing would ever be able to match it.

Instead, his amazement had grown.

Though he knew his thoughts would only confirm Elena's opinion that all men were pigs, he couldn't help the delight it gave knowing only *he* had discovered Elena's hidden passion. Every response was his and his alone. And every time she touched him, it thrilled his selfish ego to know he was the only man she'd touched in this way. The only man she'd *ever* touched.

Her desire for him was not something she could hide— he had learned to read his wife very well. Her eyes responded in an honest way she still wouldn't allow her body to fully do.

He hoped the day would come when *she* seduced *him*. When she would press her lips to his and breathe into him.

If she would only let go, set all her inhibitions and doubts about him free and embrace with everything she had what could be explosive.

She had no reason to trust him. He knew that.

By the time he earned it, their marriage would be over. One way or another.

But then her fingers dug even harder into him and her

thighs trembled and his thoughts vanished, his concentration solely on her and her pleasure.

Only when he felt her go limp did he look back at her, smiling to see the dazed expression now echoing back at him.

Taking a firm hold of her hips, he got to his feet and lifted her into the air, a lock of her white-blonde hair falling into his face.

In three strides he carried her to the bed and laid her down.

She parted her legs for him and with one thrust he was inside her.

Until that moment he hadn't realised how deep his own ache had been.

It was an ache he carried with him on an almost permanent basis.

CHAPTER ELEVEN

IF ELENA'S NERVES got any tighter she would go springing across Piazza del Duomo.

Gabriele, who had earlier massaged her shoulders in an effort to relieve her tension, rubbed her wrist with his thumb.

'I'm sure your family will behave themselves,' he said. In the five-minute walk to the hotel they were throwing the party at, he'd made a variety of assurances at least seven times.

'It's not their behaviour that concerns me.' She was only half lying. Over one hundred people would be attending their 'celebration'. Every single one of them knew of the animosity between her father and her husband.

The media furore had died down in the past week, but today talk of their wedding celebration was everywhere. Rumours had circulated of paparazzi offering thousands of euros for an invitation. All anyone seemed to care about was who would hit who first—her husband or her father...?

Since when had she started thinking of Gabriele as her husband?

There was no time to ponder this strange turn of events as they'd arrived at the hotel.

A media scrum greeted them but the hotel had beefed up its security and cordoned the media away from the hotel steps.

Clinging tightly to his hand, she climbed the stairs under a hail of flashing bulbs and shouted questions.

Hotel staff greeted them in the foyer, welcoming them with glasses of champagne. Gabriele had booked the whole hotel, one of the oldest and most prestigious in Florence, for the evening, bedrooms and all.

Anna Maria was in the dance room waiting for them. Gabriele left them to it while he went to greet the band, infamous hell-raisers who'd had half a dozen global best-selling albums and who had flown in from America especially for the evening. While they milled by the free bar, their roadies were setting up on the stage.

'What do you think?' Anna Maria asked.

As Elena gazed around the room, taking it all in, she couldn't help the wistfulness that raced through her. The high vaulted ceiling and frescoed walls were magnificent on their own but the tables decorated with silver balloons and the scattering of tiny silver horseshoes, the streams of ribbon twisted around the pillars in the room's corners, gave it a romantic effect that made her ache that this was all a lie.

'It looks beautiful,' she said.

She looked over at Gabriele, deep in conversation with the band's singer, and wished...

Wished for what? That this could be real? That their marriage could be born out of love, not hatred and ven-geance?

He caught her eye and made a drinking motion, asking if he could get her anything.

Touched, she raised her still-full glass of champagne.

He winked and indicated he would be with her in a mo-ment.

Shaking off the wish that he were with her right now, she turned her attention back to Anna Maria, taking in the creased trouser suit she wore. 'Are you going to change soon?'

'I'm only here to oversee events,' the PA replied.

'That's what the hotel management's for,' Elena said. 'Take the evening off and join us.'

'I can't.'

Rooting through her small clutch bag, Elena found her credit card. 'There's a boutique and a hairdresser here in the hotel. Take this and buy yourself something. I'm sure the hotel will have a room you can get ready in.'

Anna Maria shook her head, now looking ill at ease. 'I truly can't.'

'You can. I insist. I'll clear it with Gabriele for you.'

At the mention of his name, something flickered on Anna Maria's face.

For the briefest moment Elena wondered if the PA was in love with him but immediately discounted the idea. She wasn't an expert on relationships but not once had she felt any vibes that suggested they were anything but boss and employee.

Maybe the PA disapproved of their farce of a marriage and didn't think it appropriate to join in with the mock celebrations?

'Please,' she said, touching her hand and deciding to change tack. 'We both know the truth about my marriage, there's no need to pretend otherwise, but that doesn't mean you can't enjoy the evening. I won't know many people here and it will be nice to have a familiar face in the crowd.'

Anna Maria bit into her lip. When she looked at Elena there was something in her expression that set off a fresh warning of something being wrong. But then she smiled and nodded her head.

'Thank you. That's very kind of you.'

'Go and make yourself look beautiful.'

Anna Maria spoke briefly to Gabriele, who sent Elena another wink, then she disappeared from the room.

Elena continued gazing at him, happy to observe from afar. He looked gorgeous in his black tuxedo and bow tie, a powerhouse of masculinity that perfectly complemented the femininity she could feel racing through her blood.

Tonight she truly felt like a woman.

Of all the dresses she'd bought on Liana the stylist's recommendation, this was the one she'd never had any intention of wearing. For a start, it showed off flesh. *Her* flesh. Made of silk crepe de Chine that felt heavenly against her skin, the spaghetti straps and low-cut front skimmed both sides of her breasts, making the wearing of a bra impossible. Monochrome swirl prints interspersed with turquoise fell in layers, one side to mid-thigh, the other to mid-calf, and swayed when she walked. And speaking of walking...

She'd squeezed her feet into a pair of blush-coloured five-inch-high sandals with one simple strap across her toes that was nonetheless crystal embellished, and a thin ankle strap. She'd never felt so tall. Her legs had never felt so shapely.

A visit to a salon had seen her hair swept into a loose but elegant chignon, her fringe swept to one side and tendrils left loose around her ears and her nape. She'd kept her make-up simple but after weeks of determined practice she was finally getting the hang of it.

As vain and silly as she knew it to be, she now loved wearing make-up and felt nothing but sadness that she had spent so many years denying this side of her nature, not just denying it but pretending it didn't exist.

Gabriele had taken one look at her and wolf-whistled.

That man...how could the one person she should hate more than any other on the planet be the one to make her look in a mirror and find the real woman beneath the skin?

With a start she realised she didn't hate him any more. And when he came over and took her hand in his, she squeezed it, her heart so full, her chest so tight she couldn't speak.

'That was a lovely thing you did for Anna Maria,' he said quietly, handing her credit card back to her. 'I've told her to put whatever she buys on the account. I should have thought of it myself.'

The temptation to reach out and touch his face was strong but some last resistance lay within her and she slipped the card back into her bag, saying, 'She looked so tired I almost ordered her home.'

He gazed into her eyes as if he were searching for something.

The urge to touch him grew and she raised her chin towards his, parting her lips...

A loud noise from the stage broke the moment and she quickly looked away, trying desperately to regain control of herself.

'The guests are arriving,' she murmured, glad of the distraction, horrified that she had been about to kiss him, not for show but because at that moment she had wanted nothing more than to feel his mouth upon hers.

Soon the dance room was filled with guests, all of whom had to congratulate the happy couple. Even though they'd put on the invitations that the only present they required was their guests' company, many came with gifts, which Elena felt terrible about accepting. She kept staring at the table laden down with beautifully wrapped packages with that same tugging wistfulness in her belly she had felt when she'd walked into the room; that sensation of wishing that this could really be...

She knew from Gabriele's body language when her family arrived.

They were talking to a couple whose names she couldn't remember when he stiffened and his hold on her hand tightened.

'Elena's family are here,' he said politely. 'We need to go and welcome them.'

Her heart pounding so loudly it muffled her hearing, she walked with him to the bar, where her father and brothers were standing, champagne flutes in hand, although she would bet that any moment they would be ordering double Scotches.

The four Ricci men stood in a row facing them.

It was like a Mexican stand-off and, judging by the

looks in their eyes, they were all waiting for her to decide which side she was on.

How could she tell them that there was no choice and that if she didn't stay on her side of the invisible dividing line, they would likely all go to prison?

You don't know if you even want to return to their side of the divide.

Fixing a smile to her face, she embraced them in turn, wishing so hard she didn't feel like such a traitor, not just by her actions but by her emotions too. She had as little control over the latter as she had the former.

'Thank you so much for coming,' she said brightly, then stood back as Gabriele extended his hand to her father, forcing Ignazio to shake it.

She winced. She didn't know who tried the hardest to crush the other but any moment she expected to hear the sound of snapping bone.

When Gabriele shook her brothers' hands, it was their turn to wince.

After the 'niceties' had been observed, Roberto, the youngest of her brothers, looked her up and down, a smirk on his face. 'What's Mantegna done to you? You look like a girl.'

'More like a whore,' Franco muttered under his breath, yet audible enough for Elena to hear.

Her whole body flushed at the insult she had spent her entire life trying to avoid being on the receiving end of.

Before she could think of a suitable response—her brothers' guffaws only added to the brain-melting humiliation—Gabriele fixed them all with a stare that stopped their laughter in its tracks.

He took her hand in his and held it possessively.

'Your sister is a beautiful, intelligent woman,' he said, undisguised contempt in his voice, 'and I would appreciate it if you kept any sexist digs you may have in mind out of her earshot and definitely out of mine.'

All four Ricci men gaped at him, then identical fury flashed over their features.

Her father elbowed Franco, a silent but painful warning to keep his mouth shut.

The problem for her father and brothers was that they knew Gabriele had an agenda in marrying her but they didn't know what it was or how he intended for it to work out. They couldn't afford to antagonise him any further.

'Excuse us, but some new guests have arrived.' Gabriele's tone was like ice but his smile did not falter. 'I'm sure we'll have a chance to catch up later. The buffet will open soon so you'll have much to occupy you.'

When he bore her away, Elena didn't know whether to shout at him for his subtle rudeness or laugh at the memory of her brothers' gawping faces.

What she really didn't want to do at that moment, though, was shed the tears clamouring behind her eyes.

For the first time in her life she had looked at her immediate family and *really* seen them. She had seen four squat, overweight men who looked as if they were auditioning for the role of petty gangsters in a Scorsese film.

And then Gabriele introduced her to someone who made all thoughts of her father and brothers take a back seat.

'Elena?' said the elegant blonde woman before her.

'Aunt Agnes?' So shocked was she that she could hardly get the words out. She didn't have to say anything else for Agnes yanked her into her arms for a tight embrace.

'It is so good to see you,' Agnes said in perfect Italian. 'I have missed you terribly.'

By the time her mother's sister let her go, the threatening tears had spilled out.

'Are you here alone?' Elena asked after she'd blown her nose on a tissue Gabriele had thrust into her hands before he'd kissed her neck and whispered that he would leave them to it.

'Henrick is in Canada on business but Lisbeth travelled

with me—she's just changing Annika's clothes. Did you know she had a baby?'

Elena shook her head.

'Malin wanted to come too but she's due to give birth in three weeks herself so she wasn't allowed to fly, but she sends her love. Is your father here?'

'Yes.'

Agnes grimaced but didn't elaborate on her thoughts. Before Elena could ask, Agnes waved over Elena's shoulder. 'There's Lisbeth and baby Annika now.'

More embraces were shared and then they found a table to sit around and catch up on. Baby Annika was handed to her and Elena gazed down at the chubby little face with awe.

'I can't believe you've had a baby,' she said in wonderment. 'The last time I saw you, you were still in a training bra.'

Lisbeth laughed. 'The last time I saw you, you called me a silly girl and pulled my hair.'

Elena winced.

Lisbeth took her hand. 'I forgive you,' she said, so earnestly Elena smothered a laugh.

'I feel so bad that I haven't kept in touch,' she confessed a short while later.

'That wasn't your fault,' Agnes interjected. 'I take responsibility for that. I never should have suggested to your father that you come and live with us.'

'Did you?' Something else she hadn't known.

'When you were twelve. You were so unhappy and I—rightly or wrongly—thought it unfair of your father to lock you away as he did. I thought he would be happy for you to have some female guidance but he thought…otherwise.'

'Is that why we stopped seeing you?' They had never seen a huge amount of her mother's family, just the odd family party here and there, but it had stopped completely around the time of Elena's early adolescence.

'You know what your father's like. He rules with an iron fist and does not appreciate dissent, especially from a woman.'

Elena gazed at Gabriele, standing with a crowd of men, all of them roaring with laughter.

Gabriele would never treat a woman as anything but an equal. And he would never lock a child away. He might have stipulated that no child they had be allowed anywhere near her father or brothers but once a child came he would change his mind if he could see it would be in the child's best interests.

She kissed baby Annika's sweet scented head.

A pang rippled through her to think of the child she and Gabriele would have together.

There might be a little cluster of cells in her that very second, steadily forming into an embryo that would be part her and part Gabriele.

He had done this for her. He had brought her family over from Sweden without her knowledge. He'd given her back the family she hadn't known how much she needed.

It was the best present she had ever had.

Agnes followed her gaze. A smile tugged at her lips. 'I think your husband could not be less like your father. He must love you very much.'

No. He didn't love her. Gabriele could never love someone with Ricci blood. But what he'd done in bringing her family to Italy…

But of course this went unsaid. Elena forced a smile to her face and took a sip of champagne.

A few minutes later he was at their table.

'Excuse me, ladies, but I need to borrow my wife. It's time for us to say a few words to our guests.'

Taking his hand, Elena got up, promising to continue their talk later.

'Can you give me a minute to use the bathroom?' she said, wanting some time to compose herself and fix her face.

'Of course.' He rubbed a finger up her cheekbone and smiled, his eyes flashing. 'You really do look incredibly beautiful. You *are* incredibly beautiful.'

She wanted to thank him, not just for the compliment, which she truly believed he meant, but for what he'd done in bringing her family here. But her throat had closed and she couldn't get the words out.

'I'll wait for you by the bar,' he said before placing the softest of kisses to her lips.

Diving into the ladies', she went straight to the mirror and took a deep breath.

What was happening to her? Her emotions were all over the place, pulling her in directions she knew could never lead anywhere.

Was she suffering from a version of Stockholm syndrome? She'd heard of kidnapped women falling for their captors and making excuses for them but had never understood how such a thing could happen.

But she *hadn't* fallen for Gabriele, she told herself stubbornly. She'd just come to accept he wasn't the complete bastard she had thought him to be. He was much more complex than that.

And so were her emotions.

Satisfied her face was repaired as well as it could be, she left the sanctuary of the ladies' to find her father waiting for her.

He opened his arms and she gratefully slipped into his embrace.

How could she have such doubts about him? He was her father. He'd raised her alone and while he had certainly made mistakes he'd only ever done his best by her.

Hadn't he?

'You are happy, Elena?' he asked, stepping back a little but keeping a tight hold on her arms to peer at her closely.

What was he looking for? Signs of her doubt?

The disloyal thought made her feel even worse.

'Mantegna, he treats you well?'

'He treats me very well and I'm very happy with him.'
And as she spoke the words she knew them to be true.

She *was* happy with Gabriele.

There were times—many times—when she forgot why
she was with him and would feel full to the brim. And he
treated her better than she had ever been treated in her
life. He listened to her. He took her opinions as seriously
as he took his own. He made love to her as if she meant
something to him.

If he could treat her, a Ricci, like that, she could only
imagine how he would treat a woman he was in love with.

His ex-fiancée needed her head examined. If she'd been
Sophia she would have fought to clear his name. She would
never have doubted him.

Her head began to swim.

'When are you coming back to work?' her father asked,
still holding her arms. 'Your staff miss you.'

'I need to sort some things out,' she said, avoiding a
straight answer. Because what her father hadn't mentioned
was that she hadn't stopped working. She might not have
physically gone to work since marrying Gabriele but she
communicated with her staff daily and dealt with any problems as and when they occurred. Which was rarely. 'I'm
sure I'll be back in the office soon.'

*Back in the office, running myself ragged around Eu-
rope, trying desperately to justify why I have the position
I worked so hard for but which is ultimately worthless.*

These weeks away had forced her to see the truth. Her
job was nothing but a sop. She was nothing but a highly
paid supervisor. The divisions she managed didn't need
her. They were well run by their individual management
teams and functioned perfectly well without her.

She didn't even enjoy it!

Why had it taken her so long to see the truth?

But what else could she do?

She wasn't qualified to do anything else.

'I'll let you know very soon,' she promised, kissing his cheek and gently extracting her arms from his hold.

'If he hurts you…'

'I know.' She nodded wryly. 'I'll tell you. But he won't hurt me.'

'What does he say about me?' he asked as she made to move away.

She had dreaded this question, had been certain that when confronted with it the temptation to confess all would be too great, that she wouldn't be able to lie to him.

It was the look in his eyes that made her keep her confessions to herself.

He was worried about something.

And it *terrified* her to think what that something could be.

She was saved from having to answer by the singer of the band doing a call-out for her from his vantage point on the stage. Gabriele was standing by the stage, his arms folded and a mock-scowl on his face.

She gave her father one last impulsive hug, cleared the lump in her throat, and made her way through the laughing crowd to the stage.

Gabriele watched his wife walk to him, so much flittering over her face he couldn't discern one distinct emotion. Until she looked at him that was, and all her features softened and something flickered in her eyes he'd never seen before.

He didn't think he'd ever seen a more beautiful woman than Elena that night. When she finally reached him and took his hand, a tightness pooled in his gut that almost doubled him over.

The singer from the band said a few words then handed the microphone to Gabriele, who jumped straight into his thanks to everyone for attending and apologised for marrying in such haste.

'You know what it's like,' he drawled, pitching his speech between humour and sincerity, 'you meet someone and within a day the life you know is gone and you find yourself signing the *rest* of your life away.'

He waited for the laughter to subside before continuing. 'But that's what love does to you. It turns everything on its head and marks you to the person you've fallen for.'

His intention had been to direct those last words at Ignazio, to hammer home the message that Ignazio's beloved daughter had got into bed with the enemy, but he couldn't do it. He couldn't tear his gaze away from the woman who wore his ring.

He thought of Ignazio's right-hand man, who was on the brink of defecting to him with all the incriminating documents. He thought of how Elena would react when she learned of this and learned that he still intended for her father to spend the rest of his miserable life in prison.

But then he thought of his own father, dying within days of Gabriele being incarcerated, knowing full well that his only son was innocent and the man he'd considered a brother had betrayed him in the most heinous way.

He thought of his mother, so full of life if a little forgetful when this nightmare had started, the stress of seeing her son imprisoned and the sudden death of her husband accelerating the loss of her mental capacity at an alarming rate.

That was all Ignazio's doing.

It came to him that he hadn't added Sophia to that list.

But then Sophia paled in comparison to Elena. Elena would never have abandoned him. She would have been one of those wives who visited every weekend, the first to arrive and the last to leave. She would have believed in his innocence.

She *did* believe in his innocence. After everything he was doing to her, she believed him.

If he took the proof to the FBI as he intended then she would never believe in him again.

It would devastate her.

Could he really do that to her?

Hadn't she suffered enough?

The cheers from their guests brought him back to the present.

His silence had been so long they clearly assumed he'd finished. He couldn't remember the rest of what he was going to say anyway.

The band started playing again.

'Shall we dance?' he said.

Her hand was still in his. She gave one of those shy smiles he adored so much and nodded.

He led her to the centre of the dance floor and took her into his arms.

Smiling, she looped her arms around his neck and sighed, gazing up at him. 'Thank you for bringing my family here.'

He knew she didn't mean the Mantegnas.

'You're welcome. They seem like nice people.'

'They do.' Her eyes shone. 'Thank you.'

She moved closer to him, their legs touching, his groin pressing into her abdomen, even with the height of her sandals giving her an extra lift. And then she raised herself onto her toes and, her eyes still gazing into his, pressed her mouth tentatively to his.

He stilled, unsure whether this was a kiss of gratitude or something more.

Only when she tightened her hold around his neck and parted her lips did he dare believe it was something more.

Her sweet breath suffused him. Her sweet scent filled him. The softness of her lips…

He forgot that only weeks ago this party had been arranged with the sole purpose of showing Elena off on his arm in front of her father and letting him know in no uncertain terms that she belonged to him.

None of that mattered.

Elena was kissing him with feather-light movements and the tiniest darts of her tongue, and it was the most erotic, moving kiss he had ever experienced.

Running his hand up her spine, he captured the nape of her slender neck and kissed her back with the same languidness she kissed him.

When she eventually broke away, she buried her head in his shoulder and gave a muffled laugh.

He squeezed her tightly, adoring the feel of her pressed so close to him. And wished that everything could be different.

CHAPTER TWELVE

THE REST OF the evening passed in a happy daze. Elena had never expected to enjoy the party but she did. Meeting her Swedish family had been the pinnacle and when she and Gabriele left it was with promises to visit them very soon.

They took the short walk back to the apartment in silence, hands clasped, tension thick between them. Gabriele had long since removed his dinner jacket and bow tie, but the night air was so warm he slung it over his shoulder rather than put it back on. Or was it the heat swirling between them keeping him warm?

She had never felt such *depth* for someone, or such gratitude. Every time she remembered her brothers' faces when he'd reprimanded them she wanted to laugh. Every time she thought of what he'd done in bringing her Swedish family there she wanted to cry. It had been the most thoughtful thing she could imagine and he'd done it without any selfish motive. He'd done it for *her*.

She could never explain how much it meant.

The only way she'd been able to think to show how much it meant was by giving him the one thing she'd been denying him. She'd kissed him.

And now she knew it hadn't just been him she'd been denying by her refusal to kiss but herself too.

In the apartment they went straight to the bedroom, Gabriele throwing his dinner jacket onto a chair as they passed.

Elena closed the door behind them and leant against it, tugging at the ankle straps of her sandals and kicking them off, staring at *him*, the most beautiful man in the world.

And he stared right back, a fever in his eyes that filled every crevice.

She held out a hand. When he reached to take it, she took a step towards him and placed his palm on her chest, letting him feel the hammering of her heart. Her lonely heart that had somehow, without her knowing when or how, become whole.

His breathing was as heavy as her own, his eyes dark, molten.

Stepping even closer, she placed a kiss on his neck and inhaled his scent, then slowly moved her lips up, over his jawline, across his cheeks and then to his mouth.

She breathed him in as she kissed him and wound her arms around his neck, exploring him with her lips and her tongue, heat filling her trembling body.

He held her securely to him, letting her take the lead.

Dragging her fingers down his chest, she undid the buttons on his shirt, their kisses deepening.

One hand still splayed on the base of her back, he undid his trousers. Between them they removed his shirt and tugged his trousers and underwear down until he stood naked, his erection jutting against her belly.

She'd never known she could feel such need for someone. She'd never dreamt there would come a day when she would physically ache for a man and that her heart would race so hard it would feel bruised.

Now she broke the kiss and took a step back.

Gabriele thought he might be drowning.

He'd never known one kiss could make his entire body ignite with something more combustible than mere lust.

Whatever this was, he'd never felt it before. There was a voice in his head warning him of danger but he was helpless to obey it.

He didn't want to obey it.

Right now, this moment, Elena kissing him as if she

would consume him, every one of her looks spearing him...
it would be easier to slice a limb off than walk away.

'Get on the bed,' she whispered, standing as still as a
statue, only the rise and fall of her chest showing life...and
those mesmeric eyes that bore into him.

On legs that felt strangely boneless, he did as she bid,
not taking his eyes off her.

Only when he was leaning back against the headboard
on the bed did she come back to life.

She took a deep, trembling breath then gathered her
dress in her hands and pulled it up and over her head. The
movement dislodged whatever had been holding her hair
in place, white-blonde locks spilling over her shoulders.

All she had on now was a pair of lacy white panties.

She gazed at him, colour on her face, but made no attempt to cover herself as she usually did.

He swallowed the moisture in his mouth, gripping hold
of the bed sheets lest he jumped out, threw her onto the
bed and plunged inside her as the aching jut between his
legs longed to do.

She walked to him, not taking her gaze from him, until
she stood at the edge of the bed and slowly, *torturously*
slowly, tugged her panties down.

Climbing onto the bed, she straddled him, then her hot,
sweet mouth was back on his and she was kissing him as
if she needed his breath for life.

And then that beautiful mouth was dragging down his
throat, her tongue darting out, and she was kissing him everywhere, moving down his chest, his abdomen, her fingers exploring, so many sensations igniting that it was a
struggle to breathe.

When she took him into her mouth his hands clenched
into fists and he had to force air into his lungs.

He'd never experienced anything like it, such pure, deep
desire. It burned him.

Groaning, he watched her head bob up and down, desperate to reach out and touch her but not wanting to do anything that might scare her or break her from the moment.

Just at the point when he felt he might burst, she trailed her tongue back up his chest, her breasts brushing against his skin, until she found his lips. At the same moment her tongue swept back into his mouth, she sank down on him, taking him inside her sweet tightness in one long movement.

He watched her eyes close and a look of bliss spread over her beautiful face.

Wrapping his arms around her, he held her tightly, fusing her to him as she began to move, little cries escaping from her mouth that soon turned into moans and then gasps.

For so many nights he'd dreamed of her submitting to the desire gluing them together and letting herself go.

He'd never imagined it would be like this or dreamt it would *feel* like this.

He didn't want it to end.

When he felt his orgasm welling up inside him, he gritted his teeth to hold on, but the softness of her skin against him, the feel of being so perfectly fitted inside her, the friction of her movements, her breath and scent filling his senses…it was a battle he was about to lose.

And then she was crying out his name and sinking as hard onto him as she could, thickening around him, somehow pulling him even deeper into her.

He let go.

'Elena, God, Elena,' he breathed with the last of his air, white light flickering behind his eyes and pulsations ravaging him, taking him to a place he had never known existed.

His heart had never beaten so fast.

Much later, when lethargy had crept through his bones and sleep arrived to claim him, Elena entangled in his arms and breathing rhythmically, he opened his eyes for one last look at her and pressed the lightest of kisses to her forehead. Then he fell into the deepest, most content sleep of his life.

* * *

Gabriele gave his morning run a miss. Or, rather, his morning run gave *him* a miss. Today the sun had beaten him awake. And so had Elena.

He found her on the balcony, drinking coffee and gazing out at waking-up Florence.

Her face lit up with a smile to see him.

They'd shared a bed for almost three weeks yet this morning it felt as if he were handling the morning-after for the very first time.

He wanted to scoop her up and carry her back to bed.

Conversely, he wanted to get his training shoes on and run away as fast as he could.

He settled on taking a seat next to her and pouring himself a coffee.

'I hope you don't mind me wearing this,' she said shyly, indicating his navy robe, which she had wrapped herself in.

Seeing her dwarfed in *his* robe, her hair mussed from a night of lovemaking, a sparkle in her eyes…

His chest constricted, the palms of his hands dampening.

'Not at all.' He added a splash of milk to his cup. 'You're up early.'

The sparkle faded a little and she took a sip of her coffee. 'I woke up with cramps.'

'Are you okay?' he asked, immediately concerned.

'I've taken some painkillers. But it does mean I'm not pregnant.'

Relief surged through him in a whoosh.

He hadn't even realised this was news he'd been hoping for.

Elena wasn't pregnant. He got to keep her for longer.

He stared at her, trying to read her expression. 'You're disappointed?'

Was she really that keen for them to be over? When she conceived their child she could walk away.

But surely she didn't want to walk away after the night they'd just shared?

She would walk away if she learned what you were up to.

'A little.' She took another sip. 'I don't know why I thought it would happen so quickly.'

'It will happen when it's ready.' He ran a thumb against her cheek, thrilling when she rubbed into his touch. He adored her cheekbones; they were made for touching. 'You really do want to have a baby?'

He should have asked her before. Before he made her sign a contract where her only means of escaping him was by carrying his child.

What had he been *thinking*?

What kind of monster had he become?

And what could he do about it?

Her eyes were wide as she nodded. 'Very much. I never thought I would...'

'Because only girls have babies and you didn't want to be a girl?' he supplied.

She laughed, visibly relaxing. 'That was certainly a part of it. But don't forget I'd intended to stay a virgin until I died and seeing as a man's help is needed in making a baby...' She laughed again. 'I just never thought I would be in the position where a baby could be possible.'

She made it sound as if he'd given her a choice in the matter when the choice he'd presented her with had been no choice at all.

How could she even exchange a civil word with him?

Her hand crept onto his and squeezed. 'You need to get going soon, don't you?'

'Yes.'

He didn't want to leave her.

He couldn't wait to get away.

What was happening to him?

'I'll be back Tuesday,' he said, getting to his feet then leaning over to capture her lips.

He'd told her yesterday morning that he needed to go to America on business. He hadn't specified which American continent and she hadn't asked. She had no idea he was travelling to Brazil.

It would be the first time they'd been parted since he'd rescued her from those thugs on Nutmeg Island.

Her arm looped around his neck and she kissed him back, her teeth razing gently along his bottom lips when she pulled away, still holding him, and gazed into his eyes.

'When you get home…' She swallowed, colour flooding her cheeks. 'We can enjoy trying again to make a baby.'

How could she be like this around him? How could she even bear to look at him?

He took a deep breath and gave her one final, lingering kiss.

He prayed it wouldn't be their last.

As he got into his waiting car an hour later, he knew he would have to come to a decision soon. Tomorrow he would meet Carlos in Brazil. If Gabriele played his cards right, the original documents would be handed over. If he could meet Carlos's price, he should be able to persuade him to testify in person.

If everything went as he hoped, Ignazio would be arrested within days.

And he would lose Elena.

Elena got out of the test car and pulled the helmet off her head, unable to wipe the beam from her face.

That had to count as one of the best experiences of her life.

Monty, the official test driver, had called her that morning to say he had an unexpected free window and the test car was available for her to take out on the track. She hadn't needed asking twice. She'd jumped straight into the small Mantegna sports car Gabriele had given her the keys to before he'd left, and only just kept within the speed limit in her rush to Mantegna HQ.

Monty had driven the first couple of laps, explaining all the pertinent information before letting her loose. After a cautious first lap, she had put her foot down, the speedometer reaching one hundred and ten miles an hour before she'd lost her nerve and slowed it to a more reasonable ninety.

It had been an amazing experience.

What had made it extra special was knowing she had enjoyed it for herself; not as a means of proving a point to the men of the world—specifically her father and brothers—but for the sheer exhilaration.

Finally she understood what Gabriele meant about her having desires that were specific to *her* and not her gender. She was a woman learning to embrace the feminine side of her nature but also learning that the feminine side didn't exclude the traditionally masculine pursuits she enjoyed.

She suspected she would have enjoyed punching her brothers when she'd been a child even if she'd been dressed in pretty pink dresses and had her hair tied in neat little plaits.

Gabriele had done this for her. He'd opened her eyes and forced her to see and accept who she really was: a flesh and blood woman.

Knowing he was mid-air, flying back to Florence, she hadn't bothered calling to tell him she would be testing the car. He'd told her to expect him home late afternoon so she would tell him about it then. And tell him she'd decided to resign from her job. That was something that had solidified in her mind over the past couple of days, when Gabriele's absence had given her time to really think.

She'd missed him so much it scared her. It was like a great hollow ache in her entire being.

She knew the day would soon come when she would have to live with missing him permanently. They had no future. They never would.

However her feelings had developed, she still had Ricci blood running through her veins.

But something *had* passed between them the night of their party; changed them fundamentally. Whether it was enough…

Enough for what though? For a life together? A real life?

After Monty had put the boiler outfits they'd been wearing away, they headed back to the car park.

About to walk through the double doors, Elena did a double take at a car parked at the front and the driver leaning against its door smoking a cigarette.

'Is Gabriele here?' she asked the receptionist when she'd got inside the main building.

'He arrived an hour ago,' the receptionist said, recognising her. 'He's in his office.'

'Thanks.' Checking her phone for any missed calls or messages, of which there were none from Gabriele, she climbed the stairs.

What was he doing here? When she'd spoken to him last night he hadn't mentioned anything about coming back early.

Excited to see him, Elena hurried her pace, heading in the direction she recalled his office being in.

Taking a left at the top of the stairs on the third floor, she passed a skinny man in a garish silver suit. Thinking he looked familiar but unable to place where from, she arrived at Gabriele's office door.

She knocked, not wanting to presume too much and barge in without invitation.

The door was opened by Anna Maria, whose eyes widened to see her.

From behind the desk, visible from her vantage point at the threshold, Gabriele shot to his feet.

'Elena? What are you doing here?' he asked hoarsely.

They were both clearly shocked to see her. No, make

that horrified. They looked like a couple of children caught in the act of stealing.

Anna Maria appeared frozen, making no attempt to get out of her way. Elena pushed past her and strode to the desk.

'What's going on?' she demanded, half expecting to see discarded underwear on the floor.

'Nothing.' A sheath of papers was strewn over the desk, which he was gathering together. 'I wasn't expecting you.'

'I've been on the test drive you suggested Monty take me on.' As she spoke, she tried to see what was on the papers. Whatever they were, Gabriele didn't want her to see them, not if the way he was rushing to file them away was anything to judge by.

Something icy cold snaked up her spine.

That man in the corridor...

She snatched the papers from Gabriele's hand.

'Elena—'

He tried to take them back but it was too late.

She only needed a quick scan for her eyes to swim and her brain to fill with cold fog.

That man. *She knew who he was.*

'No,' she whispered, shaking her head violently. 'No.'

Discarded underwear would have been preferable to this.

Not taking her eyes from Gabriele's white face, she said, 'Anna Maria, leave us.'

The door slammed sharply.

'I suppose this explains why Anna Maria has been so uneasy around me,' she said in a voice that sounded distant to her ears. 'She's known from the beginning?'

Gabriele dropped the papers onto the desk and stared at her with black ringing eyes. 'Elena, let me explain.'

The coldness cleared, replaced with red-hot fury that she controlled by a whisker.

'What do you want to explain? How you've been lying to me all this time? How you tricked me into marrying you to save my father from a prison sentence when all the time you were still plotting against him?'

Of all the things she'd struggled to believe since that fateful night on Nutmeg Island, this was the hardest. Of everything, this was the one thing she didn't want to believe or accept, harder even than believing her father could have betrayed his best friend so heinously.

She'd given Gabriele everything of herself and *it had all been a lie*.

Sharply pointed talons clawed at her heart, slashing into her belly, slicing great chunks out of her.

'I never lied to you.' He spoke calmly but his chest rose and fell rapidly, his strong nose flaring. 'The contract never said anything about me not continuing my fight to clear my name and finding the evidence to prove your father was behind the fraud.'

'You're lying to me now!' Her control failed her. She grabbed a pile of the papers and began ripping into them, wishing it were his flesh she was tearing into. 'You've been lying to me from the beginning. You knew damn well I thought it meant you would leave my father alone, that marrying you meant my family would be safe. God, I was starting to think you were someone special—I was prepared to have your baby! And you were lying to me and using me, you manipulative *bastard*.'

He yanked at his hair, his eyes black with feverish emotion. 'Goddammit, Elena, I spent two years in prison for a crime *your father* committed. My dad died of a broken heart and you've seen how my mother is with your own eyes—do you really think I could just let that go? Your father deserves to pay for those crimes.'

'If my father did it then yes, he *does* deserve to pay, but *I don't*. I have done nothing, not to you, not to your family, not to anyone.' Furious, heartbroken tears fell like a waterfall from her eyes. 'And you know that's true. You know I'm innocent but you couldn't give a damn, so long as you get your vengeance.'

The colour that had returned to his face paled again. 'Elena…'

'How much did you pay Carlos to turn traitor?' she screamed. 'How much are you paying him to lie for you?'

Sadness now rang from his eyes and he raised a hand as if to reach for her before dropping it back down to his side. 'It's not lies. It's the truth. That's all I ever wanted—for the truth to be told and my family's good name to be restored. But I swear to you, I didn't know you were innocent. I would never have involved you in any of this if I had.'

'And that's supposed to make it all right? As if I will *ever* believe another word that comes from your mouth.' She gave a maniacal laugh that ripped through her throat. 'I'm nothing but a pawn in your game and I will hate you for the rest of my life.'

She couldn't look at him, couldn't look at the lying mouth she had kissed with such love. Couldn't look in the eyes that had devoured her and made her feel so wanted and *necessary*.

It had all been a lie.

'Where are you going?' A trace of panic resonated from his voice.

Facing him for the last time, she said with all the loathing she muster, 'As far away from you and your ugly vendetta as I can get. I never want to see you again.'

The door slammed shut and she was gone.

Gabriele stared at the blank space where only a moment before Elena had stood, his heart pounding and nausea rising from his stomach to his throat.

Dear God, what had he done?

What had he done?

CHAPTER THIRTEEN

ELENA STOPPED LONG enough at Gabriele's apartment to get her passport and leave his car keys on the sideboard. Everything else could go to hell.

From Florence, she took a flight to Sweden, hired a car and headed for the sleepy town her mother had been raised in. She didn't think she had ever needed her more.

During the long drive she did not allow herself to think of Gabriele. As far as she was concerned, he didn't exist. She would spend the rest of her life scrubbing clean her memories of him if she had to.

Eventually she arrived at a large timber chalet on the edge of a lake.

She switched the engine off and gazed at it with a lump in her throat and an ache in her heart.

This was where her mother had spent her childhood. And here was the second-best thing to the woman who had given birth to her.

The front door opened and a tall white-blonde woman appeared, staring at the car with a quizzical expression.

Elena got out and gazed at her aunt.

'Elena?'

She tried to speak but the words wouldn't form.

Agnes must have seen something in her expression for concern flittered over her face and she hurried over to her. Instead of bombarding her with questions, her kindly aunt simply pulled her into an embrace and whispered into her hair, 'Oh, Elena, it is so wonderful to have you here.'

And with those words, Elena burst into tears.

Hours later Elena sat at a scrubbed wooden kitchen table drinking sweet tea. Her aunt had sent Henrick, her husband, out on errands, with the words, 'Don't hurry back.'

Elena told her everything. Every sordid detail.

Agnes didn't say much, seemingly content to listen and provide cakes and biscuits for the never-ending supply of tea.

'Do you think your father's involved?' was the first question she asked when Elena finished talking.

'I don't know,' Elena whispered. 'I know there are many things I've been kept in the dark about.'

For the first time she forced herself to really think about her father, not just as the man who had raised and loved her but as something else. Someone else. Someone who could be cruel enough to frame his best friend and allow his own godson to go to prison for a crime he himself had committed.

'Do *you* think he's capable of doing it?'

'If you had asked me that twenty-five years ago I would have said no,' Agnes answered matter-of-factly. 'But losing your mother...' She closed her eyes and shook her head. When she opened them to look at Elena, sadness emanated from them. 'Do you know much about your parents' marriage?'

'Not really.' She attempted a smile. 'I know they met when my mother was on holiday in Italy.'

Agnes returned the smile. 'They did. It was love at first sight for them both. They were smitten with each other. I had never seen Hilde so happy.'

'I'm sensing a "but" coming.'

Her aunt grimaced. 'Your father is a very possessive man. He couldn't bear to let her out of his sight. He hated her talking to other men.'

'He didn't...?' She couldn't bring herself to say the words.

'Hit her?' Agnes supplied. 'No. Never. But he never thought twice about beating up any man who disrespected her or who your father felt was getting too close to her. Hilde was a very gentle woman—it upset her very much.'

Elena couldn't think of anything to say to that. This was a side to her father she had never seen.

'I am telling you this so you can understand how your father became the man he is now,' Agnes said gently. 'They *were* happy. They loved each other very much. When your mother died...' She tapped the side of her head. 'I don't think he ever got over it. He threw a protective cloak around his children and hardened himself to the rest of the world. He loved his boys but you were always the apple of his eye. He doted on you. You were a fighting tomboy but you have your mother's gentle heart. I don't think your father could bear for you to see him as less than perfect.'

Elena put her hand to her throat and closed her eyes.

Trying to forget thoughts of disloyalty, and trying to think dispassionately about Gabriele when all she wanted to do was spend the rest of her life crying, she took a deep breath and mentally counted off some indisputable facts.

She ran the European division. It was the division where nothing creative happened. It was an outpost for selling stock. Nothing more. All the meat and bones of her father's company was conducted in Asia and South America. She had never travelled to either continent. She was kept ignorant of whatever happened there.

Alfredo Mantegna had been her father's best friend. When Alfredo had emigrated with his family to open his car empire to the North American market, her father had used Alfredo's new contacts to expand his own empire.

Her father no longer had any business dealings in North America.

A decade ago, her father and Alfredo had merged the overlapping parts of their two business entities into a new business that they owned fifty-fifty. The headquarters were based in Brazil, where her own father had plenty of businesses and where Alfredo had none. That business was proven to have been used as a front for fraud and money laundering. The trail had led to the Mantegnas.

Even through her loathing of Gabriele she could not believe he would be involved in something like that. Gabriele's mother...

Is he in prison yet?

Elena clamped a hand over her mouth and swallowed back the rising nausea.

'It is natural to want to see only the best in the people we love,' Agnes said in a quiet, sympathetic voice. 'You and your father have always been exceptionally close. If your father *was* behind it I am certain he would do everything in his power to protect you from it.'

'I need to talk to him, don't I?' Elena whispered.

Agnes nodded and reached across the table to take her hand. 'I suspect you're the only person who could ever get the truth from him.'

Elena blew out a long breath of air.

She'd buried her head in the sand for long enough.

She needed to speak to him face to face, now, before Gabriele and Carlos went to the FBI. If they hadn't already.

Her father answered his phone after the first ring and, while he hesitated at first, agreed to her request to meet her in Sweden.

He arrived at Agnes's cabin the very next day.

That he was still at liberty soothed her. It meant Gabriele knew his evidence wasn't strong enough, or the FBI had discounted it, or Carlos had changed his mind about being a turncoat.

She greeted him at the door and was immediately engulfed in a huge embrace.

'It's been many years since I've been in this house,' he said as she led him to the kitchen, where Agnes had laid out lunch for them. Clearly ill at ease, he craned his neck at every turn, looking at everything. 'What brought you here?'

'I wanted to see Aunt Agnes,' she said. 'Don't worry—they've gone out. It's just you and me.'

'Mantegna's not with you?'

She shook her head, taking a seat. 'I've left him.'

He paused, staring hard at her, then a smile spread across the tension-strewn face. 'If I had known that I would have brought champagne.'

She didn't respond, taking the lid off the casserole dish. Even if he'd magically produced a bottle of champagne she felt too heartsick to drink.

She didn't think her heart would ever beat normally again.

Why couldn't she forget him? Why was it that every time she closed her eyes, all she could see was Gabriele? After everything he'd done, why did she *ache* so much for him?

You would have done the same if you were in his shoes. If someone had destroyed your family the way Gabriele believes your father destroyed his, you would have stopped at nothing for revenge.

She would never have hurt an innocent though.

He didn't know you were innocent.

'So you have seen the light,' her father said, nodding his approval. 'I told your brothers, I said, "Don't worry about Elena, she's a good girl, she knows where her loyalty lies."'

She ladled some casserole into a bowl, holding it tightly to stop her shaking hands from spilling the hot liquid onto the table.

'Gabriele's loyalty is to his father,' she said, choosing her words with care.

Something flickered on her father's face.

And in that moment all her doubts crystallised and the truth came crashing down on her.

It was all true. All of it. Everything Gabriele had said. All true.

'Elena?'

She looked into her father's concerned face, the room swimming, darkness seeping into her pores, infecting her blood.

The truth was what her heart had been telling her for weeks but she had been too wilfully blind to see.

Gabriele tied a cufflink to his sleeve and smiled at his reflection.

It made no difference.

He still looked shot.

He tried again. This time his mouth wouldn't co-operate.

His driver was waiting outside for him. At Mantegna HQ, over two dozen media journalists were congregating for the launch of the new Alfredo car, along with over a hundred of the staff members who had worked most closely on it. Caterers had delivered enough canapés to feed an army and enough champagne to get a battalion drunk.

This was the culmination of the past year's hard work, a car made to honour his father, and he could no longer bring himself to care.

How could he ever care about anything when the best part of him wouldn't be by his side?

She would never be by his side again.

Having got increasingly frantic that Elena had seemingly dropped off the face of the earth, he'd hired a bunch of private detectives on all continents to find her. Just to satisfy him that she was well. Four hours ago he'd got the message that she'd landed in Rome.

The relief had been indescribable.

After five days of silence he at least had confirmation that she was alive.

She wouldn't see him. He knew that. She refused to answer his calls or his messages. His emails bounced back as undeliverable.

How could he stand up in front of one hundred and fifty people and make a speech when he couldn't think of

a single thing to say that wasn't a plea for Elena to come
back to him?

Why had he attempted to defend himself?

There was no defence for what he'd done and the more
he tortured himself by thinking about it, the more he accepted how blinded and despicably wrong he'd been.

He could hear his housekeeper hovering behind his bedroom door, knew she wanted to remind him of the time and
how late he was going to make the launch.

Instead of getting into gear, he slipped into Elena's
dressing room.

All her clothes were still neatly hung up or folded away,
as if waiting for her to return to claim them.

He knew she would never reclaim them.

He spotted the silver top she'd worn on their first night
out together and pulled it off the hanger, burying his nose
in it, hoping to catch her scent before it faded completely.

It had already gone.

A sharp burn at the backs of his eyes caught him. He
blinked it away as a commotion outside caught his attention. Swaying slightly, he went back into his room and
opened the door.

Anna Maria stood there, looking flushed.

'Have you seen the news?'

Elena's house was in a quiet, affluent street in Rome's Pari-
oli district. Soft lights glowed behind the shuttered windows When Gabriele found the red door he was searching
for, he put his hands to his knees and allowed himself to
breathe.

It had been two hours since Anna Maria had shown him
the coverage dominating the Italian news channels and,
he suspected, the US ones too. In that time he'd comman-
deered a helicopter to fly him from Florence and taken the
cab ride from hell across Rome's streets, which were only
marginally better to drive through than Florence's. Ten

minutes ago he'd thrown a hundred-euro bill at the driver and got out, figuring it had to be quicker walking.

Taking one last apprehensive breath, he climbed the steps and pressed the doorbell. He banged on the door for good measure too.

When there was no answer, he rang and banged again. He would ring and bang on the door all night if he had to.

After what was probably only a minute but felt much, much longer, he heard a clicking noise followed by the slow turning of the door handle.

The door opened a fraction and a green eye appeared in the gap.

'Elena...' He couldn't say anything more. His throat had closed up.

She didn't say anything, her mostly concealed face staring at him blankly as if a stranger were on her doorstep.

'Can I come in?' he asked hoarsely.

Still not speaking, she shook her head.

'Please? I will only take a minute of your time.'

Another shake of her head.

He bowed his head and exhaled heavily. 'I understand.'

He raised his head to look back at her. She had almost entirely closed the door. Only the tiniest of gaps remained open.

'I don't expect you to believe me but I had nothing to do with your father's arrest,' he said quietly, certain she was listening. 'I destroyed the evidence I had. I just wanted you to know that and to tell you that I'm sorrier than words can say for what I've done to you.'

He bowed his head again and swallowed.

He expected no response and none followed.

But she was still there, still listening.

Gabriele sank to the floor and pressed his cheek to the door. 'My father would be heartbroken if he knew what I'd done in his name. I forced you into a marriage you didn't want. I made you dress in clothes you didn't want. I made you sign a contract stating the only way you could leave was if my baby was in your belly. I took your virginity.' He sucked in a breath and gazed up at the starry night sky. 'I did all that for revenge against your father, not against you. But you were my pawn and I was going to play you—I *did* play you. I told myself that you *had* to be in league with your father, as if that could excuse what I was doing. But you were nothing like my prejudices expected. You were everything. You *are* everything. *My* everything. I fell in love with you, Elena, but I was so blinded by revenge I couldn't see it.'

Placing a palm against the door, he prayed she was still there, still listening to him.

'You told me once that there wouldn't be a minute of the day when I didn't regret what I'd done to you. Well, that day is here. I know you will never forgive me but I wanted you to know that I will never forgive myself either. You wanted to see me burn in hell and you have your wish; I'm there. Every day without you is agony.'

He pinched the bridge of his nose and blinked rapidly, then got to his feet. He'd said everything he wanted to say. Everything he could say.

Almost stumbling back down the steps on legs that felt filled with lead, he stood on the pavement not having a clue where to go.

Elena leaving him had left him rudderless.

'I know it wasn't you who had my father arrested.'

The hairs on the back of his neck stood on end.

He turned slowly.

Elena stood clinging to the open doorway. Her face was pinched, her hair loose but lank around her shoulders. All she wore was a pair of leggings and a long-sleeved baggy top.

'It was me.'

And then she was crying, her hand clasped over her

mouth, her face a stream of tears, her whole body trembling with the force of her misery.

He flew back up the steps and took hold of her, pulling her to him.

When she wrapped her arms around him and sobbed into his chest, he held her tight, devastated to see the depths of her despair.

This was all his fault.

She tilted her head back to look at him with red-rimmed eyes, tears still pouring down her cheeks.

'It was me,' she repeated, biting into her lip.

He brushed her tears away and gazed into her distraught face. 'What was you?'

'My father.' She hiccupped. 'I made him confess. I told him if he didn't he would never see me again.' Her face crumpled. 'Oh, Gabriele, I'm so sorry. He did frame your father and let you go to prison for it. He's been laundering money for years. You were right all along but I couldn't see it.'

Unable to bear her distress any longer, he pulled her back into his arms and stroked her hair. 'My love, please, no, you have nothing to apologise for.'

'I didn't believe you.'

'Of course you didn't. He's your father. We all want to believe the best of our parents.' He burrowed his nose in her hair, breathing her in, hardly able to believe she was allowing him to hold her and that she held him in turn.

'You should be at the launch,' she suddenly wailed. 'This was your big night for your father…'

'It doesn't matter,' he cut in. '*You* are all that matters. My father would understand.'

When she was finally still, he took her face in his hands and stared intently into her eyes. 'Elena…why? Why did you make him confess?'

Incredulity came into her eyes. 'Because what he did was despicable. What he did to you and your family…' She shook her head, her chest shuddering. 'I'm still struggling to believe he could do such a thing. The money laundering and fraud… I might have been able to accept that, but to set your family up like he did and watch you be imprisoned for it…'

Her entire body shook, fresh tears falling over his hands.

'He was jealous of your father's success. When my mother died his jealousy grew—he saw your father with a happy family and thriving business and it turned him. When he learned the FBI was monitoring him, he framed your father without any remorse. I'm trying to understand how he could do it but…' She blew a breath of air out. 'I can never forgive him for what he's done to you.'

'Listen to me,' he said, speaking quietly. 'Whatever he's done, he's still your father. You will always love him and he will always love you. Never forget that.'

'I feel tainted,' she whispered.

A dog barked from across the street, its walker staring at them with curiosity.

'Can we go inside and talk before someone accuses me of bothering you?' he asked.

She attempted a laugh. 'You want to come inside a Ricci house?'

'The Ricci blood can't be all bad if it made you.'

She gazed at him, her brow furrowed.

'Can't you see how special you are that your father would willingly go to prison rather than lose you?' He kissed her forehead. 'And you're so special to me that I ripped up the documents and sent Carlos on his way rather than have your father arrested because your happiness and peace of mind mean more to me than anything. More than revenge. More than clearing my name. I had lost all faith in humanity and you gave it back to me—you, the woman with Ricci blood in her veins. I love you more than I knew was possible and I will never, ever forgive myself for what I've done to you.'

'Your name *will* be cleared now,' she said softly.

'That means a lot to me,' he admitted. 'I'm just sorry it comes with such a heavy price for you.'

'I'll survive.' She swallowed and gazed into his eyes. 'I'll survive if you're with me.'

Speech suddenly became impossible.

Elena stared at the man she loved, wishing he could see into her heart and read what was there. 'You saved me.'

His eyes didn't leave her face.

'You saved me from those men and then you saved me from myself. You opened my eyes to who I really am. You taught me there's nothing to be ashamed of in being a woman; in being *me*.' She looked up at the starry sky. 'Without you in my life, it feels like all the stars have gone out.'

When she gazed back at him, stark, silent hope and disbelief were etched on his face.

Now it was her turn to touch *him*. She pressed her palm to his cheek, a shiver racing through her to feel the smooth skin she'd dreamed of every night since she'd left him.

'I love you, Gabriele, and I forgive you.'

His eyes widened and he nestled into her palm.

'You love me?' he asked in a choked voice. 'You *forgive* me?'

'What you did... I can't say in all honesty that I wouldn't have done the same in your shoes. What you've been through—what we've both been through...'

'If you give me a second chance I will never lie to you again,' he said, with such sincerity the last doubts in her heart fluttered away.

'I know,' she said softly.

Suddenly he dropped to one knee and took her hand. 'Elena Ricci, will you do me the honour of divorcing me?'

'What?'

A smile tugged at his lips, the heavy lines that had marred his face since his arrival on her doorstep lifting.

'Divorce me…and then do me the even greater honour of marrying me, but this time for real. I love you and I want to spend the rest of my life with you. I want to have little Mantegna and Ricci babies with you.'

If her heart could expand any further it would explode out of her chest.

All the misery of the past five days was pushed aside as a wave of joy ripped through her.

'So will you?' he asked, still on one knee, his finger rubbing the gold band on her wedding finger. 'Do you want it too?'

'More than anything,' she said, a beam she had no control over spreading over her face. 'I love you, Gabriele.'

With that, he pulled the ring off, threw it over his shoulder and kissed the space on her finger where it had been. Gazing back up into her eyes, he said, 'The next ring I put there will be for keeps. All the rings I put on this finger will be for keeps just as my heart is yours to keep for ever.'

'My heart belongs to you too and it always will.' She laughed, then planted the most enormous kiss she could muster on his welcoming mouth. 'Shall we go inside now?'

'Yes. Let's go and make some Mantegna-Ricci babies.'

And they did.

EPILOGUE

'YOU'RE GOING to be late,' Lisbeth squealed the second Elena stepped into the hotel bedroom. Lisbeth was already dressed in her mint bridesmaid dress.

'No, I'm not.'

Malin stuck her head out of the bathroom. 'You're here. Thank God. Your ex-husband has been driving us crazy.'

'He knew I was on my way back.'

'You didn't speak to him?' Lisbeth demanded. 'That's bad luck.'

'I'm sure it's only *seeing* them before the wedding that's bad luck.' Elena hid a grin. She swore her Swedish cousins had sucked all the nerves out of her and channelled them into themselves.

She herself had only felt mild anxiety at her journey taking an hour longer than anticipated. There was plenty of time. Besides, Gabriele would wait for her. He would always wait.

There was a bang on the door.

'Stay there,' Lisbeth hissed. 'It's probably your ex-husband.' She tugged the door open a fraction.

'Is she back?' came Gabriele's voice.

'Yes, she's here. Now go away. You can't see her.'

'How was her father?'

'He was good,' Elena called, ignoring the glares from her cousins. 'He's holding up well. Now go before Lisbeth and Malin spontaneously combust.'

She'd left before breakfast to visit her father at the prison he was being held at as he awaited sentencing. She couldn't get married without seeing him first. It had lifted her heart to hear him give them his blessing.

She visited him whenever she could. It would be easier after sentencing as he'd be transferred to a prison in Italy, so she'd be able to visit much more regularly.

He liked her visits. While she would never be able to forgive him for what he'd done to Gabriele and his family, she still loved him and he loved her. He must have taken a lesson in selflessness from her ex-husband as he'd completely exonerated her brothers from any blame. Unfortunately he hadn't been able to save them from financial ruin. That they still had roofs over their heads was entirely down to Gabriele.

Gabriele chuckled from the other side of the door. 'I'll see you in a couple of hours.'

A couple of hours?

From feeling as if she had all the time in the world, she suddenly saw the time with the same eyes as her panicking cousins.

In a flurry, she got herself into gear.

After she'd had a quick shower, Lisbeth and Malin got to work.

Her hair was dried and styled, her face made up and then it was time to get her into her dress.

When she was done she truly felt like a bride.

Her ivory dress, which hugged her figure, had a five-foot train. It sparkled and shimmered under the light. She could feel the rest of her shimmering with it.

The Somerset County church they were marrying in shimmered too, the autumn sunshine bouncing light off its white walls.

This was it. This was her wedding day. This was the day she committed the rest of her life to the man she loved.

With Aunt Agnes on her arm to walk her down the aisle and her cousins behind her, Elena took the first step towards Gabriele, her ex-husband and, any moment now, to be her husband for ever.

He stood at the front in his black tuxedo and did nothing but gaze at her adoringly as she walked towards him.

Elena beamed hugely to see his mother sitting beside Loretta in the family seats. It had been touch and go whether she would make it—it could only be feasible if she was having a good day—but they had decided to take the risk of marrying in Somerset County in the hope she would be well enough,

The gamble had paid off.

Finally they exchanged their vows and Gabriele was sliding a gold band onto her finger with their names and the date engraved on it so it rested above the diamond engagement ring he'd given her the day after they'd embraced the love they had.

And then they were pronounced man and wife. Gabriele and Elena Mantegna-Ricci.

The little life growing in her belly would get the best of them both.

* * * * *

AT THE COUNT'S BIDDING

BIDDING

CAITLIN CREWS

CHAPTER ONE

"I MUST BE hallucinating. And may God have mercy on you if I am not."

Paige Fielding hadn't heard that voice in ten years. It wrapped around her even as it sliced through her, making the breezy Southern California afternoon fade away. Making the email she'd been writing disappear from her mind in full. Making her forget what year it was, what day it was. Rocketing her right back into the murky, painful past.

That voice. *His voice.*

Uncompromisingly male. As imperious as it was incredulous. The faint hint of sex and Italy in his voice even with all that temper besides, and it rolled over Paige like a flattening heat. It pressed into her from behind, making her want to squirm in her seat. Or simply melt where she sat. Or come apart—easily and instantly—the way she always had at the sound of it.

She swiveled around in her chair in instant, unconscious obedience, knowing exactly who she'd see in the archway that led into the sprawling Bel Air mansion high in the Hollywood Hills called La Bellissima in honor of its famous owner, the screen legend Violet Sutherlin. She knew who it was, and still, something like a premonition washed over her and made her skin prickle in the scant seconds before her gaze found him there in the arched, open door, scowling at her with what looked like a healthy mix of contempt and pure, electric hatred.

Giancarlo Alessi. The only man she'd ever loved with every inch of her doomed and naive heart, however little good that had done either one of them. The only man who'd made her scream and sob and beg for more, until she was hoarse and mute with longing. The only man who still haunted her, and who she suspected always would, despite everything.

Because he was also the only man she'd ever betrayed. Thoroughly. Indisputably. Her stomach twisted hard, reminding her of what she'd done with a sick lurch. As if she'd forgotten. As if she ever could.

She hadn't thought she'd had a choice. But she doubted he'd appreciate that any more now than he had then.

"I can explain," she said. Too quickly, too nervously. She didn't remember pushing back from the table where she'd been sitting, doing her work out in the pretty sunshine as was her custom during the lazy afternoons, but she was standing then, somehow, feeling as unsteady on her own legs as she had in the chair. As lost in his dark, furious gaze as she'd been ten years ago.

"You can explain to security," he grated at her, each word a crisp slap. She felt red and obvious. Marked. As if he could see straight through her to that squalid past of hers that had ruined them both. "I don't care what you're doing here, Nicola. I want you gone."

She winced at that name. That hated name she hadn't used since the day she'd lost him. Hearing it again, after all this time and in that voice of his was physically upsetting. Deeply repellant. Her stomach twisted again, harder, and then knotted.

"I don't—" Paige didn't know what to say, how to say

it. How to explain what had happened since that awful day ten years ago when she'd sold him out and destroyed them both. What was there to say? She'd never told him the whole truth, when she could have. She'd never been able to bear the thought of him knowing how polluted she was or the kind of place, the kind of people, she'd come from. And they'd fallen in love so fast, their physical connection a white-hot explosion that had consumed them for those two short months they'd been together—there hadn't seemed to be any time to get to know each other. Not really. "I don't go by Nicola anymore."

He froze solid in the doorway, a kind of furious astonishment rolling over him and then out from him like a thunderclap, deafening and wild, echoing inside of her like a shout.

It hurt. It all hurt.

"I never—" This was terrible. Worse than she'd imagined, and she'd imagined it often. She felt an awful heat at the back of her eyes and a warning sort of ache between her breasts, as if a sob was gathering force and threatening to spill over, and she knew better than to let it out. She knew he wouldn't react well. She was lucky he was speaking to her at all now instead of having Violet's security guards toss her bodily from the estate without so much as a word. But she kept talking anyway, as if that might help. "It's my middle name, actually. It was a— my name is Paige."

"Curiously, Paige is also the name of my mother's personal assistant."

But she could tell by the way his voice grew ominously quiet that he knew. That he wasn't confused or asking her to explain herself. That he'd figured it out the moment he'd seen her—that she'd been the name on all those emails from his mother over the past few years.

And she could also tell exactly how he felt about that revelation. It was written into every stiffly furious line of his athletic form.

"Who cannot be you." He shifted and her breath caught, as if the movement of his perfect body was a blow. "Assure me, please, that you are no more than an unpleasant apparition from the darkest hour of my past. That you have not insinuated yourself into my family. Do it now and I might let you walk out of here without calling the police."

Ten years ago she'd have thought he was bluffing. *That* Giancarlo would no more have called the police on her than he would have thrown himself off the nearest bridge. But this was a different man. *This* was the Giancarlo she'd made, and she had no one to blame for that but herself.

Well. Almost no one. But there was no point bringing *her* mother into this, Paige knew. It was his he was concerned about—and besides, Paige hadn't spoken to her own in a decade.

"Yes," she said, and she felt shaky and vulnerable, as if it had only just occurred to her that her presence here was questionable, at best. "I've been working for Violet for almost three years now, but Giancarlo, you have to believe that I never—"

"*Stai zitto.*"

And Paige didn't have to speak Italian to understand that harsh command, or the way he slashed his hand through the air, gruffly ordering her silence. She obeyed. What else could she do? And she watched him warily as if, at any moment, he might bare his fangs and sink them in her neck.

She'd deserve that, too.

Paige had always known this day would come. That this quiet new life she'd crafted for herself almost by accident was built on the shakiest of foundations and that all it would take was this man's reappearance to upend the whole of it. Giancarlo was Violet's son, her only child. The product of her fabled second marriage to an Italian count that the entire world had viewed as its own, personal, real-life fairy tale. Had Paige imagined this would end in any other manner? She'd been living on borrowed time from the moment she'd taken that interview and answered all the questions Violet's managers had asked in the way she'd known—thanks to her insider's take on Violet's actual life away from the cameras, courtesy of her brief, brilliant affair with Giancarlo all those years ago—would get her the job.

Some people might view that harshly, she was aware. Particularly Giancarlo himself. But she'd had good intentions. Surely that counted for something? *You know perfectly well that it doesn't,* the harsh voice in her head that was her last link to her mother grated at her. *You know exactly what intentions are worth.*

And it had been so long. She'd started to believe that this might never happen. That Giancarlo might stay in Europe forever, hidden away in the hills of Tuscany building his überprivate luxury hotel and associated cottages the way he had for the past decade, ever since she'd set him up and those sordid, intimate photographs had been splashed across every tabloid imaginable. She'd lulled herself into a false sense of security.

Because he was here now, and nothing was safe any longer, and yet all she wanted to do was lose herself in looking at him. Reacquainting herself with him. Reminding herself what she'd given up. What she'd ruined.

She'd seen pictures of him all over this house in the years she'd worked here. Always dark and forbiddingly elegant in his particularly sleek way, it took no more

than a glance to understand Giancarlo was decidedly not
American. Even ten years ago and despite having spent so
much time in Los Angeles, he'd had that air. That *thing*
about him that whispered that he was the product of long
centuries of European blue bloods. It was something in
the way he held himself, distant and disapproving, the
hint of ancient places and old gods stamped into his aristocratic bones and lurking behind his cool dark gaze.

Paige had expected Giancarlo would still be attractive,
of course, should she ever encounter him again. What
she hadn't expected—or what she'd allowed herself to
forget—was that he was so *raw*. Seeing him was like a
hard, stunning blow to the side of her head, leaving her
ears ringing and her heart thumping erratically inside
her chest. As if he knew it, his head canted to one side
as he regarded her, as if daring her to keep talking when
he'd ordered her to stop.

But she couldn't seem to do anything but stare. As if
the past decade had been one long slide of gray and here
he was again, all of him in bold color and bright lights.
So glaring and hot she could hardly bear to look at him.
But she did. She couldn't help herself.

He stood as if he was used to accolades, or simply
commanding the full and rapt attention of every room
he entered. It was partly the clothes he wore, the fabrics
fitting him so perfectly, almost reverently, in a manner
Paige knew came only at astronomical expense. But it
was more than that. His body was lean and powerful,
a symphony of whipcord strength tightly leashed, the
crackle of his temper and that blazing sensuality that felt
like a touch from ten feet away, carnal and wild. Even
though she knew he'd never willingly touch her again.
He'd made that clear.

Giancarlo was still so beautiful, yes, but there was

something so *male* about him, so rampantly masculine, that it made Paige's throat go dry. It was worse now, ten years later. Much worse. He stood in the open doorway in a pair of dark trousers, boots, and the kind of jacket Paige associated with sexy Ducati motorcycles and mystical places a girl like her from a ramshackle desert town in Nowhere, Arizona, only fantasized about, like the Amalfi Coast. Yet somehow he looked as effortlessly refined as if he could walk straight into a black-tie gala as he was—or climb into a bed for a long, hot, blisteringly feral weekend of no-holds-barred sex.

But it did her no good to remember that kind of thing. For her body to ready itself for his possession as if it had been ten minutes since they'd last touched instead of ten years. As if it knew him, recognized him, wanted him—as deeply and irrevocably as she always had. As if *wanting him* was some kind of virus that had only ever been in remission, for which there was no cure.

The kind of virus that made her breasts heavy and her belly too taut and shivery at once. The kind of virus that made her wish she still danced the way she had in high school and those few years after, obsessively and constantly, as if that kind of extended, heedless movement might be the only way to survive it. *Him.* His marvelous mouth tightened as the silence dragged on and she sent up a prayer of thanks that he hadn't thought to remove his mirrored sunglasses yet. She didn't want to know what his dark gaze would feel like when she could actually see his eyes again. She didn't want to know what that would do to her now. She still remembered what it had been like that last time, that short and harsh conversation on the doorstep of her apartment building that final morning, where he'd confronted her with those pictures and had truly understood what she'd done to him. When he'd looked at her as if he'd only then, in that moment, seen her true face—and it had been evil.

Pull yourself together, she ordered herself fiercely. There was no going back. There were no do-overs. She knew that too well.

"I'm sorry," she managed to get out before he cut her off again. Before she melted into the tears she knew she'd cry later, in private. Before the loss and grief she'd pretended she was over for years now swamped her. "Giancarlo, I'm so sorry."

He went so rigid it was as if she'd slapped him, and yet she felt slapped. She hurt everywhere.

"I don't care why you're here." His voice was rough. A scrape that tore her open, ripping her right down her middle. "I don't care what game you're playing this time. You have five minutes to leave the premises."

But all Paige could hear was what swirled there beneath his words. Rage. Betrayal, as if it was new. Hot and furious, like a fire that still burned bright between them. And she was sick, she understood, because instead of being as frightened of that as she should have been, something in her rejoiced that he wasn't indifferent. After all this time.

"If you do not do this of your own accord," Giancarlo continued with a certain vicious deliberation, and she knew he *wanted* that to hurt her, "I will take great pleasure in dumping you on the other side of the gates myself."

"Giancarlo—" she began, trying to sound calm, though her hands nervously smoothed at the soft blouse and the pencil skirt she wore. And even though she couldn't see his eyes, she felt them there, tracing the curve of her hips and her legs beneath, as if she'd deliberately directed his gaze to parts of her body he'd once claimed he worshipped. Had she meant to do that? How could she not know?

But he interrupted her again.

"You may call me Count Alessi in the remaining four minutes before I kick you out of here," he told her harshly. "But if you know what's good for you, whatever name you're using and whatever con you're running today and have been running for years, I'd suggest you stay silent."

"I'm not running a con. I'm not—" Paige cut herself off, because this was all too complicated and she should have planned for this, shouldn't she? She should have figured out what to say to someone who had no reason on earth to listen to her. And who wouldn't believe a word she said even if he did. Why hadn't she prepared herself? "I know you don't want to hear a single thing I have to say, but none of this is what you think. It wasn't back then, either. Not really."

He seemed to *expand* then, like a great wave. As if the force of his temper soared out from him and crashed over the whole of the grand terrace, the sloping lawn, the canyons all around, the complicated mess of Los Angeles stretched out below. It crackled as it cascaded over her, making every hair on her body seem to stand on end. That mouth of his flattened and he swept his sunglasses from his face at last—which was not an improvement. Because his eyes were dark and hot and gleamed a commanding sort of gold, and as he fastened them on her he made no attempt at all to hide the blistering light of his fury.

It made her want to sit down, hard, before she fell. It made her worry her legs might give out. It made her want to cry the way she had ten years ago, so hard and so long she'd made herself sick, for all the good that had done. She felt dangerously, dizzyingly hollow.

"Enlighten me," he suggested, all silken threat and that humming sort of violence *right there* beneath his elegant surface. Or maybe not really *beneath* it, she thought, now that she could see his beautiful, terrible face in all its furious perfection. "Which part was not what I thought? The fact that you arranged to have photographs taken of us while we were having sex, though I am certain I told you how much I hated public exposure after a lifetime in the glare of my mother's spotlight? Or the fact that you sold those photos to the tabloids?" He took a step toward her; his hands were in fists at his side, and she didn't understand how she could simultaneously want to run for her life and run *toward* him. He was a suicide waiting to happen. She should know that better than anyone. "Or perhaps I am misunderstanding the fact that you have now infiltrated my mother's house to further prey on my family?" He shook his head. "What kind of monster *are* you?"

"Giancarlo—"

"I will tell you exactly what kind." His nostrils flared and she knew that look that flashed over his face then. She knew it far too well. It was stamped into her memories and it made her stomach heave with the same shame and regret. It made her flush with terrible heat. "You are a mercenary bitch and I believe I was perfectly clear about this ten years ago. I never, ever wanted to see your face again."

And Paige was running out of ways to rank which part of this was the worst part, but she couldn't argue. Not with any of what he'd said. Yet rather than making her shrink down and curl up into the fetal position right there on the terra-cotta pavers beneath their feet, the way she'd done the last time he'd looked at her like that and called her names she'd richly deserved, it made something else shiver into being inside her. Something that made her straighten instead of shrink. Something that gave her the strength to meet his terrible glare, to lift her chin despite all of that furious, condemning gold.

"I love her."

That hung there between them, stark and heavy. And, she realized belatedly, an echo of what she'd said ten years ago, when it had been much too late. When he'd believed her even less than he did now. When she'd known full well that saying it would only hurt him, and she'd done it anyway. *I'm so sorry, Giancarlo. I love you.*

"What did you say?" His voice was too quiet. So soft and deliberately menacing it made her shake inside, though she didn't give in to it. She forced her spine even straighter. "What did you *dare* say to me?"

"This has nothing to do with you." That was true, in its way. Paige wasn't a lunatic, no matter what he might think. She'd simply understood a long time ago that she'd lost him and it was irrevocable. She'd accepted it. This wasn't about getting him back. It was about paying a debt in the only way she could. "It never did have anything to do with you," she continued when she was certain the shaking inside her wouldn't bleed over into her voice. "Not the way you're thinking. Not really."

He shook his head slightly, as if he was reeling, and he muttered something in a stream of silken, shaken Italian that she shouldn't have felt like that, all over her skin. Because it wasn't a caress. It was its opposite.

"This is a nightmare." He returned his furious glare to her and it was harder. Fiercer. Gold fury and that darkness inside it. "But nightmares end. You keep on, all these years later. It was two short months and too many explicit pictures. I knew better than to trust a woman like you in the first place, but this ought to be behind me." His lips thinned. "Why won't you go away, Nicola?"

"Paige." She couldn't tolerate that name. Never again. It was the emblem of all the things she'd lost, all the terrible choices she'd been forced to make, all the sacrifices she'd made for someone so unworthy it made her mouth taste acrid now, like ash and regret. "I'd rather you call me nothing but *mercenary bitch* instead of that."

"I don't care what you call yourself." Not quite a shout. Not quite. But his voice thudded into her like a hail of bullets anyway, and she couldn't disguise the way she winced. "I want you gone. I want this poison of yours out of my life, away from my mother. It disgusts me that you've been here all this time without my knowing it. Like a malignant cancer hiding in plain sight."

And she should go. Paige knew she should. This was twisted and wrong and sick besides, no matter the purity of her intentions. All her rationalizations, all her excuses, what did any of them matter when she was standing here causing *more* pain to this man? He'd never deserved it. She really was a cancer, she thought. Her own mother had always thought so, too.

"I'm sorry," she said, yet again, and she heard the bleakness in her own voice that went far beyond an apology. And his dark, hot eyes were on hers. Demanding. Furious. Still broken, and she knew she'd done that. It stirred up sensations inside of her that felt too much like ghosts, an ache and a fire at once. But Paige held his gaze. "More than you'll ever know. But I can't leave Violet. I promised her."

Giancarlo's dark gaze blazed into a brilliant fury then, and it took every bit of backbone and bravado Paige had not to fall a step back when he advanced on her. Or to turn tail and start running the way she'd wanted to do since she'd heard his voice, down the expansive lawn, through the garden and out into the wild canyon below, as far as she could get from this man. She wanted to flee. She wanted to run and never stop running. The urge to do it beat in her blood.

But she hadn't done it ten years ago, when she should have, and from far scarier people than Giancarlo Alessi. She wouldn't do it now. No matter how hard her heart catapulted itself against her chest. No matter how great and painful the sobs she refused to let loose from inside.

"You seem to be under the impression I am playing a game with you," Giancarlo said softly, so very softly, the menace in it like his hand around her throat. What was the matter with her that the notion moved in her like a dark thrill instead of a threat? "I am not."

"I understand that this is difficult for you, and that it's unlikely you'll believe that was never my intention." Paige tried to sound conciliatory. She did. But she thought it came out sounding a whole lot more like panic, and panic was as useless as regret. She had no space for either. This was the life she'd made. This was what she'd sown. "But I'm afraid my loyalty is to your mother, not to you."

"I apologize." It was a snide snap, not an apology. "But the irony rendered me temporarily deaf. Did you—*you*—just utter the word *loyalty?*"

Paige gritted her teeth. She didn't bow her head. "You didn't hire me. She did."

"A point that will be moot if I kill you with my bare hands," he snarled at her, and she should have been afraid of him, but she wasn't. She had no doubt that he'd throw her off the estate, that if he could tear her to shreds with his words he would, and gladly, but he wouldn't hurt her. Not physically. Not Giancarlo.

Maybe that was the last remnant of the girl she'd been,

she thought then. That foolish, unbearably naive girl, who'd imagined that a bright and brand-new love could fix anything. That it was the only thing that mattered. She knew better now; she'd learned her lessons well and truly and in the harshest of ways, but she still believed Giancarlo was a good man. No matter what her betrayal had done to him.

"Yes," she said, and her voice was rough with all the emotion she knew she couldn't show him. He'd only hate her more. "But you won't."

"Please," he all but whispered, and she saw too much on his face then, the agony and the fury and the darkness between, "do not tell me you are so delusional as to imagine I wouldn't rip you apart if I could."

"Of course," she agreed, and it was hard to tell what hurt when everything did. When she was sure she would leave this encounter with visible bruises. "If you could. But that's not who you are."

"The man you thought you knew is dead, *Nicola*," he said, that hated name a deliberate blow, and Paige finally did step back then, it was so brutal. "He died ten years ago and there will be no breathing him back to life with your sad tales of loyalty and your pretty little lies. There will be no resurrection. I might look like the man you knew, for two profoundly stupid months a lifetime ago, but mark my words. He is gone as if he never was."

It shouldn't be so sad, when it was nothing more than a simple truth. Not a surprise. Not a slap, even, despite his harsh tone. There was absolutely no reason she should feel swollen anew with all that useless, unwieldy, impossible grief, as if it had never faded, never so much as shifted an inch, in all this time. As if it had only been waiting to flatten her all over again.

"I accept both responsibility and blame for what happened ten years ago," she said as matter-of-factly as she could, and he would never know how hard that was. How exposed she felt, how off balance. Just as he would never know that those two months she'd lost herself in him had been the best of her life, worth whatever had come after. Worth anything, even this. "I can't do anything else. But I promised Violet I wouldn't leave her. Punish me if you have to, Giancarlo. Don't punish her."

Giancarlo Alessi was a man made almost entirely of faults, a fact he was all too familiar with after the bleakness of the past decade and the price he'd paid for his own foolishness, but he loved his mother. His complicated, grandiose, larger-than-life idol of a mother, who he knew adored him in her own, particular way. It didn't matter how many times Violet had sold him out for her own purposes—to combat tales of her crumbling marriage, to give the tabloids something to talk about other than her romantic life, to serve this or that career purpose over the years.

He'd come to accept that having one's private moments exposed to the public was par for the course when one was related to a Hollywood star of Violet's magnitude—which was why he had vowed never, ever to have children that she could use for her own ends. No happy grandchildren to grace magazine articles about her *surprising depths*. No babies she could coo over in front of carefully selected cameras to shore up her image when necessary. He'd never condemn a child of his to that life, no matter how much he might love Violet himself. He'd pass on his Italian title to a distant cousin of his father's and let the sharp brutality of all that Hollywood attention end with him.

He forgave his mother. It was who she was. It was *this* woman he wanted to hurt, not Violet.

This woman who could call herself any name she wanted, but who was still Nicola to him. The architect of his downfall. The agent of his deepest shame.

The too-pretty dancer he'd lost his head over like a thousand shameful clichés, staining his ancient title, his relationship with his late father, and himself in the process. The grasping, conniving creature who had led him around by his groin and made him a stranger to himself in the process. The woman who had made him complicit in the very thing he hated above all others: his presence in the damned tabloids, his most private life on parade.

He'd yet to forgive himself. He'd never planned on forgiving her.

Standing here in this house he'd vowed he'd never enter again, the woman he'd been determined he'd cut from his memory if it killed him within his reach once more, he told himself the edgy thing that surged in him, making him feel something like drunk—dangerously unsteady, a little too close to dizzy—was a cold, clear, measured hatred. No more and no less than she deserved.

It had to be cold. Controlled. He wouldn't permit it to be anything else. He wouldn't let it run hot, burn within him the way loving her had, take charge of him and ruin him anew. He wasn't that trusting, gullible fool any longer, not as he'd been then—so sure he'd been the experienced one, the calloused and jaded one, that no one could take advantage of. She'd made certain he'd never be that idiot again.

He would save that kind of heated, brooding dislike for the sprawling, sunbaked city of Los Angeles itself. For California, brown and gold with only its manufactured, moneyed swaths of green as relief in another breathless summer. For the elegant monstrosity that was La Bellissima. For his heedless, callow twenties playing silly playboy games with films and a parade of famous and beautiful lovers, which *this woman* had brought to a screeching, excruciatingly public halt. For that dry blast of relentless heat on the wind, spiced with smoke from far-off brushfires and the hint of the Pacific Ocean that never cooled it, that made him feel too edgy, too undone. For his mother's recklessness in lovers and husbands and assistants, in all her personal relationships to the endless delight of the predatory press, a trait of hers Giancarlo had long despaired of and had shared but once.

Once.

Once had been enough.

He studied Nicola—*Paige*—as she stood there before him, gazing back at him from her liar's eyes that were neither blue nor green, that fall of thick, dark hair with a hint of auburn that she'd tamed into a side plait falling over one bare, exquisitely formed shoulder. Back then her hair had been redder, longer. Less ink, more fire, and he wished he found the darker shade unpleasant, unattractive. She was still as tall as he remembered but had gone skinny in that way they all did here, as if the denial of every pleasure in the world might bring them the fame they wanted more than anything. More than breath, more than food. Much, much more than love, as he knew all too well.

Don't even think that word, he snarled at himself.

She stiffened as he let his gaze roam all over her, so he kept doing it, telling himself he didn't care what this woman, whatever the hell she called herself now, thought or felt. Because she'd made it clear that the only things she'd ever seen when she'd looked at him—no matter how many times he'd made her scream his name, no matter how many ways they'd torn each other up and turned each other inside out, no matter how deeply he'd fallen

for her or how enthusiastically he'd upended his life for
her in those two months they'd spent almost entirely in
his bed—were Violet's fame and a paycheck to match.

It wasn't only his heart she'd broken. She'd ground
his pride, his belief that he could read anyone's intentions at a glance and keep himself safe from the kind of
grasping predators who teemed over this city like ants,
under her heel. She'd completely altered the way he'd
seen himself, who he was, as surely as if she'd severed
one of his limbs.

Yet she still held herself well, which irritated him. She
still had that dancer's easy grace and the supple muscle
tone to match. He took in her small, high breasts beneath
that sleeveless white shirt with the draped neck, then the
efficient pencil skirt that clung to the swell of her hips,
and his hands remembered the lush feel of both. The
slick perfection of her curves beneath his palms, always
such a marvel of femininity in such a lean frame. The
exquisite way she fit in his hands and tasted against his
tongue. She'd left her legs bare, toned and pretty, and all
he could think about was the way she'd wrapped them
around his hips or draped them over his shoulders while
he'd thrust hard and deep inside of her.

Stop, a voice inside him ordered, *or you will shame
yourself anew.*

Her disguise—if that was what it was—did nothing to
hide her particular, unusual beauty. She'd never looked
like all the other girls who'd flocked around him back
then. It was that fire in her that had called to him from
that first, stunning clash of glances across the set of
the music video where they'd met. She'd been a backup
dancer in formfitting tights and a sport bra. He'd been
the high-and-mighty pseudo director who shouldn't
have noticed her with a band full of pop stars hanging

on his every word. And yet that single look had singed him alive.

He could still feel the same bright flames, even though she'd darkened her hair and wore sensible, professional clothes today that covered her mouthwatering midriff and failed to outline every last line of her thighs. Like the efficient secretary to his mother that he knew she'd proved herself to be over these past years, for some reason—and Giancarlo refused to let himself think about that. About her motives and intentions. Why she'd spent so long playing this game and why she'd bothered to excel in her position here while doing it. Why he couldn't look at her without wanting her, even with all of this time between them. Even knowing exactly what she'd done.

"Is this where you tell me your sob story?" he asked coldly, taking a grim pleasure in the way she reacted to his voice. That little jump, as if she couldn't control this crazy thing between them any more than he could. "There's always one in these situations, is there not? So many reasons. So many excuses."

"I'm not sobbing." He couldn't read that lovely oval of a face, with cheekbones made for a man to cradle between his palms and that wide mouth that begged to be tasted. Plundered. "And I don't think I've made any excuses. I only apologized. It's not the same thing."

"No." He let his gaze move over her mouth. That damned mouth. He could still feel the slide of it against his, or wrapped hot and warm around his hardness, trailing fire and oblivion wherever she used it. *And nothing but lies when she spoke.* "I'll have to see what I can do about that."

She actually sighed, as if he tried her patience, and he didn't know whether he wanted to laugh or throttle her. He remembered that, too. From before. When she'd broken over his life like a hurricane and hadn't stopped tearing up the trees and rearranging the earth until she was gone the same way she'd come, leaving nothing but scandal and the debris of her lies in her wake.

And yet she was still so pretty. He found that made him angrier than the rest of it.

"Glaring ferociously at me isn't going to make me cry," she said, and he wanted to *see things* in those chameleon eyes of hers. He wanted something, anything, to get to her—but he knew better, didn't he? She hadn't simply destroyed him, this time. She'd targeted his mother and she'd done it right under his nose. How could he imagine she was anything but evil? "It only makes the moment that much more uncomfortable." She inclined her head slightly. "But if it makes you feel better, Giancarlo, you should go right ahead and try."

He did laugh then. A short, humorless little sound.

"I am marveling at the sight of you," he said, sounding cruel to his own ears, but she didn't so much as blink. "You deserve to look like the person you really are, not the person you pretended you were." He felt his mouth thin. "But I suppose this is Hollywood magic in action, no? The nastiest, most narcissistic things wrapped up tight in the prettiest packages. Of course you look as good as you did then." He laughed softly, wanting it to hurt. Wanting something he said or did to have *some* effect on her—which told him a bit more than he wanted to know about his unresolved feelings about this woman. "That's all you really have, is it not?"

CHAPTER TWO

GIANCARLO HAD FANCIED himself madly in love with her.

That was the thing he couldn't forgive, much less permit himself to forget, especially when she was *right here* before him once again. The scandal that had ruined his budding film career, that had cast that deep, dark shadow over what had been left of his intensely private, deeply proper father's life, that had made him question everything he'd thought he'd known about himself, that had made him finally leave this damned city and all its demons behind him within a day of the photos going live—that had been something a few shades worse than terrible and it remained a deep, indelible mark on Giancarlo's soul. But however he might have deplored it, he supposed he could have eventually understood a pampered, thoughtless young man's typical recklessness over a pretty girl. It was one of the oldest stories in the world.

It was his own parents' story, come to that.

It was the fact that he'd been so deceived that he'd wanted to *marry* this creature despite his lifelong aversion to the institution, make her his countess, bring her to his ancestral home in Italy—he, who had vowed he'd never marry after witnessing the fallout from his parents' tempestuous union—that made his blood boil even all these years later. He'd been plotting out weddings in his head while she'd been negotiating the price of his disgrace. The fury of it still made him feel much too close to wild.

She only inclined her head again, as if she was perfectly happy to accept any and all blame he heaped on her, and Giancarlo didn't understand why that made him even more enraged.

"Have you nothing to say?" he taunted her. "I don't believe it. You must have lost your touch in all these years, Nicola." He saw her jerk, as if she really did hate that name, and filed that away as ammunition. "I beg your pardon. *Paige*. You can call yourself whatever you want. You've obviously spent too much time with a lonely old woman if this is the best you can do."

"She *is* lonely," Paige agreed, and he thought that was temper that lit up her cheeks, staining them, though her voice was calm. "This was never meant to be a long-term situation, Giancarlo. I assumed you'd come home and recognize me within the month. Of course, that was three years ago."

It took him a moment to understand what it was he was feeling then, and he didn't like it when he did. *Shame.* Hot and new and unacceptable.

"The world will collide with the sun before I explain myself to you," he bit out. Like how he'd managed to let so much time slip by—always so busy, always a crisis on the estate in Italy, always *something*. How he'd avoided coming here and hurt his mother in the process. Those things might have been true—they were why he'd finally forced himself to come after an entire eighteen months without seeing Violet on one of her usual press junkets around the globe—but they certainly weren't *this* woman's business.

"I didn't ask you to explain anything." She lifted one

shoulder, still both delicate and toned, he was annoyed to notice, and then dropped it. "It's simply the truth."

"Please," he scoffed, and rubbed his hand over his face to keep from reacting like the animal he seemed to become in her presence. Ten years ago he'd thought that compulsion—that need—was passion. Fate. He knew better now. It was sheer, unadulterated madness. "Do not use words you cannot possibly know the meaning of. It only makes you look even more grasping and base than we both know you are already."

She blinked, then squared her shoulders, her chin rising as she held his gaze. "Do I have time to get a list of approved vocabulary words in what remains of my five minutes? Before you have me thrown over Violet's walls and onto the street?"

Giancarlo looked at her, the breeze playing in her inky dark hair with its auburn accents, the sun shifting through the vines that stretched lazily above them in a fragrant canopy, and understood with a painful surge of clarity that this was an opportunity. This woman had been like a dark, grim shadow stretching over his life, but that was over now. And he was so different from the man he'd been when she'd sunk her claws in him that he might as well have been a stranger.

She had never been the woman she'd convinced him she was. Because *that* woman, he had loved. *That* woman had been like a missing piece to his own soul that he'd never known he lacked and yet had recognized instantly the moment he'd seen her.

But that was nothing but a performance, a stern voice whispered in his head.

And this was the second act.

"Does my mother know that you are the woman who starred in all those photos a decade ago?" he asked, sounding almost idle, though he felt anything but. He slid his hands into his pockets and regarded her closely, noting how pale she went, and how her lips pressed hard together.

"Of course not," she whispered, and there was a part of him that wondered why she wanted so badly to maintain his mother's good opinion. Why should that matter? But he reminded himself this was the way she played her games. She was good—so good—at pretending to care. It was just another lie and this time, he'd be damned if he believed any part of it.

"Then this is what will happen." He said it calmly. Quietly. Because the shock of seeing her had finally faded and now there was only this. His revenge, served nice and cold all these years later. "I wouldn't want to trouble my mother with the truth about her favorite assistant yet. I don't think she'd like it."

"She would hate it, and me," Nicola—*Paige* threw at him. "But it would also break her heart. If that's your goal here, it's certainly an easy way to achieve it."

"Am I the villain in this scenario?" He laughed again, but this time, he really was amused, and he saw a complex wash of emotion move over her face. He didn't want to know why. He knew exactly what he did want, he reminded himself. His own back, in a way best suited to please him, for a change. This was merely the dance necessary to get it. "You must have become even more delusional than your presence here already suggests."

"Giancarlo—"

"You will resign and leave of your own volition. Today. Now."

She lifted her hands, which he saw were in tight fists, then dropped them back to her sides, and he admired the act. It almost looked real. "I can't do that."

"You will." He decided he was enjoying himself. He couldn't remember the last time that had happened. "This isn't a debate, *Paige*."

Her pretty face twisted into a convincing rendition of misery. "I can't."

"Because you haven't managed to rewrite her will to leave it all to you yet?" he asked drily. "Or are you swapping out all the art on the walls for fakes? I thought the Rembrandt looked a bit odd in the front hall, but I imagined it was the light."

"Because whatever you might think about me, and I'm not saying I don't understand why you think it," she rasped, "I care about her. And I don't mean this to be insulting, Giancarlo, but I'm all she has." Her eyes widened at the dark look he leveled at her, and she hurried on. "You haven't visited her in years. She's surrounded by acolytes and users the moment she steps off this property. I'm the only person she trusts."

"Again, the irony is nearly edible." He shrugged. "And you are wasting your breath. You should thank me for my mercy in letting you call this a resignation. If I were less benevolent, I'd have you arrested."

She held his gaze for a moment too long. "Don't make me call your bluff," she said quietly. "I doubt very much you want the scandal."

"Don't make me call *your* bluff," he hurled back at her. "Do you think I haven't looked for the woman who ruined my life over the years? Hoping against hope she'd be locked up in prison where she belongs?" He smiled thinly when she stiffened. "Nicola Fielding fell off the face of the planet after those pictures went viral. That suggests to me that you aren't any more keen to have history reveal itself in the tabloids than I am." He lifted his brows. "Stalemate, *cara*. If I were you, I'd start packing."

She took a deep breath and then let it out, long and slow, and there was no reason that should have bothered him the way it did, sneaking under his skin and making him feel edgy and annoyed, as if it was tangling up his intentions or bending the present into the past.

"I genuinely love Violet," she said, her eyes big and pleading on his, and he ignored the *tangling* because he knew he had her. He could all but taste it. "This might have started as a misguided attempt to reach you after you disappeared, I'll admit, but it stopped being that a long time ago. I don't want to hurt her. Please. There must be a way we can work this out."

He let himself enjoy the moment. Savor it.

This wasn't temper, hot and wild, making him act out his passions in different ways, the line between it and grief too finely drawn to tell the difference. Too much time had passed. There was too much water under that particular bridge.

And she should never have come here. She should never have involved his mother. She should never have risked this.

"Giancarlo," she said, the way she'd said it that bright and terrible morning a decade ago when he'd finally understood the truth about her—and had seen it in full color pictures splashed across the entirety of the goddamned planet. When he'd showed up at the apartment she'd never let him enter and had that short, awful, final conversation on her doorstep. Before he'd walked away from her and Los Angeles and all the rest of these Hollywood machinations he hated so deeply. Five painful minutes to end an entire phase of his life and so many of his dreams. "Please."

He closed the distance between them with a single step, then reached over to pull on the end of that dark, glossy hair of hers, watching the auburn sheen in it glow and shift in the light. He felt more than heard her quick intake of breath and he wanted her in a thousand ways. That hadn't dimmed.

It was time to indulge himself. He was certain that whatever her angle was, her self-interest would win out over self-preservation. Which meant he could work out what remained of his issues in the best way imaginable. Whatever else she was, she was supple. *He had her.*

"Oh, we can work it out," he murmured, shifting so he could smell the lotion she used on her soft skin, a hint of eucalyptus and something far darker. *Victory,* he thought. His, this time. "It requires only that you get beneath me. And stay there until I'm done with you."

She went still for a hot, searing moment.

"What did you say?"

"You heard me."

Her changeable eyes were blue with distress then, and he might have loathed himself for that if he hadn't known what a liar she was. And what an actress she could be when it suited her. So he only tugged on her plait again and watched her tipped-up face closely as comprehension moved across it, that same electric heat he felt inside him on its heels.

That, Giancarlo told himself, was why he would win this game this time. Because she couldn't control the heat between them any more than he could. And he was no longer fool enough to imagine that meant a damned thing. He knew it was a game, this time.

"I want to make sure I'm understanding you." She swallowed, hard, and he was certain she'd understood him just fine. "You want me to sleep with you to keep my job."

He smiled, and watched goose bumps rise on her

smooth skin. "I do. Often and enthusiastically. Wherever and however I choose."

"You can't be serious."

"I assure you, I am. But by all means, test me. See what happens."

Her lips trembled slightly and he admired it. It looked so real. But he was close enough to see the hard, needy press of her nipples against the silk of her blouse, and he knew better. He knew she was as helpless before this *thing* between them as he was. Maybe she always had been. Maybe that was why it had all got so confused— she'd chosen him because he was Hollywood royalty by virtue of his parents and thus made a good mark, but then there'd been all of *this* to complicate things. But he didn't want to sympathize with her. Not even at such a remove.

"Giancarlo…" He didn't interrupt her but she didn't finish anyway, and her words trailed off into the afternoon breeze. He saw her eyes fill with a wet heat and he had to hand it to her, she was still too good at this. She made it so *believable*.

But he would never believe her again, no matter the provocation. No matter how many tears she shed, or *almost* shed. No matter how convincingly she could make her lips tremble. This was Hollywood.

This time, he wouldn't be taken by surprise. He knew it was all an act from the start.

"Your choices are diminishing by the minute," he told her softly. It was a warning. And one of the last he'd give her. "Now you have but two. Leave now, knowing I will tell my mother exactly why you've left and how you've spent these past years deceiving her. It might break her heart, but that will be one more black mark on your soul, not mine. And I'd be very surprised if she didn't find some way to make you pay for it herself. She didn't become who she is by accident, you must realize. She's a great deal tougher than she looks."

"I know she is." Her gaze still shimmered with that heat, but none of it spilled over—and he reminded himself that was *acting talent,* not force of will. "And what's the second choice?"

He shrugged. "Stay. And do exactly as I tell you."

"Sexually." She threw that at him, her voice unsteady but her gaze direct. "You mean do as you tell me *sexually.*"

If she thought her directness would shame him into altering his course here, she was far stupider than he remembered. Giancarlo smiled.

"I mean do as I tell you, full stop." He indulged himself then, and touched her. He traced the remarkable line of her jaw, letting the sharp delight of it charge through his bones, then held her chin there, right where he could stare her down with all the ruthlessness he carried within him. "You will work for me, *Paige.* On your back. On your knees. At your desk. Whatever I want, whenever I want, however I want."

He could feel her shaking and he exulted in it.

"Why?" she whispered. "This is *me,* remember? Why would you want to…?"

Again, she couldn't finish, and he took pleasure in these signs of her weakness. These cracks in her slick, pretty armor. Giancarlo leaned in close and brushed his mouth over hers, a little hint of what was to come. A little test.

It was just as he remembered it.

All that fire, arcing in him and in her, too, from the shocked sound she made. All that misery. Shame and fury and ten years of that terrible longing. He'd never quite got past it, and this was why. This thrumming, pounding excitement that had only ever happened here, with her. This unmatched hunger. This beautiful lie that would not wreck him this time. Not this time.

He needed to work it all out on that delectable body she'd wielded like a weapon, enslaving him and destroying him before she'd finally got around to killing him, too. He needed to make her pay the price for her betrayal in the most intimate way possible. He needed to work out his goddamned issues in the very place they'd started, and then, only then, would he finally be free of her. It had only been two months back then. It would have burned out on its own—he was sure of it, but they hadn't had time. He wanted time to glut himself, because only then would he get past this.

Giancarlo had to believe that.

"I know exactly who you are," he told her then, and he didn't pretend he wasn't enjoying this. That now that the shock had passed, he wasn't thrilled she'd proved herself as deceitful as he remembered. That he wasn't looking forward to this in a way he hoped scared her straight down into her bones—because it should. "It's long past time you paid for what you did to me, and believe me when I tell you I have a very, very detailed memory."

"You'll regret it." Her voice was like gauze and had as much effect.

"I've already regretted you for a decade, *cara*," he growled. "What does it matter to me if I add a little more?"

He leaned in closer, felt her quiver against him and thrilled to it. To her, because he knew her true face this time. He knew *her*. There would be no losing himself. There would be no fanciful dreaming of marriage and happy-ever-afters in the Tuscan countryside, deep in all the sweet golden fields that were his heritage. There would only be penance. Hers. Hard, hot, bone-melting penance, until he was satisfied.

Which he anticipated might take some time.

"This doesn't make sense." Did she sound desperate or did he want her to? Giancarlo didn't care. "You hate me!"

"This isn't hate," he said, and his smile deepened. Darkened. "Let's be clear, shall we? This is revenge."

Paige thought he would leap on her the moment she agreed.

And of course she agreed, how could she do anything *but* agree when Violet Sutherlin had become the mother her own had been far too addicted and selfish and hateful to pretend to be? How could she walk away from that when Violet was therefore the only family she had left?

But Giancarlo had only smiled that hard, deeply disconcerting smile of his that had skittered over her skin like electricity.

Then he'd dropped his hand, stepped away from her and left her alone.

For days. Three days, in fact. Three long days and much longer nights.

Paige had to carry on as if everything was perfectly normal, doing her usual work for Violet and pretending to be as thrilled as the older woman was about the return of her prodigal son. She'd had to maintain her poise and professionalism, insofar as there *was* any professionalism in this particular sort of job that was as much about handling Violet's personal whims as anything else. She'd had to try not to give herself away every time she was in the same room with Giancarlo, when all she wanted to do was scream at him to end this tension—a tension *he* did not appear to feel, as he lounged about, swam laps in the pool and laughed with his mother.

And every night she locked herself into the little cottage down near the edge of the canyon that was her home on Violet's property and tortured herself until dawn.

It was as if her brain had recorded every single moment of every single encounter she'd ever had with Giancarlo and could play it all back in excruciating detail. Every touch. Every kiss. That slick, hard thrust of his possession. The sexy noise he'd made against her neck each time he'd come. The sobs echoing back from this or that wall that she knew were hers, while she writhed in mindless pleasure, his in every possible way.

By the morning of the fourth day she was a mess.

"Sleep well?" he asked in that taunting way of his, his dark brows rising high when he met her on the back steps on her way into the big house to start her day. Violet took her breakfast and the trades on a tray in her room each morning and she expected to see Paige there, too, before she was finished.

Giancarlo stood on the wide steps that led up to the terrace, not precisely blocking her way, but Paige didn't rate her chances for slipping past him, either. Had she not been lost in her own scorching world of regret and too many vivid memories as she'd walked up the hill from her cottage, she'd have seen him here, lying in wait. She'd have avoided him.

Would you? that sly voice inside her asked.

A smart woman would have left Los Angeles ten years ago, never to return to the scene of so much pain and betrayal and heartache. A smart woman certainly wouldn't have got herself tangled up with her ex-lover's mother, and even if she had, she would have rejected Giancarlo's devil's bargain outright. So Paige supposed that ship had sailed a long time ago.

"I slept like a baby," she replied, because her memories were her business.

"I take it you mean that in the literal sense," he said drily. "Up every two hours wailing down the walls and making life a misery, then?"

Paige gritted her teeth. He, of course, glowed with health and that irritating masculine vigor of his. He wore an athletic T-shirt in a technical fabric and a pair of running shorts, and was clearly headed out to get himself into even better shape on the surrounding trails that scored the mountains, if that were even possible. No wonder he maintained that lean, rangy body of his that appeared to scoff at the very notion of fat. She wished she could hate him. She wished that pounding thing in her chest, and much lower, was *hate*.

"I've never slept better in my life," she said staunchly.

Her mistake was that she'd drifted too close to him as she said it, as if he was a magnet and she was powerless to resist the pull. She remembered that, too. It had been like a tractor beam, that terrible compulsion. As if they were drawn together no matter what. Across the cavernous warehouse where she'd met him on that shoot. Across rooms, beds, showers. Wherever, whenever.

Ten years ago she'd thought that meant they were made for each other. She knew better now. Yet she still felt that draw.

Paige only flinched a little bit when he reached over and ran one of his elegant fingers in a soft crescent shape beneath her eye. It was such a gentle touch it made her head spin, especially when it was at such odds with that harsh look on his face, that ever-present gleam of furious gold in his gaze.

It took her one shaky breath, then another, to realize

he'd traced the dark circle beneath her eye. That it wasn't a caress at all.

It was an accusation.

"Liar," he murmured, as if he was reciting an old poem, and there was no reason it should feel like a sharp blade stuck hard beneath her ribs. "But I expect nothing else from you."

Bite your tongue, she ordered herself when she started to reply. Because she might have got herself into this mess, twice, but that didn't mean she had to make it worse. She poured her feelings into the way she looked at him, and one corner of that hard, uncompromising mouth of his kicked up. Resignation, she thought. If they'd been different people she might have called it a kind of rueful admiration.

But this was Giancarlo, who despised her.

"Be ready at eight," he told her gruffly.

"That could cover a multitude of sins." So much for her vow of silence. Paige smiled thinly when his brows edged higher. "Be ready for what?"

Giancarlo moved slightly then on the wide marble step, making her acutely aware of him. Of the width of his muscled shoulders, the long sweep of his chiseled torso. Of his strength, his heat. Reminding her how deadly he was, how skilled. How he'd been the only man she'd ever met, before or since, who had known exactly what buttons to push to turn her to jelly, and had. Again and again. He'd simply looked at her, everything else had disappeared and he'd known.

He still knew. She could see it in that heat that made his dark eyes gleam. She could feel it the way her body prickled with that same lick of fire, the way the worst of the flames tangled together deep in her belly.

She felt her breath desert her, and she thought she saw

the man she remembered in his dark gaze, the man as lost in this as she always had been, but it was gone almost at once as if it had never been. As if that had been nothing but wishful thinking on her part.

"Wear something I can get my hands under," he told her, and there was a cruel cast to his desperately sensual mouth then that should have made her want to cry—but that wasn't the sensation that tripped through her blood, making her feel dizzy with something she'd die before she'd call excitement.

And as if he knew that too, he smiled.

Then he left her there—trying to sort out all the conflicting sensations inside of her right there in the glare of another California summer morning, trying not to fall apart when she suspected that was what he wanted her to do—without a backward glance.

"I think he must be a terribly lonely man," Violet said.

They were sitting in one of the great legend's favorite rooms in this vast house, the sunny, book-lined and French-doored affair she called her office, located steps from her personal garden and festooned with her many awards.

Violet lounged back on the chaise she liked to sit on while tending to her empire—"because what, pray, is the point of being an international movie star if I can't conduct business on a chaise?" Violet had retorted when asked why by some interviewer or another during awards season some time back—with her eyes on the city that preened before her beneath the ever-blue California sky and sighed. She was no doubt perfectly aware of the way the gentle light caught the face she'd allowed age to encroach upon, if only slightly. She looked wise and gorgeous at once, her fine blond hair brushed back from her face and only hinting at her sixty-plus years, dressed in her preferred "at home" outfit of butter-soft jeans that had cost her a small fortune and a bespoke emerald-green blouse that played up the remarkable eyes only a keen observer would note were enhanced by cosmetics.

This was the star in her natural habitat.

Sitting in her usual place at the elegant French secretary on the far side of the room, her laptop open before her and all of Violet's cell phones in a row on the glossy wood surface in case any of them should ring, Paige frowned and named the very famous director they'd just been discussing.

"You think *he's* lonely?" she asked, startled.

Violet let out that trademark throaty laugh of hers that had been wowing audiences and bringing whole rooms to a standstill since she'd appeared in her first film in the seventies.

"No doubt he is," she said after a moment, "despite the parade of ever-younger starlets who he clearly doesn't realize make him look that much older and more decrepit, but I meant Giancarlo."

Of course she did.

"Is he?" Paige affected a vague tone. The sort of tone any employee would use when discussing the boss's son.

"He was a very lonely child," Violet said, in the same sort of curious, faraway voice she used when she was puzzling out a new character. "It is my single regret. His father and I loved each other wildly and often quite badly, and there was little room for anyone else."

Everyone knew the story, of course. The doomed love affair with its separations and heartbreaks. The tempestuous, often short-lived reunions. The fact they'd lived separately for years at a time with many rumored affairs, but had never divorced. Violet's bent head and flowing tears at the old count's funeral, her refusal to speak of him publicly afterward.

Possibly, Paige thought ruefully as she turned every last part of the story over in her head, she had studied that Hollywood fairy tale with a little more focus and attention than most.

"He doesn't seem particularly lonely," Paige said when she felt Violet's expectant gaze on her. She sat very still in her chair, aware that while a great movie star might *seem* to be too narcissistic to notice anyone but herself, the truth was that Violet was an excellent judge of character. She had to be, to inhabit so many. She read people the way others read street signs. Fidgeting would tell her much, much more than Paige wanted her to know. "He seems as if he's the sort of man who's used to being in complete and possibly ruthless control. Of everything."

The other woman's smile then seemed sad. "I agree. And I can't think of anything more lonely," she said softly. "Can you?"

And perhaps that conversation was how Paige found herself touching up what she could only call defensive eyeliner in the mirror in the small foyer of her cozy little cottage when she heard a heavy hand at her door at precisely eight o'clock that night.

She didn't bother to ask who it was. The cartwheels her stomach turned at the sound were identification enough.

Paige swung open the door and he was there, larger than life and infinitely more dangerous, looking aristocratic and lethal in one of the suits he favored that made him seem a far cry indeed from the more casual man she'd known before. *This* man looked as if he'd sooner spit nails than partake of the Californian pastime of surfing, much less lounge about like an affluent Malibu beach bum in torn jeans and no shirt. *This* man looked as forbidding and unreachable and haughtily blue-blooded as the Italian count he was.

Giancarlo stood on the path that led to her door and let his dark eyes sweep over her, from the high ponytail she'd fashioned to the heavy eye makeup she'd used because it was the only mask she thought he'd allow her to wear. His sensual mouth crooked slightly at that, as if he knew exactly what she'd been thinking when she'd lined her eyes so dramatically, and then moved lower. To the dress that hugged her breasts tight, with only delicate straps above, then cascaded all the way to the floor in a loose, flowing style that suggested the kind of casual elegance she'd imagined he'd require no matter where he planned to take her.

"Very good, *cara*," he said, and that wasn't quite *approval* she heard in his voice. It was much closer to *satisfaction,* and that distinction made her pulse short-circuit, then start to drum wildly. Erratically. "It appears you are capable of following simple instructions, when it suits you."

"Everyone can follow instructions when it suits them," she retorted despite the fact she'd spent hours cautioning herself not to engage with him, not to give him any further ammunition. Especially not when he called her that name—*cara*—he'd once told her he reserved for the many indistinguishable women who flung themselves at him. *Better that than "Nicola,"* she thought fiercely. "It's called survival."

"I can think of other things to call it," he murmured in that dark, silken way of his that hurt more for its insinuations than any directness would have. "But why start the night off with name-calling?" That crook of his mouth became harder, deadlier. "You'll need your strength, I suspect. Best to conserve it while you can."

He's only messing with you, she cautioned herself as she stepped through the door and delivered herself into his clutches, the way she'd promised him she would. *He wants to see if you'll really go through with this.*

So did she, she could admit, as she made a show of locking the front door, mostly to hide her nerves from that coolly assessing dark gaze of his. But it was done too fast, and then Giancarlo was urging her into a walk with that hand of his at the small of her back, and their history seemed particularly alive then in the velvety night that was still edged with deep blues as the summer evening took hold around them.

Everything felt perilous. Even her own breath.

He didn't speak. He handed her into the kind of low-slung sports car she should have expected he'd drive, and as he rounded the hood to lower himself into the driver's seat she could still feel his hand on that spot on her back, the heat of it pulsing into her skin like a brand, making the finest of tremors snake over her skin.

Paige didn't know what she expected as he got in and started to drive, guiding them out of Violet's high gates and higher into the hills. A restaurant so he could humiliate her in public? One of the dive motels that rented by the hour in the sketchier neighborhoods so he could treat her like the whore he believed she was? But it certainly wasn't the sharp turn he eventually took off the winding road that traced the top of the Santa Monica Mountains bisecting Los Angeles, bringing the powerful car to a stop in a shower of dirt right at the edge of a cliff. There was an old wooden railing, she noted in a sudden panic. But still.

"Get out," he said.

"I, uh, really don't want to," she said, and she heard the sheer terror in her own voice. He must have heard it too, because while his grim expression didn't alter, she thought she saw amusement in the dark eyes he fixed on her.

"I'm not going to throw you off the side of the mountain, however appealing the notion," he told her. "That would kill you almost instantly."

"It's the 'almost' part I'm worried about," she pointed out, sounding as nervous as she felt suddenly. "It encompasses a lot of screaming and sharp rocks."

"I want you to suffer, *Paige*," he said softly, still with that emphasis on her name, as if it was another lie. "Remember that."

It told her all manner of things about herself she'd have preferred not knowing that she found that some kind of comfort. She could have walked away, ten years ago or three days ago, and she hadn't. He'd been the one to leave. He'd hurled his accusations at her, she'd told him she loved him and he'd walked away—from her and from his entire life here. This was the bed she'd made, wasn't it?

So she climbed from the car when he did, and then followed him over to that rail, wary and worried. Giancarlo didn't look at her. He stared out at the ferocious sparkle, the chaos of light that was this city. It was dark where they stood, no streetlamps to relieve the night sky and almost supernaturally quiet so high in the hills, but she could see the intent look on his face in the reflected sheen of the mad city below, and it made her shake down deep inside.

"Come here."

She didn't want to do that either, but she'd promised to obey him, so Paige trusted that this was about shaming her, not hurting her—at least not physically—and drifted closer. She shuddered when he looped an arm around her neck and pulled her hard against the rock-hard wall of his chest. The world seemed to spin and lights flashed, but that was only the beaming headlights of a passing car.

Giancarlo stroked his fingers down the side of her face, then traced the seam of her lips.

Everything was hot. Too hot. He was still as hard and male as she remembered, and his torso was like a brand beside her, the arm over her shoulders deliciously heavy, and she felt that same old fire explode inside of her again, as if this was new. As if this was the first time he'd touched her.

He didn't order her to open her mouth but she did anyway at the insistent movement, and then he thrust his thumb inside. It was hotter than it should have been, sexy and strange at once, and his dark eyes glittered as they met hers with all of Los Angeles at their feet.

"Remind me how exactly it was I lost my head over you," he told her, all that fury and vengeance in his voice, challenging her to defy him. "Use your tongue."

Paige didn't know what demon it was that rose in her then, some painful mixture of long lost hopes and current regrets, not to mention that anger she tried to hide because it was unlikely to help her here, but she did as she was told. She grabbed his invading hand with both of hers and she worshipped his thumb as if it were another part of his anatomy entirely, and she didn't break away from him while she did it.

She didn't know how long it went on.

His eyes were darker than the night around them, and the same hectic gold lit them, even as it burned within her. She felt molten and wild, reckless and lost, and none of that mattered, because she could taste *him*. He might hate her, he might want nothing more than to hurt her, but Paige had never thought she'd taste him again. She'd never dreamed this could happen.

She told herself it didn't matter, those things she felt deep inside her that she didn't want to acknowledge. Only that this was a gift. It didn't matter what else it was.

He pulled his thumb out then and shifted her so they were facing each other, and the space between them seemed dense. Electric.

"I'm glad to see you haven't lost your touch," he said, and though his tone was cruel his voice was rougher than it had been, and she told herself that meant something. It meant the same thing her breathlessness did, or that manic tightening deep in her belly, that restlessness she'd only ever felt with him and knew only he could cure.

He smiled, and it was so beautiful it made her throat feel tight, and she should have known better. Because he wasn't finished.

"Get on your knees, *Paige,*" he ordered her. "And do it right."

CHAPTER THREE

FOR A MOMENT Paige thought she really had pitched over the side of the hill, and this taut, terrible noise in her head was her own scream. But she blinked and she was still standing there before Giancarlo, he was still waiting and she didn't want him to repeat himself.

She could see from that faintly mocking lift to his dark brows and that twist to his lips that he knew full well she'd heard him.

"Not *here*, surely," she said, and her voice sounded thin and faraway.

"Where I want. How I want. Was I unclear?"

"But I—" She cleared her throat. "I mean, I don't—"

"You appear to be confused." His hands were still on her, and that didn't help. The offhanded sweep of his thumbs against the tender skin of her bare shoulders made her want to scream, but she didn't think she'd stop if she started. "*I* this, *I* that. This isn't about you. This is about me."

"Giancarlo."

"I told you what to do," he said coolly. "And what will happen if you don't."

She jerked back out of his grip, furious in a sudden jolt, and not only because she knew he could have held her there if he liked. But because he hated her and she hated that he did. Because he was back in her life but not really, not in the way she'd refused to admit to herself she'd wanted him to be.

God, in those first months, those first years, she'd expected him to appear, hadn't she? She'd expected him to seek her out once his initial anger passed, once the last of the scandal had died down. To continue that conversation they'd had outside her apartment the morning the pictures had run, so swift and terrible. Because they might have been together only a short time, but he'd known her better than anyone else ever had. *Or ever would.* Maybe not the details of her life, because she'd never wanted anyone to know those, but the truth of her heart. She'd been so sure that somehow, he'd understand that there had to have been extenuating circumstances....

But he'd never come.

So perhaps it was a very old grief that added to the fury and made her forget herself completely.

"Is this really what you want?" she demanded, forgetting to hold her tongue, the taste of his skin still a rich sort of wine in her mouth, making her feel something like drunk. "Is this what a decade did to you, Giancarlo?"

"This is what you did to me." He didn't use that name then, but she was sure they could both hear it, *Nicola* hanging in the air and weaving in and out of the scent of the night-blooming jasmine and rosemary all around them. "And this is exactly what I want."

"To force me. To make me do things I don't want to do. To—" She found she couldn't say it. Not to the man who was the reason she knew that love could be beautiful instead of dark and twisted and sick. Not to the man who had made her feel so alive, so powerful, so perfect beneath his touch. "There are words, you know. Terrible words."

"None of which apply." He thrust his hands in the pockets of that suit, and she wondered if he found it hard to keep them to himself. Was she as sick as he was if that made her feel better instead of worse? How could she tell anymore—what was the barometer? "You don't *have* to do anything. I have no desire to force you. Quite the opposite."

"You told me I had to do this—to—to—"

"Don't stutter like the vestal virgin we both know you are not," he said silkily, and she wondered if he'd forgotten that she'd been exactly that when she'd come to him ten years ago. If he thought that was another lie. "I told you that you had to obey me. In and out of bed."

"That I had to have sex with you *at your command* or leave," she gritted out.

He didn't quite shrug, or smile. "Yes."

"So then I do, in fact, have to do something. You *are* perfectly happy to use force."

"Not at all." He shrugged as if he didn't care what happened next, but there was a tension to those muscled shoulders, around his eyes, that told her otherwise. And it wasn't in the least bit comforting. "You're welcome to leave. To say no at any time and go about your life, such as it is, using whatever name appeals to you. I won't stop you."

It was as if her heart was in her mouth and she felt dizzy again, but she couldn't look away from that terrible face of his, so sensual and impassive and cruel.

"But if I do that, you'll tell Violet who I am. You'll tell her I…what? Stalked you? Deliberately hunted her down and befriended her to get to you?"

"I will." His face hardened and his voice did, too. "It has the added benefit of being the truth."

But Paige knew better, however little she could seem

to express it to him. She knew what had grown between her and Violet in these past years, and how deeply it would wound the other woman to learn that Paige was yet one more leech. One more user, trying to suck Violet dry for her own purposes. It made her feel sick to imagine it.

"That's no choice at all."

"It's a choice, *Paige*," he said with lethal bite. "You don't like it, perhaps, but that doesn't make it any less of a choice, which is a good deal more than you offered me."

"I can't hurt her. Don't you care about that? *Shouldn't* you?"

"There are consequences to the choices you make," he said with a certain ruthless patience. "Don't you understand yet? This is a lesson. It's not supposed to be fun." That smile of his was a sharp blade she was certain drew blood. "For you."

For a moment she thought she'd bolt, though it was a long walk to anywhere from high up on this hill. She didn't know how she kept herself still, how she stayed in one piece. She didn't know how she wasn't already in a thousand shattered bits all over this little pull out on the side of the deserted road, like a busted-out car window.

"Tell me, then," she managed after a moment, keeping her head high, though her eyes burned, "how does this lesson plan work, exactly? You say you don't want to force me, but you're okay with me forcing myself? When it's the last thing I want?"

"Is it?" He shook his head at her, that smile of his no less painful. "Surely you must realize how little patience I have for lies, *Paige*." He let out a small sound that was too lethal to be a laugh. "If I were to lift your dress and stroke my way inside your panties, what would I find? Disinterest?"

Damn him.

"That's not the point. That's biology, which isn't the same thing as will."

"Are you wet?"

It wasn't really a question, and her silence answered it anyway. Her bright red cheeks that she was sure were like a flare against the night. A beacon. Her shame and fury and agony, and none of that mattered because she was molten between her legs, too hot and too slippery, and he knew it.

He knew it by looking at her, and she didn't know which one of them she hated more then. Only that she was caught tight in the grip of this thing and she had no idea how either one of them could survive it. How anything could survive it.

"Please," she said. It was a whisper. She hardly knew she spoke.

And the worst part was that she had no idea what she was asking for.

"We'll get to the begging," he promised her.

Giancarlo looked as ruthless as she'd ever seen him then, and it only made that pulsing wet heat worse. It made her ache and hunger and *want*, and what the hell did that make her? *Exactly what he thinks you are already,* a voice inside her answered.

And he wasn't finished. "But first, I want you on your knees. Right here. Right now. Don't make me tell you again."

He didn't think she'd do it.

They stood together in the dark, close enough that any observer would think them lovers a scant inch away from a touch, and Giancarlo realized in a sudden flash that he didn't want her to do it—that there was a part of him that wanted her to refuse. To walk away from this thing before it consumed them both whole and then wrecked them all over again.

To stop him, because he didn't think he could—or would—stop himself.

Seeing her had taken the brakes off whatever passed for his self-control and he was careening down the side of a too-steep mountain now, heedless and reckless, and he didn't care what he destroyed on the way down. He didn't care about anything but exploring the phrase *a pound of flesh* in every possible way he could.

She didn't blink. He didn't think either one of them breathed. He saw her clench her hands into fists, saw her stiffen her spine. He wanted to stop her from running. From not running. From whatever was about to happen next in this too-close, too-dark night, where the only thing that moved was that long dress of hers, rippling slightly against the faint breeze from the far-off sea.

Then she moved, in a simple slide of pure grace that was worse, somehow, than all the rest. It reminded him of so many things. The supple strength and flexibility of her body, her lean curves, and all the ways he'd worshipped her back before he'd known who she really was. With his hands. His mouth. His whole body. She was his memory in lovely action, a stark and pretty slap across his face, and when she was finished she was settled there on her knees before him.

Just as he'd asked. *Demanded.*

Giancarlo stared down at her, willing back all of his self-righteous fury and the armor it provided, but it was hard to remember much of anything when she was staring up at him, her eyes wide and mysterious and her lips slightly parted, making the carnal way she'd taken his thumb inside her mouth seem to explode through him all over again.

Making him realize he was kidding himself if he thought he was in control of this.

As long as *she* didn't realize that, Giancarlo thought, he'd manage. So he waited, watching her as he did. The night seemed much darker than it was, heavy on all sides and far fewer stars above than in the skies over his home in Tuscany, and he *felt* the ragged breath she took. That same old destructive need for her poured through him, rocketing through his veins and into his sex, making him clench his jaw too tight to keep from acting on it.

He felt like granite—everywhere—when she tilted herself forward and propped herself against his thighs, her palms like fire, her mouth much too close to the part of him that burned the hottest for her.

"Your mother thinks you're lonely," she said.

It took him a moment to understand the words she spoke in that husky tone of voice, and when he did, something he didn't care to identify coursed through him. He told himself it was yet more anger. He had an endless well where this woman was concerned, surely.

Giancarlo reached down and took her jaw in his hand, tugging her face up so he could look down into it, and it was the hardest thing he'd done in a long, long time to keep himself in check. In control. To crush the roaring thing that wanted only to *take her, possess her* and force himself to *think*, instead.

"That's not going to work," he told her softly. He was so hard it very nearly hurt, but he stood there as if he could do this all night, and he felt the faintest shiver move through her, making it all worthwhile.

"What do you mean? That's what she said."

"It doesn't matter if she hauled out her photo albums and wept over pictures of me as a fat, drooling infant," he said mildly, though his hand was hard against her jaw and he could feel how much she wanted to yank herself back, away from him. He could feel the flat press of her hands on his thighs, and the heat there that neither one of them had ever been any good at harnessing. "You're not bringing it up now, on your knees in the dirt because I ordered it, because you have a sudden interest in my emotional well-being."

"I could be interested in nothing *but* your emotional well-being and you'd tell me I was only running a con," Nicola—*Paige* said, with more bravado than he might have displayed were he the one kneeling there in the dark. "I don't know why I bother to speak."

"In this case," he said silkily, moving his hand along the sweet line of her jaw, her cheek, cradling her head with a softness completely belied by the lash in his words, "it is because you hope to shame me into stopping this. Why else bring up my mother when you're about to take me into your mouth at last?"

Her mouth fell open slightly more, as if in stunned astonishment, and he laughed, though it wasn't a very nice sound.

"Fine," she said, though her voice sounded like a stranger's. "Whatever you want."

"That is the point I am trying to make to you, *Paige*," he bit out then, holding her immobile, so she had no choice but to gaze back at him, and he was a terrible man indeed, to revel in the temper he saw in her changeable eyes. "'Whatever I want' isn't an empty phrase. It could mean pleasuring me by the side of the road without any consultation whatsoever about your feelings on the subject. It is what *I* want. Are you beginning to understand me? How many object lessons do you think you will require before this sinks in?"

She said something in reply but the night stole her

words away, and she cleared her throat. She was trembling fully then, and he might have felt like the monster all that accusation in her gaze named him, but he could see the rest of it, too. The stain of color on her cheeks. That glassy heat in her eyes. And beneath the hand he still held to her face and against her neck, the wild drumming of her pulse, pounding out her arousal in an unmistakable beat.

He knew that rhythm better than he knew himself. He thought it might have been the only honest thing about her, then and now.

"How long?" she whispered.

"Until what?"

"Until this is done." She moistened her lips and he felt it like her wicked mouth, wet and soft and deep, and nearly groaned where he stood.

"Until I'm bored."

"A few hours, then," she said, with a remnant of her usual fire, and he smiled.

"I don't imagine you'll be that lucky." He traced a pattern from that stubborn chin of hers to the delicate shell of her ear, then back. "I've had a long time to think about all the ways I'd like to make you crawl. Then pay. Then crawl some more. There's no telling how long it could take."

"And yet when you had the chance, you talked to me for three seconds and then disappeared for a decade," she pointed out.

He felt that same wash of betrayal, that same kick in the gut he'd felt that long-ago day when he'd realized she'd used him the way his own mother always had—and it had been far more shattering, because Violet had only sold him out when he was clothed.

"I don't want to *talk* to you," he said, as harshly as he

could in that same soft voice. "I didn't then. I don't now. I thought I'd made that clear."

A car passed by on the winding mountain drive, the headlights dancing over them, and he saw something bleak in her eyes, across her lovely face. He told himself there was no echo at all inside him, no hollow thing in his chest.

"Then we'd better get started with the humiliation and sexual favors, hadn't we?" she said with a cheerfulness that was as pointed as it was feigned, and he felt her hands tighten against his thighs. She moved them up toward his belt and he didn't know he meant to stop her until he did.

He watched her face as he helped her rise to her feet, and he didn't let go of her arm when she was standing, the way he should have done.

"And here I thought we were right on target to get arrested for public indecency," she whispered, her voice still sharp but something raw in her chameleon gaze. "They could throw me in jail and charge me for solicitation and it would be like all your dreams come true in one evening."

"This is my dream," he growled at her, his hand wrapped tight around her arm and that fever in his blood. His revenge, he thought. At last. "It's not the act itself that matters, *cara*. That's a privilege you haven't earned. It's the surrender. It's all about the surrender." He laughed then, a dark sound he felt in every part of him, as if it was a part of the night and as dangerous, and then he let her go. It was harder than it should have been. "You'll learn."

It became clear to Paige in the week that followed that it wasn't Giancarlo's intention to *actually* make her have sex with him whenever and wherever he chose, no matter what provocative things he might say to the contrary.

That would have been easy, in its way. He was far more
diabolical than that.

He wanted her in a constant state of panic, with no idea
what he might do next. He wanted her to think of nothing at all but him and the little things he made her do to
prove her obedience that were slowly driving her insane.

It's all about the surrender, he'd said. Her surrender.
And she was learning what he'd meant.

One day—after nearly a week filled with anticipation and the faintest of touches, always in passing and
always unexpected, all of which still felt like a metal collar around her neck that he tightened at will—he found
her in Violet's expansive closet, putting together a selection of outfits with appropriate accessories for Violet to
choose between for the event the star was scheduled to
attend that evening.

"Pull up your skirt, take off your panties—if you are
foolish enough to be wearing any—and hand them to
me," Giancarlo said without preamble, making Paige
jump and shiver into a bright red awareness of him, especially because her mind had been a long way away.

Ten years ago away, in fact, and treating her to a play-
by-play, Technicolor and surround-sound replay of one
of their more adventurous evenings in the Malibu house
down on the beach she had no idea if he still owned.

"What?" she stammered out, but her body wasn't in
any doubt about his instructions. Her breasts bloomed
into an aching heaviness, making her bra feel too tight
and too scratchy against her skin. Her stomach flipped
over, and below, that shimmering heat became scalding.

And that was only at the sound of his voice. What
would happen if he touched her this time?

"Is this your strategy, *cara*? To feign ignorance every
time I speak to you?" He loomed in the doorway, look-

ing untamed and edgy, furious and male. He'd forgone
the exquisite suits and running apparel today and looked
more like the Giancarlo she remembered in casual trousers and a top that was more like a devotional poem ex-
tolling the perfection of his torso than anything so prosaic
as a *T-shirt*. "It's already tiresome."

She was standing too straight, too still, on the other
side of the central island that housed Violet's extensive
jewelry collection, entirely too aware that she resembled
a deer stuck fast in the glare of oncoming headlights. But
she couldn't seem to move.

Anything besides her mouth, that was. "I did try to
warn you that this would get boring."

Giancarlo's mouth crooked slightly and made hers
water. His eyes were so dark the gold in them felt as
much like a caress as a warning, and she was terribly
afraid she could no longer tell the difference.

"Show me that you know how to follow directions."
He folded his arms over that chest of his and propped a
shoulder against the doorjamb, but Paige wasn't the least
bit fooled. He looked about as casual and relaxed as a
predator three seconds before launching an attack. "And
I'd think twice before making me wait, if I were you."

"It's all the threats," she grated at him. "They make
me dizzy with fear. It's hard to hear the instructions over
all the heart palpitations."

"I'm certain that's true." That crook in his mouth deepened. She was fascinated. "But I think we both know it
isn't fear."

Paige couldn't really argue with that, and she certainly didn't want him to wander any closer and prove
his point—did she? She glanced down at her outfit, the
short, flirty little skirt with nothing on beneath it, and
realized that she'd obeyed him without thinking about it

when she'd dressed this morning. *Make sure that I have access to you, should I desire it,* he'd told her two nights ago, a harsh whisper in the hallway outside Violet's office. She'd obeyed him and in so doing, she'd revealed herself completely.

When she raised her gaze to his again, he was smiling, a fierce satisfaction in his dark gold eyes and stamped across that impossibly elegant face of his. He jerked his chin at her, wordlessly ordering her to show him, and her hands moved convulsively, as if her body wanted nothing more than to prove itself to him. To prove *herself* trustworthy again, to jump through any hoop he set before her—

But that wasn't where this was headed. This wasn't a love story. No matter how many memories she used to torture herself into imagining otherwise.

"Come over here and find out for yourself, if you want to know," she heard herself say. Suicidally.

Giancarlo only shook his head at her, as if saddened. "You seem to miss the point. Again. This is not a game that lovers play, *cara.* This is not some delightful entertainment en route to a blissful afternoon in bed. This is—"

"Penance," she finished for him, with far more bitterness than she should have allowed him to hear. "Punishment. I know."

"Then stop stalling. Show me."

Paige could see he meant it.

She told herself it didn't matter. That he'd seen all of her before, and in a far more intimate setting than this. That more than that, he'd had his mouth and his hands on every single inch of her skin, in ways so devastating and intense that she could still feel it ten years later. So what did it matter now? He was all the way across the

room and he *wanted* her to balk. To hate him. That was
why he was doing this, she was sure.

So instead, she laughed, like the carefree girl she'd
never been. Paige stepped out from behind the center
island so there could be no accusations of hiding. She
watched his hard, hard face and then, slowly, she reached
down and pulled her skirt up to her hips.

"Satisfied?" she asked when she was fully bared to
his view—because she was.

She'd been so lost in her guilt, her shame, her own
anger at everything that had happened and Giancarlo
too, that she'd forgotten one very important fact about
this thing between them that Giancarlo had been using
to such great effect.

It ran both ways.

He stared at her—too hard and too long—and she
saw the faintest hint of color high on those gorgeous
cheeks of his. And that hectic glitter in his dark eyes
that she recognized. Oh yes, she recognized it. She remembered it.

She knew as much about him as he did about her,
after all. She knew every inch of *his* body. She knew
his arousal when she saw it. She knew he'd be so hard
he ached and that his control would be stretched to the
breaking point. The chemistry between them wasn't only
his to exploit.

She stood there with her skirt at her waist, supposedly
debasing herself before the only man she'd ever loved,
and Paige felt better than she had in years. Powerful.
Right, somehow.

"Looked your fill?" she asked sweetly when the silence stretched on, taut and nearly humming. He swallowed as if it hurt him, and she felt like a goddess as he
dragged his gaze back to hers.

"Come here." His voice was a rasp, thick and hot, and it moved in her like joy.

She obeyed him and this time, she was happy to do it. She walked toward him, reveling in the way her blood pounded through her and her skin seemed to shrink a size, too tight across her bones. Because he could call this revenge. He could talk about hatred and penance. But it was still the same thick madness that felt like a rope around her neck. It was still the same inexorable pull.

It was still *them*.

Paige stopped in front of him and let out a surprised breath when he moved, reaching down to gather her wrists in his big hands and then pull them behind her, securing them in one of his at the small of her back. Her skirt fell back into place against the sensitized skin of her thighs, her back arched almost of its own accord, and Giancarlo stared down at her, a hard wildness blazing from his eyes.

Paige remembered that, too.

She didn't know what he looked for, much less what he saw. He stared at her for a moment that dragged out to forever and she felt it like panic beneath the surface of her skin. Like an itch.

And then he jerked her close, her hands still held immobile behind her back, and slammed his mouth to hers.

It wasn't a brush of his mouth, a tease, like before. It wasn't an introduction.

He took her mouth as if he was already deep inside of her. As if he was thrusting hard and driving them both toward that glimmering edge. It was more than wild, more than carnal. He bent her back over her own arms, pressing her breasts into the flat planes of his chest, and he simply possessed her with a ruthless sort of fury that set every part of her aflame.

She thrilled to his boldness, his shocking mastery. The glorious taste of him she'd pined for all these years. The sheer *rightness*.

Paige kissed him back desperately, deeply, forgetting about the games they played. Forgetting about penance, about trust. Forgetting her betrayal and his fury. She didn't care what he wanted from her, or how he planned to hurt her, or anything at all but this.

This.

There was too much noise in her head and too much heat inside of her and she actually moaned in disappointment when he pulled back, holding her away from him with that iron strength of his that reminded her how gentle he was with it. How truly demanding, because he knew—as he'd always known—exactly what she wanted. How far away from *force* all of this really was.

"You kiss like a whore," he said, and she could see it was meant to be an insult, but it came out sounding somehow reverent, instead.

She laughed. "Have you kissed many whores, then? You, the exalted Count Alessi, who could surely have any proper woman he wished?"

"Just the one."

She should be wounded by that, Paige thought as she studied him. She should feel slapped down, put in her place, but she didn't. She cocked her head to one side and saw the fever in his dark gaze, and she knew that whatever power he had over her, she had it over him, too. And more, he was as aware of that as she was.

"Then how would you know?" she asked him, her voice like a stranger's, breathy and inviting. Nothing like hurt at all. "Maybe the whore is you."

"Watch your mouth." But he'd moved closer again, his shoulders filling her vision, her need expanding to swallow the whole world. Or maybe it was his need. Both of theirs, twined together and too big to fit beneath the sky.

"Make me," she dared him, and he muttered something in Italian.

And then he did.

He let go of her hands to take her face between his hard palms, holding her where he wanted her as he plundered her mouth. As he took and took and then took even more, as if there was no end and no beginning and only the madness of their mouths, slick and hot and perfect. The fire between them danced high and roared louder, and he didn't stop her when Paige melted against him. When she wound her arms around his neck and clung to him, kissing him back as if this was the reunion she'd always dreamed of. As if this was a solution, not another one of his clever little power games.

And she didn't know when it changed. When it stopped being about fury and started to taste like heat. When it started to feel like the people they'd been long ago, before everything had gone so wrong.

He felt it, too. She felt him stiffen, and then he thrust her aside.

And for a long moment they only stared at each other, both of them breathing too fast, too hard. Paige tried to step back and her legs wobbled, and Giancarlo scowled at her even as his hand shot out to steady her.

"Thank you," she said, because she couldn't help herself. Her mouth felt marked, soft and plundered, and Giancarlo was looking at her as if she was a ghost. "That certainly taught me my place. All that punitive kissing."

She didn't know what moved across his face then, but it scraped at her. It hurt far worse than any of his words had. She had to bite her own tongue to keep from making the small sound of pain that welled up in her at the sight of it.

"It will," he promised her, a bleakness in his voice that settled in her bones like a winter chill. Like the fate she'd been running from since the day she'd met him, loath as she was to admit it. "I can promise you that. Sooner or later, it will."

Kissing her had been a terrible mistake.

Giancarlo ran until he thought his lungs might burst and his legs might collapse beneath him, and it was useless. The Southern California sun was unforgiving, the blue sky harsh and high and cloudless, and he couldn't get her taste out of his mouth. He couldn't get the feel of her out of his skin.

It was exactly as it had been a decade ago, all over again, except this time he couldn't pretend he'd been blindsided. This time, he'd walked right into it. He'd been the one to kiss her.

He cursed himself in two languages and at last he stopped running, bending over to prop his hands on his knees and stare down the side of the mountain toward his mother's estate and the sprawl of the city below it in the shimmering heat of high summer. It was too hot here. It was too familiar.

Too dangerous.

It was much too tempting to simply forget himself, to pick up where he'd left off with her. With the woman who was no longer Nicola. As if she hadn't engineered his ruin, deliberately, ten years ago. As if she hadn't then tricked her way to her place at his mother's side with a new name and God only knew what agenda.

As if, were he to bury himself in her body the way he wanted to do more than was wise and more than he cared to admit to himself, she might transform into the woman she'd already proved she wasn't in the most spectacular way imaginable.

He was already slipping back into those old habits he'd thought he'd eradicated. The work he'd left in Italy was piling up high, and yet here he was, running off steam in the Bel Air hills the way he'd done when he was a sixteen-year-old. She was the first thing he thought of when he woke. She was what he dreamed about. She was taking over his life as surely as she ever had, very much as if this was *her* revenge, not his.

He was an addict. There was no other explanation for the state he was in, hard and ready and yearning, and he didn't want that. He wanted her humbled, brought low, destroyed. He wanted her to feel how he'd felt when he'd woken that terrible morning to find his naked body splashed everywhere for the entire world to pick over, parse, comment upon, like every other time his private life been exploited for Violet's gain—but much worse, because he hadn't seen the betrayal coming. He hadn't thought to brace himself for impact.

He wanted this to hurt.

Giancarlo straightened and shoved his hair back from his forehead, the past seeming to press against him too tightly. He remembered it all too well. Not just the affair with Nicola—*Paige,* he reminded himself darkly—in all its blistering, sensual perfection, as if their bodies had been created purely to drive each other wild. But the parts of that affair he'd preferred to pretend he didn't remember, all these years later. Like the way he'd always found himself smiling when they'd spoken on the phone, wide and hopeful and giddy, as if she was sunshine in a bottle and only his. Or the way his heart had always thudded hard when she'd entered a room, in the moment before she'd seen him and had treated him to that dazzling smile of hers that had blotted out the rest of the world. The way she'd held his hand as if that connection alone would save them both from darkness, or dragons, or something far worse.

Oh yes, he remembered.

And he remembered the aftermath, too. After the pictures ran in all those papers. After those final, horrible moments with this woman he had loved so deeply and known not at all. After he'd done the best he could to clear his head and then made his way back to Italy. To face, at last, his elderly father.

His father, who had felt denim was for commoners and had thought the only thing more tawdry than Europe's aristocracy was the British royals, with their divorces and dirty laundry and *jeans*. His father, Count Alessi, who could have taught propriety and manners to whole nunneries and probably had, in his day. His father, who had been as gentle and nobly well-meaning as he was blue-blooded. Truly the last of his kind.

"It is not your fault," he'd told Giancarlo that first night in the wake of the scandal. He'd hugged his errant son and greeted him warmly, his body so frail it had moved in Giancarlo like a winter wind, a herald of the coming season he hadn't wanted to face. Not then. Not yet. "When I married your mother I knew precisely who she was, Giancarlo. It was foolish to imagine she and I could raise a son untainted by that world. It was only a matter of time before something like this happened."

Perhaps his father's disappointment in him had cut all the deeper because it had been so matter-of-fact. Untouched by any hint of anger or vanity or sadness. There was nothing to fight against, and Giancarlo had understood that there had been no one to blame but himself for his poor judgment. His father might have been anti-quated, a relic of another time, but he'd instilled his values in his only son and heir.

Strive to do good no matter what, he'd told Giancarlo again and again. *Never make a spectacle of oneself. And avoid the base and the dishonorable, lest one become the same by association.*

Giancarlo had failed on all counts. It was why he knew that the vows he'd made when he was younger were solid. Right. No marriage, because how could he ever be certain that someone wanted *him*? And no heirs of his own, because he'd never, ever, subject a child to the things he'd survived. He might not be able to save himself from his own father's disappointment, he might find his life trotted out into public every time his mother starred in something new and needed to remind the world of her once upon an Italian count fairy-tale marriage, but it would end with him.

Damn Nicola—*Paige*—for making him think otherwise, even if it had only been for two mostly naked months a lifetime ago.

It was that, he thought as he broke into a run again, his pace harder and faster than before as he hurtled down the hill, that he found the most difficult to get past. He hated that she had betrayed him, yes. But far worse was this *thing* in him, dark and brooding, that yearned only for her surrender no matter how painful, and that he very much feared made him no different than she was.

He thought he hated that most of all.

CHAPTER FOUR

AFTER A LONG shower and the application of his own hand to the part of him that least listened to reason, Giancarlo prowled through the house, his fury at a dull simmer. An improvement, he was aware.

La Bellissima was the same as it ever was, as it had been throughout his life, he thought as he moved quietly through its hushed halls, gleaming with Violet's wealth and consequence in all its details. The glorious art she'd collected from all over the planet. The specially sourced artisan touches here and there that gave little hints of the true Violet Sutherlin, who had been born under another name and raised in bohemian Berkeley, California. Old Hollywood glamor mixed with contemporary charm, the house managed to feel light and airy rather than overfed, somehow, on its own affluence.

Much like Violet herself, all these years after her pouty, sex kitten beginnings in the mid-seventies. He should know, having been trotted out at key moments during her transition from kitten to lion of the industry, as a kind of proof, perhaps, that Violet could do more than wear a bikini.

There was the time she'd released a selection of cards he'd written her as a small child, filled with declarations of love that the other kids at school had teased him about all the way up until his high school graduation. There was the time she'd spent five minutes of her appearance in a famous actor's studio interview telling a long, involved anecdote about catching him and his first girlfriend in bed that had humiliated fourteen-year-old Giancarlo and made his then-girlfriend's parents remove her to a far-off boarding school. He knew every inch of this house and none of it had ever been his; none of it had ever been safe. He was as much a prop as any of the other things Violet surrounded herself with—only unlike the vases, he loved her despite knowing how easily and unrepentantly she'd use him.

He followed the bright hall toward Violet's quarters, knowing how much she liked to spend her days in the office there with its views of the city she'd conquered. He had memories of catapulting himself down this same hallway as a child, careening off the walls and coming to a skidding halt in that room, only to climb up on the chaise and lie at his mother's feet as she'd run her lines and practiced her voices, her various accents, the postures that made her body into someone else's. He'd found her fascinating, back then. He supposed he still did, and Giancarlo couldn't remember, then, at what age he'd realized that Violet was better admired than depended upon. That her love was a distantly beautiful thing, better experienced as a fan than a family member. The first time she'd released a photo of him he'd found embarrassing? Or the tenth, with as little remorse?

He only knew they'd both been far happier once he'd accepted it.

Giancarlo paused in the doorway, hearing his mother's famous laugh before he saw her. She wasn't in her usual place today, reclining on her chaise like the Empress of Hollywood. She was standing at the French doors instead, bathed in soft light from the summer day beyond with a mobile phone in her hand, and even though there was no denying her celebrated beauty, his gaze went straight to the other woman in the room as if Violet wasn't there at all.

Paige sat at the fussy little desk in the corner, typing something as a male voice responded to whatever Violet had said from her mobile phone, obviously on speaker. Paige was frowning down at her laptop as her fingers flew over the keys, and when Violet turned toward her to roll her eyes at her assistant, Giancarlo could see the face Paige made in immediate response.

Sympathetic. Fully on Violet's side. Staunch and true, he'd have said, if he didn't know better.

He'd seen that expression before. *That* was the woman he'd loved in all the passionate fury of those two months of madness. Stalwart. Loyal. Not in any way the kind of woman who would sell a man out and print it all up in the tabloids. He'd have sworn on that. He'd have gambled everything.

Giancarlo still couldn't believe how wrong he'd been.

His stomach twisted, and it took everything he had not to make a noise, not to bellow out his fury at all of this—but mostly at himself.

Because he wanted to believe, still. Despite everything. He wanted there to be an explanation for what had happened ten years ago. He wanted Paige—and when had he started thinking about her by that name, without stumbling over it at all?—to be who she appeared to be. Dedicated to his mother. Deeply sorry for what had gone before, and with some *reason* for what she'd done. And not the kind of self-serving reason Violet always had...

He wanted her back.

And that was when Giancarlo woke up with a jolt and recognized the danger he was in. History could not repeat itself. Not with her. Not ever.

"Darling," Violet said when she ended her call, turning from the window and smiling at him. "Don't lurk in the hallway. It was only my agent. A whinier, more demanding fool I have yet to meet, and yet I'm fairly certain he's the best there is."

But what Giancarlo noticed was the way Paige straightened in her chair, her eyes wide and blue when they flew to him, then quickly shuttered when she looked back to her keyboard.

He could think of a greater fool than his mother's parasitical agent. It was something about finding himself back in Los Angeles, he thought as he fought back his own temper, as well as seeing Paige again. It would have been different if he'd encountered her in some other city. Somewhere that held no trace of who they'd been together. But here, their history curled around everything, like a thick, encroaching smog, and made it impossible to inhale without confronting it every time.

With every goddamned breath.

"I must return to Italy," he said shortly. Almost as if he wasn't certain he'd say it at all if he didn't say it quickly and that, of course, made him despise himself all the more.

"You can't leave," Violet said at once. Giancarlo noticed Paige seemed to type even more furiously and failed to raise her head at all. "You've only just arrived."

"I came because it had been an unconscionably long time, Mother," he said softly. "It was never my intention to stay away so long. But I have a solution."

"You are moving back to Los Angeles," Violet said, a curve to her mouth that suggested she didn't believe it even as she said it. "I'm delighted. That Malibu house is far too nice to waste on all those renters."

"Not at all." He wanted to study Paige instead of his mother but he didn't dare. Still, he was as aware of her as if she was triple her own size. As if she loomed there in his peripheral vision, a great dark cloud, consuming everything. "You must come to Italy. Bring your assistant. Stay for the rest of the summer."

Violet looked startled for a moment, but then in the next her face smoothed out, and he recognized the mask she wore then. As impenetrable as it was graceful. A vision of loveliness that showed only what she wanted seen, and nothing else. Violet Sutherlin, the star. Giancarlo didn't know what it said about him that he found this version of her easier to handle than the one who pretended motherhood was her primary concern.

"Darling, you know my feelings about Italy," she murmured, and a stranger might have believed her wry, easy tone. "I love it with all my heart. But I'm afraid I buried that heart with your father."

"Not that Italy," he said. He smiled, though he understood he was speaking as much to the silent woman in the corner of his eye as to his mother. "My Italy."

"Do you have your own?" Violet asked. She laughed again. "You have been busy indeed."

"I've completely transformed the estate," Giancarlo said quietly. "I know we've discussed all these changes over the years, but I'd like you to see them for yourself. I think Father would be proud."

"I know he would," Violet said with a glimmer of something raw in her gaze and the sound of it in her voice, and Giancarlo knew he had her. Paige knew it too, he could tell. He felt more than saw her stiffen at her desk, and it took everything he had to keep the triumph from his voice, the sheer victory from his face. "Of course, Giancarlo. I'd love to see Tuscany again."

He only let himself look at Paige again when he was certain he had himself under complete control. *Like iron,* he thought fiercely. Like the old houses he'd rebuilt on the ancestral estate in Tuscany, stone by ancient stone, forcing his will and vision onto every acre.

He would take her away from Los Angeles, where history seemed to infuse every moment between them with meaning he didn't want. He didn't know why he hadn't thought of this sooner.

In the far reaches of Tuscany, as remote as it was possible to get in one of the most famous and beloved regions of the world, she would be entirely dependent on him. Violet could relax in the hands of his world-class staff, her every need anticipated and met, and he would have all the time in the world to vanquish this demon from his past, for good. All the time he needed to truly make her pay.

Because that was what he wanted, he reminded himself. To make her pay. Everything else was memory and fantasy and better suited to a long night's dream than reality.

"Wonderful." Giancarlo tried not to gloat, and knew he failed when Paige frowned. And it was still a victory. It was still a plan. And it would work, he was sure of it. Because it had to. "We leave tonight."

Paige had dreamed of Italy her whole life.

When she was a child, she'd sneaked library books into her mother's bleak trailer in the blistering heat of the rocky Arizona desert. She'd waited for Arleen to pass out before she'd lost herself in them, and she'd dreamed. Fierce dreams of cypress trees in stern columns marching across a deep green undulation of ancient fields. Monuments to long lost gods and civilizations gone centuries before her birth, red-roofed towns clustered on gentle hills beneath a soft, Italian sun.

Then she'd met Giancarlo, who carried the lilt of Italy in every word he spoke, and her dreams had taken on a more specific shape. Even back then, when he'd wanted to play around in Hollywood more than he'd wanted to tend to his heritage, he'd spoken of the thousands of rural acres that his father had only just started to reclaim from the encroaching wilderness of a generation or two of neglect. They were his birthright and in those giddy days ten years ago she'd dared to imagine that she was, too.

And now she was finally here, and it turned out it was extraordinarily painful to visit a place that she'd once imagined might be her home and now knew never, ever would be. More than painful—but she told herself it was the jet lag that made her ache like that. Nothing a good night's sleep on solid ground wouldn't cure.

Even if it was *this* solid ground.

The vast estate sprawled across a part of Tuscany that had been in the Alessi family in one form or another since the Middle Ages. It was dotted with old farmhouses Giancarlo had spent the past decade painstakingly renovating for a very special class of clientele: people as wealthy as his mother and as allergic to invasions of their privacy as his father had been. As Paige supposed he must be himself now, after his too-public shaming at her own hands.

Here at Castello Alessi and all across its hilly lands, thick with olive groves and vineyards, lavender bushes and timeless forests of oak trees—according to the splashy website Paige had accessed a hundred times before and once again from the plane when she'd accepted she was really, truly coming here at last—such privacy-minded people could relax, secure in the knowledge that the "cottages" they'd paid dearly either to rent or to buy outright and fashion to their liking were as private and remote as it was possible to get while still enjoying world-class service akin to that of the finest hotels, thanks to Giancarlo's private, around-the-clock staff.

But none of that applied to Paige, she was well aware.

They'd landed on a private airstrip in a nearby valley after flying all night. It had been a bright, somehow distinctly Italian summer morning, filled with yellow flowers and too-blue skies, and a waiting driver had whisked them off to the estate some forty minutes away. It was a long, gorgeous drive, winding in and around the hills of Tuscany that looked exactly as Paige had imagined them while also being somehow so much *more* than she'd anticipated. Violet had been installed in the lavishly remodeled *castello* itself, arrayed around a welcoming stone courtyard with heart-stopping views and her own private spa with waiting staff to pamper her at once, as if she was truly the High Queen of Italy.

Paige, on the other hand, Giancarlo ushered into a Jeep and then personally drove far out into the heart of the property, until all she could see in all directions was the gently rolling countryside and one lone house at the top of the nearest hill. All of it so gorgeous and yet so *familiar*, as if she'd been here before and recognized it like a homecoming, and yet, she was forced to keep telling herself, none of this was hers. Not the perfect sky, the charming lane, the pretty little houses on this or that ridge. *Not hers.* The man beside her least of all.

"Are you deliberately stranding me out here as some kind of punishment?" she asked him, when it became clear that a smaller cottage down in the valley beneath that lone house was where he was headed. She was doing her best not to look at him, braced beside her in the smaller-by-the-moment front of his Jeep as they bumped along the lazy dirt road that meandered toward the little stone house, because she was afraid it might make all these raw emotions inside of her spill over into tears. Or worse. "Don't you think that looks a little bit strange?"

"My mother will be waited on hand and foot in the *castello*," he said, his gruff voice either impatient or triumphant, and Paige couldn't tell which. She wasn't sure she wanted to know. "And if by some chance she needs you while undergoing a battalion of spa treatments, never fear, the Wi-Fi is excellent. I trust she can manage to send out an email should she require your presence."

"So the answer is yes," Paige said stiffly as he pulled up in front of the cottage. He turned the key in the ignition and the sudden quiet seemed to pour in through the open windows, as terrifying as it was sweet. "This is a punishment."

"Yes," he said in that low way of his that wrapped around her and made her yearn, then made her question her own sanity. "I am punishing you with Tuscany. It is a fate worse than death, obviously. Just look around."

She didn't want to look around, for a thousand complicated reasons and none she'd dare admit. It made her feel scraped to the bone and weak. So very weak. So she looked at him instead, which wasn't really any better.

"You think I don't know why you brought me here, but of course I do." She laughed, though it was a hollow little sound and seemed to make that scraped sensation expand inside of her. "You're making sure I have nowhere to run. I think that counts as the most basic of torture methods, doesn't it?"

"Correction." He aimed a smile at her that didn't quite

reach the storm in his eyes, but made her feel edgy all the same. "I don't care if you know. It isn't the same thing."

Paige pushed her way out of the Jeep, not surprised when he climbed out himself. Was this all a prologue to another one of these scenes with him—as damaging as it was irresistible? She tucked her hands into the pockets of the jeans she'd worn on the long flight and wished she felt like herself. *It's only jet lag,* she assured herself. Or so she hoped. *You've read about jet lag. Everyone says it passes or no one would ever go anywhere, would they?* But she didn't feel particularly tired. She felt stripped to the bone instead. Flayed wide-open.

And the way he looked at her didn't help.

"How long?" she asked, her voice not quite sounding like her own. "How long do you think you can keep me here?"

Giancarlo pulled her bags from the back and carried them to the door of the cottage, shouldering it open and disappearing inside. But Paige stayed where she was, next to the Jeep with her eyes on the rolling green horizon. The sweet blue of the summer sky was packed with fluffy white clouds that looked as if they were made of meringue and were far more beautiful than all of her dreams put together, and she tried her best not to cry, because this was a prison—she knew it was—and yet she couldn't escape the notion that it was *home*.

"I'll keep you as long as I like," he said from the doorway, his voice another rolling thing through the morning's stillness, like a dark shadow beneath all that shine. "This is about my satisfaction, *cara*. Not your feelings. Or it wouldn't be torture, would it? It would be a holiday."

"By your account, I imagine I don't have any feelings anyway, isn't that right?" She hadn't meant to say that, and certainly not in that challenging tone. She scowled at the stunning view, and reminded herself that she'd never really had a home and never would. Longing for a place like this was nothing more than masochistic, no matter how familiar it felt. "I'm nothing but a mercenary bitch who set out to destroy you once and is now, what? A delusional stalker who has insinuated herself into the middle of your family? For my own nefarious purposes, none of which have been in evidence at all over the past three years?"

"I find *parasite* covers all the bases." Giancarlo drawled that out, and it was worse, somehow, here in the midst of so much prettiness. Like a creeping black thing in the center of all that green, worse than a mere shadow. "No need to succumb to theatrics when you can merely call it what it is."

She shook her head, that same old anguish moving inside of her, making her shake deep in her gut, making her wish for things she knew better than to want. A home, at last. Love to fill it. A place to belong and a person to share it with—

Paige had always *known better*. Dreams were one thing. They were harmless. No one could have survived the hard, barren place where she'd grown up, first her embittered mother's teenage mistake and then her meal ticket, without a few dreams to keep them going. Much less what had happened ten years ago. What her mother had become. What Paige had nearly had to do in a vain attempt to save her.

But *wishes* were nothing but borrowed trouble. And she supposed, looking back, that had been the issue from the start—being with Giancarlo had made her imagine she could dare to want things she knew, *she knew,* could never be hers. Never.

You won't make that mistake again in a hurry, her mother's caustic voice jeered at her.

Paige risked a look at Giancarlo then, despairing at the way her heart squeezed tight at the sight of him the way it always had, at that dark look on his face that was half hunger and half dislike, at the way she had always loved him and understood she always would, and to what end? He would have his revenge and she would endure it and somehow, somehow, she would survive him, too.

It hurts a little bit more today than it usually does because you're here and you're tired, she tried to tell herself. *But you're fine. You're always fine. Or you will be.*

"I know you don't want to believe me," she said, because she had always been such an idiot where this man was concerned. She had never had the slightest idea how to protect herself. Giancarlo had been the kind of man who had blistering affairs the way other people had dinner plans, but *she* had fallen head over heels in love with him at first glance and destroyed them both in the process. And now she wanted, so desperately, for him to *see* her, just for a moment. The real her. "But I would do anything for your mother. For a hundred different reasons. Chief among them that she's been better to me than my own mother ever was."

"And here I thought you emerged fully grown from a bed of lies," he said silkily. He paused, his dark eyes on her, as if recognizing how rare it was that Paige mentioned her own mother—but she watched him shrug it off instead of pursuing it and told herself it was for the best. "I was avoiding the city my mother lived in all these years and the kind of people who lived in it, not my mother. A crucial distinction, because believe me, *Paige*, I would also do anything for my mother. And I will."

There was a threat in the last three words. A promise. And there was no particular reason it should thud into her so hard, as if it might have taken her from her feet if she hadn't already been braced against all of this. The pretty place, the sense of homecoming, the knowledge he was even more lost to her when he stood in front of her than he had been in all their years apart.

"I loved my mother, too, Giancarlo," Paige said, and she understood it was that scraped raw feeling that made her say such a thing. Giancarlo would never understand the kind of broken, terrible excuse for love that was the only kind Paige had ever known, before him. The sharp, scarring toll it exacted. How it festered inside and taught a person how to see the world only through the lens of it, no matter how blurred or cracked or deeply twisted. "And that never got me anything but bruises and a broken heart." And then had taken the only things that had ever mattered to her. She swallowed. "I know the difference."

He moved out of the doorway of the cottage then, closing the distance between them with a few sure steps, and Paige couldn't tell if that was worse or better. Everything seemed too mixed up and impossible and somehow *right*, too; the gentle green trees and the soft, lavender-scented breeze, and his dark gold eyes in the center of the world, making her heart beat loud and slow inside her chest.

Stop it, she ordered herself. *This is not your home. Neither is he.*

"Is this an appeal to my better nature?" Giancarlo asked softly. Dangerously. "I keep telling you, that man is dead. Killed by your own hand. Surely you must realize this by now."

"I know." She tilted up her chin and hoped he couldn't see how lost she felt. How utterly out of place. How hideously dislocated if it seemed that *he* was the only steady thing here, this man who detested her. "And here I am. Isolated and at your beck and call. Just think of all the ways you can make me pay for your untimely death."

She couldn't read the shadow that moved over his face then. His hand moved as if it was outside his control and he ran the backs of his fingers over the line of her jaw, softly, so softly, and yet she knew better than to mistake his gentleness for kindness. She knew better than to trust her body's interpretations of things when it came to this man and the things he could do to it with so seemingly careless a touch.

The truth was in that fierce look in his eyes, that flat line of his delectable mouth. The painful truth that nothing she said could change, or would.

He wanted to hurt her. He wanted all of this to *hurt*.

"Believe me," he said quietly. Thickly, as if that scraped raw thing was in him, too. "I have thought of little else."

Paige thought he might kiss her then, and that masochist in her *yearned* for it, no matter what came after. No matter how he made her pay for wanting him, which she knew he would. She swayed forward and lifted her mouth toward his and for a moment his attention seemed to drift toward her lips—

But then he muttered one of those curses that sounded almost pretty because it was in Italian. And he stepped back, staring at her as if she was a ghost. A demon, more like. Sent to destroy him when it was clear to her that if there was going to be any destruction here, it would be at his hands.

It was going to be her in pieces, not him. And Paige didn't understand why she didn't care about that the way she should. When he looked at her, she didn't care about anything but him and all these terrible, pointless wishes that had wrecked her once already. She should have learned her lesson a long time ago. She'd thought she had.

"I suggest you rest," he said in a clipped tone, stalking back toward the driver's side of the Jeep. "Dinner will be served at sunset and you'll wake up starving sometime before then. That's always the way with international flights."

As if he knew she'd never left the country before, when she'd thought she'd hidden it well today. His knowing anyway seemed too intimate, somehow. The sort of detail a lover might know, or perhaps a friend, and he was neither. She told herself she was being ridiculous, but it was hard to keep looking at him when she felt there had to be far too much written across her face then. Too much of that Arizona white trash dust, showing him all the things about her she'd gone to such lengths to keep him from ever knowing.

"At the *castello*?" she asked, after the moment stretched on too long and his expression had begun to edge into impatience as he stood there, the Jeep in between them and his hand on the driver's door. "That seems like a bit of a walk. It was a twenty-minute drive, at least."

"At the house on the hill," he said, and jerked his head toward the farmhouse that squatted at the top of the nearest swell of pretty green, looking sturdy and complacent in the sunlight, all light stones and an impressive loggia. "Right there. Unless that's too much of a hike for you these days, now that you live on a Bel Air estate and are neck deep in opulence day and night. None of it earned. Or yours."

Paige ignored the slap. "That really all depends on who lives there," she replied, and it was remarkably hard to make her voice sound anything approximating *light*.

"A troll? The Italian bogeyman? The big, bad wolf with his terrible fangs?"

His mouth moved into that crooked thing that made her stomach flip over and her heart ache. More. Again. *Always.*

"That would be me," he said softly, and she thought he took a certain pleasure in it. "So that's all of the above, I'd think. For your sins."

A long nap and a very hot shower after she woke made Paige feel like a new person. Or herself again, at last. She had been too weary and inexplicably sad to explore the cottage when Giancarlo had driven away, so she did it now, with the whisper-soft robe she'd found in the master bathroom wrapped around her and her feet bare against the reclaimed stone floors, her wet hair feeling indulgent against her shoulders as she moved through the charming space.

It was a two-story affair in what had looked from the outside like a very old stone outbuilding. Inside, it was filled with the early-evening light thanks to the tall windows everywhere, the exposed beams high above, and the fact the interior was wholly open to best take advantage of what would otherwise have felt like a small space. Stairs led from the stone ground floor to the loft above, which featured a large, extraordinarily comfortable bed in the airy room nestled in the eaves, a small sitting area with a balcony beyond, and the luxurious master bath Paige had just enjoyed.

The main floor was divided into an efficient, cheerful kitchen with a happily stocked refrigerator, a cozy sitting area with deep sofas arranged around a wide stone fireplace, a small dining area that led out to a patio that spanned the length of the cottage and led into a small, well-tended garden. And everywhere she looked, behind everything and hovering near and far and more beautiful by the moment, the Tuscan view.

Home, she thought, despite herself.

Evening had crept in with long, deep shadows that settled in the valley and made art out of the soft green trees, the cypress sentries and the rounded hills on all sides. The road that had felt torturously remote when Giancarlo had driven her here looked like something from one of her beloved old books now, winding off into the distance or off into dreams. Paige stood there in the window until the air cooled around her, and realized only when she started back up the stairs that she hadn't breathed like that—deeply and fully, all the way down to her feet, the way she had when she'd danced—in a very long time.

Almost as if she was comfortable here. As if she belonged. She'd felt that way in only one other place in her whole life, and had been as wrong. Giancarlo's Malibu home, all wood and glass, angled to best let the sea in, had only been a pretty house. This was a pretty place.

And when you leave here, she told herself harshly, *you will never come back. The same as that house in Malibu. Everyone feels at home in affluent places. That's what they're built to do.*

Paige dressed slowly and carefully, her nerves prickling into a new awareness as she rifled through her suitcase. Should she wear the sort of thing she would wear if this was a vacation in Italy she happened to be taking by herself? Or should she wear something she suspected Giancarlo would prefer, so he could better enact his revenge? On the one hand, jeans and a slouchy sweatshirt, all comfort and very little style. On the other, a flirty little dress he could *get his hands under,* like before. She didn't have the slightest idea which way to go.

"What do *you* want?" she asked her sleepy-eyed reflection in the bathroom mirror, her voice throaty from all that sleep.

But that was the trouble. She still wanted the same things she'd always wanted. She could admit that, here and now, with Giancarlo's Italy pressing in on her from all sides. The difference was that this time, she knew better than to imagine she'd get it.

Paige dried her hair slowly, her mind oddly empty even as the rest of her felt tight with all the things she didn't want to think about directly. Taut and on edge. She pulled on a pair of soft white trousers and a loose sort of tunic on top, a compromise between the jeans she'd have preferred and what she assumed Giancarlo would likely want to see her wear, given the circumstances.

"What he'd really like is me, as naked as the day I was born and crawling up that hillside on my hands and knees," she muttered out loud and then laughed at the image, the sound creaky and strange in the quiet of the cottage. She kept laughing until a wet heat pricked at the back of her eyes and she had to pull in a ragged breath to keep the tears from pouring over. Then another.

Paige frowned as she slipped her feet into a pair of thonged flat sandals. When was the last time she'd laughed like that? About anything?

What a sad creature you've become, she scolded herself as she dug out her smartphone from her bag and scrolled through her messages. But the truth was, she had always been a fairly sad thing, when she looked back at the progression of her life. Sad and studious or determined and stubborn, from the start. It had been the only way to survive the chaos that had been her mother. There had only been one two-month stretch of laughter in her life, gleaming and overflowing and dizzy with joy, and she'd ruined it ten years ago.

"My goodness," Violet said in her grand way when she picked up her private line, after Paige apologized for disappearing and then sleeping for hours, "this is *Italia*, Paige. One must soak in *la dolce vita*, especially when jet-lagged. I plan to spend the night in my lovely little castle, getting fat on all the *marvelous* local cuisine! I suggest you do the same."

And Paige would have loved to do the same, she thought when she finally stepped out of her cottage into the cool evening, the Tuscan sky turning to gold above her. But she had a date with her sins instead.

Sins that felt like wishes granted, and what was wrong with her that she didn't want to tell the difference between the two?

She took her time and yet the walk was still too short. Much too short.

And Giancarlo waited there at the crest of the hill, his eyes as hard as his body appeared loose and relaxed, in linen trousers and the sort of camel-colored sport coat that made her think of his aristocratic roots and her lack of them. And Paige was suddenly as wide-awake as if she'd drowned herself in a vat of espresso.

He looked like something more than a man as he waited there, at first a shadow next to the bold upright thrust of a thick cypress tree, then, as she drew closer, very distinctly himself. He'd clearly watched her come all the way up the side of his hill, and she wasn't sure if she'd seen him from afar without realizing it or if it was that odd magnetic pull inside of her that had done it, pointing her toward him as unerringly as if she'd been headed straight to him all along.

Home, that thing in her whispered, and she didn't have

the strength to pretend she didn't feel it when she did. Not tonight.

She stopped when she was still some distance away and looked back the way she'd come, unable to keep the small sigh of pleasure from escaping her lips. There was the hint of mist in the valley the lower the sun inched toward the hills, adding an elegant sort of haunting to the shadows that danced between them, and far off in the distance the *castello* stood tall and proud, lights blazing against the coming night. It was so quiet and perfect and deeply satisfying in a way Paige hadn't known anything could be. Gooseflesh prickled up and down her arms and she felt it all like a heavy sob in her chest, rolling through her, threatening her very foundations.

Or maybe that was him. Maybe it had always been him.

"It's gorgeous here," she said, which felt deeply inadequate. "It doesn't seem real."

"My father believed that the land is our bones," Giancarlo said. "Protect it, and we strengthen ourselves. Conserve it and care for it, and we become greater in its glory. Sometimes I think he was a madman, a farmer hiding in an aristocrat's body." His gaze moved over her face, then beyond her, toward the setting sun. "And then another sunset reminds me that he was right. Beauty is always worth it. It feeds the soul."

"He sounds like some kind of poet."

"Not my father. Poets and artists were to be championed, as one must always support art and culture for the same reason one tends the land, but Alessis had a higher calling." He shook his head. "Endless debt and responsibility, apparently. I might have been better off as an artist, come to that."

"If I had a home like this, I don't think I'd mind doing

whatever it took to keep it," Paige said then. She remembered herself. "I don't think anyone would."

She thought Giancarlo smiled, though his face was obscured in the falling dark and then she knew she must have imagined it, because this wasn't that kind of evening no matter how lovely it was. He wasn't that kind of man. Not anymore. Not for her.

"Come," he said. He reached out his hand and held it there in the last gasp of golden light, and Paige knew, somehow, that everything would be divided into before and after she took it. The world. Her life. This *thing* that was still between them. And that precarious, wildly beating creature inside her chest that was the battered ruins of her heart.

His mouth crooked slightly as the moment stretched out. She made no move; she was frozen into place and wasn't sure she could do anything about it, but he didn't drop his hand.

"Did you make me dinner?" she asked, her voice shockingly light when there was nothing but heaviness and their history and her treacherous heart inside of her, and she thought neither one of them was fooled. "Because food poisoning really would be a punishment, all joking aside."

"I am Italian," he said, with a note of amused outrage in his voice, which reminded her too strongly of all that laughter they'd shared a lifetime ago. As if the only things that had mattered in the whole world had been there in his smile. She'd thought so then. She thought maybe she still did, for all the good that would do her here. "Of course I can cook." He paused, as if noticing how friendly he sounded and remembering how inappropriate that was tonight. As if he, too, was finding it hard to recall the battle lines he'd drawn. "But even if I couldn't, the estate has a fleet of chefs on call. Meals are always gourmet here, no matter who prepares them."

"Careful," she said softly, more to her memories and her silly heart than the man who stood there before her, still reaching out to her, still her greatest temptation made flesh. Still the perfect embodiment of all the things she'd always wanted and couldn't have. "I might forget to be suitably intimidated and start enjoying myself. And then what would happen?"

He definitely smiled that time, and Paige felt it like a deep, golden fire, lighting her up from the inside out. Making her shiver.

"Surrender takes many forms," he replied into the indigo twilight that cloaked them both, now that the sun had finally sunk beneath the furthest hill. "I want yours every way I can get it."

"I can surrender to *la dolce vita*," she said, as airily as possible, as if her tone of voice might make it so. "I understand that's the point of Italy."

He still stood there, his hand out, as if he could stand like that forever. "That's as good a place to start as any."

And there was no real decision, in the end. There had been so many choices along the way, hadn't there? Paige could have got a different job three years ago. She could have left Violet's house and employ the moment Giancarlo had appeared, or anytime since. She could have declined the offer of that "date" that night, she could have stayed standing up instead of sinking to her knees by the side of that road, she could have shown him nothing in Violet's closet that day but her back as she walked away from him. She could have refused to board his plane, refused to leave her cottage tonight, locked herself inside rather than climb this hill to stand before him like this.

He hadn't *happened* to her, like the weather. She'd

chosen this, every step of the way, and even here, even
stranded in the countryside with this man who thought
so ill of her, she felt more at home than she had in years.
Maybe ever. She supposed that meant she'd made her
decision a long time ago.

So Paige reached out her hand and slid it into his. She
let the heat of him wash through her at that faintly rough
touch, his palm warm and strong and perfect, and told
herself it didn't matter what happened next.

That she'd surrendered herself to Giancarlo a long
time ago, whether he understood that or not.

CHAPTER FIVE

"IF THIS IS your revenge," Paige said, a current of laughter in her voice though her expression was mild, "I think I should confess to you that it tastes a whole lot like red wine."

He should do something about that, Giancarlo thought, watching her move through the refurbished ground floor of his renovated house. She was still so graceful, so light on her feet. Like poetry in motion, and he'd never been able to reconcile how she could flow like that and have turned out so rotten within. He'd never understood it.

It doesn't matter what you understand, he snapped at himself. *Only what you do to make this* thing *for her go away—*

But something had happened out there as the sun set. Something had shifted inside him, though he couldn't quite identify it. He wasn't certain he'd want to name it if he could.

"It may prove to be a long night, *cara,*" he told her darkly, pouring himself a glass of the wine they made here from Alessi grapes. "This is merely the beginning."

"The civilized version of revenge, then," she murmured, almost as if to herself, running her fingers along the length of the reclaimed wood table that marked his dining area in the great, open space he'd done himself.

In soothing yet bright colors and historically contextual pieces, all of which dimmed next to that effortless, off-handed beauty of hers. "I'll keep that in mind."

This didn't feel like revenge. This felt like a memory. Giancarlo didn't want to think too closely about that, but the truth of it slapped at him all the same. It could have been any one of the long, lush evenings they'd shared in Malibu a decade back that still shimmered in his recollection, as if the two of them had been lit from within. It shimmered in him now, too. Again. As if this was the culmination of all the dreams he'd lied and told himself he'd never had, in all those years since he'd left Los Angeles and started bringing the estate back to life.

There was too much history between them, too much that had gone wrong to ever fix, and yet he still caught himself watching her as if this was a new beginning. But then, he had always been such a damned fool where this woman was concerned, hadn't he?

Earlier he'd stood in the courtyard of the *castello* with Violet, toasting her first night back in Italy since his father's funeral eight years ago, and he'd felt a sense of deep rightness. Of homecoming, long overdue. These hills held his happiest childhood memories, after all. When his parents had both been alive, and in those early years, so much in love it had colored the air around them.

"You've done a marvelous thing here, darling," Violet had said, smiling as much at him as at the achingly perfect view.

"I remember the days when we couldn't drive out the gates in Bel Air without having to fight our way through packs of photographers," he'd said, gazing out at the slumbering hills, all of them his now, his birthright and his future. His responsibility. And not a single paparazzo in a thousand miles or more. No lies. No stories. Only the enduring beauty of the earth. "Just to get to school in the morning."

"The tabloids giveth and the tabloids taketh away," Violet had said drily, looking as chic and elegant as ever though she wore her version of lounge wear and what was, for her, a practically cosmetic-free face. "It's never been particularly easy to navigate, I grant you, but there did used to be a line. Or perhaps I'm kidding myself."

"I want this place to be a refuge," he'd told her then. "It's nearly fifteen miles to the nearest main road. Everything is private. It's the perfect retreat for people who can't hide anywhere else."

Violet had tasted her wine and she'd taken her time looking at him again, and he'd still been unsure if she was pausing for dramatic effect or if that was simply how she processed emotion. She was still a mystery to him and he'd long since accepted she always would be. Or anyway, he'd been telling himself he'd accepted it. It might even have been true.

"Yes," she'd said, "and it's very beautiful. It's always been beautiful. I imagine I could live here quite happily and transform myself into one of those portly, Italy-maddened expatriates who are forever writing those merry little Tuscan memoirs and waxing rhapsodic about the *light*." Her brows had lifted. "But which one of us is it that feels they need a hiding place, Giancarlo? Is that meant to be you or me?"

"Never fear, Mother," he'd replied evenly. "I have no intention of having children of my own. I won't have any cause to hide away, the better to protect them from prying eyes and a judgmental world. Perhaps I, too, will flourish in the heat of so many spotlights."

She'd only smiled, enigmatic as ever, seemingly not in the least bit chastised by what he'd said. Had he expected otherwise? "Privacy can be overrated, my darling boy. Particularly when it better resembles a jail."

And now he stood in the cheerful lounge of the house he'd taken apart and put back together with his own two hands, and watched the woman he'd once loved more than any other walk through the monument—he wouldn't call it a *jail*—he'd built to his own unhappiness, his lonely, broken, betrayed heart.

How had he failed to realize, until this moment, that he'd built it for her? That he'd been hiding here these past ten years—deliberately keeping himself some kind of hermit, tucked away on this property and in this very cottage? That it was as much his refuge *for* her as it was *from* her?

That notion made something like a storm howl in him, deep and long. And as if she could read his mind, Paige turned, a small smile on that distracting mouth of hers.

"I always liked your films," she said, her voice the perfect complement to the carefully decorated great room, the furnishings a mix of masculine ease and his Italian heritage, as if he'd planned for her to stand there in its center and make it all work. "I suppose it shouldn't surprise me that that kind of attention to detail should spill over into all the things you do."

"My films were laughable vanity projects at best," he told her, that storm in his voice and clawing at the walls of his chest. "I should never have taken myself seriously, much less allowed anyone else to do the same. It's an embarrassment."

Paige wrinkled her nose and he thought that might kill him, because finding her *adorable* was far more dangerous than simply wanting her. One was about sex, which was simple. The other had consequences. Terrible consequences he refused to pay.

"I liked them."

"Shall we talk about the things you like?" Giancarlo asked, and he sounded overbearingly brooding to his own ears. As if he was performing a role because he thought the moment needed a villain, not because he truly wanted to put her back in her place. "Your interest in photography and amateur porn, for instance?"

Some revenge, he thought darkly. *Next you'll try to cuddle her to death with your words.*

But she only smiled in that enigmatic way of hers, and moved closer to one of the paintings on the wall, her hands cupped around her glass of wine and that inky black hair of hers falling in abandon down her back, and it wasn't cuddling he thought about as he watched her move. Then bite her lower lip as she peered up at the painting. It wasn't *cuddling* that made his blood heat and his mouth dry.

"I don't understand why I'm here," Paige said, so softly that it took him a moment to realize she'd spoken. She swiveled back to look at him, framed there like a snapshot, the woman who had destroyed him before the great, bright canvas that stretched high behind her, all shapes and emotion and a swirl of color, that he hadn't understood until tonight had reminded him of her.

Giancarlo told himself it was a sour realization, but his sex felt heavy and the air between them tasted thick. Like desire. Like need.

Like fate.

"It seems as if you've achieved what you set out to do," she continued as if she couldn't feel the thickness, though he knew, somehow, that she could. "You've separated me from Violet without seeming to do so deliberately, which I'm assuming was your purpose from the start. But why bring me all the way here? Why not leave me in California and spirit Violet away? And having made me come all the way here," Paige continued, something he couldn't identify making her eyes gleam green in the mellow light, "why not simply leave me to rot in my little cottage? It's pretty as prison cells go, I grant you. Very pretty. It might take me weeks to realize I'm well and truly trapped there."

He let his gaze roam over her the way his hands itched to do. "You've forgotten the most important part."

"The sex, yes," Paige supplied, and she didn't sound particularly cowed by the idea, or even as outraged as she'd been back in Los Angeles. Her tone was bland. Perhaps too bland. "On command."

"I was going to say obedience," he said, and he didn't feel as if he was playing a game any longer. He was too busy letting his eyes trace over her curves, letting his hands relish the tactile memory of her face between them as if she'd burned her way into his flesh. He could still taste her, damn it. And he wanted more.

"Obedience," she repeated, as if testing each syllable of the word as she said it. "Does that include feeding me a gourmet dinner in this perfect little mansion only a *count* would call a cottage? Are you entirely sure you know what *obedience* involves?"

Giancarlo smiled, or anyway, his mouth moved. "That's the point. It involves whatever I say it involves."

He took a sip of his wine as he walked over to the open glass doors that led out to the loggia, nodding for her to join him outside. Stiffly, carefully—as if she was more shaken by their encounter than she appeared, and God help him, he wanted that to be true—she did.

Because the truth was so pathetic, wasn't it? He still so badly wanted her to be real. To have meant some part of the things that had happened between them. All these years later, he still wanted that. Giancarlo despaired of himself.

A table waited out in the soft night air, bright with candles and laden with local produce and delicacies prepared on-site, while a rolling cart sat next to it with even more tempting dishes beneath silver covers. It was achingly romantic, precisely as he'd ordered. The hills and valleys of the estate rolled out beneath the stars, with lights winking here and there in the distance, making their isolation high up on this terrace at a remove from all the world seem profound.

That, too, was the point.

He moved to pull her chair out for her like the parody of the perfect gentleman he had never quite been and waited as she settled in, taking a moment to inhale her scent. Tonight she smelled of the high-end bath products he had his staff stock in the cottages, vanilla and apricots, and that hint of pure woman beneath.

"This house was a ruin when I started working on it," he told her, still standing behind her, because he didn't know what his face might show and he didn't want her to see it. To see *him*. He succumbed to a whim and ran his fingers through her hair, reveling in the heavy weight of the dark strands even as he remembered all the other times she'd wrapped him in the heat and sweetness of it. When she'd crawled over him in that wide bed in Malibu and let her hair slip and tumble all over his skin as she tortured him with that sweet mouth of hers, driving them both wild. Giancarlo hardened, remembering it, and her hair was thick silk in his hands. "It sits on its original foundation, but everything else is changed. Perhaps the walls still stand, but everything inside is new, reclaimed, or altered entirely. It might look the same from a distance, but it isn't."

"I appreciate the metaphor," Paige said, with a certain grittiness to her voice that he suspected meant her teeth were clenched. He smiled.

"Then I hope you'll appreciate this, too," he said as he rounded the table and sat down across from her, stretching out his legs before him as he did. "This is the Italian countryside and everything you can see in every direction is mine. You could scream for days and no one would hear you. You could try to escape and, unless you've taken up marathon running in your spare time, you'd run out of energy long before you found the road. You claimed to be obedient in Los Angeles because it suited you. You wanted your job more than you minded the loss of your self-respect, such as it is. Here?" He shrugged as he topped up their wineglasses with a bottle crafted from grapes he'd grown himself and then sat back, watching her closely, as she visibly fought not to react to his cool tone, his calmly belligerent words. "You have no other choice."

"That's not at all creepy," Paige said, though he could have sworn that gleam of green in her chameleon gaze was amusement, however beleaguered. "I'm definitely the terrifying stalker in this scenario, not you."

Giancarlo laughed. "Not that I would care if it really was creepy, but I don't think you really think so, do you? Shall we put it to the test?"

He wanted her to push him, he understood. He wanted to see for himself. He wanted to peel those crisp white trousers from her slim hips and lick his way into her wetness and heat and know it was all for him, the way he'd once believed it was. The way he'd once believed *she* was.

Soon, he assured himself as his body reacted to that image with predictable enthusiasm. *Soon enough.*

"Again," Paige said tightly, taking a healthy gulp of

her wine, "it seems to me that there are more effective forms of payback than a romantic dinner for two, served beneath the starry night sky on what might be the most intimate terrace on the entire planet." She looked out at the view as the heavens sparkled back at her, as if they were performing for her pleasure. "I suspect you might be doing it wrong."

"Ah, Paige," Giancarlo said softly. "You lack imagination." Her eyes swung back to his and he smiled again, wider, pleased when that seemed to alarm her. "The romantic setting will only make it more poignant, will it not, when I order you to strip and sit there naked as we eat. Or when I demand that you please me with your mouth while I soak in the view. Or when I bend you over the serving table and make you scream out my name until I'm done." He let his smile deepen as her eyes went very green, and very round. "The more civilized the setting, the more debauched the act," he said mildly. "I find there is very little more effective."

She looked stunned, and then something like wistful, and he almost broke and hauled her into his arms—but somehow, *somehow*, he reined himself in. *Just a little bit longer,* he promised himself. She blinked, then coughed, and then she folded her hands together in her lap with such precision that Giancarlo knew she was torturing *herself* with all those images he'd put in her head.

Va bene.

"You say that as if this isn't the first time you've done this." Her voice was his own little victory, so raspy was it then, with that stunned heat in her gaze and that band of color high on her cheeks. "Do you spend a lot of time enacting complicated revenge fantasies, Giancarlo? Is that another one of your heretofore hidden talents—like architecture and interior design, apparently?"

"I went to architecture school after university," he said, and something about the fact she didn't know that bothered him. Had he never told her his own story? Had he been as guilty of wearing a false persona ten years ago as she had been? Had it simply been the rush, the need that had kept them in bed and focused on other things? Had it been by her design—or had it been his own selfishness at play? He shoved that disconcerting thought aside. "But when I was finished, I decided I wanted to leverage my position as Violet's son, instead. That didn't work out very well for either one of us, did it?" He reached over and removed the silver cover from the plate of antipasti in front of her, then from his own, and smiled at her when she looked confused. "The *salsicce di cinghiale* is particularly good," he told her. "And you should be certain to eat well. We have a very long night ahead of us."

He expected her to do as she was told. It took a moment or two for him to realize that she hadn't moved. That she appeared to have frozen solid where she sat and was staring at him with a stricken sort of expression on her face.

Giancarlo lifted a brow. "Was I unclear?"

"I appreciate all the tension and drama," Paige said after a moment. "I don't think I realized how very much you take after your mother until now. That's a compliment," she added in a hurry when he frowned at her. "But I'll pass."

"That is not an option you have." He shrugged. "You persist in thinking what you want comes into play here. It doesn't."

"What will you do?" she asked softly, so softly it took a moment for him to hear the challenge beneath the words, and then to see it there in her chameleon eyes.

"Make me scream for people who won't hear me? Make me walk for days in search of a road that's still hours from anywhere? Force me to stay in that gorgeous little cottage down the hill like a bird in a cage?"

"Or, alternatively, merely call my mother and tell her exactly who you are," he suggested. "A fate you felt was worse than death and far more terrible than anything I might do a week ago."

But tonight she only shook her head and she didn't avert her gaze, reminding him of that moment in his mother's closet across the world. Reminding him he'd never controlled this woman, not even when she'd agreed to let him.

"I think if you were going to do that, Giancarlo, you would have. You wouldn't have dragged me across the planet and then presented me with wine and a four-course meal."

He laughed, a smoky little sound against the night. It did nothing to ease the mounting tension. "Do you really want to test that theory?"

She leaned forward, holding his gaze, and his laughter dried up as if it had never been. He was aware of everything at once. The stars above them, the faint breeze that teased him with the intoxicating scent of her. The rich food before them, the dancing candlelight. The way she sat now, the wide neck of her brightly patterned tunic falling open as she leaned toward him, hinting at the soft curves beneath.

And all that fire, as bright as it had ever been, burning them both where they sat.

Her gaze was like a touch on his, and he felt it everywhere. "I have a different theory."

"I'm all ears, of course. Every inmate is innocent, every killer was merely misunderstood, every con man an artist in his soul, et cetera. Tell me your sob story, *cara*." He felt his mouth crook. "I knew you would, sooner or later."

But Paige only smiled, and her eyes were so green tonight they rivaled his own lush fields. It moved in him like summer, an exultation of all that boundless heat that spiked the air between them.

"You don't want revenge. Not really. You want sex."

Her smile deepened when he only stared back at her, that mouth of hers still an utter distraction, still his undoing. Her gaze proud and unwavering and he had no defense against that, either.

"You don't want to admit it, given what happened the last time we had sex, but look where we are." She lifted a shoulder, somehow encompassing the whole of the estate in that simple little gesture. "You've made sure there couldn't possibly be a camera here. You've cut us off from the rest of the world. And you're calling it *revenge* because you're furious that you still want me."

"Or because *wanting* you is only part of it," he replied, stiffer than he should have sounded, because it was that or let loose the wild thing in him that wanted nothing but her however he could have her. That didn't give a toss about the rest of it as long as he got his hands on her one more time. Just one more time. "And not mutually exclusive with revenge, I assure you."

Her smile seemed to pierce straight through him then, heat and fire and danger, and it sank straight to his sex.

Making him nothing at all but that wildness within.

"Call it whatever you want," she suggested in that rough voice of hers that hinted at her own dark excitement, that called to him like a song the way it always had. That sang in him still, no matter how he tried to deny it.

"Call it *hate sex*. I don't care, Giancarlo." She shrugged. "Whatever it is, whatever you need to call it to feel better about it, I want it, too."

"I beg your pardon?" Giancarlo's voice was a rough whisper that somehow sounded in Paige like a bellow.

It was the wine, Paige told herself as she stared back at him, her own words seeming to cavort between them on the heavily laden tabletop, making it impossible to see or hear much of anything else. Of course it was the wine—though she'd only had a few sips—and the lingering jet lag besides, though she didn't feel anything like tired at the moment.

Nothing else could possibly have made her say such things, she was sure, much less throw down the gauntlet to a battle she very much feared might be the end of her.

She opened her mouth to take it back, to laugh and claim she'd been kidding, to break the strange, taut spell that stretched between them and wrapped them tight together, caught somewhere in that arrested expression that transformed his beautiful face. But Giancarlo lifted an aristocratic hand that stopped her as surely as if he'd placed it over her mouth, and she knew she really shouldn't have shivered in a rush of dark delight at the very image.

"I find I'm not as trusting as I used to be," he told her, though *untrusting* wasn't how she would have described the wolfish look in his dark eyes then. "It is a personality flaw, I am sure. But I'm afraid you'll have to offer proof."

She was watching his mouth as if it was a show, which was only part of the reason Paige didn't understand what he'd said. She blinked. "Proof?"

"That this is not another one of your dirty little games

that will end up painting the front page of every godfor-saken gossip rag in existence." He lounged back in his chair, but his eyes were hot, and she had the notion that he was coiled to strike. "You understand my reticence, I'm sure."

"And I'd offer you my word," she said, not sure how she kept her tone so light, as if *dirty little games* hadn't pricked at her and hurt while it did, because he had no idea what kind of dirt she'd been drowning in back then, "but somehow, I'm betting that won't be enough for you."

"Sadly, no," he agreed. He sounded anything but sad. "Though it pains me to cast such aspersions on your char-acter, even if only by insinuation."

"Oh, that's what that look on your face is." Her tone was arch and if she hadn't known better, if she hadn't known it was impossible, she might have thought she was enjoying herself here. "It looks a bit more like glee than pain from this side of the table, I should tell you."

Giancarlo smiled, dark and intent. "I can't imagine why."

The night air seemed to shimmer in the space between them, in the flickering light of the candles and in the vel-vety dark that surrounded the table like an embrace. He settled even farther back in his chair and stretched his legs out again, like an indolent god awaiting a sacrifice, and Paige knew she should put a stop to this before it got out of control—but she didn't. The truth was she didn't want to stop it. She didn't want to do anything but this.

"Strip." It was a hoarse command, rich and dark, like the finest chocolate poured over her skin, and she should have been outraged by his arrogance. Instead, she wanted to bathe in it. In him.

Wasn't that always what she'd wanted?

She didn't pretend she hadn't heard him or that she didn't understand. "Here?"

"Right here." His dark gaze burned, gold and onyx, daring her. "Unless there is some new reason you refuse to obey me this time?"

"You mean, besides the fact that we're sitting outside? Where anyone could see us engaged in all manner of shocking acts? I thought you had a horror of public displays of anything."

"How shocking could a simple strip show be?" he asked, and there was something else in his gaze then, sharp and hard. "It has slipped your mind, perhaps, that the entire world has already seen us having sex. I doubt anything we do could possibly shock them now. Unless you've learned new tricks since I last saw you?"

"Nothing but the same old tricks here," she said, keeping her tone the same as it was, as if that slap of history hadn't made her feel dizzy at all. It was too bad nothing seemed to keep her from wanting him. She was that masochistic. "I'm sorry to disappoint you. Should I keep my clothes on?"

Paige saw that flash of fury in his gaze once more, but it melted into molten heat in the space of a heartbeat, as if they were both masochists here. Somehow, that made her feel better.

"No," he said in a low voice. "You most certainly should not."

"Then it seems I have no choice but to obey you, as promised," she said quietly. "Despite your poor, apparently unshockable neighbors and the things they might see."

"The closest resident aside from my mother is over forty miles away tonight," Giancarlo said, as if impatient. But she could see the fire in his gaze. She could practically taste his need. "Your modesty is safe enough, such as it is. What other excuses do you have?" He let out a bark of something not quite laughter. "We might as well address them all now and be done with them."

"What happens after I strip for you?" Paige asked, almost idly, but she was already pushing her chair back with a too-loud scrape against the stones, then rising to her feet. "This is daring, indeed, to get me naked and then leave me standing here all alone. Is that the plan? It's something of a waste, I'd think."

"First we'll worry about whatever cameras you might have secreted on that body of yours," he told her, and if she hadn't known him she might have thought him cold. Unmoved by all of this. But that wild, uninhibited lover she'd known lurked there in the sensual curve of his lips, that gleaming thing deep in his gaze. Giancarlo might hate her, but he wanted her as much as she did him. And Paige clung to that, perhaps harder than she should have. She clung to it as if it was everything and opted not to listen to the alarms that rang out in her at the thought. "Then we'll worry about what to do with that body."

"Whatever you say, Count Alessi," she murmured, which was as close to obedient as she'd ever come. She saw a certain appreciation for that—or for her wry tone, more like—in his dark eyes, but then it was time to dance.

Because that was what this was. Paige didn't pretend otherwise. The only music was his breath and hers, the only audience the primeval explosion of stars above them. She hadn't danced in years. Ten years, in fact. But she could feel him in her feet, in her hips. In the glorious stretch of her arms over her head. Her pulse and her breath. She could feel him everywhere, better than any sound track with her own hopeful heartbeat like the kick of drums, and she danced.

She poured herself into each undulation of her hips, each exultant reach of her hands. She'd kicked off her shoes when she'd stood and she curled her toes down hard into the smooth stones beneath her, feeling what was left of the day's heat against her soles and that wildfire that only arced higher between the two of them as she moved. She tried her best to catch the sensation in the movement of her hips, her legs, her torso. She took her time peeling off her trousers, managing to kick them aside with a flourish, and then she moved closer to him as she rid herself of her shirt, as if his intent expression beckoned her to him.

She took her time with her bra, offering her breasts to him when she finally dropped it at her side, and she smiled at the way he moved in his chair, his gaze a wild touch on her skin, so fierce it made her nipples pull taut. And she wasn't done. She kept up the dance, the ecstatic dance, and she made it her apology, her regret. She told him all about her love and her silly, shattered hopes with every move she made, and when she stepped out of her panties she didn't know which one of them was breathing more heavily.

Paige only knew that he was standing, too. And that she was naked before him and she still wasn't done.

Naked in the Tuscan night, she danced for all those dreams she'd let carry her away as a girl. For the dream she'd destroyed with a single phone call and a cashed check ten years ago, and none of it worth the sacrifice, in the end. It was like skinny-dipping, warm and cool at once, the summer air a sensual caress against her flesh. She danced for the joy she'd only ever felt in this man's presence, the laughter she still missed, the love she'd squandered for good reasons that seemed nothing but sad in retrospect.

She danced and she danced, and she might have danced all night, but Giancarlo swept her into his arms instead, high against his chest, and that was like a much better dance. Hotter and more intense, and then his mouth came down on hers, claiming her and destroying her that easily.

He came down hard on top of her and she loved it. That lean, hard body of his crushing her with his delicious weight, his narrow hips keeping her legs apart, and it took her a moment to realize that he'd moved them over to one of the sun chaises that sat around the gleaming, sleek pool that jutted out from the loggia toward the vineyards. And that he'd lost his jacket in the move.

And he looked as gorgeously undone as she felt, and very nearly as wild.

"Giancarlo," she whispered, the dance still running madly in her veins, almost as addictive as he was. "Don't stop."

"I give the orders, not you," he growled, but his lips were curved when they took hers all over again.

And then everything slowed down. Turned to honey, thick and sweet.

Giancarlo feasted on her as if she were the gourmet meal his chefs had prepared for him, and beneath his talented mouth she felt almost that cherished, that perfect. She wanted his naked skin pressed to hers more than she could remember wanting anything else, ever, but he kept her too busy to peel his shirt back from his strong shoulders.

He kissed her until her head spun, and then he followed the line of her neck, tasting her and muttering dark things in Italian that she told herself she was happy she didn't understand.

Even if they moved in her like music, dark and compelling, sex and magic and *Giancarlo,* at long last.

He found her breasts and pulled one of the proud nipples deep into his hot mouth, and she didn't care what he *said*. Or in what language. She arched into him, mindless and needy, and he punished and praised her with his lips, his tongue, the scrape of his teeth. He played with her until she begged him to stop and then he only laughed and kept going, sending a catapult of pure wildfire straight down into her core.

She thought for a panicky, wondrous second that he might throw her straight over the edge with only this—

But he stopped, as diabolical as ever, raising his dark head to take in the flushed heat on her face and all down her neck. Her sensual distress. Her driving need.

"This punishment appears to be far more effective than you imagined it would be, *cara*," he murmured, his voice another sensual shiver against her sensitive skin, with its echoes of the playfully wicked lover she'd met so long ago. "It's almost as if you forgot what I can do to you."

"Thank you for the harsh lesson, Count Alessi," she whispered, not trying too hard to keep her tone anything approaching respectful when she was this close to the edge. "May I have another?"

He laughed, and she did too, and she didn't know if she'd been kidding or if she'd meant it when he returned his attention to her body, shifting to crawl down farther. If these were harsh lessons indeed, or gifts. He left a shimmering trail of fire from her breasts to her belly, and when he paused there, his breath fanning out over the hungriest part of her, Paige realized she was breathing as heavily as if she was running a race. The marathon he'd mentioned earlier, God help her.

"You'd better hold on," he warned her, dark and stirring and *right there* against her sex. "I'm going to stop when I'm done, not when you are."

And then he simply bent his head and licked his way into her.

Paige ignited.

She went from the mere sensation of burning straight into open flame. She couldn't seem to catch her breath. She arched against the exquisite torment of his wickedly clever mouth, or she tried to escape it, and either way, it didn't matter. He gripped her hips in his strong hands and he tasted her molten heat as if it was his own greatest pleasure, and before she knew it she was bucking against him, her hands buried deep in his thick, dark hair.

Calling out his name like a prayer into the night.

And he was as good as his word. He didn't stop. He didn't wait for her to come back down, to come back to herself. He simply kept on tasting her, settling in and taking his time, laughing against her tender flesh when she begged him to stop, laughing more when she begged him to keep on going.

The fire poured back into her, hotter and higher than before, and then he plunged two fingers deep inside of her and threw her over the side of the world. Again.

This time, when she shuddered her way back to earth, Giancarlo had moved off her to stand beside her, his hard hands impatient as he pulled her to her feet. It took her a moment to realize he'd finally stripped but she had no time to appreciate it, because he was lying back on the chaise and pulling her down to sit astride him.

"I want to watch," he told her, his voice dark and nearly grim with need, and it lit that flame inside of her all over again.

And then he simply curled his strong hands around her hips the way he had a thousand times before, the way she'd never dreamed he would again, and thrust home.

CHAPTER SIX

HE WAS INSIDE her again. At last.

Finally.

Giancarlo thought the sensation—far better than all his pale memories across these long years, far better than his own damned hand had ever been—might make him become a religious man.

She was so damned hot, molten and sweet and slick and *his,* and she still held him so tightly, so snugly, it was nearly his undoing. Her hair was that deep black ink with hints of fire and it tumbled all around her in a seductive tousle, falling to those breasts of hers, still high and pert, the tips already tight again and begging for his mouth.

Paige looked soft and stunned, exactly how he liked her best, exactly how he remembered her, and then she made everything better by reaching out to prop her hands against his chest. The shift in position made her sink down even farther on him, making them both groan.

He let his hands travel back to cup the twin globes of her delectable bottom, and tested the depth of her, the friction. God help him, but she was perfect. She had always been perfect. The perfect fit. The perfect fire.

Perfect for him.

Giancarlo had somehow forgotten that, in all the long years since he'd last been inside her. He'd convinced himself he'd exaggerated this as some kind of excuse for his own idiocy—that she'd been nothing more than a pretty girl with a dancer's body and all the rest had been a kind of madness that would make no sense if revisited.

But this was no exaggeration. This was pure, hot, bliss. This was that same true perfection he remembered, at last.

Paige looked down at him, her gaze unreadable. Bright and something like awed. And then she started to move.

He had watched her dance ten years ago, and he had wanted her desperately. He'd watched her dance tonight, that astonishing performance for him alone, equal parts sensual and inviting, and he'd thought he might die if he didn't find a way inside her. But nothing compared to *this* dance. Nothing came close.

She braced herself against him, her hands splayed wide over his pectoral muscles, while her hips set a lazy, shattering, insistent rhythm against his. And Giancarlo was lost.

He forgot about revenge. He forgot about their past. Her deceit, his foolish belief in her. All the terrible lies. The damned pictures themselves, grainy and humiliating. He lost his plans in the slide of her body against his, the sleek thrill that built in him with every rocking motion she made. Every life-altering stroke of the hardest part of him so deep, so very deep, in all of her soft heat.

"Make me come," he ordered her, in a stranger's deep growl. He saw her skin prickle at the sound of it, saw the way she pulled her lower lip between her teeth as if she was fighting back the same wave of sensation he was. "Make it good."

Not that it could be anything but good. Not that it ever had been. This was a magical thing, this wild, hot fire that was only theirs. He could feel it every time he sank within her. He knew it every time he pulled back. He felt it in the sure pace she set with her hips, the tight hold of her flesh against his. He wanted it to go on forever, the way he'd thought it would when he'd met her that first time.

The way it should have, that little voice that was still in love with her, that had never been anything but in love with her, whispered deep inside him.

But she was following his orders and this was no time for regrets. She moved against him, lush and lovely, her hips a sinuous dance, a well-cast spell of longing and lust and too many other things he refused to name. He'd thought he'd lost her forever and yet she was here, moving above him, her lovely body on display because he'd wanted it, holding him so deep inside her he couldn't tell where he ended and she began. He didn't want to know.

"Your wish is my command, my count," she teased him, her voice a husky little dream, and then she did something complicated with her hips and the world turned to flames all around them.

When he finally exploded, a bright rush of fire turned some kind of comet, rocketing over the edge of the night, he heard her call out his name.

And then follow him into bliss.

Giancarlo did not welcome reality when it reasserted itself.

Paige lay slumped over him, her face buried in his neck, while he was still deep inside of her. He opted not to think about how easy it was to hold her, or how she still seemed to have been crafted especially to fit in his arms, exactly this way. It took him much longer than it should have to get his breathing under control again. He held her the way a lover might, the way he always had before, and stared out over the top of her head at the faint lights on distant hills and the smear of starlight above.

He wished he didn't care about the past. More than that, he wished he could trust her the way he had once. He wished so many things, and yet all of the stars were fixed tonight, staring down at him from their cold positions, and he knew better.

Paige was an accident waiting to happen. He'd been caught up in that accident once—he wouldn't subject himself to it again. Even he wasn't foolish enough to walk into the same trap twice. No matter that it felt like glory made flesh to touch her again, like coming home after too long away.

He would learn to live without that, too. He had before.

She shifted against him, and he felt the brush of her lips over his skin and told himself it was calculated. That everything about her was calculated. There was no use remembering the afternoons they'd spent curled around each other in his huge bed surrounded by the Malibu sea. When she'd tasted him everywhere with her eyes closed, as if she couldn't help herself, as if her affection was as elemental as the ocean beyond his windows or the sky above and she had no choice but to sink into it with all of her senses.

That had been an act. This was an act. He needed to remember it.

But that didn't mean he couldn't enjoy the show.

"You've obviously been practicing," he said, to be horrible. To remind them both that this was here and now, not ten years back. "Quite a lot, I'd say, were I to hazard a guess."

He felt her tense against him, but almost thought he'd imagined it when she sat up a moment later, displaying her typical offhanded grace. And then she smiled slightly as she looked down at him.

"I was about to compliment you on the same thing," she said, a brittle sort of mischief and something else lighting up her gaze. "You must have slept with a thousand women to do that so well! My congratulations. Especially as I would have said there weren't ten women you could sleep with in a hundred miles, much less a thousand. The privileges of wealth, I presume?"

"You're hilarious." But he couldn't help the crook of his mouth. "I have them flown in from Rome, of course."

"Of course." She wrinkled her nose at him, and it was as dangerous as it had been earlier. It made him want things he knew he couldn't have. He couldn't have them, and more to the point, she couldn't give them. Hadn't he learned anything? "You realize, Giancarlo, that people might get the wrong idea. They might begin to think you're a playboy whore."

"They won't."

"Because you tell them so?" She shook her head, her expression serious though her mysterious eyes laughed at him. "I think that tactic only works with me. And not very well."

"Because," he said, his hands moving to her bottom again, then higher along the tempting indentation in her lovely back to tug her down to him, "a man is only a playboy whore when he appears to be having too much of a certain kind of uncontrolled fun in public. I can do all the same things in private and it doesn't count. Didn't you know?"

Her attention dropped to his mouth and he wanted it there. He was already hardening within her again and she shifted restlessly against him as if she encouraged it, making the fire inside him leap to new life that easily.

"It all counts," she breathed. "Or none of it does."

"Then I suppose that makes us all whores, doesn't

it?" he asked. He indulged himself and sank his hands deep into her hair, holding her head fast, as he tested the depth of her again and found her hotter around him. Wetter. Better, somehow, than before. That quickly, he was like steel. "But let's be clear. How many lovers have you taken in the last ten years?"

"Less than your thousand," she said, her voice a thin little thing, as her hips met his greedily. Deliciously. He grunted, and then pulled out to flip them around, coming down over her again and drawing her legs around his waist. He teased her heat with the tip of his hardness, and he didn't know what it was that drove him then, but he didn't let her pull him into her.

"How many?" he asked. He had no idea why he cared. He didn't care. He'd imagined it a thousand times and it scraped at him and it changed nothing either way. But he couldn't seem to stop. "Tell me."

Her eyes moved to his, then away, and they looked blue in the shadows. "What does it matter? Whatever number I pick, you'll think the worst of me."

"I already think the worst of you," he said, the way he might have crooned love words a lifetime ago, and he couldn't have said what he wanted here. To hurt her? Or himself? To make this all worse? Or was this simply his way of reminding them both who they were? "Why don't you try the truth?"

"None," she said, and there was an odd expression on her face as she said it. He might have called it vulnerable, were she someone else. "I told you there were no new tricks."

It took another beat for him to process that, and then something roared in him, a primal force that was like some kind of howl, and he thought he shook though he knew he held himself perfectly still.

"Is that a joke?" But he was whispering. He barely knew his own voice.

Her wide mouth twisted and her gaze was dark with something he didn't want to understand. Something that couldn't possibly be real.

"Yes," she said, her voice broken and fierce at once. "Ha ha, what a joke. I meant ten. Twenty. How many lovers do you imagine I've taken, Giancarlo? What number proves I'm who you think I am?"

He heard her voice break slightly as she asked the question, and a kind of ripple went through her lush body. He felt it. This time when she urged him into her, he went, slick and hard and even better than before, making him mutter a curse and press his forehead to hers. And he didn't have the slightest idea if this was his form of an apology, or hers.

"I don't care one way or the other," he lied, and he didn't want to talk about this any longer. He didn't want to revisit all those images he'd tortured himself with over the years. Because his sad little secret was that he'd never imagined her in prison, the way he'd told her he had. He'd imagined her wrapped around some other man exactly like this and he'd periodically searched the internet to see if he could find any evidence that she was out there somewhere, doing it with all that same joy and grace that had undone him.

And it had killed him, every time. It still killed him.

So he took it out on her instead, in the best way possible. He set a hard pace, throwing them headfirst into that raging thing that consumed them both, and he laughed against the side of her neck when she couldn't do anything but moan out her surrender.

He held on, building that perfect wildness all over again, making her thrash and keen, and when he thought he couldn't take it any longer he reached between them and pressed hard against the center of her need, making her shatter all around him.

And he rode her until he could throw himself into that shattering, too. Until he could forget the truth he'd heard in her voice when she'd told him there hadn't been anyone since him, because he couldn't handle that—or what he'd seen on her face that he refused to believe. *He refused*.

He rode her until he could forget everything but this. Everything but her. Everything they built between them in this marvelous fire.

Until he lost himself all over again.

"Violet is asking for you," Giancarlo said.

Paige had heard him coming from a long way off. First the Jeep, the engine announcing itself high on the hill and only getting louder as it wound its way down toward her cottage. Then the slam of the driver's door. The thud of the cottage's front door, and then, some minutes later, the slide of the glass doors that led out to where she sat, curled up beneath a graceful old oak tree with her book in her lap.

"That sounds like an accusation," she said mildly, putting her book aside. He stood on the terrace with his hands on his lean hips, frowning at her. "Of course she's asking for me. I'm her assistant. She might be on vacation here, but I'm not."

"She needs to learn how to relax and handle her own affairs," he replied, somewhat darkly. Paige climbed to her feet, brushing at the skirt she wore, and started toward him. It was impossible not feel that hunger at the sight of him, deep inside her, making her too warm, too soft.

"Possibly," she said, trying to concentrate on something, anything but the sensual spell he seemed to weave simply by existing. "But I'm not her therapist, I'm her personal assistant. When she learns how to relax and handle her own affairs, I'm out of a job."

Her heart set up its usual clatter at his proximity, worse the closer she got to him, and she didn't understand how that could still happen. They'd been here almost a week. It should have settled down by now. She should have started to grow immune to him, surely. After all, she already knew how this would end. Badly. Unlike the last time, when she'd been so blissfully certain it would be the one thing in her life that ended well, this time she knew better. Their history was like a crystal ball, allowing her to see the future clearly.

Maybe too clearly. Not that it seemed to matter.

She stopped when she was near him but not too near him, and felt that warm thing in the vicinity of her heart when he scowled. He reached over and tugged her closer, so he could land a hard kiss on her mouth. *Like a mark of possession,* she thought, *more than an indication of desire*—but she didn't care.

It deepened, the way it always deepened. Giancarlo muttered something and angled his head, and when he finally pulled back she was wound all around him and flushed and there was that deep male satisfaction stamped all over his face.

"Later," he told her, like a promise, as if she'd been the one to start this.

And in this past week, Paige had learned that she'd take this man any way she could have him. She imagined that said any number of unflattering things about her, but she didn't care.

"I might be busy later," she told him loftily.

He smiled that hard smile of his that made her ache,

and he didn't look particularly concerned. "I will take that chance."

And she would let him, she knew. Not because he told her to. Not because he was holding anything over her head. But because she was helpless before her own need, even though she knew perfectly well it would ruin her all over again....

Later, she told herself. *I'll worry about it later.*

Because *later* was going to be all the years she got to live through on the other side of this little interlude, when he was nothing but a memory all over again. And she wasn't delusional enough to imagine that there was any possibility that when this thing with Giancarlo ended he might permit her to remain with Violet, in any capacity. He was as likely to fall to his knees and propose marriage.

She moved around him and into the house then, not wanting him to read that epic bit of silliness on her face, when that notion failed to make her laugh at herself the way it should have. When it made everything inside of her clutch hopefully instead. *You are such a fool,* she chided herself.

But then again, that wasn't news.

Paige swept up her bag and hung it over her shoulder, then followed Giancarlo out to his Jeep. He climbed in and turned the key, and she clung to the handle on her side of the vehicle as he bumped his way up the old lane and then headed toward the *castello* in the distance.

It was another beautiful summer's day, bright and perfect with the olive trees a silvery presence on either side of the lane that wound through the hills toward Violet, and Paige told herself it was enough. This was enough. It was more than she'd ever imagined could happen with Giancarlo after what she'd done, and why did she want to ruin it with thoughts of *more*?

But the sad truth was, she didn't know how to be anything but greedy when it came to this man. She wanted all of him, not the parts of himself he doled out so carefully, so sparingly. Not when she could feel he kept so much of himself apart.

She'd woken the morning after that first night to find herself in his bed. Alone. He'd left her there without so much as a note, and she'd lectured herself about the foolishness of her hurt feelings. She'd told herself she should count herself lucky he hadn't tossed her out his front door at dawn, naked.

What she told herself and what she actually went right on feeling, of course, were not quite the same thing.

Modify your expectations, girl, she'd snapped at herself on the walk down the hill to her cottage. The birds had been singing joyfully, the sun had been cheerful against her face, she was in *Italy* of all places, and Giancarlo had made love to her again and again throughout the night. He could call it whatever he wanted. She would hold it in her battered little heart and call it what it had meant to her.

Because she hadn't lied to him. She hadn't touched another man since him, and she'd grown to accept the fact she never would. At first it had hurt too much. She'd seen nothing but Giancarlo—and more important, his back, on that last morning when he'd walked away from her rather than talk about what had happened, what she'd done. Then she'd started working for Violet and it had seemed as if Giancarlo was everywhere, in pictures, in emails, in conversation. Paige had had the very acute sense that so much as going out to dinner with another man was some kind of treason—which she'd known was absurd. Beyond absurd, given the way in which she'd betrayed him. She'd made certain he hated her. He'd walked away from her without a single backward glance. Why should he care what she did?

And yet somehow, each of these ten years had crept by and he was still the only man she'd ever slept with. She'd been unable to contain the small, humming thing inside her then as that thought had kept her company on her walk. It had felt a little bit too much like a kind of silly joy she ought to have known better than to indulge.

But he'd turned up that night, his face drawn as if he'd fought a great battle with himself, and he hadn't seemed interested in talking about whether he'd lost or won. He'd led her up her stairs, thrown her on her bed, and kept them up for another night—this time, she'd noted, with the condoms they'd failed to use before.

They hadn't talked about that first night and its lack of birth control. Just like ten years ago, they hadn't talked about a thing.

And that was how it had been since her arrival, Paige thought now, as they drew closer to the *castello*. She'd never spent much time wondering what it felt like to be a rich man's *kept woman* before now. What she thought people in this part of the world might call a *mistress*. But she imagined it must be something like this past week.

Nothing but the pleasures of their flesh. No unpleasant topics, save the odd bout of teasing that never quite landed a hard punch. Nothing but sex and food and sex again, until she felt glutted on it. Replete. Able to know him at a touch, taste him when he wasn't there, scent him on any breeze.

The last time she'd felt so deeply a part of her own body, her own physical space, she'd been dancing more hours of the day than she'd slept.

She didn't tell him that, either. That she filled these golden, blue-skied days with dancing, as if the first dancing she'd done on that initial night with him had freed her. Paige hadn't understood how lost she'd been until she found herself out in the field near her cottage, dancing in great, wide circles beneath the glorious Tuscan sky with tears running down her face and her arms stretched toward the sun. She wanted nothing more than to share that with him.

But Giancarlo drove the Jeep with the same ferocity he did everything else—except in bed, where he indulged every sense and took his sweet time—and with that same hard edge of his old dark fury beneath it.

Almost as if he, too, preferred the little fairy tale they'd been living this past week, where she existed purely to please him, and did, again and again.

Paige knew better than to ask him about it. Or to tell him the things that moved in her, sharp and sweet, in this place that felt more like home every day. This was a no-talking zone. This was a place of sun and sex and silence. It was the only possible way it could work.

Like all temporary things, all stolen moments, it could only be a secret, or it would implode.

"What have you been up to all this time?" Violet asked, peering at Paige from her position on one of the *castello*'s lovely couches, her iPad in her lap and her voice no more than mildly reproving. "I thought perhaps you'd been sucked into one of the olive groves, never to be seen again."

"You should have told me you needed me!" Paige exclaimed instead of answering the question. Because she didn't want to know what Violet would think about the help touching her son. She didn't want to risk her relationship with either one of them. "I thought I was giving you some much-needed time and space to yourself!"

"My dear girl," Violet said, sounding amused, "if I

wanted time and space to myself, I would have chosen a different life altogether."

Paige was too aware of Giancarlo's dark, brooding presence on the other side of the living room then, lounging there against the massive stone fireplace, supposedly scrolling through his phone's display. She was certain he was hanging on every word. Or did she simply want to be that important to him?

There was no answer to that. Not one that came without a good dose of pain in its wake.

"I'm here now," Paige said stoutly, trying to focus on the woman who had always been good to her, without all these complications and regrets. *Not that she'd give you the time of day if she knew who you really were,* that rough voice that was so much like her mother's snarled at her.

"Then I have two questions for you," Violet replied, snapping Paige back to the present. "Can you operate a manual transmission?"

That hadn't been what Paige was expecting, but that was Violet. Paige rolled with it. "I can."

It was, in fact, one of the few things she could say her mother had taught her. Even if it had been mostly so that Paige could drive the beat-up car she owned to pick her up, drunk and belligerent, from the rough bars down near the railroad tracks.

"And do you want to drive me to Lucca?" Violet smiled serenely when Giancarlo made an irritated sort of noise from the fireplace across the room and kept her eyes trained on Paige. "If memory serves, it has wonderful shopping. And I'm in the mood for an adventure."

"An adventure with attention or without?" Paige asked without missing a beat, though she was well aware it had been a long time since Violet had gone out on one of her excursions into the public without expecting attention from the people who would see her out and about.

"Without," Giancarlo snapped, from much closer by, and Paige had to control a little jump. She hadn't heard him move.

"With, of course," Violet said, as if he hadn't spoken. "No one has fawned over me in a whole week, and I require attention the way plants require sunlight, you know. It's how I maintain my youthful facade."

She said it as if she was joking, but in that way of hers that didn't actually allow for any argument. Not that it was Paige's place to argue. Her son, however, was a different story.

"You're one of the most famous women in the world," Giancarlo pointed out, and the dark thing Paige heard in his voice was a different animal than the one he used when he spoke to her. More exasperated, perhaps. Or more formal. "It's not safe for you to simply wander the streets alone."

"I won't be alone. I'll have Paige," Violet replied.

"And what, pray, will Paige do should you find yourself surrounded? Mobbed?" Giancarlo rolled his eyes. "Hold the crowd off with a smart remark or two?"

"I wouldn't underestimate the power of a smart remark," Paige retorted, glaring at him—but his gaze was on his mother.

"That was a long time ago," Violet said softly. With a wealth of compassion that made Paige stiffen in surprise and Giancarlo jerk back as if she'd slapped him. "I was a very foolish young woman. I underestimated the kind of interest there would be—not only in me, but in you. Your father was livid." She studied her son for a moment and then rose to her feet, smiling faintly at Paige. "We were in the south of France and I thought it would be a marvelous idea to go out and poke around the shops by myself. Giancarlo was four. And when the crowds surrounded us, he was terrified."

"The police were called," he said, furiously, Paige thought, though his voice was cold. "You had to be rescued by armed officials and you never went out without security again—and neither did I. I hope you haven't spent your life telling this story as if I was an overimaginative child who caused a fuss. It wasn't a monster in my closet. It was a pack of shouting cameramen and a mob of fans."

"The point is, my darling, you were four," Violet said quietly. "You are not four any longer. And while I flatter myself that I remain relevant, I am an old woman who has not commanded the attention of packs of paparazzi in a very long time. I'm perfectly capable of enjoying an afternoon with my assistant and, if you insist, *one* driver."

"And you wonder why I refuse to have children," he growled at her, and it took every shred of self-preservation Paige had to keep from reacting to that. To Giancarlo and the pain she could hear beneath the steel in his voice. "Why I would die before I'd subject another innocent to this absurd world of yours."

"I didn't wonder," Violet replied. "I knew. But I hoped you'd outgrow it."

"Mother—"

"I don't like being locked away in Italian castles, Giancarlo," she said, and there was steel in the way she said it, despite the smile she used. It was the famous star issuing a command, not a mother. "If you cast your memory back, you'll remember that I never have."

There was a strange tension in the room then. And though she knew better, though it would no doubt raise the suspicions of the woman who could read anyone, standing right there beside her, Paige found herself looking to Giancarlo as if she could soothe him somehow. As if he'd let her—

And she found that great darkness blazing in his eyes as he slowly, slowly turned his attention from Violet to her.

As if this was something she'd done, too.

Because, of course, she had. When he'd been far older than four. And what she'd done to him hadn't been an accident.

The truth of that almost knocked her sideways, and she would never know how she remained standing. She wanted to tell him everything, and who cared what Violet thought? She wanted to explain about her mother's downward spiral. The money owed, the threats from the horrible Denny, the fear and panic that she'd thought were just the way life was. Because that was how it had always been. Paige wanted him to understand—at last—that she never, ever would have sacrificed him if she hadn't believed she had no other choice. If she hadn't been trapped and terrified herself, with only hideous options on all sides.

But this wasn't the place and she knew—*she knew*—he wouldn't want to hear it anyway. He didn't want to know *why*. He only wanted her to pay.

He didn't realize that she had. That she still did. Every moment since.

And so she stood there, she said nothing the way she'd always said nothing and somehow she managed not to fall to her knees. Somehow Paige managed not to break into pieces. Somehow, she stared back at him as if she'd never broken his heart and she wished, hard and fierce and utterly pointless, that it were true.

"Don't worry," he said quietly, as if he was answering

his mother. All of that darkness in his gaze. All of the betrayal, the loss. The terrible grief. It made Paige's chest ache, so acutely that she forgot to worry that Violet would be able to sense it from a few feet away. So sharp and so deep she thought it might have been a mortal blow, and how could anyone hide that? "I remember everything."

CHAPTER SEVEN

LUCCA WAS A walled city, an old fortress turned prosperous market town, and it was enchanting. Paige dutifully followed Violet through the bustle of tiled red roofs, sloped streets and the sheer tumult of such an ancient place, and told herself there was no reason at all she should feel so unequal to the task she'd done so well and well-nigh automatically for years.

But her heart wasn't with her in the colorful city. It was back in the hills with the man she'd left there, with that look on his face and too much dark grief in his gaze.

And the longer Violet lingered—going in and out of every shop, pausing for cell phone photos every time she was recognized, settling in for a long dinner in a restaurant where the chef came racing out to serenade her and she was complimented theatrically for her few Italian phrases, all while Paige looked on and/or assisted—the more Paige wondered if the other woman was doing it deliberately. As if she knew what was going on between her son and her assistant.

But that was impossible, Paige kept telling herself.

This is called guilt, that caustic voice inside her snapped as Violet flirted outrageously with the chef. *This is why you're here. Why you work for his mother. Why you accept how he treats you. You deserve it. You earned it.*

More than that, she missed him. One afternoon knowing Giancarlo wasn't within reach, that there was no chance he'd simply appear and tumble her down onto the nearest flat surface, the way he'd done only yesterday with no advance warning, and she was a mess. If this was a preview of what her life was going to be like after this all ended, Paige thought as she handled Violet's bill and called for the car, she was screwed.

"Like that's anything new," she muttered under her breath as she climbed into the car behind Violet, nearly closing the heavy door on the still-grasping hands of the little crowd that had gathered outside the restaurant to adore her.

"Pardon?" Violet asked.

Paige summoned her smile. Her professional demeanor, which she thought she'd last seen weeks ago in Los Angeles. "Did that do? Scratch the attention itch?"

"It did." Violet sat across from her in the dark, her gaze out the window as the car started out of the city. "Giancarlo is a solitary soul. He doesn't understand that some people recharge their batteries in different ways than he does. Not everyone can storm about a lonely field and feel recharged."

Said the woman who had never passed a crowd she couldn't turn into a fan base with a few sentences and a smile. Paige blinked, amazed at her churlishness even in her own head, and found Violet's calm gaze on hers.

"You're an extrovert." Paige said evenly. "I'm sure he knows that by now. Just as he likely knows that therefore, his own needs are different from yours."

"One would think," Violet agreed in her serene, untroubled way, which shouldn't have sent a little shiver of warning down Paige's back. "But then, the most interesting men are not always in touch with what they need, are they?"

Violet didn't speak much after that, yet Paige didn't feel as if she could breathe normally until the car pulled off the country road and started along the winding drive into the estate. And she was impatient—the most impatient she'd ever been in Violet's presence, though she tried valiantly to disguise it—as she helped the older woman into the *castello* and oversaw the staff as they sorted out her purchases.

And only when she was finally in the car again and headed toward her cottage did Paige understand what had been beating at her all day, clutching at her chest and her throat and making her want to scream in the middle of ancient Italian piazzas. Guilt, yes, but that was a heavy thing, a spiked weight that hung on her. The rest of it was panic.

Because any opportunity Giancarlo had to reflect on what was happening between them—not revenge, not the comeuppance he'd obviously planned—was the beginning of the end. She knew it, deep inside. She'd seen it in his eyes this morning.

And when she got to her cottage and found not only it but the house above it dark, it confirmed her fears.

Paige stood there in the dark outside her cottage long after the driver's car disappeared into the night, staring up the hill, willing this shadow or that to separate from the rest and become Giancarlo. She was too afraid to think about what might happen if this was it. If that kiss he'd delivered in the garden was their last.

Too soon, she thought desperately, or perhaps that was the first prayer she'd dared make in years. *It's too soon.*

She stared up the side of the hill as if that would call him to her, somehow. But the only thing around her was the soft summer night, pretty and quiet. Still and empty, for miles around.

When she grew too cold and he still didn't appear, she made her way inside, feeling more punished by his absence than by anything else that had happened between them. Paige entertained visions of marching up the hill and taking what she wanted, or at least finding him and seeing for herself what had happened in her absence today, but the truth was, she didn't dare. She was still so uncertain of her welcome.

Would he throw back the covers and yank her into his arms if she appeared at his bedside? Or would he send her right back out into the night again, with a cruel word or two as her reward? Paige found she was too unsure of the answer to test it.

There were red flags everywhere, she acknowledged as she got ready for bed and crawled beneath her sheets. Red flags and dark corners, and nothing safe. But maybe what mattered was that she knew that, this time. She'd known the moment she'd decided to apply for that job with Violet. She'd always known.

She would have to learn to live with that, too.

Later that night, Paige woke with a sudden start when a lean male form crawled into her bed, hauling her into his arms.

Giancarlo. Of course.

But her heart was already crashing against her ribs as he rolled so she was beneath him. Excitement. Relief. The usual searing hunger, sharper than usual this time.

"Why didn't you come to me?" he gritted at her, temper and need and too many other dark and hungry things in his voice. Then the scrape of his teeth against the tender flesh of her neck, making her shudder.

Paige didn't want to think about the contours of her fears now, her certainty he'd finished with this. With her. Not now, while he was braced above her, his body so familiar and hot against hers, making the night blaze with the wild need that was never far beneath the surface. Never far at all.

Not even when she thought she'd lost him again.

"I thought you'd gone to bed already." *I didn't know if you'd want me to come find you,* she thought, but wisely kept to herself. "All of your lights were out."

She thought she saw a certain self-knowledge move over his face then, but it was gone so quickly she was sure she must have imagined it.

"Did you have a lovely day out with my mother?" he asked in a tone she wasn't foolish enough to imagine was friendly, his dark eyes glittering in the faint light from the rising moon outside her windows. "Filled with her admirers, exactly as she wished?"

"Of course." Paige ran her hands from his hard jaw to the steel column of his neck, as if trying to imprint the shape of him on her palms. Trying to make certain that if this was the last time, she'd remember it. That it couldn't be snatched from her, not entirely. "When Violet decrees we are to have fun, that is precisely what we have. No mere crowd would dare defy the crown jewel of the Hollywood establishment."

Giancarlo didn't laugh. He shifted his body so he was hard against her and she melted the way she always did, ready to welcome him no matter his mood or hers, no matter the strange energy that crackled from him tonight, no matter the darkness that seemed wrapped around him even as he wound himself around her.

There were other words for what she was with this man, she knew, words she hadn't heard in a long time but still remembered all too well. Words she'd dismissed as the unhealthy rantings of the worst person she'd ever known, the person who had taken everything she'd wanted from her—but it turned out dismissing them wasn't the same thing as erasing them.

Even so, the hollow, gnawing thing that had sat inside her all day and made her feel so panicked was gone, because he was here. She filled it with his scent, his touch, his bold possession.

Him. Giancarlo.

The only man she'd ever touched. The only man she'd ever loved.

And this was the only way she could tell him any of that. With her body. Paige shifted so he was flush against her entrance and hooked her legs over his hips, letting him in. Loving him in the only way she knew. In the only way he'd let her.

"Maybe that didn't always work out when you were a child," she whispered, hoping he couldn't read too much emotion in her eyes, across her face. "But my relationship with Violet is much easier. She pays, I agree, the end."

Giancarlo bent his head to press hot, open kisses along the ridge of her collarbone. Paige moved restlessly, hungrily against him, tilting her head back to give him greater access. To give him anything—everything—he wanted.

Because this won't last forever, that harsh voice that was too much an echo of her mother's reminded her. That was what today had taught her. There were no fairy tales. This situation had an expiration date, and every moment she had with him was one moment closer to the end.

"In a way," Giancarlo said, still too dark, still too rough, his mouth against her skin so Paige could feel the rumble of his words inside of her as he spoke, "that is every relationship that Violet has."

She heard that same tense grief that had been in him in the *castello* that morning and this time, no one was watching. She could soothe him, or try. She ran her fingers through his thick hair and smiled when he pressed into her touch, like a very large cat.

"I don't think it can be easy to be a great figure," Paige said after a moment, concentrating on the feel of his scalp beneath her fingertips, the drag of his thick hair as she moved her hands through it, the exquisite sensation of stroking him. "Too many expectations. Too much responsibility to something far bigger than oneself. The constant worry that it will be taken away. But it must be harder still to be that person's child."

He shifted away from her, propping himself up on his elbows, though he kept himself cradled there between her thighs, his arousal a delicious weight against her softness. A promise. The silence stretched out and his face was in shadow, so all she could see was the glitter of his dark gold eyes, and the echo of it deep inside her.

"It's not hard," he said, and she'd never heard that tone before, had she? Clipped and resigned at once. And yet somehow, that pit in her belly yawned open again as he spoke. "As long as you remember that she is always playing a role. The *grande dame* as benevolent mother. The living legend as compassionate parent. The great star whose favorite role of all is *mom*. When she was younger there were different roles threaded into the mix, but the same principle applied. You learn this as a child in a thousand painful ways and you vow, if you are at all wise, never to inflict it on another. To let it end with you."

Paige tried to imagine Giancarlo as a small boy, all stubborn chin and fathomless eyes, and ached for him, though that didn't explain her nervousness. It was something in the way he held himself apart from her, a certain danger rippling down the length of his body, as hard and as steel-hewn as he was. It was the way he watched her, too still, too focused.

"I'm sorry," she said, though she wanted to say so much more. She didn't dare. Just like before, when she'd stood outside and wanted him and had known better than to go and find him, she was too uncertain. "That can't have been easy."

"Is that sympathy for me, *cara*? Don't bother."

He wasn't quite scoffing at her. Not quite, though his face went fierce in the darkness, edging toward cruel the way he'd been in the beginning, and she found she was bracing herself—unable to open her mouth and stop him. Unable to defend herself at all. *Whatever he's about to say,* that hard voice reminded her, like another slap, *you deserve.*

"Here is what I learned from my mother, the great actress," Giancarlo said. "That she is a mystery, unknowable even to herself. That she prefers it that way. That intimacy is anathema to her because it cannot be controlled, it cannot be directed, it cannot cut to print when she is satisfied with her performance. It is one long take with no rehearsal and no do-overs, and she goes to great lengths indeed to avoid it."

Paige wasn't sure why she felt so stricken then, so stripped raw when he wasn't talking about her—but then he moved again, dropping his weight against her to whisper in her ear, hot and close and dark. So very dark.

You deserve this, she told herself. *Whatever it is.*

"I want a woman I can trust, *Paige*," he said with a ruthless inevitability. And it didn't even hurt. It was like a deep slice of a sharp blade. She knew he'd cut her and now there was only the wait for blood. For the pain that would surely follow. And he wasn't finished. "A woman I can know inside and out. A woman who carries no secrets, who does not hide herself away from me or from the world, who never plays a role. A woman who wants a partner, not an audience."

"Giancarlo." She felt torn apart even though he was holding her close. Wrecked as surely as if he'd thrown her from the roof of the towering *castello*. "Please."

But the worst part was, he knew what he was doing. She'd seen it in the cast of his sensual mouth. She'd felt it in the way he'd very nearly trembled as he'd held himself above her.

He knew he was hurting her. And he kept going.

"I want a woman I can believe when she tells me she loves me," he said, raw and fierce and she knew she deserved that, she knew she did, even though it felt a little bit like dying. And then he lifted his head to look her straight in the eyes, making it that much worse. "And that can never be you, can it? It never was. It never will be."

Later, she thought she might take that apart and live awhile in the misery he'd packed into those last two sentences. Later, she thought she might cry for days and check herself for scars, the way she'd done ten years ago. But that was later.

Tonight Paige thought the pain in him was far greater than the hurt he'd caused—that she deserved, that voice kept telling her, and she agreed no matter how it cut her up—and she couldn't bear it.

She didn't care if he still hated her, even now, after another week in his bed when he'd tasted every part of her and had to have recognized the sheer honesty in her response to him. She told herself she didn't care about that at all and some part of her believed it.

Or wanted to believe it.

But worrying about that was for later, too. Later, when she could put herself together again. Later, when she could think about something other than the man who stretched over her and broke her heart, again and again and again. Because he could.

"Giancarlo," she said again, with more force this time. "Stop talking."

And he surrendered with a groan, thrusting deep and hard inside of her where there was nothing but the two of them—that shimmering truth that was only theirs, wild and dizzying and hotter every time—and that perfect, wondrous fire that swept them both away in its glory.

And Paige did her best to make them both forget.

Two more weeks passed, slow and sweet. The Tuscan summer started to edge toward the coming fall. The air began to feel crisp in the mornings, and the sky seemed bluer. And if she'd allowed herself to think about such things, Paige might have believed that the tension between her and Giancarlo was easing, too—all that heavy grief mellowing, turning blue like the sky, gold like the fields, lighter and softer with age.

Or perhaps she'd taught them both how to forget.

Whatever it was, it worked. No more did she spend her days trapped in her isolated cottage, available only to him and only when he wanted—and she told herself she didn't miss it, all that forced proximity and breathlessness. Of course she didn't miss it.

Paige's days looked a great deal as they had back home. She met with Violet most mornings, and helped her plan out her leisure time. Violet was particularly fond of day trips to various Italian cities to soak in all the art and culture and fashion with a side helping of adulation from the locals, which she often expedited by taking Giancarlo's helicopter that left from the roof of the *castello* and kicked up such a ruckus when it returned it could be heard for miles around.

"I've always preferred a big entrance," Violet had murmured the first time, that famous smile of hers on her lips as the helicopter touched down.

But when Violet was in between her trips—which meant days of spa treatments and dedicated lounging beneath artfully placed umbrellas at the side of the *castello*'s private pool instead—Paige was left to her own devices, which usually meant she was left to Giancarlo's.

One day he stopped the Jeep the moment it was out of sight of the *castello*'s stout tower and knelt down beside the passenger door, pulling her hips to his mouth and licking his way into Paige right there—making her sob out his name into the quiet morning, so loud it startled the birds from the nearby trees. Another time he drove them out to one of the private lakes that dotted the property and they swam beneath the hot sun, then brought each other to a shuddering release in the shallow end, Giancarlo holding her to him as she took advantage of the water's buoyancy to make him groan.

Other times, they talked. He told her of his father's dreams for this land, its long history and his own plans to monetize it while conserving it, that it might last for many more generations. He showed her around the Etruscan ruins that cropped up in the oddest spots and demonstrated, as much as possible, that a man who knew the ins and outs of three thousand acres in such extraordinary detail seemed something like magical when the landscape in question was a woman's body. *Her* body.

Paige didn't know which she treasured more. His words or his body. But she held them to her like gifts, and she tried not to think about what she deserved, what she knew she had coming to her. She tried to focus on what she had in her hands, instead.

One lazy afternoon they lay together in the warm sun, the sweet breeze playing over their heated skin. Paige propped her chin against his chest and looked into his eyes and it was dizzying, the way it was always dizzying. And then he smiled at her without a single stray shadow in his gorgeous eyes, and it was as if the world slammed to a stop and then started in the other direction.

"I saw you dancing in the garden the other night," he said.

There was no reason to blush. She told herself the heat she felt move over her was the sun, the leftover fire of the way he'd torn her to pieces only moments before, and nothing more.

"I haven't danced in a long while," she said, and she wanted to tear her gaze away from his, but she didn't. Or she couldn't. He ran his hand through her hair, slow and sweet, and she was afraid of the things he could see in her. And so afraid of the things she wanted.

"Why not?"

And Paige didn't know how to answer that. How to tell him the why of it without blundering straight into all the land mines they'd spent these weeks avoiding. That they'd managed to avoid entirely after that night she'd come back late from Lucca.

I want a woman I can trust, he'd said, and she wanted him to trust her. She might not deserve his trust, but she wanted it.

"I was good," she said after a moment, because that was true enough, "but I wasn't *amazing*. And there were so many other dancers who were as good as I was, but wanted it way more than I did."

Especially after he'd left and she hadn't had the heart

for it any longer, or anything else involving the body she'd used to betray the one man she'd ever given it to. She'd auditioned for one more gig and her agent had told her they'd said it was like watching a marionette. That had been her last audition. Her last dance, period.

Because once she'd lost Giancarlo, she'd lost interest in the only other thing she'd had that'd ever had any meaning in her life. Her mother had descended even further into that abyss of hers and Paige had simply been *lost*. And when she'd run into a woman she'd met through Giancarlo on one of those Malibu weekends, who'd needed a personal assistant a few days a week and had kind of liked that Paige was a bit notorious, it had seemed like a good idea. And more, a way to escape, once and for all, the dark little world her mother lived in.

A year later, she'd been working for a longtime television star who had no idea that competent Paige Fielding was related to *that* Nicola Fielding. A few years after that, she had enough experience to sign with a very exclusive agency that catered to huge stars like Violet, and when Violet's previous assistant left her, to put herself forward as a replacement. All of those things had seemed so random back then, as they happened. But now, looking back, it seemed anything but. As if Paige's subconscious had plotted out the only course that could bring her back to Giancarlo.

But she didn't want to think about that now. Or about what she'd do when she was without him again. How would she re-create herself this time? Where would she go? It occurred to her then that she'd never really planned beyond Violet. Beyond the road she'd known would bring her back to him.

I want a partner, he'd said, and the problem was, she

was a liar. A deliberate amnesiac, desperate to keep their past at bay. That wasn't a partner. That was a problem.

Giancarlo was still smiling, as if this was an easy conversation, and Paige wished it was. For once, *just once,* she wanted something to be as easy as it should have been.

"I'm surprised," he said, and there was something very much like affection in his gaze, transforming his face until he looked like that younger version of himself again. She told herself that it didn't make her ache. That it didn't make her heart twist tight. "I would have said dancing was who you were, not something you did."

"I was twenty years old," she heard herself say, in a rueful sort of tone that suggested an amusement she didn't quite feel. "I had no idea who I was."

You're his toy, Nicola, her mother had screamed at her in those final, dark days, when Paige had believed she'd somehow navigate her way through it all unscathed— that she'd manage to keep Giancarlo, please her mother and her mother's terrible friends, and pay off all of that debt besides. *He'll play with you until he's done and then he'll leave you broken and useless when he moves on to the next dumb whore. Don't be so naive!*

Giancarlo's face changed then, and his hand froze in her hair. "I think I always forget you were so young," he said after a moment, as if remembering her age shocked him. "What the hell was I doing? You were a kid."

She laughed then. She couldn't help it.

"My life wasn't exactly pampered and easy before I came to Hollywood," she told him, knowing as she said it that she'd never talked about that part of her life. He had been so bright, so beautiful—why would she talk about dark, grim things? "And I did that about ten minutes after I graduated from high school. My mom had the car packed and waiting on the last day of classes."

She shook her head at him as her laughter faded. "I was never really much of a kid."

She hadn't had the opportunity to be a kid, which wasn't quite the same thing, but she didn't tell him that. Even though she had the strangest idea that his childhood hadn't been that different from hers, really. The trappings couldn't have been more opposite, but she'd spent her whole life tiptoeing around, trying to predict what mood her mother would be in, how much she might have drunk, and how bad she could expect it to get of an evening. She wasn't sure that was all that different from trying to gauge one of Violet's moods.

It had never occurred to her that she'd traded one demanding mother for another, far classier one—and she wasn't sure she liked the comparison. *At least Violet cares for you in return,* she told herself then. *Which is more than Arleen ever did.*

"I'm not sure that excuses me," Giancarlo was saying, but then he laughed, and everything else shot straight out of her head and disappeared into that happy sound. "But then, I never had any control where you were concerned."

"Neither did I," she said, smiling at him, and they both stilled then. Perhaps aware in the same instant that they were straying too close to the very things they couldn't let themselves talk about.

Or the words they couldn't say. Words he'd told her he wouldn't believe if she did dare speak them out loud.

But that didn't keep her from feeling them. Nothing could.

He studied her face for a long moment, until she began to feel the breeze too keenly on her exposed skin. Or maybe that was her vulnerability. Having sex was much easier, for all it stripped her bare and seemed to involve every last cell in her body. It required only feeling and action. *Doing.* It was this *talking* that was killing her, making her want too much, making her imagine too many happy endings when, God help her, she knew better.

Paige pushed away from him, not willing to ruin this with a conversation that could only lead to more hurt. Or worse, something good that would be that much harder to leave behind when the time came. She sat up and gathered her clothes to her, pulling the flirty little sundress over her head as if the light material was armor. But she only wished it was.

"Was it ever real?" he asked quietly.

Paige didn't ask him what he meant. She froze, her eyes on the rolling hills that spread out before her in the afternoon light, the glistening lake in the valley below. That stunning Tuscan sky studded with chubby white clouds, the vineyards and the flowers, and she didn't think he understood that he was holding her heart between his palms and squeezing tight. Too tight.

Maybe he wouldn't care if he did.

"It was for me," she said, and her voice was too rough. Too dark. Too much emotion in it. "It always was for me, even at the end."

She didn't know what might happen then. What Giancarlo might say. Do. She felt spread open and hung out in all the open space around them, as if she was stretched across some tightrope high in the sky, subject to the whims of any passing wind—

His hand reached out and covered hers and he squeezed. Once.

And then he pulled on his clothes and he got to his feet and he never mentioned it again.

Giancarlo watched her sleep, and he did not require the chorus of angry voices inside of him to remind him that this was a bad idea.

He didn't know what had woken him, only that he'd come alert in a rush and had turned to make sure she was still there beside him—the way he'd done for years after the photographs hit. He'd lost count long ago of the number of times he'd dreamed it all away, dreamed she'd never betrayed him, dreamed that things had been different. He'd grown uncomfortably well used to lying there in his empty bed, glaring at the ceiling and wishing her ill even as he'd wanted her back, wherever she was.

But this time, she was right here. She was curled up beside him and sound asleep, so that she didn't even murmur when he stretched out on his side, his front to her back, and held her there. The way he knew he wouldn't do if she was awake, lest it give her too many ideas...

So much for your revenge plot, he chided himself, but it all seemed so absurd when she was lying beside him, her features taking on an angelic cast in the faint light that poured in from the skylight above them, the stars themselves lighting her with that special glow.

He found himself tracing the line of her cheek with his finger, the memories of ten years ago so strong he could almost have sworn that no time had passed. That the pictures and the separation had been the bad dream. Because he might be wary of her, but every day it seemed that was only because he thought he should be, not because he truly was. And every day it seemed to make less and less sense.

She had been so young.

He didn't know how he'd forgotten that. How he'd failed to factor it in. When he'd been twenty he'd been a bona fide idiot, making an ass of himself at Stanford and enjoying every minute of it. He certainly hadn't been performing for a living, running from this audition to that gig with no guarantee he'd ever make his rent or make some money or even get cast. When Violet had been twenty years old she'd been famously divorcing the much, much older producer who had married her and made her when she'd been only seventeen. No one had called her a mercenary bitch, at least, not to her face. She'd been lauded for her powerful choices and the control she'd taken over her career.

Maybe that was why he'd spent a decade *this furious* with Paige. Because he loved his mother, he truly did, but he'd wanted something else for himself. He'd wanted a girl who wouldn't think of herself first, second, last and always. He'd wanted a girl who would put *him* first. Had he known Paige wouldn't stick with dancing? Had he assumed she would gravitate toward the life she had here in Tuscany, which was more or less arranged around pleasing him?

He'd told her he wanted a partner, but nothing he'd done supported that. Back in Malibu, he'd been jealous of the time she spent practicing and really anything else that took her away from him. This time around he was jealous of her devotion to his own mother. Did he want a partner? Or did he want her to *treat* him like a partner while he did whatever he liked?

Giancarlo didn't much care for the answers that came to him then, in the quiet night, the woman he couldn't seem to get over lying so sweetly beside him. All he knew was that he was tired of fighting this, of holding her at arm's length when he wanted her close. He was tired of the walls he put up. He hated himself more every time he hurt her—

We all must practice what we preach if we are to achieve anything in this life, his father had told him a long time ago as they'd walked the land together, plotting out the placement of vineyards the older man hadn't lived to see to completion. *The trouble is we're all much better at the preaching and not so good at the listening, even to ourselves.*

It had to stop. *He* had to stop. There was no point demanding her trust if he refused to give his own.

He shifted beside her, pulling her close and burying his face in the sweet heat of her neck.

It was time to admit what he'd known for years. She was the only woman he'd ever loved, no matter what she called herself. No matter what she'd done when she was little more than a kid. And he'd never stopped loving her.

"Come sei bella," he whispered into the dark. *How beautiful you are.* And, *"Mi manchi." I miss you.* And then, "I love you," in English, though he knew she couldn't hear him.

Giancarlo understood then, in the soft darkness, Paige snuggled close in his arms as if she'd been there all along, that he always had. He always would.

He just needed to tell her when she could hear him.

Paige woke up the next morning in her usual rush when the morning light danced over her face from the skylights above. Giancarlo was next to her, his big body wrapped around her, and she thought, *this is my favorite day.*

She thought that every day, lately. No matter what that voice in her head had to say about it.

And she continued to think it until her stomach went funny in a sudden, hideous lurch, and she had to pull away from him and race for the toilet.

"I must have eaten something strange," she said when she came out of the bathroom to find him frowning with concern, sitting on the side of his bed. She grimaced. "Your mother insisted we eat those weird sausages in Cinque Terre yesterday. One must not have agreed with me."

But Violet wasn't affected. "I have a stomach of steel, my dear girl," she proclaimed when Paige called her to check in, "which is handy when one is living off craft service carts for weeks at a time in all the corners of the earth." And it happened again the next morning. And then the morning after that.

And on the fourth morning, when Paige ran for the bathroom, Giancarlo came in after her and placed a package on the floor beside her as she knelt there, pale and sick and wishing for death. It took her a long moment to calm the wild, lurching beat of her heart. To force back the dizziness as that awful feeling in her stomach retreated again. To feel well enough to focus on what he'd put there in front of her.

Only to feel even more light-headed when she did.

It was a pregnancy test.

"Use it," Giancarlo said, his voice so clipped and stern she didn't dare look up at him to see if his expression matched. She didn't think her stomach could take it. She knew her heart couldn't. "Bring me the result. Then we'll talk."

CHAPTER EIGHT

PAIGE CLIMBED SHAKILY to her feet after his footsteps retreated. She rinsed her mouth out with a scoop of water from the sink and then she followed the directions on the package. She waited the requisite amount of time—she timed it on her phone, to the second—and when the alarm chirped at her she let herself look.

And just like that, everything was forever altered. But all she could do was stare at the little stick with its unmistakable plus sign and wish she wasn't naked.

That didn't merely say things about her character, she thought dimly. It said far more dire things about the kind of mother she'd be to the tiny little life that was somehow there inside her—

That was when it hit her. It was a tidal wave of raw *feeling,* impossible to categorize or separate or do anything but survive as it all tore through her. Terror. Joy. *Panic*. How could she be someone's mother when all she'd ever known of mothering was Arleen? How could she be someone's *mother*?

She was holding on to the sink in a death grip when it passed, tears in her eyes and her knees weak beneath her. It was hard to breathe, but Paige made herself do it. In, then out. Deep. Measured.

Then she remembered Giancarlo was waiting for her,

and worse, what he'd said before he'd gone downstairs. And Paige understood then. That this was her worst fear come to life, literally.

That this was the other shoe she'd spent all this time knowing would drop.

She dressed before she went downstairs, glad she'd worn something more substantial than a silly dress the night before. That meant she could truly wrap herself up in her clothes as if they would offer her protection from whatever was about to come. She pulled her hair back into a tight knot at the nape of her neck and she took longer than she should have, and she only went to find him when she understood that dragging this out was going to make it worse. *Was* making it worse.

This will be fine, she told herself as she walked down the wide, smooth stairs, aware that she was delivering herself to her own execution. But there was, despite everything, that teeny tiny sliver of hope deep inside of her that maybe, just maybe, she'd be wrong about this. That he'd surprise her.

We're both adults. These things happen...

Giancarlo waited for her in the open doors that led out to the loggia—which, she supposed with the faintest hint of the hysteria she fought to keep away for fear it might swamp her, was appropriate, given where this baby had likely been conceived. He didn't turn when she came up behind him, he merely held out his hand.

Demonstrating how little he trusted her, she realized, when she finally understood what he was doing and what he expected her to put in his palm. Not her hand, for comfort. The pregnancy test. For proof.

Because he expected tricks and lies from her, even now. Even about this.

She felt something topple over inside of her, some

foundation or other, but she couldn't concentrate on that now. There was only Giancarlo, scowling down at the slender stick in his hand before he bit out a curse and flung it aside.

A thousand smart responses to that moved through her, but she was still shaky from that immense emotional slap that had walloped her upstairs, and she kept them all to herself. He stood there, every muscle tight, even his jaw a hard, granite accusation, and he didn't look at her for a long time.

When he did, it was worse.

Paige waited for him to speak, even as something inside her protested that no, she did not deserve his anger here. That she hadn't done this alone. But she shoved that down, too.

"I thought you were on the pill."

She blinked at the ferocity in his tone. The bite.

"No, you didn't. You used condoms after the first night. Why would you do that if you thought I was on the pill?" He stared at her, and the truth of that rolled over her. For a moment, she couldn't breathe through it. Then she could, and it hurt. It more than hurt. Another foundation turned to dust in an instant. "Oh."

"Tell me," he said in that vicious, cruel way she hadn't heard in almost a month now, so long she'd forgotten how awful it was, how deeply it clawed into her, "what possible reason you could have for sleeping with a man without protection?"

"You did the same thing." But her tongue felt too thick and her head buzzed and she'd known this would happen. Maybe not *this*. Maybe not a pregnancy. But that look on his face. She'd always known she'd see that again. She hadn't understood, until now, how very much she'd wanted to be wrong. "You were right there with me."

"I thought you were on the pill."

She felt helpless. Terrified. Sick. "Why?"

He swore again, not in Italian this time, and she flinched. "What kind of question is that? Because you were before."

"That was different." She was too shaken to think about what she was saying, so she told him the truth without any varnishing. "My mother was terrified I'd end up pregnant at sixteen and forced to raise the baby, like she was with me, so she had me on the pill from the moment I hit puberty."

"And you stopped?" He sounded furious and disbelieving, and Paige didn't understand. How could he think she'd planned this? How could she have, even if she'd wanted to? *You knew he didn't use anything that first night. Why didn't you say something?* But she knew. She hadn't wanted him to stop. She'd wanted him more than anything. "Why the hell would you do something like that?"

"I told you."

Paige was whispering, and she'd backed up so her spine was against the far side of the open doorway as if the house might keep her from collapsing to the floor, but Giancarlo hadn't moved at all. He didn't have to move. His black fury took up all the air. It blocked out the sun.

This is what you deserve, her mother's voice said in her head, filled with a sick glee. *This is what happens to little whores like you, Nicola. You end up like me.*

"You're the only man I've slept with the past ten years," she told him, bald and unflinching. He let out a sound she couldn't interpret and so she kept going, because she was certain she could explain this to him so he would understand. He had to understand. They were going to be parents whether he liked it or not. "You're the only man I've ever slept with, Giancarlo."

"Do not try to sell me that nonsense, not now," he barked at her, as if the words were welling up from somewhere deep inside of him. "I didn't believe the story that you were a virgin then, not even when I thought I could trust you. I'll hand it to you, though. You really do remember all the tortured details of the lies you spin."

"What are you talking about?" Paige shook her head, trying to keep her panic at bay, trying to keep the tears from her voice, and not really succeeding at either. "Who lies about being a virgin at twenty?"

"I can't believe I fell for this twice," he spat, his gaze a molten fury of dark gold, his mouth grim. "I can't believe I walked straight into this. Let me guess. You've never given motherhood a moment's thought, but today, as you gazed upon the test that confirmed your pregnancy, something stirred within you that you'd never felt before." His laugh felt like acid. "Is that about right?"

"Why are you talking to me like I planned this?" she cried. "No one forced you to have sex with me! And no one forced you to do it without a condom!"

"You're good," he said, still in that horrible way that curled inside of her, oily and thick. "I'll give you that. I never saw this coming. I thought I was being too hard on you. I was falling in love with you all over again, but in the end, you're just like her. You always have been. *I'm such an idiot.*"

"For all you know I have no intention of keeping it," she threw at him, desperate to make him look at her like a person again, not like a scam with two legs. Exactly the way he had ten years ago, when he'd waved that magazine in the air outside her apartment and she'd almost wished he'd thrown it at her—because that would be better, she'd thought then, and less violent than that look on his face in that moment before he'd turned and walked away.

But the look of contempt he gave her now was not an improvement.

And his words finally penetrated. *I was falling in love with you.*

"Am I to understand that this is your threat?" he asked in that low, lethal way of his that made her shudder. That made that hollow thing inside of her grow wide and grow teeth. That made it perfectly clear any love he might have felt for her was very much past tense. "I applaud you, *Nicola,*" and that name was worse than acid. If he'd hauled off and hit her, he couldn't have hurt her more. "Most women would dance around the issue. But you, as ever, go right to the heart of it."

"I'm not threatening you," she said wildly, only realizing when her cheeks felt cool in the breeze that tears were running down her face. "This wasn't planned. I don't know why you insist on thinking the worst of me—"

"Stop." It was a command, harsh and cold. "I'm not doing this with you again. I'm not pretending it matters what you say. You'll do what you like, *Nicola.* You always do. And like a cockroach I have no doubt you'll survive whatever happens and come back even stronger. Violet's protégé in more ways than I realized."

"Why would I force a child on you?" she demanded. "Why?"

"Perhaps you thought your payday last time wasn't enough," he bit out. "Perhaps you want to make certain you really will make it into Violet's will. Perhaps you're looking forward to selling as many tabloid stories as you can. It wouldn't take much effort to position yourself as one of those celebrities for no apparent reason, not with

Violet's grandchild in your clutches. To say nothing of the Alessi estate. You must know by now I'd never keep my heritage from my own child." He was nearly white with fury. "Which are only a few of the reasons I never wanted one."

"Giancarlo—"

But he straightened, his expression changed, and it was as if he disappeared, right there in front of her. As if the man she knew was simply…gone.

"If you decide to have the baby, inform my lawyers," he told her with a hideous finality that shuddered through her like an earthquake. There was none of that bright gold fury in his eyes any longer when he looked at her. There was only emptiness. A dark, cold nothing that made everything inside her twist into blackness. "I will pay whatever child support you deem necessary, and I will pay more if you honor my wish for privacy and keep my name to yourself. But I don't expect that's in your nature, is it? How can you leverage my privacy to your best advantage?"

"Please," she said, pleading with him now, unable to stop the sobs that poured out of her, worse, perhaps, because she'd always known this was coming. But not today. Not like this. She still wasn't ready. "You can't—"

"Do not attempt to contact my mother again." His voice got dangerous then. Flint and fury, and still, he was a stranger. "I will have you arrested and thrown in jail and no judge in any country would ever grant a woman with mental problems and a prison record custody of a child over me. I want you to remember that. You so much as text Violet and you'll never see that child again."

"Stop," she threw at him, in a terrible whisper. "You can't think—"

"A driver will pick you up in an hour," he told her, and

he was merciless. Pitiless. As if he was made of marble and was that soft, that bendable. "I want you gone. And I never, ever want to see you again. Not in ten minutes. Not in another ten years. Is that clear?"

Paige couldn't reply. She was shaking so hard she was afraid she'd fall over, the tears were hot and endless, and he looked at her as if she was a stranger. As if he was. Crafted of marble, but far crueler. Marble might crush her. But he'd torn her into pieces first.

"Do you understand?" he asked, even harsher than before.

"Yes," Paige managed to say. "I understand." She scrubbed her hands over her face and sucked in a breath and tried one last time. "Giancarlo—"

But he was already gone.

It was over.

The slippery December roads were treacherous but the wind outside was even worse, rattling his SUV and shaking the skeletons of the trees on either side of the New England country roads.

And inside him, Giancarlo knew, it was colder and darker still.

He had not been in a good mood to begin with when he'd left Logan International Airport in Boston more than two hours earlier on this latest quest to find Paige. It was fair to say he'd been in a black mood for the past three months.

The tiny, lonely little Maine town a hundred miles from anywhere sat under a fresh coat of snow, lights twinkling as the December evening fell sudden and fast in the middle of what other places might still consider the afternoon, and he felt the stirrings of adrenaline as he navigated through the very few streets that comprised the village to the small, white clapboard house that was his destination.

He'd hired detectives. He'd scoured half of the West Coast and a good part of the East Coast himself. This was the last place on earth he'd have thought to look for her—which was, he could admit, why it had no doubt made such a perfect hiding place.

This time, he knew she was here. He'd seen the photo on his mobile when he'd landed in Boston from Italy, taken this very morning. But he wouldn't believe it until he saw her with his own eyes.

He could admit the place held a certain desolate charm, Giancarlo thought grimly as he climbed from the car, the boots he only ever wore at ski resorts in places like Vail or St. Moritz crunching into the snow beneath him. The drive from Boston into the remote state of Maine had reminded him of the books he'd had to read while in his American high school. Lonely barns in barren fields and the low winter sky pressing down, gray and sullen. Here and there a hint of the wild, rocky Atlantic coast, lighthouses the only bit of faint cheer against the coming dark.

It felt like living inside his own bleak soul, in the great mess he'd made.

Giancarlo navigated his way over the salted sidewalk and up the old front steps to the clapboard house's front door, able to hear the faint sound of piano music from inside. DANCE LESSONS, read the sign on the door, making his chest feel tight.

He stopped there, frozen on the porch with his hand on the doorknob, because he heard her voice. For the first time since that last, ugly morning in his Tuscan cottage. Counting off the beat.

Wedging its way into his heart like one of the vicious icicles that hung from the roof above him.

He wrenched the door open and walked inside, and then she was right there in front of him after all this time. *Right there*.

She took his breath away.

Giancarlo's heart thundered in his chest and he forced himself to take stock of his surroundings. The ground floor of this house was its dance studio, an open space with only a few pillars and a class in session. And the woman he'd accused of a thousand different scams was not lounging about being fed bonbons she'd bought with his mother's money or her own infamy, she was teaching the class. To what looked like a pack of very pink-faced, very uncoordinated young girls.

He was standing in what passed for the small studio's lobby and if the glares from the women sitting in the couches and chairs along the wall were anything to go by, he'd disrupted the class with his loud entrance.

Not that Giancarlo cared about them in the slightest.

Paige, he noted as he forced himself to breathe again and not do anything rash, did not look at him at all, which was a feat indeed, given the mirrors on every available wall. She merely carried on teaching as if he was nothing to her.

But he refused to accept that. Particularly if it were true.

The class continued. And Giancarlo studied her as she moved in front of the small collection of preadolescents, calling out instructions and corrections and encouragement in equal measure. She looked as if she hadn't slept much, but only when he studied her closely. Her hair was still that inky black, darker now than he remembered, and he wondered if it was the sun that brought out its auburn hints. She moved the way she did in all his dreams, all of that grace and ease, as if she flowed rather than walked.

And she was still slim, with only the faintest thickening at her belly to tell him what he hadn't known until now, what he'd been afraid to wonder about until he'd finally tracked her down in what had to be, literally, one of the farthest places she could go in the opposite direction of Bel Air. And him.

That she was keeping the baby. *His* baby.

Giancarlo didn't know what that was inside of him then. Relief. Fury. A new surge of determination. All the rest of the dark things he'd always felt for this woman, turned inside out. All mixed together until it felt new. Until he did.

She was keeping their baby.

He would have loved her anyway. He did. But he couldn't help but view her continuing pregnancy as a sign. As hope.

As far more than he deserved.

It seemed like twenty lifetimes before the class ended, and the women in the chairs collected their young. He paid them no attention as they herded their charges past him out into the already-pitch-black night; he simply waited, arms crossed and his brooding gaze on Paige.

And eventually, the last stranger left and slammed the door shut behind her small town curiosity, and it was only the two of them in the glossy, bright room. Paige and him and all their history, and she still didn't look at him.

"You decided to keep it." He didn't know why he said it like that, fierce and low, and he watched her stiffen, but it was too late to call it back.

"If you came here for an apology," she said in a low voice he hardly recognized, and then she turned to face him fully and he blinked because she hardly looked like herself, "you can shove it right up your—"

"I don't want an apology." It was temper, he realized belatedly. Pure fury that transformed her lovely face and turned her eyes nearly gray. As if she would kill him with her own hands if she crossed the wide, battered floor and got too close to him, and there was no reason that should shock him and intrigue him in equal measure. "I spent three months tracking you down, Paige."

Her eyes narrowed and if anything, grew darker.

"Are you sure that's what you want to call me?" she threw at him. "I know that historically you've had some trouble keeping my name straight."

Giancarlo felt a muscle move in his cheek and realized he was clenching his jaw.

"I know your name."

"I can't tell you how that delights me." Her temper was like a fog in the air between them, thick and impenetrable, and he thought she might even have growled at him. "The only thing that would delight me more would be if you'd turn around and go away and pretend we never met. That's what I've been doing and so far? It's been the best three months of my life."

He had that coming. He knew that. He told himself it didn't even sting.

"I understand," he began as carefully as he could, "that—"

"Don't bother," she snapped, cutting him off. He couldn't recall she'd ever done that before. In fact, there was only one person in the world who interrupted him with impunity and she'd given birth to him—and wasn't terribly thrilled with him at the moment, either. "I don't want your explanations. I don't care."

She turned away from him, but the mirrors betrayed her, showing him a hint of the Paige he knew in the way her face twisted before she wrestled it back under control. Another sliver of hope, if he was a desperate man. He was.

Giancarlo walked farther into the studio, still studying her. She was in bare feet and a pair of leggings, with a loose tunic over them that drooped down over one shoulder. She was the most beautiful thing he'd ever seen. He wanted to press his mouth to the bare skin of her shoulder, then explore that brand-new belly of hers. Then, perhaps, that molten heat of hers that he knew had only ever been his. He was primitive enough to relish that.

He'd believed her. It had taken him longer than it should have to admit that to himself. He'd believed her then, and he believed her now—but the fact she'd only ever given herself to him had meanings he'd been afraid to explore. He wasn't afraid anymore.

Giancarlo had lost her once. What was there to fear now? He'd already lived through the worst thing that could happen to him. Twice.

"How did you find this place?" he asked as he walked toward her. He meant, *how did you settle on this small, faraway, practically hidden town it took me three months to find?* "Why did you come here in the first place?"

"I can't imagine why you care." Paige shoved her things into a bag and then straightened. "I doubt that you do." She scowled at him when he kept coming, when he only stopped when he was within touching distance. "What do you want, Giancarlo?"

"I don't know." That wasn't true, but he didn't know how to express the rest of it, and not when she kept throwing him like this. He realized he'd never seen her angry before. Or anything but wild—wildly in love, wildly apologetic, wild beneath his hands. Never cold like this. Never furious. He supposed he deserved that, too. "You're so angry."

Paige actually laughed then, and it wasn't her real laugh. It was a bitter little thing that made his chest hurt.

More than it already did, than it had since that morning in Tuscany.

"You're unbelievable," she whispered. Then she shook her head. "I could be angry about any number of things, Giancarlo, but let's pick one at random, shall we? You told me you never wanted to see me again, and I happen to think that's the best plan you've had yet. So please, go back to wherever you came from. Go back to Italy and ruin someone else's life. Leave me—leave *us*—alone."

He wanted to pull her close to him. He wanted to taste her. He *wanted*. But he settled for shaking his head slightly and watching her face, instead, as if she might disappear again if he took his eyes off her.

"I'm sorry," he said into the tense quiet. "It's not that I'm not listening to you. But I've never seen you angry, ever. I didn't think it was something you knew how to do."

Paige blinked, and pulled the bag higher on her shoulder, gripping the strap with both of her hands.

"It wasn't," she said simply. "Especially around you. But it turns out, that's not a very healthy way to live a life. It ends up putting you at the mercy of terrible people because you never say no. You never tell them to stop. You never stand up for yourself until it's too late."

And when her eyes met his, they slammed into him so hard it was like a punch, and Giancarlo understood she meant him. That *he* had done those things to her. That he was one more terrible person to her. It tasted sour in his mouth, that realization. And he hated it with almost as much force as he understood, at last, that it was true. That he'd treated her horribly. That he was precisely the kind of man he'd been raised to detest. That was why he'd come after her, was it not? To face these things.

But that didn't make hearing it any easier.

"That is not the kind of life my baby is going to live, Giancarlo," Paige told him fiercely. "Not if I have anything to say about it." She tilted her chin up as if she expected him to argue. "This baby will have a *home*. This baby will be *wanted*. Loved. Celebrated. This baby is not a mistake. Or a problem. This baby will *belong* somewhere. *With me*."

As if she really had punched him, and hard, it took Giancarlo a moment to recover from all her fierceness, and more, what it told him. And when he did, it was to see her storming across the room.

Away from him. Again.

"Come have dinner with me," he began.

"No."

"Coffee then." He eyed her, remembering that tiny bump. "Or whatever you can drink."

"And again, no."

"Paige." He didn't have any idea what he was doing and he thought he hated that almost as much as the distance between them, which seemed much, much worse now that they were standing in the same room. "It's my baby, too."

She whirled back around, so fast he thought someone without her grace might have toppled over, and then she jabbed a finger in the air in a manner he imagined was meant to show him how very much she wished it was something sharp she could stick in a far more tender area.

"She is *my* baby!" And her voice grew louder with each word. "Mine. I knew I was pregnant with the baby of a man who *hated me* for *five whole minutes* before you ripped me into shreds and walked away, but believe me, Giancarlo, I heard you. You want nothing to do with me. You want nothing to do with this baby. And that is *fine—*"

"I never said I wanted nothing to do with the baby," he protested. "Quite the opposite."

"We can debate that when there's a baby, then," she hurled at him, hardly stopping to take a breath. "Which by my calculations gives me six months and then some of freedom from having to talk to you."

"But I want to talk to you." And he didn't care that he sounded more demanding than apologetic, then. She might truly want nothing to do with him, ever again, and he understood he deserved that. But he had to be sure. "I want to see how you're doing. I want to understand what happened between us in Italy."

"No, you don't."

And her face twisted again, but her eyes were still that dark gray and they still burned, and he couldn't tell what she wanted. Only that as ever, he was hurting her. The way he always did.

"You don't want to understand *me,*" Paige told him. "You want me to understand *you.* And believe me, I already do. I understood you when you were the very wealthy, semifamous director who took an unexpected interest in a backup dancer. I understood you when you were the noble son standing up for his mother against the potential lunatic who had infiltrated her home behind your back. I even understood you when you were the beleaguered, betrayed ex, drawn back into an intense sexual relationship against his better judgment by the deceitful little seductress he couldn't put behind him. I *understood* myself sick."

She pulled in a breath, as if it hurt her, which was when Giancarlo realized he hadn't breathed throughout this. That he couldn't seem to draw a breath at all.

"And then," Paige continued, her voice strong and even, "once I left, I understood that you have never, ever pretended to be there for me in any way. Not ten years ago. Not now. It never crossed your mind to *ask me* why I did something like sell those pictures, just as it never occurred to you to ask me how *I* felt about finding myself pregnant. The only thing you care about is you."

"Paige."

She ignored him. "You never asked me anything at all. You've never treated me liked anything but a storm you had to weather." She shook her head. "You're the damned hurricane, Giancarlo, but you blame me for the rain." She shifted then, her hands moving to shelter that little bump, as if she needed to protect it from him, and he thought that might be the worst cut, the deepest wound. He was surprised to find he still stood. "All I want from you is what you've always given me. Your absence."

The room seemed dizzy with her words when she'd stopped speaking, as if the mirrors could hardly bear the weight of them. Or maybe that was him. Maybe he'd fallen down and he simply couldn't tell the difference.

"You said *she*."

"What?"

Giancarlo didn't know where that had come from. He hadn't known he meant to speak at all. He was too busy seeing himself through her eyes—and not liking it at all. "Before. You called the baby a *she*."

"Yes." She seemed worn-out then, in a sudden rush. As if she'd lanced a wound with a surge of adrenaline and the poison had all run out, leaving nothing behind it. "I'm having a little girl in May."

"A daughter." His voice was gentle, yet filled with something it took him a moment to identify. *Wonder.* He heard it move through the room and he saw her shudder as she pulled in a breath, and he knew, somehow, that everything wasn't lost. Not yet. Not quite yet. "We're having a daughter."

"Go away, Giancarlo," she said, but it was a whisper. Just a whisper with none of that fury behind it, and a hint of the kind of sadness he'd become all too familiar with these past few months. And he wanted nothing more than to protect her, even if it was from himself.

Perhaps especially then.

"I can do that," he said gruffly. "Tonight. But I'll keep coming back, Paige. Every day until you talk to me. I can be remarkably persuasive."

"Is that a threat?" She rubbed a hand over the back of her neck, and he thought she looked tired again, but not threatened. "This isn't your land in Italy. I'm not a prisoner here."

"I don't want to keep you prisoner," he said, which was not entirely true. He reminded himself he was a civilized man. Or the son of one anyway, little as he might have lived up to his father's standards lately. "I want to have dinner with you."

She eyed him, and he could see the uncertainty on her pretty face. "That's all?"

"Do you want me to lie to you?" he asked quietly. "It's a start. Just give me a start."

She shook her head, but her eyes seemed less gray now and more that changeable blue-green he recognized, and Giancarlo couldn't help but consider that progress.

"What if I don't want a start?" she asked after a moment. "Any start? We've had two separate starts marked by ten years of agony and now this. It's not fun."

He smiled. "Then it's dinner. Everyone needs to eat dinner. Especially pregnant women, I understand."

"But not with you," Paige said, and there was something different in her voice then. Some kind of resolve. "Not again. It's not worth it."

She turned away again and headed toward the door he could see in the back, and this time, he could tell, she was really going to leave.

And Giancarlo knew he should let her go. He knew he'd done more than enough already. The practical side of him pointed out that six months was a reasonable amount of time to win a person over, to say nothing of the following lifetime of the child they'd made. *Their daughter.* He had all the time in the world.

He'd spent three months trying to find her—what was another night? He knew he should forfeit this battle, the better to win the war. But he couldn't do it.

Giancarlo couldn't watch her walk away again.

CHAPTER NINE

LATER, PAIGE THOUGHT, she would hate herself for how difficult it was to march across the studio floor toward the door, her car beyond, and the brand-new life she was in the middle of crafting.

Later, she would despair of the kind of person she must be, that her heart had somersaulted nearly out of her chest when Giancarlo had stormed in, startling her so profoundly it had taken her a long moment to remember why that instant sense of relief she'd felt was more than a little sick. Later, she would beat herself up about how little she wanted to walk away from him, even now.

But first she had to really do it. Walk away. Mean what she said. Leave him standing—

Her first clue that he'd moved at all was a rush of air over her shoulder and then his hands were on her, gentle and implacable at once. He turned her, lifted her, and in a single smooth shift she was in his arms. Held high against his chest, so she was surrounded. By his scent. By his strength.

A scant breath away from that cruel mouth, that sensual mouth.

Much too close to everything she wanted, so desperately, to forget.

"Put me down."

Her voice was so quiet it was hardly a breath of sound—but she knew, somehow, what that dark gold fury in his gaze was now. It was a warning that this situation could get out of control quickly, with a single kiss, and Paige rather doubted she'd be able to maintain any kind of moral high ground if she let him deep inside her again.

Especially because she wanted him there. Even now.

"First of all," Giancarlo said, in that low and lethal way that still moved over her like a seduction, making her very bones feel weak, "I do not hate you. I have never hated you. I have spent years trying to convince myself that I hated you only to fail miserably at it, again and again."

"Then you only *act* as if you hate me," she grated at him, refusing to put her arm over his shoulders, holding herself tight and unyielding against him as if that might save her. From herself. "That's much better."

He stopped next to the line of old armchairs and love seats that sat against the wall and set her down in the biggest one, then shocked her to the core by kneeling down in front of her. She froze, which was why it took her a moment to notice that he'd caged her in, his hands gripping the back of the chair behind her, putting his face about as close as it could get to hers without actually touching her.

"Why did you sell those photographs?" he asked. Quietly, his dark gaze trained on her face. So there was no chance at all he didn't see the heat that flashed over her, making her cheeks warm.

"What can that possibly matter now?"

"I think you're right about a lot of things," he said, sounding somewhere between grim and determined. And something else she wasn't sure she'd ever heard before. "But especially this. I should have asked. I'm asking now."

And the trouble was, she loved him. She'd always loved him. And she'd waited a decade for him to ask. If he'd asked in Italy, she might have sugarcoated it, but things were different now. *She* was different now.

She owed it to the life inside of her to be the kind of woman she wanted her daughter to become. That strong. That unafraid. That unflinching when necessary.

"My mother was a drunk," Paige said flatly. "Her dreams of riches and fame and escape from our awful little hometown came to a screeching halt when she got pregnant with me in high school, so it worked out well that I could dance. The minute I was done with high school she took me to Los Angeles. She made me use my middle name as a stage name because she thought it was fancy, and everyone knew you had to be fancy to be famous. She decided she made an excellent stage mother, if your definition of a stage mother is that she took all the money and then yelled at me to get out there and make more."

"That is the common Hollywood definition, yes," Giancarlo said drily, but she couldn't stop now. Not even to laugh.

"A drunk Arleen was one thing," Paige told him. "But a little while before I met you, my mother met a meth dealer. His name was Denny, and let me tell you, he was *so* nice to us. A new best friend." Her mouth twisted. "A month later, she was thousands of dollars in the hole and he was a little less friendly. Two months later, she was hundreds of thousands of dollars in debt to him, there was no possible way she could get out of it and he stopped pretending. He laid it out for me." She met Giancarlo's gaze and held it. *Unflinching,* she told herself. No matter that she'd never wanted him to know the kind of dirt that clung to her. Not when his whole life was so clean, so pretty, so bathed in light. "I could work it off on my back, or I could watch him kill her. Or—and this was an afterthought—I could make some money off my rich new boyfriend instead."

"Paige." He breathed her name as if it was one of his Italian curses, or perhaps a prayer, and she didn't know when he'd dropped his hands down to take hers, only that his hands were so warm, so strong, and she was far weaker than she wanted to be if he was what made her feel strong. Wasn't she? "Why didn't you tell me this? Why didn't you let me help you?"

"Because I was ashamed," she said, and her voice cracked, but she didn't look away from him. "Your mother was *Violet Sutherlin*. My mother was a drug addict who sold herself when she ran out of money, and it still wasn't enough. Who wanted to sell *me* because until I met you, I was a virgin."

He paled slightly, and she felt his hands tighten around hers, and she pushed on.

"The first night I spent with you, she realized I'd slept with you," Paige said, aware that she sounded hollow, when still, she couldn't regret it. Not a moment of that long, perfect night. Not even knowing what came after. "And when I got home that next day, she slapped me so hard it actually made my ears ring. But not enough to block her out. I'd already ruined her life by being born, you see. The least I could have done was let her sell the one commodity she had—I mean my virginity—to the highest bidder. She'd had the whole thing planned out with some friends of Denny's."

"How did I miss this?" Giancarlo asked, his voice a hoarse scrape in the empty studio.

"Because I wanted you to miss it." Her voice was fierce. "Because you were my single rebellion. My escape. The only thing I'd ever had that was good. And all mine. And you came without any strings." She dropped her gaze then, to where their hands were clasped tight. "But she was my mother."

He muttered something in Italian.

"I think," Paige said, because she had to finish now, "that if I hadn't met you, even if I'd had a different boyfriend, I would have just slept with whoever Denny told me to sleep with. It would have been easier."

"It would have been prostitution," Giancarlo said, viciously, but she knew that this time, it wasn't directed at her.

"What difference would it have made?" she asked, and she meant that. She shrugged. "I didn't know anything else. A lot of the dancers slept around and let the men help with their rent. They didn't call it prostitution— they called it dating. With benefits. Maybe I wouldn't have minded it, if I'd started there. But I'd met you." She blew out a breath and met his dark gold gaze. "And I was twenty years old. My mother told me a thousand times a day that men like you had a million girls like me. That I'd thrown myself away on you, that you would get sick of me sooner rather than later and we'd have nothing to show for it. And she, by God, wanted something to show for all her suffering."

"How, pray, had *she* suffered?" His tone was icy, and it warmed something inside of her. As if maybe all those foundations she'd thought he'd shattered in Italy had only frozen and were coming back now as they warmed. As she did.

"It wasn't my idea," Paige said quietly, because this was the important part. "Denny insisted that sex sold.

That you were worth an outrageous amount of money. And I thought—I really thought—that I owed her something. That it was just what love looked like. Because I might have ruined her life, but she was my mother. I loved her. I owed her."

"You don't have to tell me any more," Giancarlo said, his voice a deep rumble. "I understand."

"I loved you, too," Paige whispered. "But I'd had twenty years of Arleen and only a couple months of you. I thought she was the real thing and you were just a dream. I thought if it was really a true thing between you and me, you'd try to understand why I did it. But I wasn't surprised when you didn't."

He let out a breath, as if he'd suffered a blow.

"I'm so sorry," he said quietly. So quietly she almost didn't notice the way it sneaked into her, adding fuel to that small fire that still burned for him, for them. That always would. "I wish you'd come to me. I wish I'd seen what was happening beneath my nose. I wish I'd had any idea what you were going through."

"It doesn't matter now." And she found she meant that. She kept going, because she needed to finish. To see it through. "I did it. I got half a million dollars for those pictures and I lost you. I gave the money to my mother. It was enough to pay Denny and then some. I was such an idiot—I thought that meant we'd be fine."

"How long?" he asked, and she knew what he meant.

"Another month or so and the money was gone. Then she was in debt again. And it turned out Denny was even less understanding than he'd been before, because there was no rich boyfriend any longer. There was only me. And he was pretty clear about the one thing I was good at. How could I argue? The entire world had seen me in action. I was a commodity again."

"My God."

"I don't know about God," Paige said. "It was the LAPD who busted Denny on something serious enough to put him away for fifteen years. My mother lost her supplier, which meant she lost her mind. The last time I saw her, she was on the streets and she might be there still. She might not have made it this long. I don't know." She lifted her chin to look him in the eye. "And that's what happened ten years ago."

"You can't possibly feel guilty about that." He sounded incredulous. He frowned at her. "Paige. Please. You did everything you possibly could for that woman. Literally. You can't stop people when they want to destroy themselves—you can only stop them from taking you along with them."

She shrugged again, as if that might shift the constriction in her throat. "She's still my mother. I still love…if not her, then who she was supposed to be."

Giancarlo looked at her for a long time. So long she forgot she'd been too ashamed to tell him this. So long she lost herself again, the way she always did, in that face of his, those dark eyes, that mouth.

"I'm so sorry," he said, his voice so low it seemed to move inside of her, like heat. "I wouldn't blame you if you hated me. I don't think I understand why you don't."

"Because my whole life, Giancarlo," she whispered, unable to hide anything from him, not after all this time and all the ways they'd hurt each other, not any longer, "you're the only person I've ever loved. The only one who loved me back."

He shifted back and then he reached over to brush moisture from beneath her eyes, and Paige reminded herself that she was supposed to be resisting him. Fighting him off. Standing up for herself. She couldn't understand how she could feel as if she was doing that when, clearly, she was doing the opposite.

"Violet adores you," he said then. "And despite her excursions around the Tuscan countryside purely to be recognized and adored, she does not, in fact, like more than a handful of people. She trusts far fewer."

Paige made a face. "She has no idea who I really am."

He smiled then. "Of course she does. She tells me she's known exactly who you are from the moment she met you. Why else would she let you so deep into the family?"

But Paige shook her head at that, confused. And something more than simply confused.

"Why would she do that?" she whispered.

"Because my father was a good man," Giancarlo said, his hands hard and warm and tight on hers again, "and a kind man, but a cold one. And shortly after I told her you'd left she informed me that the only time in my life when I didn't act just like him, inaccessible and aloof and insufferable—her words—" and his mouth crooked then "—was when I was with you. Ten years and three months ago."

"She knew," Paige whispered, trying to take it in. "Is that why she was so kind to me?"

"That," Giancarlo said, a certain urgency in his voice that made her shift against the chair and tell herself it was only nerves, "and the fact that no matter what you might have been taught, it is not that difficult to be kind to you."

"You've found it incredibly difficult," she pointed out, and it was getting harder by the moment to control the things shaking inside her, the things shaking loose. "Impossible, even."

"I am a selfish, arrogant ass," he said, so seriously that she laughed out loud.

"Well," she said when the laughter faded. "That's not the word I would have used. But if the shoe fits…"

"I am my mother's son," he said simply. "I was born wealthy and aristocratic and, apparently, deeply sorry for myself. It took me all of an hour to realize I'd been completely out of line that day in Italy, Paige. It wasn't about you. It was about my own childhood, about the vows I'd made that only you have ever tempted me to break—but I have no excuse." He shook his head, his mouth thinning. "I know you didn't try to trick me. I considered chasing you down at the airfield and dragging you back with me, but I thought you needed space from the madman who'd said those things to you. I took the earliest flight I could the following day, but when I got to Los Angeles, you weren't there. Your things were packed up and shipped out to storage, but you never went there in person."

"That storage facility is in Bakersfield," she said, blinking. "Did you go there?"

"I haunted it," he said, his gaze dark and steady on hers. "For weeks."

There was no denying the heat that swirled in her then, too much like hope, like light, when she knew better than to—

But he was here. He was kneeling down in front of her even after she'd told him the kind of person she'd been at twenty. The kind of life she'd have led, if not for him. The kind of world she'd been raised in. He was *trying,* clearly.

And Paige didn't want to be right. She wanted to be happy. Just once, she wanted to be *happy.*

"I was going to ship it wherever I settled," she told him, letting that revolutionary thought settle into her bones. "There was no point carting it all around with me when I didn't know where I was going."

"What 'all' are you talking about?" he asked, his tone

dry. "It is perhaps three boxes, I am informed, after bribing the unscrupulous owner of that facility a shockingly small amount of money to see for myself." His expression dared her to protest that, but she didn't. If anything, she had to bite back a smile. "My mother requires more baggage for a long afternoon in Santa Monica."

Paige shook her head, realizing she was drinking in his nearness instead of standing up for herself and the little life inside of her. That she owed both of them more than that. That the fact she felt lighter than she had in years was nice, but it didn't change anything. That wasn't happiness, that was chemistry, and she'd already seen where that led, hadn't she? She needed more.

Paige might not be certain what *she* deserved, but her daughter deserved everything. *Everything.* She would use Arleen as her base and do the exact opposite. That meant many things, among them, not settling for a man—even if it was Giancarlo Alessi—simply because he was in front of her. Paige had watched that dynamic in action again and again and again. Her baby would not.

"How did you find me?" she asked, keeping all of her brand-new hopes, all of her wishes and all of her realizations out of her voice. Or she tried. "And more importantly, why?"

"The how is simple. I remembered you said you wanted to see the fall leaves change color in Vermont."

"I did?"

"When we first met. It was autumn in Los Angeles, hot and bright, and you told me you wanted to see real seasons. You also said you wanted to live near the sea and see the snow." He shrugged. "I decided that all those things pointed to New England. After that, I utilized the fact that I am a very wealthy, very motivated, very determined man to hunt you down."

"Giancarlo—"

"And the why is this." He reached into his pocket and pulled out a small box, and smiled slightly when she jerked back.

"No." It was automatic. And loud.

Giancarlo didn't seem at all fazed.

"This was my grandmother's diamond," he said. He cracked open the box and held it out, and she remembered, then, that first night with him in Italy, when he'd stood with his hand out and she'd thought he could stand like that forever, if he had to. His dark gaze met hers, and held. "I had the ring made for you ten years ago."

Paige felt her eyes flood then, and she let them, covering her mouth with her hands, unable to speak. So he did.

"Everything you said about me is true," he told her. "I can't deny any of it. But I want to understand you, Paige. I want to dedicate the next ten years to learning every single thing that makes you *you*. I don't simply want a partner, I want to be one. I want to be yours. I want you to yell at me and put me in my place and I want to help you teach our daughter never to surrender herself to terrible men like her father." His voice was scratchy then. "Not ever."

"Stop," she said, and she didn't mean to reach over to him. She didn't mean to slide her hand along his perfect, lean cheek. "I never gave you anything I didn't want to give. You must know that. It was only that I knew it would end."

"This won't," he whispered. "It hasn't in ten years. It won't in ten more, or ten after that, or ever." He leaned forward, sliding his hand over her belly to cup that small, unmistakable swell, and the smile that moved over that mouth of his broke her heart and made it leap at once. Then he made it far worse, leaning in to press a reverent kiss there. "I love you, Paige. Please. Let me show you."

"I love you, too," she whispered, because what was the point in pretending otherwise? They'd already lost so much time. "But trust is a whole lot more than a pretty ring. I'll always be the woman who sold you out."

"And I'll always be the man who greeted the news of his daughter's impending arrival like a pig," he retorted. "Based on the wild fears of the four-year-old boy I haven't been in decades."

"That sounds like a recipe for disaster."

"I know." He shifted then, pulling the ring from its box and slipping it onto her finger. It fit perfectly, and Paige couldn't seem to breathe. And his eyes were so bright, and she felt three times the size of her skin, and she didn't want to let him go this time. She didn't want to sacrifice him, ever again. "Believe me, I know, but it's not. It only means we've tested each other and we're still here."

He picked up her hand with its sparkling diamond and carried it to his lips. "Wear this and we'll work on it," he murmured, his eyes on her and the words seeming to thud straight into her heart, her flesh, her bones. "Every day. I promise I won't rest until you're happy enough to burst."

"Until we both are," she corrected him.

And then he leaned in close, and he wrapped himself around her and he kissed her. Again and again. Until she was dizzy with longing and love. Until neither one of them could breathe.

And Giancarlo gave her a detailed demonstration of his commitment to the cause, right there on one of the sofas in that bright, big room.

CHAPTER TEN

SHE MADE HIM work for it. And she made him wait.

And Giancarlo had no one to blame but himself for either.

"How do I know that you want to marry me and not simply to claim the baby in some appalling display of machismo?" she had asked him that first night, naked and astride him, when his intentions toward her, personally, could not have been more obvious.

"Set me any test," he'd told her then. "I'll pass it."

She'd considered him for a long moment, her inky hair in that tangle he loved and her eyes that brilliant green. And the way she fit him. *God, the fit.*

"Don't ask me again," she said, her tone very serious, her green gaze alight. "I'll let you know when I'm ready."

"Take your time," he'd told her with all the patience of a desperate man. "I want you to trust me."

"I want to trust you, too," she'd whispered in return.

But the truth was they learned to trust each other.

He flew back and forth from Italy as needed, and didn't argue when sometimes, she refused to go with him. He shared her tiny studio apartment with her in her snowy New England town, a hundred miles or more from anywhere, and he didn't complain. He shoveled snow. He salted paths. He made certain her car was well-maintained and he never pressured her to move.

She told him more about her childhood with that terrible woman. He told her about his childhood with a woman less terrible perhaps, but deeply complicated all the same. And they held each other. They soothed each other.

They came to know each other in all the ways they hadn't had time to get to know each other ten years ago. Layer on top of layer.

Until he came back from another trip to Italy one snowy March weekend and Paige said that maybe, if he had a better place in mind for them to live, she'd consider it.

"I don't know anything about homes," she told him, her attention perhaps *too* focused on the book she held in her lap. "But you seem to have quite a few."

"You make every house I have a home, *il mio amore,*" he told her. "Without you, they are but adventures in architecture."

And he had them back in his house in Malibu by the following afternoon, as if they'd never left it ten years ago. The sea in front of him, the mountains behind him and his woman at his side.

Giancarlo had never been happier. Except for one small thing.

"Why haven't you married her yet?" Violet demanded every time she saw him, particularly when Paige was with him. He could only raise his brows at this woman he loved more than he'd imagined it was possible to love anyone, and wait for her to answer.

Which she was happy to do.

"I'm not sure I'll have him, Violet," Paige would reply airily. She would pat her ever-larger belly and smile blandly, and Giancarlo thought that they'd both transitioned from a working relationship to family rather easily. Almost as if Violet had planned it. "I'm considering all my options."

"I don't blame you," Violet would say with a sniff. "He was horrible. I'd tell you he gets that sort of inexcusable behavior from his father but, alas, Count Alessi was the most polite and well-mannered man I ever met. It's all me."

"I don't think anyone thought otherwise," Giancarlo would say then, and everyone would laugh.

But he never asked Paige again. He kept his promise.

"And if a single photograph or unauthorized mention of my daughter appears anywhere, for any reason, in a manner which benefits you without my express, written consent," he told the great screen legend Violet Sutherlin one pretty afternoon, in her office in front of her new assistant so there could be no mistake that he meant business, "you will never see her again. Until she is at least thirty. Do you understand me, Mother? I am no longer that four-year-old. My daughter never will be."

Violet had gazed at him for a long time. She hadn't showed him that smile of hers. She hadn't said anything witty. In the end, she'd only nodded, once. Sharp and jerky.

But he knew she understood that he'd meant it.

Five months and three weeks after the night he'd turned up in Maine, when Paige was big and round and had to walk in a kind of waddle to get down the makeshift aisle, she married him at last in a tiny ceremony on Violet's terrace. Violet presided. The bride and the officiant wept.

Giancarlo smiled with the greatest satisfaction he'd known in his life. And kissed his bride. *His wife.*

"Don't ever torture me like that again," he growled

against her lips when they were in the car and headed home, finally married, the way they should have been more than ten years before.

"Surely you knew I'd marry you," Paige said, laughing. "I've been pretty open about how much I love you."

"I'm not at all certain I deserve you," he said, and was startled when that made great tears well up in her lovely changeable eyes, then roll down her cheeks. "But I've taken that on as a lifelong project."

She smiled at him, the whole world in that smile, the way it had been that long ago day on that set when they'd locked eyes for the first time. And Giancarlo knew without the slightest shred of doubt that this was merely a particularly good day on the long road toward forever. And that they'd walk the whole of it together, just like this.

And then her expression altered, and she grabbed his arm.

"We're going to have a lot of lifelong projects," Paige said, sounding fierce and awed at once. His beautiful wife. "I think my water just broke."

They named their daughter Violetta Grace, after her famous grandmother, who'd insisted, and the less famous one, who'd died before Paige was born and Arleen had gone completely off the rails, and she was perfect.

Extraordinary.

Theirs.

And they spent the rest of their lives teaching her, in a thousand little ways and few great big ones, what it meant to be as happy as they were the moment they met her.

* * * * *

LET'S TALK
Romance

For exclusive extracts, competitions
and special offers, find us online:

 facebook.com/millsandboon
 @millsandboonuk
 @millsandboon

Or get in touch on 0844 844 1351*

For all the latest titles coming soon, visit
millsandboon.co.uk/nextmonth